LIES

LIES

a novel

ENRIQUE DE HÉRIZ

Translated from the Spanish by John Cullen

NAN A. TALESE | DOUBLEDAY

New York London Toronto Sydney Auckland

PUBLISHED BY NAN A. TALESE

AN IMPRINT OF DOUBLEDAY

Copyright © 2007 by Enrique de Hériz

A different version of this book was originally published in
Spain as *Mentira* by Edhasa, Barcelona, in 2004, and in the U.K.
as *Lies* by Weidenfeld & Nicolson, a division of The Orion
Publishing Group, London, in 2007. This edition published
by arrangement with Edhasa.

Published in the United States by Nan A. Talese, an imprint
of The Doubleday Broadway Publishing Group, a division
of Random House, Inc., New York.
www.nanatalese.com

DOUBLEDAY is a registered trademark of Random House, Inc.

LIBRARY OF CONGRESS CATALOGING-IN-PUBLICATION DATA
Hériz, Enrique de.
[Mentira. English]
Lies : a novel / Enrique de Hériz ; translated from the Spanish
by John Cullen.—1st ed. in the U.S.
p. cm.
I. Cullen, John. II. Title.
PQ6658.E672M4613 2007
863'.64—dc22
2006027606

ISBN-978-0-385-51794-2

PRINTED IN THE UNITED STATES OF AMERICA

1 3 5 7 9 10 8 6 4 2

FIRST U.S. EDITION

To Héctor Orlando Chimirri,
who knew how to tell stories.
Go get 'em

And to a mother who was able to overcome death
and dedicate the victory to us.

All we don't know is astonishing. Even more astonishing
is what passes for knowing.

—PHILIP ROTH

The strongest guard is placed at the gateway to nothing. . . .
Maybe because the condition of emptiness is too shameful
to be divulged.

—F. SCOTT FITZGERALD

There is a taint of death, a flavor of mortality in lies—
which is exactly what I hate and detest in the world—what
I want to forget.

—JOSEPH CONRAD

I knew a harbor, safe and wide.
To say I knew it means something has died.

—RAÚL GONZÁLEZ TUÑÓN

[The earth] is a carpet on one side and a blanket on the
other, a thin frontier between those who walk upon it and
those who lie under it, between the armies of movement and
the armies of repose, two hosts united in mutual oblivion.

—JESÚS DEL CAMPO

LIES

Dead? Me, Isabel, dead? Not a chance. Not while I still have something to say about it. I'm in an inn, the Posada del Caribe. I've been here for nearly a month and a half without seeing a single soul. That's a lie: once a week, Amkiel brings me provisions. On Tuesdays, I believe, although my notion of time isn't too reliable. Out here, all the days look the same.

Posada del Caribe, the Caribbean Inn. What a name! Six rectangular cabins grouped around a larger square one that serves as both dining room and administration center. All the cabins have palm-frond roofs and thick tree trunks comprise the lower half of the walls. Big windows in the upper half. Awful mosquito nets. They're so dense they block out almost all of the jungle light, which is scarce enough to begin with, because this is the Petén jungle in northern Guatemala. The Caribbean is very far away.

First, a ten-hour flight from London to Miami. Two more hours to Guatemala City. Fifty minutes in a light plane to Flores. Sixty-two kilometers in a van, along the dirt roads that lead to Sayaxché. Not bad for a woman my age. In Sayaxché, you have to negotiate with the motorboat drivers. It costs more patience than money. I made a deal with Amkiel because I liked the look of him. He had the typical smile—half discouraging and half sardonic—of people who make their living from tourism, but he struck me as serious and responsible. My choice was also influenced by the fact that his flat-bottomed boat looked more stable than the others. They call them "launches" but they're really just motorized canoes. Amkiel's boat is called Pampered Girl, which would be a memorable name if they weren't all like that: Pampered, Forgetful, Jealous, Silent. If such things still interested me, I'd investigate the origins of their names. Who gave his boat the first one, and why? Who copied whom? I was good at questions like that in the old days.

Anyway, whichever launch I choose, the money's always going to wind up in the same place: the Boss's pocket. I assume he has a name, but I don't know what it is. Everyone just calls him "the Boss," and since I arrived in Sayaxché every step I've taken has required his indirect approval. Although I've never even seen his face, I know that it's to him I owe the privilege of having this inn all to myself, even though it has room enough for nearly twenty people. This doesn't exactly represent an outpouring of generosity: under normal circumstances, the Posada del Caribe would be closed at this time of year, waiting for the wet season to end and the annual mosquito plague to disappear. But mosquitoes don't bother me.

Pampered Girl *is made of aluminum. Judging by her shade of green, I'd guess she must have belonged to some sort of army in the past. She's about two and a half meters long, and I doubt she has room for more than three passengers, four at a pinch, despite Amkiel's insistence that he's transported as many as seven or eight people in the thing. He also enumerates for me, nearly every time we meet, the advantages of having an aluminum vessel to navigate these rivers. The other boats are made of carbon fiber. They're as light and maneuverable as his, but much more fragile; if they receive a sharp blow, they don't just dent, they come apart like dried stalks of cane, especially when they're already old and cracked. I explain to him that I like the few remaining wooden boats, and he replies that nobody wants them because they're heavy and impractical. In another period of my life, I would have spoken to him of ships and oceans, of sailboats and Italian steamers, of all the things I know about the sea. I would have told him my life's story, my family's story. Not now. I smile and agree from time to time, as if the conversation really mattered to me. It doesn't. It's not his fault. There aren't many things that matter to me now.*

Amkiel brought me here for eighteen dollars. I suppose his share will be five or six; the rest is for the Boss. I don't know how many kilometers we traveled on the Río Pasión. I know we were under way for quite some time, and these launches are very fast. The river is calm, unobstructed, and broad, with a channel almost thirty meters across. The vegetation on both banks grew thicker the further we left Sayaxché behind. First we passed through a zone of savanna, then a tropical forest, and finally a premonition of jungle. The thick muddy waters of the river barely reflected the sky, in reddish hues. Suddenly, Río Pasión forked into twin branches; Amkiel took the one on the right. Floating vegetation appeared, a few scattered water lilies at first, then increasingly dense clusters. As we rounded a bend, the islands came into view. Real islands, each one greener and more luxuriant than the last. We spotted bamboo growing there, or something very much like it; rushes and reeds that can reach more than three meters in height, thick tangles of vegetation, floating forests. Amkiel aimed Pampered Girl's bow at one of these little islands and approached it at such a high speed I thought he was trying to impress me, or maybe simply to scare me. Then I realized it was no mere threat, not even a last-minute maneuver could avoid the impact; we had only three seconds left, two, one . . . and then we were inside. Inside the island.

We spent more than half an hour going through these lush islets. In and out, in and out. Without ever striking anything that could be called a shore, and without ever seeing any channel except for the one our boat made when its nose plowed into the vegetation and parted it, the way you open a passage between two curtains with the slight movement of your hand.

I soon turned my back on Amkiel and fixed my gaze beyond the bow. Maybe he thought I was fascinated by the landscape, but he was wrong. I was thinking about my own affairs, pondering old memories and recent discoveries, things I might not even consider important enough to record here if it weren't that my alleged death makes me see them in a different and much brighter light. The Russian woman—I was thinking about the Russian woman. Five days in London had been enough for me to find evidence for something I'd long suspected: the Russian woman was a walking, talking lie. I didn't find this astonishing, because I already knew it to be true. What is astonishing is that the entire town of Malespina, not content with believing her lies, dedicated itself to amplifying them and turning them into genuine legends, right from the beginning. During that river journey, I thought about the Russian woman a great deal, without malice, without blaming her too much, perhaps because we basically belong to the same category. Death suits us both. I didn't think so then, but now that I'm dead, I do. Now that it's assumed I'm dead. Men win themselves a place in the history books by pushing. And yelling. Shouting enhances their stature. Some women find themselves a niche in the book of legends by means of their silence. The Russian belonged to this category. So do I, I suppose. To a more modest degree, of course, but I too have managed to make my silences so dense that other people could build a minor legend from them. This thought struck me the day before yesterday, when I read my obituaries. When I learned that my children are not capable of recognizing me.

I was also thinking about Judith on that trip up the river. Now Judith is dead. Yes, she's the one who's really dead. I can't say I knew her—we spoke for no more than twenty minutes. She sat next to me on the flight from Miami to Guatemala City. She was traveling alone, like me. She was an older woman, like me. Sixtysomething, perhaps. I didn't ask her. As a matter of fact, I hardly asked her any questions at all. I remember noticing her and thinking, "She looks like me. If I were a nun, that's the way I'd look." I went to a convent school, so I'd met a few women like that. One day they might lay their habits aside, but their look would keep giving them away: the precise length of their skirts, the propriety of their heels, their scrubbed faces, a particular sort of hairdo. But Judith was not and had never been a nun. She was a nurse. For Doctors Without Borders. She was most probably German, judging by her accent, although she spoke impeccable Spanish. She acted as a liaison among different aid projects throughout Latin America. Administrative operations. Supervising the transfer of medicines left over from one project and needed in another. Organizing emergency evacuations of sick people. She'd dedicated the past fifteen years of her life to this work. I didn't ask her if she had children. Now I'd like to know. After we landed at the airport in Guatemala City, her suitcase came out before mine. She bade me a polite farewell, and as I watched her leave, I thought, "There goes another legend." A woman on her own, surrounded by silences. Like the Russian. Like me. If I were writing a novel, I'd say that the bond that was going to link our two destinies was formed in that last moment. In novels, assertions like this—grandiose words that give some weight to chance, however ethereal chance may be—can sound appropriate. But not in real life; in real life, it's enough to say that a person I didn't know, someone with whom I happened to exchange twenty minutes' worth of small talk, died in my place. Poor Judith. Of course, nothing that happened to her was my fault, and when I thought about her, the idea that she would meet such an unpleasant end so soon was the furthest thing from my mind. But poor Judith, all the same.

While we were inside them, all the islets looked the same. But each time we broke out of one, the stretch of water separating it from the next one was narrower. I had the impression that we were lost. Every now and then, Amkiel lifted the motor out of the water to keep the propeller blades from striking the isolated tree trunks he spotted in the water ahead. His movement was automatic, instantaneous, as when you lift your foot to avoid a rock in your path without slowing your pace. At these moments, the propeller spun in the empty air above the water, and the echo multiplied the roar of the motor until it sounded as though a squad of light airplanes were flying over our heads.

After the umpteenth islet, I said, "We're lost, right?"

"No, señora. We're in the Petexbatún River."

Well, it may be a river, I thought, but it looks like a drowned planet. When it finally stopped raining and Noah stuck his head out of the ark, he must have seen something like this. A floating world. A world with no shores.

I don't know exactly how long it took us but eventually the trip was over. Amkiel slowed the boat down and approached an islet, but this time, instead of plunging into it, he pulled up alongside. It took me a while to realize what was going on, to discern the muddy sand beneath the greenery and understand that this was terra firma, solid ground you could walk on. The silence that fell upon us when Amkiel cut his motor cannot be described. He jumped out of the boat, gave a slight tug, and grounded Pampered Girl in about eight inches of mud.

"Now what?" I asked. "A breakdown?"

"No. This is it. We're here. Lake Petexbatún is behind those trees"—he gestured at the vegetation barely twenty meters ahead of us—"and that over there is the Posada del Caribe."

I looked to where he was pointing and could just about make out the first cabin among the dense foliage.

Amkiel put my bag on the ground, held out his hand for his eighteen dollars, thrust the money into his pocket, and then took his leave as if he hadn't a moment to spare: "Enjoy your stay señora this key works for all the doors the Boss gave it to me for you the radio's connected to a car battery all you have to do is press the ON button and then you operate the microphone with the switch but of course you already know that there are candles in the room under the beds I'll come back next Tuesday if you have any problems you can tell me then."

He started the motor with a jerk, put it in reverse to extract Pampered Girl from the mud, and disappeared upriver. I was puzzled. During the whole journey, he'd behaved like a man of few words, slightly shy, maybe a little proud, but never disagreeable. My professional obsession led me to think that his sudden haste might be the vestige of some ancient tribal superstition, fear of the jungle spirits or something like that. But after two seconds—or rather, two steps—I understood. Two steps into the jungle, and I was enveloped by what had caused such a hasty departure. Mosquitoes. My old friends. Millions of mosquitoes. I turned back to the shore, got the repellent out of my backpack, and smeared it over my face and hands, my ankles, my ears. I'm not afraid of mosquitoes, and I'm not overly concerned about the diseases they can *transmit. I've been living for years with sudden, prolonged bouts of high temperature, tropical fevers that doctors can't identify and whose symptoms they can scarcely mitigate. I've learned to put up with them—I don't even take antibiotics. It's part of the job. That's what I was told on my first trip to Africa, and my life has confirmed it. A real anthropologist has no choice but to make fever her friend. As for malaria, I don't underestimate it, but I've learned not to fear it. If it has respected me so far, I don't see why it would decide to consume me now, when all my body has to offer are weakened bones and sagging flesh. Malaria can be fatal in the long run, I know. Well, so is life. When I use repellent, it's only so I can avoid the mosquito bites them- selves and the stinging sensation that accompanies them. I also do it a little out of nostalgia for the jungle. That's what brought me here, among many other things. And that's why I have five cans of mosquito repellent. Too many—even if I stay here a year, I'll never use them all up. Maybe I brought so many because I didn't know when I was going to return. Or I brought them just in case, like smokers who accumulate car- tons of cigarettes because they're terrified of going without. Not any type of repellent will do. It must contain at least forty percent diethyl- toluamide. The smell of this repellent is the perfume of my life. Some- times I put a spot on even when I'm in Barcelona, just a little, like those preening ladies who dab a few drops of essence behind their ears and along their décolletage. When I die, they ought to put a can of it inside my coffin, in case the next world is a jungle or I start longing for the old days. I should put such a request in writing, but I suppose it's a little late for that. Let them ask my children. Alberto—let them ask Alberto. Let them tell him to smell me to see if he can recognize me.*

It took me barely two minutes to settle into the Posada del Caribe. I shifted my backpack onto a shaky old bed. Then I went to the central cabin and checked that the pantry had been filled in accordance with the instructions I'd passed on to the Boss the previous day. I hadn't asked for much. I've always been told I eat like a bird, so it must be true. I sup- pose my profession has accustomed me to frugality. A lot of white rice.

I can make a feast out of some pasta and a clove of garlic. After seeing that everything was in order, I went over to the radio and disconnected it. In my line of work, it's good practice not to let a battery run down even if you don't plan on using it. I could cite that as the reason why I disconnected the radio, a mere precaution, but I'd be lying. One of the advantages of these words I'm writing is that I don't need to lie, because no one's ever going to read them. I don't even think I'm going to read them myself. These pages aren't a monument to the truth, nor are they a pedestal for exhibiting it; they're more like a sewer for the truth, a place where I can get rid of it. I disconnected the radio because I had come here. To be alone. Alone and in silence. When I want to break that silence, I connect the radio, I ask the Boss for what I need, and I disconnect it again. Then Amkiel brings me what I've requested. I'd also be lying if I said I left the radio disconnected because I'd anticipated what was going to happen. No one can anticipate a thing like that.

It's a joke. The whole thing's a joke. A colossal, hysterical, monumental joke. A clumsy move on the part of chance, aggravated by an unpardonable mistake on the part of my children. The reasons don't matter much. If I insisted on uncovering whatever made this random combination of circumstances possible and—especially—what led to such a mistake, I'd wind up like my daughter Serena. Serena treats the past the way flies treat a windowpane: she runs up and down it, bangs her head against it, and wears herself out trying to reach the light, without noticing that the light and the glass are two separate things. Poor Serena. Poor all of them. When I think about them, it makes me feel like rising from the dead. Going back, in other words. But if I didn't do that the day before yesterday, when I learned about this absurd confusion, I don't see why I should do it now. I don't know. The moment will come. If it comes.

That isn't to say that their grief doesn't affect me. And I know that it's in my power to put an end to it. All I'd have to do is call on the radio and ask Amkiel to come and pick me up and take me to Sayaxché, where I could make a phone call. In fact, I wouldn't even have to do that. I could just ask the Boss to call on my behalf and say I'm alive and well. On the other hand, I don't feel I can destroy this perfect construction that fate has woven together out of several loose strands. However ridiculous it may seem, however absurd and macabre, this situation has its own categorical, transparent logic. Nobody chose it and nobody's entirely responsible for it, although if I had to distribute blame, my son Alberto would probably receive the largest share. Nonetheless, the situation is so absolutely coherent that if it were the work of a playwright, I could do nothing but beat my hands sore applauding his mastery. In the first place, think of all the times I dreamed of a solution such as this, maybe without realizing it. All the times I thought about not going back. On almost every trip, I found something that held me, something that begged me to stay, but I never dared. Fear of the sorrow my desertion would cause Julio and our children always won out. Perhaps it's different now; after all, they're grown up. My desire to remain far from them didn't mean I didn't love them. The mere thought that I could cause them irreparable harm was enough to prevent me from staying. Sometimes I imagined a brilliant solution to my problem, very much like the one that has just been handed to me on a plate: I would fake my own death. It would be the best for everyone. For me and for them. I'd avoid going back to a life that seemed less like life every day. And they . . . well, I supposed a mother's death would be easier to accept than her disappearance. But I've never been capable of plotting a situation like this. Besides, if I had been capable of doing such a thing, I would have done it twenty or thirty years ago, not now. What would be the point? Soon I'm going to be seventy. Inventing a death for myself isn't going to give me any more time. What happened may have coincided with my wishes, but that doesn't mean it was the result of my will. Sometimes life does things for you that you don't do for life.

There are many reasons to welcome this mistake. After all, death is my specialty. Not the dead, but death itself. Or rather, what we the living do with our dead. I've traveled over half the world, following the rituals of grief, trying to find out how men and women of every race and culture face up to the loss of a loved one. I've published seven books on the subject and hundreds of articles, field studies, comparative analyses. I'm supposed to know everything about how the living grieve for the dead. Had I been offered the possibility of mounting the ultimate investigation, producing the definitive thesis, I couldn't have found a better way of doing it. To live my own death without being dead. It's something I've even dreamed about. Should anyone want to blame me because chance has placed this opportunity within my reach, I'll accept that blame with a smile.

There's still another reason, no less important. This could have happened to me anywhere in the world. The jungle doesn't have exclusive rights to accidental deaths in murky circumstances. Nevertheless, it had to be here, in a place like this, a place I didn't even know about two months ago, but where I feel I absolutely belong. So much so, I could die here. So much so, I could live here. I don't exactly know why.

I often have my moments of doubt. Ever since I discovered I was dead, I've done nothing but think about righting this wrong. About putting my few soiled belongings in my bag and retracing the steps that brought me here.

I think about my children crying. How they must have wept for me, how they must be weeping for me still. I don't count the quantity of their tears as a measure of their grief; weeping is a learned skill, and everyone cries the way he knows how, the way he can. In the southeastern Bay of Bengal, in the Andaman and Nicobar Islands, when a funeral is held, the men weep with a degree of intensity inconceivable to any Westerner. They tremble and howl in such a savage way that their bodies appear to be on the point of bursting apart. They suffer a kind of acute pulmonary convulsion, yet somehow they manage to take in enough air to emit shrieks capable of shattering the thickest glass. The first anthropologists who visited the islands couldn't believe their eyes. When they returned home, they announced their discovery in the academic journals. Their essays were dense, teeming with imaginative hy-

potheses, in which the authors asserted that they had found a community which, when faced with the death of its members, manifested feelings much more profound and more authentic than those of any other group. Then the technicians, the skeptics, arrived on the scene. They landed on the islands with their cameras and their tape recorders, calculated and registered the amount of weeping per person per death, and measured the precise characteristics of every howl. Soon they came up with a whole series of explanations related to Andamanese familial structures, or to the Andamanese males' lack of inhibition around weeping, or to a particularly dolorous conception of the afterlife. Rubbish. Nobody stayed there long enough to find out the truth or ask the necessary questions at the right time. Except for me. This wasn't especially praiseworthy; the other groups were financed by large institutions and driven by the necessity to return home and publish. Return and publish, make and broadcast documentaries, place photographs in magazines, as if these were the only ways to demonstrate that they'd been there. This was all during the first flowering of anthropology. Publishing a curious photograph was beginning to prove more profitable than possessing a thorough knowledge of the reality behind it. But I digress—right now, much as I dislike doing so, I'm talking about myself.

I went about freely, my disadvantages accidentally working in my favor. I had less money than the others because Julio paid for my first trips. He sold a few paintings and told me, "We have a million pesetas. You can go wherever you want." It was the Julio Fellowship—that's what we called it. Without it, I would never have been able to travel. Official research grants for a female anthropologist at the end of the 1950s? Properly speaking, anthropology didn't even exist.

So I financed my trips with the family savings. It wasn't much money, of course. I had to travel on cut-price tickets, stay in the most uncomfortable places, and limit my field work to projects that could be carried out alone. In exchange, I was free to go wherever I liked, I could stay longer than anyone else, and, above all, I was in no hurry to pub-

lish. I traveled all over the Andamans for two months without ever having the good fortune to come across a funeral. My trip was a disaster, a waste. I decided to stay another month. I moved around constantly, from island to island. I witnessed a wedding. The men wished the bride happiness by laying their heads on her shoulder and weeping with her. They literally broke down in tears. I didn't say anything to anyone. I didn't rush to publish. A short while later, I found two men weeping in the street. Several other people were looking on. I asked where the funeral would be held, but they told me there wasn't going to be any funeral. These were two old friends; it had been years since they'd seen each other, and they were celebrating their reunion in this way. I took notes, but I continued to say nothing.

A few weeks later, the family whose house I was staying in invited me to attend a festival. Two neighboring villages, longtime enemies because of an old dispute over the ownership of a well, were sealing a peace agreement reached after years of negotiations. About two hundred people were there, mostly men and boys, sitting on the ground in two separate groups. A representative from each village stepped forward. They exchanged things: sacks of corn, some tools. Then they embraced. At that moment, everyone who was present broke down and wept. I'm certain that such weeping, such a river of collective tears, has never been seen in Europe. Not even in the most dramatic moments of its history. Almost forty years have passed since that day, and I still get goose bumps every time I remember it. Later that afternoon, I left the village to take a walk in the countryside. On my way, I met a group of farmworkers. I did what I should have done from the beginning: I asked. It was as simple as that. I stopped the four men and asked them how they could produce such heartrending tears, and how those tears could express even the most radiant jubilation. My perplexity amused them. They answered that it was easily done. Laying their staffs aside, they sat on the ground and burst into unrestrained, convulsive weeping, as though they had just received news of the death of the person dearest to them in all the world.

For them, weeping is a convention, like shaking hands to establish a bond. I went back home and published my report. The most powerful figures in the international anthropological community had to accept my theory, but not before they'd wasted two years in a polemic that seemed perfectly ridiculous to me; unfortunately, it was but the first of many. I've been at the center of disputes far more bitter than that one, although those who know me know I've never pursued notoriety. Well, the upshot of all this is that these days no one doubts that weeping is a form of cultural expression, a reaction that can be learned.

I'm not saying my family doesn't love me or their tears are false. Far from it. I'm just saying that almost everything they attribute to emotions is cultural. I admit I'd love to be watching them through a peephole, but I don't really need one. I know them well enough. The one I feel the least bad about is Julio. Maybe he doesn't even know I'm dead yet. How that man loved me! Despite all his tricks, despite that way he had of absenting himself from reality, how he loved me. Right from the beginning. So much that he ended up inventing me. Nevertheless, the news of my death may not even have registered with him. Or maybe it has; maybe he heard it one minute and forgot it the next. Better for him.

And then there are my children. Alberto will have shed the correct amount of tears. Not one more, not one less. Not because he's mean. On the contrary, he's no doubt been so busy consoling the others, so immersed in resolving the practical matters related to my death and making sure no one else has to worry, that he won't have yielded to his grief for any longer than was strictly necessary. I must be fair: even though Alberto is the principal cause of this confusion, even though I still haven't forgiven him for his mistake, I can't deny the evidence—he's a good man. Generous to a fault, always busy solving everyone else's problems. Now he'll be more devoted than ever to his son Luis. The sick boy. To tell the truth, at nineteen he doesn't seem like a boy to me anymore. And not in the least bit sick. Maybe his brain is different, but sometimes I envy him. If anyone's going to say something beautiful and true about my death, it will surely be him.

I know that Pablo, the middle one, has made up for any shortfall in Alberto's tears. He's overwhelmed. Undone. Incapable of speech. By now his face must be as swollen as a toad's. Poor Pablo. I'm sure he's smoking like a chimney. I'd give anything if I could see him for a moment. Or rather, if he could see me. I'd have a few things to tell him. Stop crying. Take a deep breath. Look at yourself. You look fifty years old. Don't smoke so much. Go to the bathroom and shave. And do me the favor of running a comb through your hair. Has he composed something in my honor? I can imagine it: a tremendous piece, like piano strings played with a bow. Or maybe not, maybe he's chosen the tribute of silence instead. In that case, he's capable of locking up the piano and leaving it untouched for years.

The one I'm most worried about is Serena, the youngest. She'll be weeping questions. I'm sure she doesn't understand a thing, as always. Where did she get that burning need to know and the naïveté to believe she can*? Serena's determined to learn the truth about the past, without realizing that the past, like the future, can only be imagined. There must be a law that requires such a silent mother to have such an imaginative daughter. And so full of questions. As a child, Serena listened to her father's stories as if her life depended on it. Her head would be filled with Simóns and Russian women and Chinese tales and medieval battles, and then she'd have bad dreams and would not be pacified. Sometimes she'd even run a fever. I should have intervened because Julio didn't notice. I did, but it never seemed important. Mistakes always come back to you in the end. By the time she was a teenager, Serena knew that stories were only stories, and whereas her brothers accepted them quite naturally and kept them stored in the musty trunk of nostalgia, she did not; she took them as an injustice, she felt deceived, and she insisted that Julio indemnify her with the truth. She started asking questions at all hours. She insisted on knowing. When she was about to turn seventeen, her father asked her what she wanted for her birthday. The truth, she said, I want you to give me the truth. The truth about what? her father said. The truth about every story you've ever told me.*

She subjected him to pitiless interrogations and noted down his replies, forever scribbling in her notebooks. She dragged some answers out of her father and worked others out for herself, without understanding that the alleged truth that was supplanting those stories was nothing but an even bigger story, much more complex and therefore more difficult to take apart. She was always striving for certitude. That's why she worries me more than her brothers. If I don't go back, if I decide not to clear up this mistake, the days will pass and life will resume its normal course for them. I'll be dead, and they'll go on as before. But not Serena.

Serena will keep asking questions and looking for explanations. Why, Mama, why that boat, that river, that jungle, since when, what for, and what happened before and before and before? She'll go back into our family history, years and years, centuries if necessary, until she finds something she can be certain of. God, how naïve she is. She's spent half her life like that, indignant and surprised when the rest of us didn't join her in the struggle. She has a fabulous memory, like her father, like—or so they say—her grandfather Simón, her father's father. But she notes everything down so she won't forget. Now that I mention it, I'm sure she's having another go at Simón's story. I can't blame her. Two imaginary shipwrecks in the same family is far too tempting for someone like her.

What obstinacy—she should have studied law. Alberto's a great lawyer, but she would have been even better. No court would have been able to resist her perseverance, that determination of hers to submit everything, including the inexplicable, to logic. Maybe I should have tried to set her straight, but I never felt capable of doing so. I don't know, I suppose I wanted to give my children the freedom of choice I never had. They've all done pretty well and that should be enough for me, but I regret not having intervened in their lives more often. Maybe I reinforced their mistakes with my silence. Maybe I spent too much time away from them. Back then, it seemed like a good idea; I was convinced it would help them mature more quickly and learn to make their own decisions.

Of course, I can't pretend that these words will correct whatever mistakes I may have made in the past. Words have formidable power, not always for the good, but they're not capable of swimming back up the river of time and changing its course. Besides, I don't want to waste them. They are life. In Africa, in northwest Uganda, the Lugbara use the same term to refer to an achievement, an event, and a word. When a man is about to die, it's his duty to gather his children around his deathbed and speak his final words to them. His final words, in a sense so literal that even if death holds back, even if the man survives for years, he will not speak again. The word is authority itself. When the man finally dies, a period of chaos begins. This is a common feature in all the cultures I know. Death introduces social chaos until the living undertake to reorder reality in some way. That's what funeral rites are for: to symbolize the arrival of a new order. In the case of the Lugbara, when someone dies, it's said that "his words have ended." Chaos recedes only when the local witch doctor makes contact "with the mouth of the dead man" to inform him that his heirs have accepted the order established by his final words. Only then can the spirit of the dead man rest in peace and cease to represent a threat to the living.

This has never happened before. Apart from my professional work, I've rarely written anything more than the occasional letter. But now the words are boiling up furiously, and I need to get them out, to leave a record of them, even though no reader is possible in this kingdom of the dead. Maybe it's because I'm alive, and I don't have anything else. Maybe it's because one day I really am going to die, and that day can't be so very far off. These will be my final words. The day before yesterday, when I learned I was dead, I decided to write them down. It's the only way to get rid of them.

SUNDAY

"Be careful what you write," Alberto says. "You don't want to tell any lies." He's come up to the terrace to make sure everything's okay. Papa and Luis have gone to bed. "You know what happens to liars."

"What happens?" I ask. I know, of course, but I feel like hearing it again.

"The usual two possibilities: imprisonment, like Simón; or exile, like Li Po." He makes a show of being serious, but a smile betrays him. He looks so much like Papa when he smiles. "Good night, Serena. Try not to stay up too late." He kisses me on the forehead. As he leaves, he can't suppress a few more big-brotherly comments: "Have you got enough light? If you want, I'll turn on the halogen lamps, but then the terrace will be full of bugs. Are you all right here? You're not cold? Shall I get you a coat?"

"Alberto," I protest, more fondly than angrily. I know he just can't help himself.

"What?"

"I'm thirty-eight years old."

"You're right. Sorry. Well. See you tomorrow."

Before going, he gives me a hug and another kiss. Ever since Mama's accident, he's been more anxious than ever, but also more affectionate.

Before he disappears, he says, "I'd give anything to know what you're writing."

So would I. I've already filled a page with scratched-out scrawls and a few isolated, disconnected words. I don't know where to begin, how to find the opening sentence. I lift my eyes from the paper at any excuse, tear out the page, crumple it into a ball, and crush it in my hand. I take another page and put the word "Sunday" at the top, even though I'm not writing a diary. The only connection between these words and the present is my hope that they'll help explain a past that made it possible.

Maybe it would be easier to relate the events of the recent past. For example: my mother died in Guatemala last week. There it is; I've said it. She drowned in a river with an absurd name: Río Pasión, "Passion River." Río Pasión really exists, it's not some ridiculous invention. (I myself saw its sandy banks myself just last week.) Mama was in a launch, a small motorboat with three other people. Everyone died except the skipper. What else can I say? That we were surprised? Well, Mama was sixty-nine and that doesn't count as old nowadays. I mean, not too old to live. Too old to take off for Guatemala, yes, and too old to be getting into launches. Whose idea was that? She was in perfect health. No one expected her to die so soon, much less to die in that way, dragged down into the water, her lungs full of mud and her face sliced to pieces.

Alberto took care of cutting through all the red tape required for bringing her ashes back to Spain, but Pablo and I had to go and identify her first. That's why we're all here in Malespina now. Even Papa has come, despite his condition. The only one missing is Pablo, and he'll arrive tomorrow. We're going to take advantage of one of Papa's lucid moments to dispose of the ashes by scattering them in the sea from the Russian woman's beach. We're assuming that's what Mama would have wanted. It's strange—she never told us what we were to do if something like this should happen, even though this was precisely her field.

That's it. There's nothing else worth saying. And what I've said is of no use to me anyway. It's all about the end, and I'm looking for the beginning. The first step that explains the next step and the one after that. I'm holding one end of a ball of tangled thread. I yank on it, trying to find the other end, but every pull tightens the knots and tangles them further.

Maybe this is how it has to be. Maybe you just have to accept that the only way to relate the history of a family—or of a person—is like this, backward in fits and starts: this is the story of Serena, daughter of a father who was the son of a father who in turn . . . And the mothers: the mother of the father of a mother, like that, swimming upriver in the current of life, always looking for a previous cause, until you come to the first monkey that stretched its legs and climbed down out of its tree, itself a remote descendant of the first amphibian, which was the distant relative of an atypical fish capable of breathing out of water and endowed with sufficient curiosity to penetrate the forest and, who knows, maybe with enough memory to recall parents and grandparents and great-grandparents, and still further back, until the inevitable end, which is the beginning of everything: the first cell, born by chance, more than 3,500 million years ago at a depth of 3,500 meters, when the core of the earth happened to release a bubble of warm air into a sea like the one I'm listening to right now as it beats against the cliff. An aberration. A monumental coincidence, an error perhaps, resulting hundreds of thousands of millions of coincidences later in me. Telling the story of any life is a work of archaeology. I can't go quite that far.

I feel a little dizzy. I never used to be like this. I used to believe in things. In signs, and in my ability to interpret them. One summer afternoon twenty years ago, in this very house, I announced to the whole family my intention of studying meteorology. Mama didn't say a word, and I assumed that meant she thought it was a good idea. Papa proposed a game, a challenge: I had to guess which wind was blowing without looking out the window. I went through the house. The *garbí*, I said. It was easy. The towels in the big bathroom, which faced south, were damp. The kitchen floor, which Mama had scrubbed almost twenty minutes ago, hadn't dried yet. The *garbí*, therefore, the moist southern wind. One plus one equals two. My brain processed this data automatically; the activity had as little to do with my will as my heartbeat. I was eighteen years old: knowing things was a source of pride, an incentive to learn more.

Now it simply makes me tired. This evening, as soon as I reached Malespina, even before I got out of the car, I saw the detritus whirling around next to the woodshed under the open window of the laundry room, and it took me only a moment to understand what that meant: at least two consecutive days of *garbí*, sweeping up all the pine needles and dead leaves that have accumulated in the back patio since autumn began and piling them against the wall.

The open window meant that someone was in the house. Since I didn't hear any music, it couldn't be Pablo. If it was Alberto, Papa and Luis would be with him. If Alberto hadn't swept the patio, it was because he couldn't leave Papa. Conclusion: Papa wasn't well. All deduced from an open window. If A, then B, followed by C, as if the only law I've ever believed in, the law of logic, truly existed. It's exhausting. It's the first time I've felt like this, of course, but it's never overwhelmed me before. I've never felt such an intense weariness, as if life has been secretly forging a metal band around my chest and now it's so tight I can barely breathe. I feel as though my life were a film I've seen too many times; it bores me because I know it by heart, and yet I don't understand it. I stayed in the car, motionless, without even taking the trouble to stop the engine, one hand on the ignition key and the other on the door handle, incapable of moving a single muscle. The chain of mechanical gestures—opening the door, lifting my leg out of the car, placing my foot on the ground—seemed to require a superhuman effort, both mental and physical. I'm thirty-eight. I probably have half my life ahead of me. And yet, at that moment, I felt as if a thousand years of knowledge were weighing on my shoulders. Which is a fancy way of saying I felt old.

I don't know how long I stayed there. I cried for a good while, I suppose. Ever since I received the news of Mama's death, weeping has become one of my habits. At first, there was grief, of course, and surprise; later, when we went to claim her body, I cried from sheer nerves. Now, I don't know. It comes over me like this, all at once, a tremendous weariness coupled with the urge to bawl my eyes out. I could also blame it on my hormones. I've been pregnant for only six weeks, but already I can detect the revolution that's taking place in my body. I've stopped using eye makeup. Like a drunk in a cartoon, I have a red nose round the clock. When I've been crying, I don't look at myself in the mirror.

All that notwithstanding, when Luis opened the door for me, he said I looked prettier than ever. Had he been anyone else, I would have raged at him for lying, but my nephew can't lie, not even for the sake of politeness. He always says what he thinks. I want to have a long talk with him, just the two of us. Prettier than ever, he says. He put a hand on my stomach. Am I showing? No, I know I'm not showing. Maybe my lips are a little thicker, but I don't think anyone's noticed. They don't know yet. It doesn't make sense to say anything to anybody until I decide whether I'm going to keep it or not. Alberto was nervous, solicitous, and clumsy all at once, as if he were walking on a carpet of eggshells. Every time I come to Malespina, he shows me the whole house, room by room, as though it were new. Or as though he's just the custodian who takes care of it in my absence. With regard to Papa, it's best for me not to say anything, although I think he at least recognized me. I don't know, it could also be that his smile is a reflex, a trick employed by his wandering brain to hide the fact that he has no idea who he's talking to. I'd rather not talk about Papa. The four of us had dinner together.

I feel better now, up here on the terrace, alone. Writing is a comfort to me. It would take a warehouse to store all the notebooks I've filled up over the years. For a long time, I kept them, but two or three years ago I decided to throw them all away because they contained nothing but questions. This afternoon, before leaving Barcelona, I bought three new notebooks like this one. I hope it's different this time—I hope some answers find their way onto these pages. I have a great deal to write about. Lies I've been told, truths I've learned, recent events. I'm in no hurry. I've requested a fifteen-day holiday, and I don't suppose this whole procedure with Mama's ashes is going to take more than three or four days. I'm going to ask Alberto to let me stay here after everyone else leaves, so I can keep writing, so I can think. He'll be put out by my request—he may even be offended. He'll say I don't need anyone's permission; he'll say it's my house too. That's a lie. I have my own key and my own room and I know I can come and go as I please, but the house is still his. I'm not complaining; I'm just calling things by their proper name.

Sometimes I write a word without knowing what the next one will be. Such uncertainty doesn't bother me. I'm confident that these words will follow the thread back to the other end of what I am and take me back to the beginning of everything I want to tell. Until that happens, at least they'll keep me awake and I'll be able to avoid the nightmare that persecutes me, the dream of churning mud, the vision of my mother's flayed hands and mangled fingers that invades my brain whenever I close my eyes to sleep. Ever since Mama died, I've been at war with my own mind. It betrays me while I sleep, and sometimes even when I'm awake, pounding me with terrible images: fantasies of shipwrecks involving not only my mother, but also myself, and even the little creature I'm going to bear. In return, I exact from my brain a miserable revenge: its punishment is to spend these endless nights with me, compelled to supply me with one word after another. If a single word remains to be written, I won't sleep. We'll see who wins.

I get up and walk toward the end of the terrace. There's a new moon tonight and I can barely make out the balustrade, but I could describe the view from here with my eyes closed. There's a pine tree over there—about three meters beyond the balustrade—that's more than a hundred years old, maybe even two hundred. It's grown almost horizontally, sticking out at a dizzying angle over the edge of the cliff, as though bewitched by the waves lapping below. When we were children, we used to clamber up it all the way from the Russian woman's beach, holding on to the tough, stout roots that protruded from the earth like so many ribs. It seemed incredible to me that the roots of a tree could run so deep and spread so wide. Like the roots of lies. But I didn't think that then; I only say it now.

Before me, on the other side of the bay, rises the headland of Cabo

San Sebastián, the site of a lighthouse built in 1857 that has a great deal to do with the story of my life. I close my eyes and play a game. I try to open them at the exact moment when the light from the lighthouse sweeps across the terrace and seems to pause on my face. I always guess correctly, but I don't deserve much credit for that, because I know that the lighthouse beam returns to this spot every 3.47 seconds, so I count to three and then I open my eyes. My father taught me that. And I have evidence that this one thing, at least, is true.

Everything else was a lie. Or a half-truth. The Battle of the Formigues Islands, for example. The Islas Formigues, the Ant Islands, are to my right, two or three miles out to sea. They barely break the line of the water, a sketchy string of rocks like ants swarming over the foaming waves. The most important battle fought in the western Mediterranean during the whole of the Middle Ages took place nearby, more than 150 vessels, their bows splintering from their crews' ferocious efforts to close with the enemy. Why do I say "vessels"? Because that's the word my father uses; I would say "ships." More than 150 ships, facing one another like angry dogs. There were thousands of deaths. When we were little, Papa would describe this battle to us as if it had been an innocent fight between children wielding nothing more harmful than slingshots.

The village of Malespina is a lie, too. It's over to my left. If it were daylight, I'd say I can't see the village from here because a pine grove blocks the view in that direction. It's just like me to try to describe a view the night prevents me from seeing. That is, a view that's not a view. Maybe it's better this way—the night hides the cranes rising above the roofs of the village and the concrete blocks starting to appear in clearings in the pine grove. From here, I can maintain the nostalgic fantasy that Malespina hasn't changed; I can pretend it's still the same idyllic fishing village where I passed the long summers of my childhood. The place near where my grandfather Simón's ship went down and he survived, after struggling against the sea for three consecutive days. The place where my father chose to build a house with his own hands, a house that looked out to sea in honor of Simón. To the right of the house, a couple of kilometers south, is the Russian woman's castle. I don't need to see it, either. I could say that the wind carries the fragrance of her botanical garden, but in fact the wind smells only of dampness and salty air. Today, that is.

Imprisonment or exile. Simón or Li Po. According to my father's tales, which I do not necessarily continue to believe, the poet Li Po was exiled for lying to the emperor. My grandfather Simón was locked up for deceiving his father. When we were little, my father used to tell us, "You've told a lie, and I've caught you out. You know the punishments. Choose for yourself: imprisonment, like Simón, or exile, like Li Po." In reality, it made no difference which one you chose, because the punishment was always the same. Go to your room. To bed without supper. Nothing serious. My parents weren't terribly strict; in fact, they were just the opposite. And, although it's true that Papa was particularly obsessed with teaching us not to lie, the punishment was usually symbolic. You had to have practiced a very great deception for your imprisonment, or your exile, to be prolonged beyond a couple of hours. But that's not what is bothering me. What bothers me is that Li Po *wasn't* exiled. And it may be true that my grandfather Simón was locked up, but there are so many obscure elements in his story that sometimes I prefer to believe the whole thing is entirely false.

You don't need a lighthouse to know that the night is strewn with lies. They're everywhere; they're evidence of life. They grow around a person by dint of his mere presence, like the lowly greenery that will spring up between two stones if oxygen and light should countenance its existence.

It took me years to accept the impossibility of knowing the past, as distinct from knowing accounts of the past. A legacy of centuries, of superimposed generations, of tales complementing or contradicting or denying or getting entangled with one another. That's why "explain" and "tell" are synonyms. A law of life: at the precise instant when someone tells a truth, that truth is transformed into a tale. Only then I stopped blaming my father. I stopped wishing him a long exile or laborious imprisonment as a punishment for his fictions. So why am I feeling that old frustration again now, when I thought I'd finally overcome it? Should I blame this, too, on my hormones? It is possible I may decide to become a mother. I wasn't looking to get pregnant, and I'm not sure I want to be pregnant. But suppose I do go ahead. Suppose I allow myself to become one more link in the chain of generations that every family represents. In that case, I'd like to be certain the other end of the chain is solidly anchored somewhere. In a beginning—no matter how remote—worthy of the name. A beginning more substantial than a bubble of air and the first cell. A beginning that will someday allow me to tell my child the story of who he is. Because that won't depend on my will or on his: we are who we're told we are. Grandfather Simón's story, if it were true, would be a good beginning.

This isn't the ends of the earth. Maybe it looks that way, but it's not. There aren't any hotels at the ends of the earth, and the Posada del Caribe, although it's not in the best of shape and is abandoned for months at a time, is indeed a hotel. Or something similar. Within two or three weeks, when the dry season begins, the mosquito plague will disappear and the human epidemic will return in small, well-organized groups. They'll be taken in canoes to see the lake and the Mayan ruins. Someone will cook black beans and rice for them; at breakfast, they'll eat scrambled eggs and ham. They'll be carrying instant coffee and powdered milk and consider themselves intrepid. At night, by the light of a lantern, they'll all check the pockets in their backpacks to make sure their return tickets are still safely stashed.

I don't know what I'm going to do when they begin to arrive. I surely won't stay here, but I don't know where I'll go. It's too bad I'm no longer young and strong enough to build myself a cabin on the other side of the lake. That's the only reason I wish I were younger: not twenty years younger, or thirty, but twelve thousand years younger. Hunting my food every day and eating it half raw, badly cooked. Maybe growing something. I know how it's done. I've seen corn growing in unlikelier places than this. Drawing an animal on a rock without knowing why. Believing that heavenly bodies can tell me things. Interpreting the flights of birds. Swimming in the lake. Well, I can still do that. Every morning, I walk down to the shore, slide slowly into the water, and swim with my eyes closed, or rather I float, holding my head up like a crocodile. I go out thirty or forty meters almost without moving my limbs, as if it were forbidden to break the glassy surface of the water with so much as a ripple. When I reach the middle of the lake, I open my eyes. It's overwhelming.

The first time, when I was standing on the shore with the water around my ankles, I decided to take off my swimsuit. After all, I thought, there's no one here to see me and even if I am being spied on, I doubt that the sight of my naked body could be much of an occasion for sin. I remember thinking about the Russian woman right before I lowered myself into the water, and I had to smile. I let the current carry me. It flows soundlessly but steadily, renewing the lake with the abundant outpourings of the river. I opened my eyes and laughed out loud, I don't know why. I was so surprised by my own guffawing that I even swallowed a little water. Then I started yelling: "I'm here!" At first, the water ignored me, as if it were shrugging its shoulders, shaming me with its silence, but suddenly the echo came rolling back: "I'mhereherehereI'mI'mI'mheeereI'mheeere!" Dozens of white herons rose in flight, and the mirror image of their undersides flashed on the surface of the water. Then I felt depressed about my apparent inability to shout something more impressive and dignified, something worth remembering. To me, "I'm here" sounded like something scrawled by a bored prisoner on an old stone wall.

The water of Lake Petexbatún is so dense that to float on it, you almost don't need to know how to swim. Every morning, I play dead, suspended in the water like a cork. I watch the sky pass by like someone watching the steady flow of time. I can't bring myself to dive, however. What am I saying, "dive"? I can't even bring myself to put my head under the water. You can't see a thing, not even a few inches away, and it makes me afraid. The dead are down there. Of course I know they aren't really there. No one knows better than I that the dead survive only in the worm that eats them; that they live again only in the apple that houses the worm; that they breathe again only in the bird that pecks at the apple; that their eternity is as short as the flight of the arrow aimed at the bird. The Great Beyond? Please. We don't even survive in the memories of the living. Science has destroyed that myth. Whenever we remember something, what we're doing is remembering the last time we remembered it; our memory doesn't go back to the original notch, the *first one that was cut, but to the last one. Human memory is virtual, like that of a computer. When we open a file, we're not opening it as it was when we first created it, but as it was the last time we used it. It's called hypercathexis and is our brain's most sophisticated recourse when it comes to confronting pain. We're often surprised by the fortitude of other people; we marvel at the instinct that enables them to overcome horrific situations and rebuild their lives: abused children, or mothers whose children have died, or survivors of massacres. But they aren't any stronger than anyone else, nor do they have a greater capacity for forgetting. It's not that their memory blocks out the source of their pain. What it does is defer it, interposing itself between the sufferer and his sorrow and offering him a recollection not of his pain, but of himself.*

Take the Wari Indians of the Amazon, for example. A few days after a Wari dies, his relatives gather in the part of the forest where he used to station himself for the hunt. They clear away the vegetation from the area and burn the leaves and brush. For a good while, until the undergrowth returns and takes possession of the place again, it remains a kind of sanctuary. The idea is that every time someone passes by, he'll remember the dead person. They don't know that they're really remembering themselves, because the most recent notch in their memory isn't the dead man, it's the gesture they made in his honor when they sanctified his hunting ground.

There are hundreds of examples. Perhaps the clearest one comes from the Laymi of Bolivia. The Laymi inherit land directly through the male line; that is, the property of a deceased father passes to his first-born son and no one else. In exchange, the son must take on the support of the rest of the family. He also inherits the moral responsibility for preserving his family's ancestral memory in a specific way: he has to remember the names of the male ancestors who preceded him in the succession—the more he remembers, the better. I claim no credit for the discovery of this custom. I went to Bolivia for the first time in 1968, and by then the practice had been recorded in the anthropological literature for more than fifteen years. But I did discover a curious coincidence:

no one remembered more than six names in his ancestral line. Most people stopped at four generations, others could go back five, but only two of the heads of families I interviewed could name six. A magic number? No, land registry. The obligatory registration of rural property in Bolivia first began in 1884. The numbers speak for themselves, and that's what I discovered: no matter how hard you squeeze them, and no matter how generous you are in attributing extraordinary precociousness to all the members of a single ancestral line, there's just no way of making room for more than six generations between 1884 and 1969. In other words, even in a society that prized memory as a moral duty, no one was able to remember what had never been written down.

Which is to say, the dead don't even survive in memory. They're not under the water. They're not anywhere; that's the essence of being dead. The word "where" is for the living. The word "word" is for the living. But I'm still afraid. I can't help it. It's a concrete, physical fear, like needles pricking my skin, as if someone's going to pull me down the moment I duck my head below the surface. I imagine the arms of the dead waving like sea anemones. In every culture I know about, the dead are associated with water. The souls of the Laymi transmigrate to a paradise called tacna. To reach this paradise, the soul has to cross the sea in the nose or the ear of a black dog. If the dog doesn't make it, the soul remains trapped in the water and turns into what we call a lost soul. If the dog succeeds in crossing the sea, it comes to a subterranean place where the happy community of the dead dedicate themselves to the cultivation of chili peppers. Once a year, the souls return to the village, where they're welcomed with great celebrations. After the festival is over, the living participants must cross a river to wash off the souls that may have attached themselves to them.

Under the water. The souls of the Wari dead live in the river, under the water. To get out, they must become incarnate in some animal; sometimes it's a fish, more often it's a bird, but wild pigs are preferred above all. White-snouted wild pigs, which the relatives of the dead hunt with the utmost respect: the dead person lives again, nourishing his loved ones. When they hunt him, his spirit returns to the river. There's not much for the dead to do in the river, beyond waiting for a new dead person to arrive. But when that happens, when a fresh soul joins them, the dead throw huge welcome banquets, at which, supposedly, gallons and gallons of corn beer are consumed. The Wari community has no leader; instead, there's a kind of council of elders which in turn is divided into various family councils. The dead Wari, however, the ones in the river, do have a leader, a giant whose name is Towira. "Towira" means "testicle"; that is to say, the leader of the dead is a gigantic testicle. The Wari would have been my great project, the high point of my whole career, the definitive study: death and life, fertility and death, sex and regeneration, virility and death. It was not to be. I was abruptly kicked out and my life threatened. For more than thirty years now, I've been barred from entering Brazil. And even if I should manage to get back in, even if I were to get hold of some fake papers and slip into the country via Ecuador, Peru, or Bolivia, as soon as I got close to the state of Rondônia, and long before I could reach the Wari villages—Tanajura, Deolinda, Negro-Ocaia—they'd arrest me and deport me back to Spain. That's if I was lucky. If not, they'd probably murder me. More than one of them has spent thirty years hoping to get their hands on me. They'd like me to give in to curiosity and nostalgia, to ignore the warnings of common sense and try to revisit the Wari. The few that are left, that is.

I've never dared to go back, and I know I'll never walk in that jungle again. I have no choice but to settle for pale imitations like Petexbatún, an inferior but beautiful substitute. Where I can be alone. Where I can swim in the lake, look at the sky, and ignore the waters beneath me. Where I can ignore the dead, and the great Towira.

MONDAY

To tell the story of my grandfather Simón, perhaps I should forget my questions and avert my eyes when contradictions appear. Maybe I should just assume that the tale is true, and tell it the way I've heard Papa tell it so many times. I'm going to try, even though my doubts are so considerable, it's as if I were trying to construct a medieval castle with bricks made of foam. I'll use borrowed words. Old, grandiloquent words. I have no others.

On the evening of January 10, 1922, Simón—who had recently passed his nineteenth birthday—obtained his father's permission to go out shortly after eight-thirty, allegedly to study for an exam with some fellow students from the university. His real intention was to attend the premiere of Jacinto Benavente's play *El collar de las estrellas* (*The Necklace of Stars*) at the Teatro Goya in Barcelona.

This innocent prank, typical of a boy his age, was the only lie Simón told his father. It seems easy to excuse, especially since it was part of the ongoing conflict that had pitted father against son for more than two years: Simón wanted to be an actor, and his father refused to allow the boy to indulge what he, the father, considered a passing fancy. The first time Simón told his father of his ambition, the reply was unequivocal: "Don't even think about it. It's not a decent profession—in fact, I don't consider it a profession at all. Besides, you already cause enough drama at home." On many subsequent occasions, Simón begged his father to reconsider, but the stern parent remained unmoved. Furthermore, he took every opportunity to make it clear that, in his view, the theater was an occupation for idlers, and that Simón would find nothing there but characters with dubious morals and opportunities to ruin his future. "I've spent half my life working like a donkey so you could have a decent education," Simón's father used to say, repeating his words so exactly and unchangingly that he seemed to be reciting them from memory, and thrusting out his hands to exhibit his extensive calluses. "And I'm not going to let you throw everything away on a whim. Besides, you don't really want to be an actor. That little seamstress has turned your head, her and your rich pals. The subject is closed. Your sainted mother, may she rest in peace, would have wanted you to take up a respectable profession, and my mind is made up: you're going to be a lawyer. If you refuse, you have only one other choice—you'll work with me in the family business."

The aforementioned "family business" was a small fruit and vegetable shop in the Born district of Barcelona. The shop was located in a narrow street adjacent to the rear of the big market; that is, in a place where customers rarely ventured, except for those who had already made their purchases, realized they'd forgotten something, and wanted to avoid going back into the market proper. It was a minuscule shop that faced north so directly it was never blessed by a single ray of sunlight. The back of the shop was a leaky atrium that harbored an ancient dampness and exuded an odor of old socks, against which even the fresh apples struggled in vain. Simón's hatred for this cranny stemmed from his childhood, when his father used to make him sit among the boxes of oranges while he did his homework, and by now it was so deeply rooted in his heart that the place caused him genuine physical revulsion. A few hours of its damp exhalations and penetrating odors was enough to provoke an allergic reaction, including an itchy rash that covered his whole body. For this reason, Simón had opted to study law, even though he felt nothing remotely resembling a vocation.

Simón's "sainted mother, may she rest in peace," who surfaced with irritating regularity in the stream of the paternal discourse, had died of dysentery many years before, when her son was barely two years old. And if his father invoked her every time he wished to criticize the boy's behavior, Simón used her as well, as the explanation and cause of all his misery, since with her premature death she had not only deprived him of maternal affection, but also left him at the mercy of this unfeeling and ignorant brute of a father. As a result, Simón, instead of venerating his mother's memory, tended to look down on her; any woman capable of loving such a man, he thought, could not have made a very good mother.

And finally, there was Amparo Ortuño, Simón's girlfriend, contemptuously dubbed "that little seamstress" by his father because she spent her time sewing and mending costumes for the Compañía del Corral, a drama company that specialized in performing the works of classical Spanish theater and in which Simón hoped to make his debut someday in the not-too-distant future. He was preparing himself by performing as the principal actor in an amateur group whose members—the "rich pals" who were the objects of his father's scorn—unceasingly praised Simón's histrionic prowess and his powerful, resonant voice. It is said, moreover, that his prodigious memory enabled him to remember entire classical works as if they were mere cradle songs, and that he was also handsome and well built. These gifts, coupled with his obsessive sense of vocation, meant that the only thing Simón was missing was a lucky break, his big chance. Simón was certain that this lack of opportunity was due solely to his humble origins, which denied him access to the necessary resources and contacts. Therefore, instead of telling his father once and for all that he felt not the slightest interest in the malodorous family business, Simón had opted for pretending to accept the paternal rules, convinced that he would be able to keep seeing Amparo and frequent the intimate world of the theater in secret.

It wouldn't be entirely correct to say that Simón led a double life, for there were not two but three existences that he found himself obliged to combine. Three lives that were completely distinct, not to say irreconcilable.

The worst of these existences, the one he most desired to leave behind, occupied his every morning, with the sole exception of Sundays. To be more precise, it occupied his every daybreak, because Simón always woke up before dawn to accompany his father to the shop. The first three hours—dedicated to sweeping and scrubbing the floor, unloading the merchandise from the trucks, and stacking it according to his father's instructions—left Simón physically exhausted. These hours were not, however, the most galling, because he could concentrate on his chores and largely ignore the maddeningly slow passage of time and the growing weariness in his muscles. The worst came later, around ten o'clock in the morning, when most of the few regular customers had come and gone, and there hung over Simón the prospect of spending yet another four hours in that detested place, praying that some confused shopper might make a wrong turn and drop in. When such a thing happened, Simón considered himself lucky. He was charming and attentive to the customers, he spoke to them most courteously, and, if they happened to live in the area, he even went so far as to offer to carry their purchases home for them; anything to avoid remaining alone in the shop with his father, exposed for long hours to the verbal pummeling that represented the paternal idea of conversation. Should no customer appear, Simón had no choice but to submit to his father's endless monologues about the obstacles lying in wait for him, the ephemeral and deceitful nature of pleasure, the necessity of strengthening and hardening his will, and a great many other interminable discourses. Simón avoided these sermons like the plague, and to this end he had developed an ample and imaginative inventory of excuses, with which he reduced to the absolute minimum the amount of time he passed in his father's company. Nevertheless, when all the daily chores were done, there was often no escape.

At such times, Simón pretended to contribute to the conversation with frequent nods of assent, but his mind would begin to drift and he would picture himself on a stage very far away, declaiming ageless verses to an enraptured audience. Although this was his chief desire, imagining it failed to bring him the relative happiness that fantasies can elicit; for the more he surrendered to his daydream, the more conscious he was of the enormous distance that separated it from his real life, the more the damp surroundings of the shop made their presence felt, and the meaner his father appeared to him. At those moments, Simón felt like a prisoner: imprisoned by his father, by that place, by his unattainable desire. Imprisoned by life.

Once or twice a week, he managed briefly to escape from his trap with the excuse of shutting himself up alone in the rear of the shop to balance his father's accounts. This was a perfect alibi, because his father was barely capable of adding small sums up on his fingers and the rear of the shop wasn't big enough for two people. A table and a single chair, both equally wobbly and wedged against the wall between sacks and crates overflowing with produce, served as an office. In this narrow, uncomfortable space, the elaborate gilded mirror that hung on the wall above the table might have seemed like a concession to luxury, except for the decades of dust that covered it and the punishment its quicksilver had sustained at the hands of time, so that every face reflected in the glass took on a phantasmagoric aspect. Simón sat at the table and raced through the accounts in a matter of minutes. Then, in order to postpone the moment when he would have to return to the paternal monologue, Simón chose to endure the dampness in the rear of the shop and tried to find some way of amusing himself. It was there that he perfected his skills as a cardsharp and juggler. He was capable of keeping six and even seven pieces of fruit in the air at the same time. At the beginning of winter, when the first smooth, firm mandarins—ideal for juggling—arrived, he was able to handle eight of them at once. When his arms grew tired, he took out the shiny deck of cards he always carried and played solitaire, but not just any old solitaire: before he began, he took all the aces and queens from the deck and hid them in his sleeves, in his pockets, and in the folds of his clothing. His trick was to complete a game of solitaire while making sure—by means of a few furtive glances into the murky depths of the mirror—that no hypothetical observer could notice how he was able to produce card after card from the most innocuous-seeming places. When he had time, Simón would also set himself the challenge of building a house of cards, which he considered successful only if he managed to use up the whole deck before the structure collapsed.

And so he spent many a stolen moment, waiting for his father to give him permission to leave the shop a little before two in the afternoon. Then, and despite his overwhelming desire to step into the street, Simón delayed his exit by performing a ritual he deemed indispensable: he would soak a sponge in bleach and scrub his hands energetically for ten minutes, as though he intended to clean them right down to the bone. He knew it was useless: the odor of onions succumbed to the bleach for a few hours, but then, in the middle of the afternoon, it would come creeping back, little by little reclaiming full possession of his skin.

That smell was the only thing Simón brought with him in his transition from one existence to the next, from the shop to the university. His humble clothing set him apart from his fellow students, and so did a barely conscious gesture: every few minutes, pretending to scratch his nose, he would sniff his fingertips. For the rest, he was a normal student; he tried not to miss classes and even dedicated a few nocturnal hours to going over his textbooks. Not too many; just enough to pass and thus ensure that his father would continue paying for his studies. Since he never imagined that he would actually become a lawyer, his classes struck him as nothing more than ridiculous monologues intoned by pompous professors, but they were infinitely preferable to his father's sermons.

A prisoner in the mornings, reluctant student in the afternoons. Only his third life—kept secret by a web of elaborate lies and delicate alibis—brought him pleasure and satisfaction, although not enough to compensate for the wretchedness of the other two. For one thing his nocturnal forays were rare. His alibi was that he was joining some fellow students, an excuse that Simón could hardly have recourse to more than a couple of nights a month. Because of this, he was prudent in availing himself of opportunities and planned his outings with great care.

Two comrades, always the same ones, from his group of theater enthusiasts would pick him up around eight o'clock in the evening. They were soberly dressed, their breath had been cleansed of all traces of alcohol, and they carried the hefty legal tomes that Simón had taken care to provide them with in advance. For ten minutes or so, they would pay court to Simón's father, making a show of agreeing with his outpourings of platitudinous advice; then, with great formality, they took their leave and disappeared with Simón down the stairs, containing their guffaws until they were sufficiently far away.

It's not surprising that Simón planned those evenings so meticulously, because they offered in concentrated form the only three pleasures of his life: theater, card playing, and Amparo. The evening would begin with two or three hours of rehearsal; afterward, while they consumed a late dinner, they played cards. To avoid giving himself away, Simón sometimes kept his cheating skills in check, but nevertheless, he almost always won. Or rather, he always won when he needed to. Since the money his father gave him barely sufficed to pay for his university textbooks and transportation, these card games, as far as Simón was concerned, were more than just entertainment; they were a secondary source of income. The stakes weren't high, but his winnings allowed him to indulge the odd whim and, above all, to buy Amparo the occasional present. Whenever he did this, she'd object—"Simón, you're crazy. Don't forget, you're even poorer than I am." But she accepted his gifts: cheap jewelry, perhaps an article of clothing, and so on. Humble objects, in short, with which Simón expressed his appreciation for Amparo's admiration at rehearsals, her silence during card games, and the liberties she allowed him to take on the way home when they embraced in the sheltering darkness of some doorway.

From time to time, money my grandfather won at cards also permitted him the luxury of attending a professional theatrical performance. Whenever he learned that an interesting troupe was scheduled to arrive in Barcelona, Simón would mark the date in the calendar, and during the two months leading up to the play he made sure to win every game. At the risk of tacitly conceding that his father was right, he soothed his guilty conscience by telling himself that his comrades were rich kids for whom the theater was little more than a passing fancy and whose money flowed through their hands like water, so they would scarcely notice their losses.

Such special skills allowed Simón and Amparo to see the opening performance of *El collar de las estrellas* on the evening of January 10, 1922. And so we return to the lie that caused Simón's terrible confinement, and I still can't get over my astonishment that a lie so insignificant—and, given the circumstances, so justifiable—was to play such a transcendent role in his life. He deceived his father with the usual story, made his exit, and set off to pick up Amparo. They went to the Goya and saw the play, which they found monotonous and vulgar, despite Mateo Alonso's efforts to bring a certain sobriety to his leading role. Their respect for the actors' work obliged Simón and Amparo to keep quiet during the performance, but it did not prevent Simón from actively participating in the rousing chorus of whistles and boos at the end of the play. We shouldn't blame him for behaving this way. He was young, he was passionate about theater, and he had every right to express his convictions. And . . .

And that's as far as we can go. The story goes on, of course, and I know it by heart. I could keep writing for pages and pages, but I just can't. It's as simple as that. My questions bring the tale to a screeching halt. To start with, how do I know all these things? I never knew Simón; I've never even seen a photograph of him. Everything I know about him was told to me by my father. The problem is that my father never knew him either, because Simón died before he was born, probably without ever even imagining that Amparo was pregnant. Amparo died years ago. I did know her, but I was too young to formulate the right questions. Nor can I ask Papa; his brain isn't capable of accounting for anything anymore. So here's my situation: it's not that there aren't any answers to the questions buzzing around my mind, it's that I don't even know to whom I should address them. I'm looking for a lighthouse in the desert.

Because my father was born without a father, I imagine that Amparo created a legend for him. She wanted to provide her son with a filtered image of his absent parent: the most flattering image possible, even the most heroic, and not necessarily false. I have no problem accepting this. What surprises me is how completely that legend turned into history. Normally, with the passage of time, the account of Simón's life would have been stripped of embellishments and hypotheses and reduced to its essentials, until the bare framework of a few certain facts was all that remained. But that's not what happened.

When I look over what I've written, I can't believe it. There are too many details; and yet there aren't enough details. It's certain that Amparo knew Simón and that she was his girlfriend, and it's probably true that she would have wound up marrying him had fate not intervened, making her a widow before she could have a wedding. But the story's so precise. Take Simón's father's shop, for example. We know how the dust gathered on the frame of the mirror in the rear of the shop, we even know the way the place smelled, but no one has ever said what street it was in. A narrow street adjacent to the market, that's all. Strange, isn't it? At one time, I thought it would be a good idea to begin my investigations with that shop. Maybe the Barcelona municipal records contain some information about the shop and its proprietor; maybe the place still exists; maybe it's still a fruit and vegetable shop to this day. But in order to find out, I'd have to know exactly where it was. It's maddening. I know what Simón's thoughts were as he sat by himself at the rear of the shop, but I can't know a simple fact like its address. Am I expected to believe that we *know* how Simón "soothed his guilty conscience" about cheating his friends in the card games they played together? We know it was Mateo Alonso who played the leading role in the play Simón and Amparo saw that night, but who in hell was Mateo Alonso? Best of all was the way Papa always introduced the passage on

Simón's three lives: "It wouldn't be completely correct to say that Simón led," et cetera. In the midst of this enormous symphony of confusion, we pay homage to meticulous accuracy.

No. I have too many doubts. I know for a fact that Papa had doubts as well and that he tried to clear them up when he was younger, just as I did twenty years ago. He interrogated his mother, he did a little investigating, but I seriously doubt that his investigations were as methodical and tenacious as mine. I suspect that in the end his imagination—or his curiosity, or his need to construct a complete history for Simón in order to alleviate the awful task of inventing himself out of nothing—was giving him answers that were more or less credible, although not necessarily correct. After we children came along, Papa took the next logical step and dedicated hours to telling us the same stories he'd been telling himself for so many years.

This story, this extravagantly shadowy legend in which my grandfather left a theater in Barcelona and almost immediately found himself fighting for his life in the sea off Malespina—and according to which, incidentally, he could suspend mandarins in the air with impossible, interplanetary weightlessness and declaim classical verses in a voice like thunder—this story wouldn't hold up. It worked for a while, of course, but only because we were children.

Indeed, I was the first to demand, as children do, that the story be told the same way, word for word, every time; I was the first to protest when Papa substituted lemons for mandarins, or when he forgot to mention Mateo Alonso, or when he took the liberty of changing any adjective applied to Simón, even if he chose that adjective's perfect synonym. Unfortunately, today I no longer believe that the successive transmission of all those words—from Simón to Amparo, from her to my father, from him to me, from me to whomever—was some sort of generous loan. The price I pay for them, the price of not knowing who I am, is too high. Nevertheless, I can't help acknowledging their power. I say that the story slips away from me whenever I try to tell it as it really was, but at the same time, I have to admit that it makes me jealous. How Simón grew in Papa's voice, how easy it was to imagine him. Until the character of Simón fell apart and revealed itself as a worm-eaten dummy with rusty metal joints. I started asking questions. I must have been fourteen, maybe fifteen. "How do you know this? Why don't you know this other? Who told you that? How did she know?" Poor Papa. Sometimes he'd forgotten, sometimes he had no idea, and he'd start blinking and saying things like, "Who knows, sweetheart? I don't remember. Ask your mother. If your grandmother were alive . . ."

I bombarded him for almost three years, opening holes in his defenses with my questions, like so many cannonballs. It was a long, extremely hard fought battle, but in the end I won, or I thought I won. And what a triumph. Not only did Papa agree to reexamine Simón's story with me, it was even his idea, my seventeenth birthday present. I remember our conversation as if it were yesterday. We talked until well past dawn. I remember Papa sitting across from me, as handsome as always and closer than ever. And above all, I remember myself, excited and proud, an adult at last, worthy of inheriting not just stories, but something more: doubts, complaints, heartaches, uncertainties. Papa was fifty-seven years old back then, but it was still a pleasure to walk by his side and watch people's eyes fasten onto him like brooches. Maybe beauty was the only legacy Simón left him. Beauty and the authority that resonated in his voice. As for the rest—his magnetism, his elegance, his composure—I don't know where they came from. Now, it's too sad. To say that he's a mere shadow of his former self would be a euphemism; he's a shadow projected onto a glass pane shattered into a million pieces.

It does me good to remember that night. Papa was chatty as usual, but more restrained, letting me do most of the talking. And like any self-respecting teenage girl, I was using my charm on my father. For the first time, I didn't have the impression that he was simply regaling me with a legend; instead I felt that he was placing the entire manuscript in my hands, complete with deletions and emendations, its undecipherable corrections, its footnotes scribbled on every page. Now I know that all the crossings out and changes made the manuscript unintelligible, but that doesn't change the fact that, at the time, I considered it a treasure.

"Before we begin, let's discuss the question of method," he said to me. We were having dinner in a restaurant. This was my present: dinner together, just the two of us, and a discussion of whatever it was I wanted to know. Of course, this arrangement didn't imply that Papa would not impose his own conditions. He said, "I'll tell you whatever you want. But when I say I don't know, that means I don't know. And if I tell you I don't remember, that means I don't remember. One more thing: don't forget that my father died before I was born. Almost everything I know about him comes from my own reinventions, which are based on a few vague stories my mother told me. In other words, when all is said and done, they're lies."

"Lies? Grandmother Amparo deceived you? I thought the liar was Simón."

"Well, maybe 'deceived' is too strong a word. Deception requires deliberation and I believe that my mother just improvised. Her portrait of my father wasn't false, but it was incomplete. I spent years trying to complete it, more or less the way you're doing now. For example, she never mentioned a single one of his flaws. All right, maybe she said he was a little stubborn, but nothing else. Doesn't that strike you as unusual?"

"Come on, it's only logical. Grandmother adored him."

"Are you sure?"

"You don't mean . . ."

"No, I don't mean anything specific, it's just an example. Sometimes you accuse me of telling you things as if they were true without offering any proof, but you do the same thing. You take it for granted that my mother adored my father. That's fine, but stop and think about it. They went out with each other for a couple of years at most, and they were never even formally engaged. I'm not saying they didn't love each other, but suppose Simón hadn't died. Or suppose she hadn't gotten pregnant. Who can tell what the passage of time would have done to them?"

"Right, but Grandmother always spoke so highly of him. . . ."

I can still remember that. For Amparo, Simón was a catalogue of virtues. Whenever she wanted to praise our conduct, she'd make some sort of comparison with him. If Alberto brought home a good report, she'd congratulate him by saying, "You're tenacious, like your grandfather. You'll go far." When Pablo started doing his first rehearsals, she remarked, "How beautifully that child sings. And such a big voice! It's natural—you can tell it's in his blood."

"Of course," Papa said, "there's nothing like dying to make people love you. Death turns you into a caricature. It seems that my father was a nice, affectionate man, and that trait was exaggerated over the years. Besides, put yourself in my mother's place. Life wasn't easy for her: she was alone with a baby and she didn't have many options. During my childhood, we never had anything like a real home. We moved from one small town to the next, following the theater company. Mama made some money on the side by doing sewing jobs for the ladies in the various towns. We didn't sleep. She'd stay up all night, and the noise of the sewing machine would wake me up every five minutes. The thing is, it wasn't easy, the life we had. I suppose she wanted to compensate me for being an orphan; maybe she thought that if this was the only father I was ever going to have, it would be worth embellishing the portrait a little."

"Fine. I have no argument with that, but it's not what I want to talk about. You admit you had the same doubts as I do and asked the same questions. So I imagine you found out something, something more than the tales Grandmother told you. Because if not, the story isn't believable. One night a man leaves the restaurant where he's had dinner after seeing a play, and the next day he's in a shipwreck who knows how many kilometers off the coast. . . ."

"All right! You want facts? Let's go over them. We know they had dinner in a restaurant after the theater. It was probably in some bar on the Ramblas, and we can assume that it was a place where the people knew them, since they were allowed to set up a card game. Maybe this seems like anecdotal evidence, but it's an important detail. Normally, the card games that Simón and his friends played after their rehearsals took place at one of their homes. But that evening was different because they had alcohol at their disposal, and everything suggests that they abused it. My mother used to say that she'd never seen such a raucous game, with table pounding and ludicrous bluffs, and higher stakes with every hand. There's another detail that's important for understanding what happened later: one of your grandfather's rich friends had a car, a brand-new Hispano-Suiza. I don't even know his name."

"Then let's give him one, so we can keep things straight."

"Very well. They used to call those cars Alfonso, in honor of the king, Alfonso XIII. So that's how we'll call him, if that makes you happy. It appears that he was extremely proud of his new car. Hispano-Suizas were made in Barcelona, but in 1921 they made a few deluxe models in Bois-Colombes, near Paris. The French ones were more expensive and extravagant than the Spanish edition, and they were a sensation. It was rare enough in those days for a young man even to own a car, so to drive an Alfonso manufactured in France was something else."

"And how do you know these details?"

"You think you're the only curious one in the family? I used to be your age too, baby girl, and I couldn't ignore that damned car. It played too important a part at the end of the story."

"I'm surprised. You never told me any of this before."

"No? Maybe you're right. I probably thought you were too young to understand. Anyway, apparently this Alfonso was interrupting the game every five minutes to enumerate the many virtues of his car and brag about what a fine machine it was, how much it had cost, how fast it could go. Although it was only a luxury touring car, Alfonso told his companions that when André Dubonnet had run it in a race in France, he beat all the professional drivers and set a new record: more than two hundred and ten kilometers in two hours. Perhaps Simón was jealous, or he was fed up with Alfonso interrupting the card game, or the alcohol had clouded his judgment; I don't know. In any case, he accused the other young man of lying, and declared the record impossible. His adversary cried out, 'Impossible?' According to Amparo, Alfonso was a good-for-nothing lout and certainly much more drunk than my father. He said again, 'Impossible? When do you want me to show you?' Now, we already know that Simón was a little hardheaded. He said, 'More than two hundred kilometers in two hours? No way. Not even a hundred and fifty. I'll bet you three hundred pesetas you can't do it.' Alfonso doubled the bet."

"Six hundred pesetas must have been a fortune in those days."

"You're right, it was a lot of money, even for someone from a well-to-do family like Alfonso, but that was the bet. He must have been confident that my father would back out because he was so much poorer. And it's true, our dear Simón could never have put together six hundred pesetas, not even if he worked for years on end, but he stuck to his guns. The debate grew more heated, the other members of the group egged them on, and finally, in spite of my mother's opposition, Simón and Alfonso left the restaurant, determined to go through with the bet. They had to reach Malespina in two hours."

"Impossible, right?"

"Naturally. Today we can do that trip in about an hour, but in those days, making it in two hours would have been a heroic feat. In fact, you'd have had to be crazy even to try it. First, there was a treacherous, winding road to Girona, and then the last stretch to Malespina was little more than a dirt track used by mules and goats."

"Wait, I want to write this down."

I was carrying a notebook with white paper, the same as the ones I still use today. Sometimes it saddens me to think that I didn't keep it. As Papa told me the story, I jotted things down. Not only the new information I was learning as he spoke, but also my questions. *List of possible Ramblas bars for after-theater gathering. Alfonso? Find out his real name. Look up history of Hispano-Suiza cars. French speed record 1921. Why Malespina? What road after Girona?*

"So what made them pick Malespina?"

"I have no idea. I asked my mother that same question many times. She said they'd never gone there before. To tell the truth, I don't imagine they'd ever traveled much at all. We're talking about poor people in 1922. They probably thought that going to what is now considered the outskirts of Barcelona was a long journey. Maybe Simón and Alfonso looked on some map and saw that the distance to Malespina was more or less right for their bet. Considering the end of the story, I'm inclined to suspect that they knew something about the tuna harvest. At that time of year, all the fishermen in the area gathered off the coast near Malespina to catch tuna. It's a shame you children never got to see it. The slaughter was so intense, it turned the sea red. . . ."

"Papa: Grandfather."

"What about Grandfather?"

"You're changing stories on me."

At that time, Papa was still active as a painter. Two more years would pass before he renounced his vocation and became a sailor. But for a long time before this, the mere mention of the sea was enough to distract him from whatever other matter was at hand. Even today, when I see that he's completely out of it, I talk to him about the sea to find out whether he's capable of holding a conversation, however short it may be.

"The thing is, there's no way of finding out the details of this part of the story. I assume Simón and Alfonso drove to some gas station in Barcelona, filled up the car, and then left town to settle their bet. Don't forget, in those days there was no such thing as road lights. . . . Anyway, if I'm right in supposing both driver and passenger were drunk, we could say that the guardian angel who later saved your grandfather's life in Malespina was already with him on the road there."

"And they got there, obviously."

"Yes, they got there. We know that the trip took them more than two hours, because your grandfather won the bet. But I don't think they were on the road for more than four hours, because the fishermen still hadn't set out by the time they arrived. Let's say they were there, on the Malespina section of the Port Bou shore, by five o'clock in the morning. In those days, there wasn't anything you could call a beach; it was more like a ribbon of sand that lay in a cove, just as it does today. The sea is calm there because the seafloor is smooth and a tongue of rock protects this cove and separates it from the next one so the fishermen could load and unload their boats with ease. People say that tourism put an end to fishing there, but that's a lie. What killed fishing was nothing other than that beach, and back in 1922, the first symptoms were already starting to appear. But let's not change the subject. I'll tell you about that another day."

"No, go on. It interests me."

Of course it interested me. More data for my notebook: *Fishing business 1922. Look up history Port Bou beach. Find out if any proof of Simón's presence in Malespina. Fishermen's Association?*

"I'll summarize it for you. Some villages had very deep coves and lots of wood. Shipyards. They started building bigger fishing boats with more extensive holds for the fish, and the fishermen in Malespina couldn't compete. No boat with a draft of more than three meters could anchor off any of their beaches. And they had no port, nor anywhere to build a port, nor money to pay for it if they did. Some fishermen sold their boats and some kept them, but they all wound up signing on with boat owners from the other villages. In any case, when your grandfather went to Malespina, this process was barely under way, and the village still had a respectable flotilla anchored in the waters off Port Bou."

"And so Grandfather and Alfonso got on a fishing boat and went out to sea? Just like that? Like going out to buy bread?"

"I don't know why you find that so surprising. Imagine that little beach at five in the morning, illuminated by only four or five torches sticking out of the sand, boats rocking in the shadows of the cove and some sixty fishermen rushing about with nets. For a young, inexperienced lad from Barcelona, that must have seemed exotic."

"Right, but the strange thing is that the boat captains took him on. They had no idea who he and Alfonso were."

"It's not so strange. Tuna fishing requires enormous physical effort. Don't forget, we're talking about potbellied wooden vessels; they had no motors, and you needed at least four strong men to hoist a lateen sail. They were maneuvered using oars, so a pair of powerful arms like your grandfather's couldn't hurt. Even so, there were problems. Alfonso had to stay ashore because he was carrying a leather wallet and refused to leave it behind. I guess he was also worried about leaving his brand-new car alone all day while he went fishing. In any case, it was forbidden to go on board carrying any leather item, including shoes or a belt, because leather was considered bad luck."

"Bad luck?"

"You can't imagine how superstitious fishermen were in those days. Supposedly, they even observed strict abstinence from sexual activity for three nights before going out. In the best years, the passage of the great tuna schools lasted for a maximum of four days and in that short period of time, practically the whole year's income for the fishermen was at stake. So it's no surprise that they became neurotic and obsessive. The fishermen were forbidden to cast their nets into the sea until permission was given by the poor wretch who served as the village healer. They brought him out every morning so he could dip a finger in the water. He was allegedly able to detect how close the tuna schools were, and not only that, he also predicted weather conditions."

Superstition? Investigate fishing customs.

"But this time he really messed up."

"Well, as it turned out, the storm rose up all of a sudden. But at six in the morning, everyone was in shirtsleeves. Simón apparently took that as a sign that the weather was going to be fine all day long. They say it was impossible to predict—but you know more about that sort of thing than I do. You spend your life looking at the sky."

It was my turn to give answers. I paid no heed back then to a paradox that grabs my attention today: Simón's story—or rather, Simón's story as told to me by my father—had a great deal to do with my childhood interest in storms. A devastating storm had turned my grandfather into a hero. I remember the summer thunderstorms in Malespina during my childhood; at an age when other girls would run to their parents for protection or hide under the bed, terrified by the roaring thunder, I'd press my nose to the window, eagerly scanning the sea and the sky, as if I were certain that a flash of lightning would illuminate the ghostly figure of Simón struggling in the water. I was obsessed with discovering some logical connection between the appearance of clouds and the downpour of rainwater. I'm not sure exactly how old I was the first time I got up enough nerve to announce that it was going to rain, but I do remember that it was a summer morning, that the sky was clear, that my brothers' mocking hurt my feelings, and that I felt vindicated later that afternoon, when the rain fell in torrents and Papa congratulated me on my accurate forecast. Perhaps I was seven. The following summer, Papa bought the first family boat, an Optimist, one of those tiny boats used to teach children how to sail. Papa called it the *Astor II*, in memory of the cargo ship that saved Simón's life. The three of us—Alberto, Pablo, and I—took turns sailing the little boat, because there was only enough room for one person in an Optimist. I remember sailing the little boat and scrutinizing the surface of the sea, as if hunting for buried treasure, looking for the wrinkles that indicated the slightest presence of wind gusts, but not because I wanted to catch the wind and sail faster; I sought the wind for its own sake. I wanted to feel it in my face, to understand it, to know where it was going.

"The low," I said.

"The what?"

"The low. If they were walking around in shirtsleeves at six in the morning in midwinter, it was probably at the critical moment in a low-pressure system so deep I'm not surprised at what happened."

"And what might cause that?"

"I don't know—I don't have enough data. To begin with, the air temperature would have to rise sharply and suddenly. Maybe in the days right before the storm, some exceptionally warm sub-Saharan winds had reached those waters, but that would be quite rare in the Mediterranean in winter. Whatever the cause, the air was very hot and humid. It would be helpful to know what kind of clouds there were."

"Simón said he saw a cloud off in the distance, an enormous black storm cloud."

"A cumulonimbus."

"If you say so. The wind was blowing in the direction of the cloud, so the fishermen thought at first that the cloud was moving away, but later it turned out to be just the opposite."

"How long did it take to reach them?"

"Long enough. They fished for more than two hours."

"That's stupid. They were right next to the chimney."

"What do you mean?"

"You'll understand better if I do you a drawing." I scribbled sketches of clouds on my notebook. "The chimney operates on a single basic principle: hot air rises, cold air sinks. Now, let's assume that the air was exceptionally warm and had been causing the seawater to evaporate for several days but without forming any clouds. Do you follow me?"

"More or less."

"Okay. Judging by where the big cloud was, I believe a high-altitude air mass was approaching the other side of the system, and this air mass was not only high, it was also exceptionally cold. When two air currents meet, the chimney effect is produced. As the warm air rises, it cools, but the evaporated humidity condenses into drops and releases energy. The cloud absorbs this energy, warms up again, and keeps rising. This process can be repeated as many as four or five times in a row. When the cloud is no longer able to warm up again, it's usually more than eight kilometers above the earth and saturated with humidity. Then it collides with the cold air that circulates at that altitude. The cloud suddenly cools and hurtles downward violently, as if it were sent by God."

"Let's not get God mixed up in all this. And be careful with that pen—you're making marks on the tablecloth."

"That's because I'm excited. What I'm describing must have looked like the wrath of God to Grandfather. Think about it: while all this was going on, the warm air above the surface of the water kept rising, and that was disastrous. Those fishermen were experienced sailors, but in such conditions experience isn't much help. You can't tell what direction the wind is blowing in, and you don't know where the torrent of water is going to come rushing down. . . ."

"That's what your grandfather said. According to him, the first moments of the storm were the worst, because the boats began to collide with one another."

"I'll never understand why they didn't go back to land. After all, they were only seven or eight nautical miles off the coast."

"Three boats did make it back. They were lucky—the wind carried them away from the others, and they were able to take refuge in the gulf. The eleven men who perished in the storm were on the other boats, the ones that couldn't reach land. You see, tuna fishermen use a huge trap net to capture their fish. The boats form a circle, and the net is spread between them. The crews also drop dozens of lines from the forward bow to catch the tuna that manage to escape the circle. When the storm struck, it spun all the boats around and caused a great tangle of nets and fishing lines that trapped the boats and took away their ability to maneuver."

"They could have cut the nets."

"There wasn't time. According to the story your grandfather told, the only voice he was able to hear gave the order to do just the opposite: grab the net and hold on to it."

"Just a moment. You're saying that my grandfather told the story, but he didn't. He died, remember?"

"Certainly, but that wasn't until several months later. I suppose we should say that Amparo was telling the story that Simón told her."

I remember making a note in my notebook: *Papa tells the story Amparo told him Simón told her.*

"It makes no difference who said it," Papa went on. "We can assume that the same fatal idea occurred to the fishermen in several of the boats at once: to hang on to the net. The result was that some of them wound up almost touching one another, and then the real tragedy began. The wind and the sea lifted the boats and flung them about so that they started colliding, then pulling apart, then colliding again, each time with greater force. According to what my mother told me, during the following months my father had recurring nightmares in which he'd hear the timbers cracking and see pieces of the boat flying through the air. The impact of one such collision threw him into the water. You know the rest."

"That's not true. All I know is that he spent three days drifting in the sea before an Italian ship picked him up. I've always thought that was the most unlikely part of the whole story. The idea that a cargo ship could spot a solitary man floating on the open sea—frankly, it sounds like a fairy tale."

"You're right, but it's happened more than once. If you think about it, the true miracle is not that they found him—that route was heavily used by merchant ships—but that he was still alive."

"Why? The Mediterranean isn't all that cold."

"You don't think so? I'd like to see you spend half an hour at night on the open sea in the middle of winter. You'd probably change your mind. The only reason he didn't die of hypothermia was that he managed to catch hold of a large, stout piece of wood he could float on. Otherwise he would have been submerged in the water up to his neck. But it wasn't only the cold: imagine his exhaustion, his hunger. . . ."

More material for my notebook: *Average water temperature in Janu-*

ary. Human body's ability to resist hypothermia. Italian shipping routes. Other cases of people rescued from shipwrecks.

"At least Grandfather knew how to swim."

"Yes, but I have a theory about this. I believe that what saved my father's life was precisely the fact that he didn't try to swim."

"How so?"

"He told my mother that as soon as he hit the water, he felt himself being dragged down. When he finally rose to the surface again, he saw that the current had carried him some distance from the boats—about twenty meters or so. He tried to swim back, but quickly realized he didn't have enough strength to make it. Luckily, a chunk of wood was floating near him, a piece of deck that I've always suspected was the hatch—it would probably have been thick and about a meter or a meter and a half square. Small but smooth, almost like a raft. He climbed on top of that and didn't swim another stroke, because he didn't want to waste his strength."

"Sounds like he was very calm."

"Exactly. Very calm and coolheaded: two qualities your grandfather completely lacked, unless my idea of him is way off the mark. And therefore—still following my theory—what saved Simón was fear; the terror of succumbing to exhaustion must have paralyzed him. It was probably accompanied by the hope that the storm would soon die down and boats would be sent out to look for survivors."

"Which didn't happen."

"No, it didn't. The storm probably lasted four or five hours. Just imagine the scene when it finally ended. My father found himself on the open sea, with no sort of vessel in sight. And for the next three days, the north wind never stopped blowing, not even for an instant, sweeping the sea from the coast and pushing him farther and farther away."

"Yes. Supposedly, the north wind always lasts for several days. Poor Grandfather."

"Poor indeed. You know what they say about the north wind? It gets into people's heads and drives them mad. Whenever anyone commits suicide in these parts, it's always blamed on the wind. And that's on dry land, on terra firma. Imagine out at sea on a raft. This was another thing that came back to haunt him in his nightmares: he'd see a thin, dark line in the distance and tell himself that it was the coast, but at the same time he realized that the wind was driving him farther away and that he was helpless against it."

"God, he must have felt completely powerless."

"Absolutely. Nevertheless, he must have tried to set up some kind of jury-rig."

"Some kind of what?"

In other circumstances, such a gap in my knowledge would have earned me a good scolding. I should have known what "jury-rig" meant. When we were young and beginning to learn about sailing, Papa placed the utmost importance on nautical terms: hatches not doors, lines and hawsers not ropes, starboard and port not right and left. He was unusually obsessed with the specifics of this language, which of course seemed so foreign to us at first.

"Jury-rig. It's when a ship can no longer be steered and the only thing you can do is invent a makeshift sail or rudder. Suppose a storm carries off your mast. You tie a bit of sail to a piece of wood and hoist it amidships so you can catch a little wind and sail along, however slowly. That's a jury-rig."

"Damn, I didn't know that."

"It seems he was able to rip off one of the side planks of his raft and tie his shirt to it. But his jury-rig was a disaster because there was no way of trimming it. And to top it all, there was so little space on the raft that Simón's own body blocked the wind from reaching his sail. It was useless."

"That's terrible! Poor Simón."

"Can you imagine?"

"I can. I always have."

I imagine Simón's surprise, the sudden fury of the sea. I imagine his frantic kicking, his frenzied effort to survive the first submersion and rise, as obstinate as a cork, driven by the sole desire to burst through the surface of the water and breathe. And then, much later, his desperation and perhaps his regret; his distress when he saw that the hours were passing, night was falling, and no one was coming for him; the terrible awareness that maybe it would have been better not to struggle, maybe he should have let himself be dragged down into the sea, maybe he should have given up and accepted death—it would have been horrible, wretched, but at least it would have been quick. Perhaps he played with the idea of letting himself go, loosening his grip on the piece of wood that was keeping him afloat. Maybe he didn't have the nerve. Or enough strength. Even letting yourself die requires an effort.

I imagine the salt. The salt in his mouth, but also coating his muscles like a second skin, making them numb and stiff. And time, too, enveloped in salt: endless, immobile, absurd. I imagine his first mouthfuls of air, the heaving bellows of his lungs.

I imagine his voice, his famous voice, and it terrifies me. He'd believed that voice was destined to recite the most exquisite speeches ever written for the stage, to touch the hearts of his audience, yet now he saw himself condemned to this pathetic, albeit genuine, monologue: a cry lost in the immensity of the sea, a wild howl for help whose only audience was solitude.

The night. Not one night, but three. Did he see the lighthouse? Maybe so—during the first night, at least. He may have been too far away from it after that. But as long as it was visible, the knowledge that the heartless light was going to pass over him every three seconds without seeing him must have driven him crazy. The same lighthouse is looking at me right now, telling me I'm alive.

I imagine his sleep, the blessing of sleep, his eyelids growing leaden, his dreams of salvation: the idea that the sea would carry him onto dry land and he'd wake up lying on a beach, or maybe even tucked up in his bed, relieved to learn that it had all been some awful nightmare. But deep sleep, its unique and blessed surrender, was not permitted him. He must have opened his eyes in fear a thousand times. How would he have kept himself awake? By going over the memories of his past life, the way people do in novels? By remembering? Perhaps. Maybe there was room only for the past in his mind, because the future was death.

I don't know if he perceived any irony in the fact that he was accompanied for most of his voyage by a brilliant sun and tranquil sea. The north wind, the same wind that was pushing him farther away from the coast, had scoured the sky and left it cloudless, prolonging his survival and perhaps nourishing his hopes. But there was also the possibility that it was also prolonging his suffering and preparing him for a crueler fate. Did he occupy himself with weighing the alternatives? Was there any moment when he believed that any of the possible deaths he was facing would be better than his life? Did he smell his hands? Did he prefer salt residue to onions? Did it occur to him that surviving this shipwreck would mean returning to his father's shop, to the paltry freedom of practicing his juggling in front of a mirror that didn't even deign to reflect his image?

Papa couldn't answer these questions. Nobody could, because Simón claimed that he remembered nothing after his first night on the water, and it's possible that he really did have amnesia, not because his memory was blocked by fear, but because memory loss was the logical consequence of having spent so many hours rocking back and forth between sleep and surrender. All we can know for certain is what happened after the crew of the *Astor* pulled Simón out of the sea some twenty miles from the coast. I like to imagine that the rescue took place at night, that the San Sebastián lighthouse picked him out in the darkness. In reality, it was most probably daytime, but there's no way of knowing. For this moment, too, we need to have partial recourse to imagination, because apparently he was unconscious when the *Astor*'s crew hauled him on board the ship. They thought he was dead and laid him on the deck until someone discovered that his heart was gently, distantly beating.

He didn't know he was alive until two days after his rescue. What finally dragged him to full consciousness was the sensation that the rocking had changed; the sea's constant slapping at his raft was gone, replaced by the gentle, side-to-side roll of the *Astor*. Nevertheless, a few impressions from his rescue must have been stored in his memory, because sometime after his return, he told Grandmother Amparo that a dream with a happy ending occasionally interrupted his nightmare of bursting timbers and elusive coastlines. In this dream, Simón saw a column of smoke appear in the distance and come toward him slowly, almost mockingly, as though it were flirting with him. At the end of the dream, the column stopped a few meters away and he knew he was saved. Did it happen like that? Did he manage to make out, in the distance, the column of smoke rising from the *Astor* as she approached to pick him up? Or did he imagine it later, driven by the need to reconstruct, if not the blank days he'd lost, at least the satisfactory end of his ordeal?

"My grandfather, the hero," I said to my father that night. "If I remember correctly, the first time you told me this story I was about six years old. You gave me the summarized version, the one you've always told up until today, without cards, cars, village healers. I told that story to my schoolmates when the teachers took us to the pool to learn how to swim. And in the summer, I told it to my other friends. You can't imagine how proud I felt as I described my grandfather's struggle, swimming for his life off the very beach where we went swimming each day. Back then I imagined that the storm had gone on for the entire three days and that the sea was infested with sharks. And, of course, the way I pictured the scene, Simón didn't float on the sea, clinging to a piece of wood; he swam and swam and swam. . . ."

"What do you think it was like for me? I spent my entire adolescence dazzled by my father's imagined heroism. Later, with the passage of time, I began to consider the whole thing less important. After all, Simón didn't really do anything other than survive."

"Shit, Papa, you don't think that's a big deal? In those circumstances?"

"They're not all that different from yours or mine. Look, Serena,

I'm very well aware that I must have made up some parts of Simón's story. The version my mother told me was summarized, too. It was heroic and easy to digest, like the one I told you. Probably, with the passage of time, my imagination has been filling in the gaps, providing answers to all the questions I never had time to ask. But there's one image I remember with absolute clarity, just the way my mother told me. The older I get, the more the other details of my father's shipwreck keep fading in my memory, but not this one. It's like the nucleus of everything that happened, the single basic fact necessary to understand the whole thing. When Simón returned to consciousness on the *Astor*, he apparently found himself in a cabin, lying on a hard bunk, weighed down by the triple layer of blankets the sailors had thrown on him to warm him up. Even before he became fully aware of the fact that he was still alive, he noticed that his hands hurt. His fingers. His knuckles. As though he'd been squeezing something for hours. He shifted about under the blankets, until he could see what was clasped in his palms. It was a piece of bread. He'd spent hours clutching a hunk of stale bread. At first, he had no idea where it had come from, but when he got up, he looked around in the dim light of the cabin and saw a tray at the foot of the bed, and on that tray was a cup of clear soup gone cold. The piece of bread—you understand? That was my father's specialty: grabbing hold of things in order to stay alive. He grabbed hold of a piece of wood or a hunk of bread, just as he always clung to his desire for a different life, to his dream of being a great actor. If that's a heroic gesture, then we're all heroes. Or almost all. I don't know whether you understand me."

"Of course I do. It's so sad."

"What is?"

"His fate. To survive a predicament like that, against all the odds, and then die just a few months later."

"The truth is, from that time on, his life was nothing but a litany of problems. In fact, you don't need much imagination to pick out the chain of events linking the circumstances of his shipwreck to his death.

But I suppose he wasn't to blame; it was his father's fault. Partly, at least."

"Your grandfather was a bit of a bastard, wasn't he?" In our family's official history, Simón's father had been assigned the role of the villain, despite my father's occasional efforts to make excuses for him.

"Well, all I can do is try to understand the people involved. My father probably didn't come up with the best way of breaking the news to his father. Remember, four weeks had passed before they entered the port in Buenos Aires. I don't know what the required protocol in such cases was. While I imagine the *Astor* had to make some sort of official report about the rescue of a shipwrecked person, it doesn't seem far-fetched to assume that no one connected that person with the fruit-and-vegetable vendor who had disappeared in Barcelona. I don't know. The fact is that no one knew anything about what had happened until Simón sent his father a telegram from Buenos Aires to let him know that he was still alive."

"Do you have a copy of that telegram?"

"I wish I did. His father probably tore it up immediately after reading it."

"Do we at least know what it said?"

"Not really. Something like, I'M ALL RIGHT STOP WHEN I GET BACK WILL TELL ALL."

"A man of few words."

"Well, put yourself in his place. What was he going to say in a telegram? SOMEONE NAMED ALFONSO STOP BET STOP MALESPINA STOP TUNA STOP SHIPWRECK STOP ASTOR STOP BUENOS AIRES STOP. Maybe he thought the most urgent thing for him to do was to let his father know he was alive; then, after he got back, he would tell him the whole extravagant story and have a better chance of convincing him that it was true."

"But he failed."

"Yes, he failed. A white lie would probably have met with a better reception from his father. There are many details that complicate this part of the story. In the first place, no one in Barcelona had heard about the storm. Not even Alfonso, the one with the car, who left for home straightaway after the fishing boats had weighed anchor and therefore never even saw the first drops of rain. Naturally, the press carried no mention of the storm. At most, there was some brief reference to the bad weather and to the cold snap that apparently followed it. Nothing else. Such a thing seems impossible to us today, but it wasn't back then. I guess the fate of some fishermen from a little coastal village wasn't considered essential news in the big city."

"But how come they didn't notify anybody? The survivors, I mean. The fishermen."

"Notify whom? No one knew anything about my father. And don't forget when this happened. The first telephone in the village was installed in 1934—that is, twelve years later. Before that, the villagers were so cut off that when a storm brewed up in the middle of the night, the fishermen gave the warning to get the boats under cover by throwing handfuls of sand at one another's windows. They probably made some sort of report to the Civil Guard, but I doubt that anyone could have given anything even remotely resembling an accurate description of Simón. Remember, none of the fishermen had seen him before. He just appeared in the middle of the night. It's possible they never even asked him his name."

"And his father didn't look for him?"

"Of course he did. Well, I don't know, but I take it for granted he did. How could he not? I'm sure he was convinced that his son had run off with some theater troupe. Maybe he reported his suspicion to the police, and as a result they didn't exactly throw themselves into the investigation. Who can tell? Don't forget, I never knew my grandfather. And my mother spoke to him only once in her life. She was alarmed at my father's absence, and so she tracked down Alfonso because she'd seen them leave together the night of the bet. Alfonso couldn't give her any explanation. He'd left Simón on a fishing boat in Malespina. She got up her courage and went looking for Simón at his house, thinking that his father had punished him. But Simón's father told her he knew nothing about the whereabouts of his son, and the fact that she didn't know anything either clearly showed that Simón had never really loved her and that his little fling with her had been nothing but a pastime—and so forth. Then, apparently, my grandfather rudely turned her out, asking her how she dared to come around asking for Simón when she was to blame for the wicked life he was leading. Whatever tenuous tie there was between my mother and my father's father was broken forever. I have no way of knowing his version of these events. I don't know what he did during the two months when my father was away. Well, to be precise, he wasn't my father yet, because Amparo wasn't pregnant yet. All I can do is infer my grandfather's attitude from the way he behaved later, when Simón returned home and—"

"Just a moment. Just a moment. What do you mean, 'returned home'? We were in Buenos Aires. How did he return home?"

"How do you think? In a ship."

"What ship?"

My doubts exasperated me. The enormous list in my notebook kept on growing, and my questions were getting more and more insistent: *Confirm duration of voyage to Buenos Aires. Telegram? Alfonso again. Newspaper archive, just in case. Find out if police report exists.*

"I don't know its name. I know that Simón spent five or six days in Buenos Aires, looking for any vessel that was leaving for Europe. I imagine he made the trip in some kind of freighter. Maybe even in the *Astor* itself . . ."

"Maybe so, but . . ."

"But nothing, Serena. You think I don't have questions, too? How did he pay for his ticket? Did he manage to find a ship whose itinerary included Barcelona, or did he have to disembark in some other European country and travel the rest of the way overland? There are more questions than answers, Serena. That's what happens with the dead."

"Okay, you're right. I apologize. Tell me what you know."

"On Sunday, March 19, 1922, Simón arrived back home. He knocked at the door. His father opened it, stood gaping for a second as though he were seeing a ghost, and then, without saying a word, he struck Simón in the face."

"What a monster."

"He wasn't a monster, he just didn't have a clue. In any case, the blow he gave Simón was nothing compared to what came next. He pushed his son down into a chair right there in the entrance hall and told him to explain himself."

"And?"

"And nothing. He didn't believe a word. Tall tales, lies, and excuses, he said. Simón couldn't even finish describing what had happened, because his father kept on interrupting him. 'Not one more lie, Simón,' his father shouted. 'Two months! I've spent two months suffering, thinking you were dead, and now you come to me with this pathetic adventure story. What's the point? You expect me to believe you're some sort of hero? Just be a man and tell me the truth.'"

"Poor Simón. What a predicament! Shipwrecked on the open sea for three days, unconscious for days on board the *Astor*, then four weeks to get to Buenos Aires, at least as many more to return home, and all he gets is a slap and a sermon. Unbearable!"

"The worst was yet to come. In the end, he—"

"Wait. Something doesn't make sense. Simón must have had some proof of where he'd been, right? I don't know, at least the ticket for his return voyage."

"Of course he did. He even had a letter from the captain of the *Astor*, describing the circumstances of his rescue at sea."

"You've read it?"

"No. My mother read it. She even said that she'd kept it for a time, but I was never able to see it. I don't know what she did with it. I imagine she lost it during our travels, when we went from village to village. But I have no idea."

Return ticket? Try to track down Astor *letter.*

"That's a shame. I would have loved to see it. Anyway, the letter wasn't enough to convince Simón's father?"

"Not so fast. It was precisely the letter that triggered the events that followed. I suppose that even if Papa had been carrying it in his hand, even if he'd brandished it as soon as the door opened, he wouldn't have been spared the first blow, but he might have escaped further punishment. In any case, he waited a long time before showing the letter to his father."

"He was foolish."

"Or proud. I think it was pride that made him hold back. Simón wanted his word to be enough for his father, and being obliged to prove what he'd said seemed demeaning. Well, at least, that's my theory. According to my mother, Simón didn't like talking about this scene. I'm sorry, Serena, but all we can do is imagine it. I don't think Simón took the letter out of his pocket until his father punched the back of his chair and threatened him: 'Don't lie to me again, Simón. You have exactly one minute to tell me the truth. Look me in the eye. If you don't, I swear I'll lock you in your room right now and you won't get out again until you're an adult.' "

"That was stupid. Wasn't he more or less an adult already?"

"Not at all. In those days, you were considered an adult when you turned twenty-one, and Simón was only nineteen. In other words, his father was threatening to shut him up for two years."

"Got it. Go on."

"Simón took the letter out of his pocket, handed it to his father, and said, 'You can think and do what you want, Father. I don't want to talk about it anymore. I only have the strength to go to bed.' "

" '. . . to go to bed.' " My voice echoed Papa's, as though we were reciting an old prayer together. I knew this speech of my grandfather's by heart.

"I see you remember."

"Of course I do. I could say those lines in my sleep. It was a story, Papa."

"You mean it was a lie?"

"No, I mean it was a story. Hamlet doesn't say, 'It's either stay alive or kill myself,' does he? He says, 'To be or not to be.' You can't tell that story without saying those words. It's the same with Grandfather. He might have said, 'All right, Father. I'm going to bed,' or something like, 'If you don't want to believe it, don't, but leave me in peace. I'm exhausted.' Or maybe he said something else, who knows? Nevertheless, if you ask my brothers, I'm sure they know Simón's words by heart as well. Because it was a story. And after saying those words, 'I only have the strength to go to bed,' Simón left his father speechless and went to his room. Later, the ogre imposed 'a severe punishment' on him. Just like that: 'a severe punishment.' He turned his room into a prison. And that's where the story ends, right?"

"Well, in reality the end was more unpleasant than that. I never told you and your brothers this part of the story. Don't forget, you were children. Simón gave up trying to convince his father he was telling the truth. He handed him the letter from the captain of the *Astor* and retired to his room. Obviously, my grandfather couldn't read Italian, but he must have realized that there was at least some truth to Simón's story, and he couldn't bear the humiliation of having made such a huge mistake. He ran after his son and began interrogating him all over again, until Simón had a moment of weakness. Maybe it was because he was exhausted and searching for a way to put an end to his father's obstinate questions. Or maybe he thought he had to make some small concession in order to make his father accept the story of his shipwreck once and for all. In any case, at some point in their wrangling, Simón confessed that after leaving home on that distant night two months before, he hadn't gone to study with his friends, but had gone to the theater instead."

"Then what happened?"

"His father went crazy. He started yelling, 'You see? You see how you keep on lying?' And he started hitting him. First with the letter in his hand, using it like a whip. Then he dropped the letter and punched

Simón a few times. Simón fell to the floor, and his father began to kick him, screaming, 'You see? You see?' "

"Jesus, Papa. You never told me that."

Papa was crying. It was the first time I ever saw him cry. The second and last time was three weeks ago, when we gave him the news about Mama's death. I put out a hand and touched his face. "I'm sorry," I said. "We can talk about something else, if you want."

"No, I'm all right. It does me good to talk about it—I don't think I've ever mentioned the beating to anyone. Well, maybe your mother, years ago. And it's not some story that's been told and retold—my father never wanted to talk about it at all, but when Amparo saw him more than two weeks later, his body still bore the marks. His face was black and blue, two of his ribs were broken, and—"

"Why didn't he defend himself? He was young and strong. He did a lot of heavy work in the shop, so he must have had powerful arms. . . ."

"Who knows? I've asked myself that question many times. I don't think he held back because he lacked a rebellious spirit. Or because he had great respect for his father. Sometimes I think his revenge was precisely that: to let himself be beaten. It's as if he allowed the deluge of blows so that he had a reason to do what he'd secretly wished to do his whole life: disappear from his father's house forever."

"He was given imprisonment, but he chose exile."

"Well, Simón didn't know the story of Li Po. But yes, I suppose you're right. When my grandfather left the room and Simón heard him lock the door, it was his first step on the path to freedom."

"Then I still don't understand."

"What don't you understand now?"

"Why he went back home. Didn't you just say he'd always wanted to disappear? To free himself of his father, once and for all? In that case, why did he go back? He could have stayed in Buenos Aires. His father would have given him up for dead, or at least missing, and Simón could have begun a new life."

"Good question, Serena. And I don't know the answer. You're right—he spends his life dreaming about freedom, and then he goes and rejects it when fate places it within his grasp. Maybe that was the problem."

"What was?"

"That it was a gift. Maybe freedom didn't seem to be worth much to him unless it required some effort."

"In that case, he deserved everything he got. He was too much like his father."

"Maybe so. But don't forget that Simón was only nineteen. Or that we're talking about 1922. You also have to remember that Simón wasn't interested solely in running away. He wanted a career in the theater. And to get into the theater, he needed Amparo. Or he needed to be in Barcelona. I don't know."

"And you never tried to contact your grandfather? Weren't you curious? Even just to see his face?"

"No. Yes. I mean no, I never tried, and yes, I was curious. I often asked my mother about him but she never wanted us to meet. Simón swore that if he succeeded in getting away, he'd never see his father again. He got away but then he died. As simple as that. And then I was born. What was my mother going to do? Present herself at my grandfather's door and say, 'Hello, I'm Amparo, and this adorable baby is your grandson Julio, son of Simón. He died right after he got me pregnant'? There wouldn't have been any sense in doing that. It might even have been disloyal to Simón. Perhaps my grandfather would have accepted me, but that would have only made things worse. It would have meant putting me in the place my father had always been desperate to run away from. Later, when I was able to make the decision for myself, I never wanted to meet him, because hatred is inherited. As the years passed, I finally began to see my grandfather as a poor wretch and not as the person responsible for all my family's misfortunes, but by then it was too late, he was probably dead. Besides, it was much more convenient to forget. My life was already set on a different course."

Simón's return home: why? Amparo's real reasons for not contacting Simón's father. Possible to find out something about him? Azuera not very common surname. Where did they live?

"In any case, I think your mother kept a lot of things hidden from you. It's simply not possible she didn't know the name of the street your father lived on."

"You may find it strange, but it is possible. I know he lived in the Ribera district and probably not far from the shop, since they walked to it every morning. But that's all I know."

"You never asked Grandmother Amparo where he lived?"

"What do you think? Of course I did."

"And?"

"And nothing."

"Impossible. She had to know."

"She did. But she never said she didn't know; she just said I didn't need to know. Those are two different things. Look, my mother decided that it would be better for me not to try to establish any sort of connection with Simón's family. You can't fault her for that. I was asking her questions about someone who, as far as she was concerned, was ultimately responsible for the death of her fiancé. So she made a decision. She drew a line in the sand and said, 'That side is the past, and it's over; this side is where life begins.' We don't have the right to judge her, because we can't put ourselves in her place."

"I don't want to judge anyone, Papa. I just want to know."

It's cold, but the air is dry and pleasant. I don't know what time it is. I walk around the terrace. I need a break. I'm a little bewildered by this muddle, this tangle of stories about what someone said someone else told someone else. I'm not complaining. This is precisely what I was seeking when I sat down to write: a little bewilderment, something that would allow me to close my eyes and collapse from pure exhaustion. I don't have my watch on, but I figure it's close to four in the morning and my notebook is nearly full.

The beam of the lighthouse keeps sweeping over my page every

3.47 seconds, almost as if it wants to make some contribution to this story. Twenty or so years ago, after that conversation with Papa, I asked him to tell me about the research he'd undertaken in his younger days. I was convinced that he'd missed a trail somewhere, an apparently insignificant detail that might serve to illuminate all the unknowns in Simón's story, like the key element that unlocks a puzzle. An answer that would permit me to link everything together.

Nothing. Not a trace of the *Astor*. No one in Malespina with any specific memory of the 1922 storm. Too much time had passed. For decades, all the civil records of events related to the village—weddings, baptisms, births or deaths, storms or miraculous catches of fish—had been kept in the church. In the first days of the Civil War, someone set fire to the church. Farewell, documents. Over a period of years, I spent scores of hours reading newspapers and magazines from 1922, any book even remotely dealing with the history of commercial fishing in the beginning of the twentieth century, old seafarers' journals, and so on. I found only one reference, which turned out to be a dead end too: *Voices of the Old Sea,* a book by Norman Lewis, in which the author describes his sojourn in Malespina in the 1940s. In a chapter dedicated to tuna fishing, Lewis mentions a man who was blown into the sea at the height of a storm in January 1922 and who was never seen again. For me the book had the value of confirming what we already knew, but it shed no fresh light. In spite of this, Papa congratulated me as if I had unearthed a precious jewel. And that was when he told me for the first time about the lighthouse log and suggested that I consult it, even though he had done so long ago to no avail.

The first time I climbed up into the lighthouse in search of the log, I was so excited my heart threatened to pound right through my chest. From the end of the nineteenth century until 1968, every lighthouse in Spain kept a record known as the "Storm Status Log." Today, the logs from all the lighthouses on the Costa Brava, one log per lighthouse per year, are preserved in the Historical Archive in Girona. I love the name "storm status," as if a storm were a permanent, hunkering presence, a wild animal whose moods must be monitored—in fact, that was the subject of my dissertation for my meteorology degree. I had the good fortune to touch those documents with my own hands: oblong notebooks, swollen by humidity, with red covers and coarse pages. When the weather grew stormy, the lighthouse keeper would start a new page and record the basic meteorological data: the time of day when the storm began and when it ended; the humidity, temperature, and wind direction and the amount of rainfall per cubic meter. On the back of the same page, writing with the aggressive strokes produced by pens with steel nibs, the keeper would add his personal impressions of the storm. For this purpose, he used the overblown style of his day, lyrically evoking peals of thunder and bolts of lightning and dwelling at length upon the thickness of clouds and the violence of the sea. Before signing, he ended every entry with the same words: "Nothing new is known to have occurred in the vicinity of this station." Dozens of storms every year, and always the same closing comment, as if the keeper's mission were to record not the storm itself but the peace that followed. I spent endless hours in the archive in Girona, fascinated by the archaic language of the lighthouse keepers and disconcerted by the sheer volume of the prose they could produce in order to describe a simple cloud. They would describe the cloud's configuration, its color, its depth, marshaling a long sequence of data with which they aspired to render as close an approximation of reality as possible. Today, the opposite view prevails: the fewer words used, the more accurate they are, and if they can be substituted by a number or a code, so much the better. In the old days, they ruined their eyes staring at the sky. Today, you can predict the weather without even looking up from your computer screen.

As I've said, I recognized all this years later, when I was doing research for my dissertation. But the first time I climbed the steps of that lighthouse, I couldn't have cared less about clouds and word counts. I had only one date engraved on my forehead: January 11, 1922. Papa had told me I wasn't going to find any page with that date written at the top. Moreover, he warned me that the page that should have corresponded to that date had been torn out: a piece of the missing page, still bound into the book, offered trenchant proof that the page had once been there. It was another dead end.

By the time I started the research for my thesis, years later, the lighthouse logs had been deposited in the Historical Archive in Girona. This arrangement was more convenient, because in the archive you could compare logs from other lighthouses. I went there so often that the archive staff ended up getting involved in my project. I told them what I was looking for and showed them where the page was torn and missing. One of the women seemed to remember that the lighthouse keepers wrote their storm notes in triplicate. The original was recorded in the lighthouse log; then they made two copies and sent one each to Barcelona and Madrid. Perhaps, she suggested, if the storm in question really had been extraordinary, the lighthouse keeper had felt a sense of urgency, torn the page out of his log, and sent it at once to Madrid or Barcelona, thinking that he would draw up copies later. But perhaps later never came, since there was no trace of such copies anywhere.

So I gave up. What else could I do? If I'd had the power to make the dead speak, I wouldn't have hesitated to use it. I would have interrogated Simón himself. Or Amparo. When she died, I had just had my tenth birthday. My grandmother appeared in my worst dreams, sitting in the dark, clicking away with her knitting needles, a modest but intrusive sound, like the ticking of a wall clock. I'd ask her to stop, but only when I got close enough to touch her did I become aware that what was issuing from her needles wasn't wool, but wet, stinking seaweed, in which the eyes of drowned men, fish skeletons, and playing cards were all entangled.

How strange, those dreams of my youth weren't very different from the ones that afflict me now. But then, it's not every family that can claim two drownings.

*There are two fundamental reasons for letting this mix-up remain un-
corrected, and I'm not certain they aren't one and the same: life and
death.*

*First life, which is going on out there. I haven't gone crazy, and I
haven't developed a taste for cut-rate philosophical jargon; "out there"
means Barcelona or Malespina. And "life" means . . . how shall I say
it? It means what everyone understands by "life": the sum of the things
you do; what happens to you and those close to you. Now, as for happening, the fact is that at my age, not much really does happen. I accepted
that years ago; I know my lot is to live by delegation. I've always
thought I'd be prepared for this moment when it came, but that doesn't
seem to be the case. I don't even have a clear idea of what options life is
offering me now. I suspect that my few friends have adapted to the passage of time better than I have. Some have dedicated themselves to their
husbands with a degree of self-denial I find ridiculous, but do not criticize. Of course, I take care of Julio—more than ever in the last few
years, since he stopped being able to look after himself—but I don't consider him the center of my life. Other friends have turned their world
into a sort of sprawling theme park. They take short courses in Japanese
cooking, collect traditional pottery, enroll in painting classes. I'm even
slightly envious. I see that they're enjoying themselves, and it's probable
that all their activities provide a strenuous neuronal workout, which has
to be important at our age. They invite me to join them; they tell me it'll
do me good to try something new. I don't know exactly what these new
things might be. I can't get myself interested.*

*What's left is my family. Watching them grow, as the saying goes.
Well, I've only one grandchild, nineteen years old, and I don't think*

there will be any more. Alberto's already too old to embark on that adventure again and the only descendants Pablo will leave will be written in musical scores. He doesn't have chromosomes in his genetic makeup, he has quavers and semiquavers. If Serena hurries up, she still has time to become a mother, but I don't see how. She's never found the right man, nor is she going to find him. Supposedly, all the females in the animal kingdom look for the most perfect available male to procreate with, but Serena's forgotten the "available" part. She's looking for the perfect male, period. And since he doesn't exist, things are as they are. Although a child might help solve some of Serena's problems, it wouldn't have any effect on mine. I'm not one of those babysitting grandmothers. I'm afraid I never paid enough attention to Luis, and I doubt that the arrival of another grandchild would make me change my ways.

Alberto, Pablo, Serena, Julio, and my grandson, they could be my life. The problem is that when I look at Julio and our children, I see the four faces of a lie I'd prefer to ignore. I'm not accusing them of anything; it's a little late to start handing out blame, and, besides, I'm afraid all the blame would go to Julio anyway. I'll just limit myself to stating a fact of which I have irrefutable proof. In the third drawer of the second filing cabinet in my office in Barcelona, there's a blue folder with a label that says JULIO. That folder contains three things: the portrait of me that he painted when we first met; the grain of sand he gave me the night we decided to get married; and a piece of paper, a document I'd rather not talk about, except to say that it provides evidence of Simón's lie. So the folder contains three distinctly different lies. The first two, if looked at a certain way, are beautiful. As the products of infatuation, they're necessarily falsehoods, or at least, as people say these days, distortions—but beautiful all the same. The third, however, is thoroughly unpleasant. In fact, the bitterness it provokes in me is one of the reasons that brought me here. I haven't come all this way to wallow in my memories; on the contrary, I've come to forget them, forget that bitterness, and bury it in the mud. I'm not judging Julio for telling the lie—after all, he was its first victim. When I discovered it, I chose to

*keep quiet, so I'm not going to accuse him now. Besides, Julio's mind
has drifted far away, and not even a traumatic confrontation with the
truth would be enough to bring him back.*

*Maybe my silence makes me an accomplice, but it hasn't made
me blind. It doesn't stop me from seeing how our existences have been
marked by Julio's lie. I look at my three children, and it pains me to see
Simón's famous three lives in them. Alberto, the attorney Simón would
have been had his father's supposed plans for him come to fruition.
Pablo, the artist Simón wanted to be. I'm proud to have such a son.
When Pablo was a small boy, he decided to become an artist and make
his father proud, and he's succeeded. I don't always understand his
music—at times I even find it painful—but I recognize his success. The
price of accomplishing this goal is that he lives in a world only he can
inhabit, a complex, well-constructed, solid world that attempts to master time.*

*As always, Serena got the worst of the deal. Of Simón's three lives,
she inherited the one that included wearisome toil in the shop of truth.
The life of futile sacrifices and eternal monologues. By the time she was
seven, she was already turning up spellbound here and there, staring at
the sky and counting clouds. Her first love was an isobar. Now she's past
thirty-eight, and she's still at it, looking for storms, dreaming about a
cyclone that will take her back in time and allow her to save her grandfather and rescue her father and maybe even save herself.*

*That's the life waiting for me if I return: a lie I can't even de-
nounce, since I've contributed to its construction by remaining silent.*

*And then there's death, my second reason for staying put. The death
that's been classified as my own: a false death, of course, but perhaps
more true than it seems. In these past few weeks, a number of people
have pronounced the words, "Isabel García Luna is dead," without realizing that they were false, that they signified nothing more than a
capricious twist of fate. Nevertheless, they do contain a grain of truth,
Isabel, Isabel García Luna, the Isabel those people knew, the daughter
of Don Ernesto, the mother of three children, a major figure in various*

absurd professional controversies, Julio's wife and lover, really is dead. Hers was not a sudden death, she was in her last throes for many years, her life miraculously held together by the threads of habit. The impostor gradually faded away, but I'm still here, happily dispossessed of all her attributes, including her name. Me. I'm the one who's alive. Neither daughter nor mother nor academic: just me. I'm still trying to find out what that might mean.

Many years ago, when I discovered Julio's lie, I was afraid and saddened at the same time. I didn't feel anger or resentment, just the immense sadness that illusions leave behind when they evaporate. I was sad for him, sad about what that grotesque fiction implied, sad about the enormous effort it must have cost him to maintain his deception. And I was afraid for myself, for all of us, afraid to look in the mirror and find that my life was as unreal as Julio's tales. I'd already spent years fighting, with a certain degree of success, to become more than the mere product of other people's imagination. At the proper time, I rebelled against my father's idea of me. If I hadn't, I would have been a house-wife or a pharmacist. I never allowed my condition as wife and mother to turn into the only facets of my existence, and in general I can say that I've been, as far as possible, the mistress of my fate. But from that day on, my own fictions were the ones that frightened me. I decided to strip myself of them, to renounce any efforts to correspond to any precon-ceived ideas of me, including my own. This went on for many years. The process was so slow that I'd almost go so far as to say that no one noticed. They did say I was "different," so perhaps that had something to do with it.

In the beginning, the story of my life was filled with husband and children, academic work and the daily grind, except for every now and then, when the parenthesis of a trip would open. For a few weeks, or a couple of months at most, I took off my everyday person, like someone who keeps her favorite coat in the closet, knowing she'll put it on again when the first cool days of autumn arrive. Then, as the years passed, things became more complicated.

In the 1960s, a Spanish woman with a degree in prehistory had very limited scope for research: proto-folkloric recordings of the Holy Week celebrations in Seville, field work on ancient Roman sites . . . My colleagues and I thought we were discovering the world, but in fact we weren't doing very much. And since I was the only woman, I cooked for everybody too. I didn't do much else apart from brushing away dirt. The site was covered by a grid, I was assigned a few sections, and I brushed and brushed. You could say it was a twofold way of passing time: first, because you could spend entire days doing nothing but systematically removing tiny layers of fine sand; and second, because the more layers you removed, the farther you burrowed into the past. The deeper the dig, the farther back the time period under investigation. Now that I think about it, it may be that the reason I came to specialize in death is not a result of the fascination it supposedly holds for me, but of my skill with the brush. I was very patient. I was able to disengage the tiniest fragment of a vase from the earth without causing the least damage. Little by little, I passed from vessels to bones. When a skeleton is discovered on a site, they call on the workers who know how to use a brush, the ones who never break anything and can recover the remains intact. I've seen many corpses. I used to spend hours staring at them, and they never said a thing to me. Dusty corpses, mute and inscrutable. I don't know that I'm explaining this very well. As far as I was concerned, those heaps of bones signified nothing but material for the laboratory. Carbon 14 put a date on them. It was never a spectacular date; no one was expecting a find that would make a revolutionary change in the foundations of archaeology. The results of my anonymous labors appeared amid a sea of data in the journal of some university. None of that meant anything to me. As many things do, the dead only made me think about the living. When we came across a skeleton, when my colleagues got excited about the contribution our discovery might offer, I thought about the dead person's family. While the others were noting the exact position of the body in order to focus more precisely on its historical implications, I thought about the tears of the dead person's friends; I thought about which Latin words they probably used to bid him farewell and about the void his death made in the lives of those he left behind.

In those days, anthropology was hardly even a secondary branch on the confused tree of history, itself lost in the impenetrable forest of philosophy and arts and letters, but I grabbed that branch and held on to it with all my might. It always surprised me that others so appreciated my contribution to the recognition of anthropology as an independent discipline and my participation in the establishment of the first university professorship in the field. Well, someone had to do it. I wasn't advocating anything particularly original. In those days, there wasn't a country in Europe where the universities weren't already thinking about setting up chairs in anthropology. It was only a matter of time. In the beginning, the creation of the professorship didn't change things very much. There still wasn't enough money for us to carry out research. Like many others, we went to some lost village in Extremadura or Teruel and recorded professional mourners at wakes and funerals. We interviewed widows and followed the trail of their grief: mourning, relief from mourning, reintegration into life.

Little by little, our research field expanded. There are many details I don't remember: the bureaucratic war and the routine boredom of offices and corridors. And then the department began to grow, and my daily presence was no longer as necessary. I had time to travel, but I didn't have money to finance my trips. During that period, the famous Julio Fellowship played an important role. Then, many years later, television came along. It's not that anthropology became fashionable, but it did attract a certain amount of interest, and now and then someone from the state television would make a documentary and ask the government to provide a scientific consultant. People . . . I don't know, people envied me. The thing is, we traveled farther each time. Mexico was first. We visited Mayan and Aztec ruins and, in passing, we caught the daily lives of the indigenous people on film. Colombia: they wanted to make a documentary film about traces of pre-Columbian cultures, and I persuaded them that we should smuggle away some time and dedicate it to the people of the Amazon Basin. Every time I had the chance to witness a funeral, I took full advantage. I turned into an expert on death. As time passed, I lost interest in the silence of ruins; I suppose the lamentations of the living seemed more eloquent to me. I started choosing my trips according to what I was really interested in. But it's a little too late to undo that now.

When I wasn't able to travel as frequently as I might have wished, I chose a method that eventually worked well, although it also caused me constant headaches: whenever anyone declared that he'd discovered something—a new custom, a hitherto unknown practice, a surprising funeral rite—I let some time pass by, maybe one or two years. Then I took advantage of any mistakes, which were almost always caused by excessive haste. When the international community of anthropologists had accepted a theory as valid, when they started to forget the matter at hand and get excited about the next novelty, I went into action. I was no better than anyone else. The most common outcome was that my research would confirm their conclusions, but from time to time, I would get hold of some subtle nuance, some different way of explaining the same thing. This gave me something of a name and a certain amount of prestige. Nonetheless, sometimes the opposite occurred; sometimes I came across a new piece of data that refuted what everyone else considered beyond doubt. That's what happened with the tears of the Andamanese, the customs of the Wari, and the regeneration of life by means of sex among the Iraqw. And I never dared explain my Iraqw findings in detail.

The learned masters in the field belittled my work. They tried to get rid of me by swatting at me, the way you try to bat away a bothersome fly. I may have been a tiny fly, but I was also stubborn and relentless. There were even some people who considered me the equivalent of a carrion feeder: they complained that they chased down the prey and then, like a vulture, I came in and swooped on the remains. At this point, I don't remember a single controversy where the passage of time hasn't eventually proven me right.

I'm not bragging here. The international community of anthropologists, prestige, science itself—none of that matters. I was talking about me. With every trip, I traveled farther, searching for the remotest tribes, the ones least contaminated by contact with Westerners, and each time I was able to stay a little longer. With every trip, returning grew harder. The parentheses had changed places: the real text of my life took place in my travels. Everything else seemed superfluous. Maybe "superfluous" isn't the right word. It's not that I was rejecting the life I'd led until then. It's not that I felt trapped in it against my will, because, after all, I'm the one who chose that life.

My absences weren't escapes from routine, either—on the contrary, people often called me an adventurer. Even today, it's one of the labels customarily pinned to my name, and my supposed death may confirm that view of my career. It wouldn't surprise me. People don't travel much. The mere mention of words such as "Africa," "tribe," "Amazon," or "rite" awakens images of inhospitable places and unheard-of risks in their imaginations. But I was traveling to such places to do my work, and when I was home in Barcelona, what I missed most was precisely the routine activity that work necessarily entailed. Whenever I boarded an airplane, I knew I was getting closer to what had gradually become my favorite routine: the routine of small things, of a more basic world, a world where life really could be summed up as birth, growth, reproduction, and death.

Then came the smells, the dampness, the mosquitoes, the dense and viscid swamps. I've never counted how many months I must have spent in awful places. I've been a working anthropologist for thirty-five years; say three to five months of travel per year. By my reckoning, that's at least 105 months. Nearly nine years. And that's the uninterrupted time I've spent in jungles, high plateaus, and deserts. Accompanied by absolute strangers, people who not only didn't know my language but had had no conception of my existence before I arrived among them.

After each trip, Barcelona seemed increasingly sick and feverish. Sometimes, I took refuge in Malespina. In the Malespina of back then, *so different from the Malespina of today, for all the efforts made by Julio and my children to keep alive a false idea of the place, the idyllic fishing village that now exists solely in their imaginations. Back then, however, it was unchanged. The streets were called "Kiln Road" or "Lower Square" or "Lemon Tree Patio." A few common words, nothing fancy. In this, Malespina resembled my world: the simplicity of nouns—water, air, forest. That was the real world.*

Nouns. Names. I wound up baptizing the Wari. The night after my first contact with them, they put me in a cabin and stationed an older woman at the door. I didn't know whether this was a demonstration of hospitality—was this woman, so to speak, at my service?—or whether she was there to keep an eye on me, which would mean I was a prisoner and would become, quite possibly, a victim. In time, I learned that her name was Tocohwet and shared with her something that, in other circumstances, would have come to look like friendship; but that first night, her face seemed impenetrable to me. I would have loved to extract from her, if only through gestures, all the information I could, but I obeyed the sacred law governing first contacts: don't interfere, let things happen on their own. I was inside the cabin, sitting on the palm-fiber mat spread out on the floor. Tocohwet occasionally pulled aside the cloth that was covering the doorway and stood looking at me for a few seconds, without saying a word. It took me a while to understand that she didn't want anything. She was just checking to see that I was still there, that the fair-haired, pale-skinned apparition hadn't vanished into thin air. It's possible they had taken me for a spirit, a strange deity come among them by magic. Explaining this embarrasses anthropologists, but in first encounters with remote tribes, the natives often take the members of the expedition group for gods or devils or creatures from space. They don't recognize us as human beings by the fact that we have a head, two arms, and two legs, nor because we have the power of speech. No, what makes us human in their eyes is our ability to carry on commerce, in its most primitive form: exchange. You give them a couple of knives or a few necklaces, and in turn they give you a bone or a carved stone. As a general rule, this is the moment when they recognize you as something similar to themselves and decide not to kill or fear you. You give to them, they give to you.

Halfway through the night, Tocohwet appeared through the curtain and, for the first time, pronounced a word. "Wari," she said, putting her right hand on her chest.

Was this her name? I didn't know how to interpret it or how to reply.

"Wari," she repeated, making the same gesture as before.

"Isabel," I said, likewise raising a hand to my chest. "Isabel."

It looked to me as though she frowned, but I couldn't tell whether it was because my response bothered her or because it cost her to process my name.

"Tsabel," she said at last, chewing the syllables.

Good, I thought, we've introduced ourselves. Tocohwet pulled the curtain closed and disappeared. After a while, she came back, accompanied by a younger woman. Tocohwet pointed to her companion and herself in turn, and then she said the same word as before: "Wari."

She repeated the word and the gesture meticulously, as though making sure I understood that the name included both of them.

There it is, I thought. Wari, woman. I got up slowly, careful not to make any sudden move and keeping my hands in view the whole time, and approached them. I indicated first the companion, then Tocohwet, and finally myself. "Wari," I said slowly, trying to imitate Tocohwet's pronunciation as closely as possible.

They answered me with a double guffaw, so loud it echoed around the cabin, and went away. Shortly afterward, the two of them returned once more, bringing with them a little boy whose eyes reflected terror and unbridled curiosity in equal measure. Tocohwet placed herself between her two companions, indicated them and herself with a circular movement of her arm, and said one more time: "Wari."

Weeks passed before I understood completely. "Wari" means "we," but also "person," "people," and "human being." From the linguistic point of view, their logic was devastating: they had never seen a human being who wasn't a Wari. That's how small their world was. They didn't have a word that included me. Other Wari subgroups had had accidental, violent encounters with Occidentals, but not their group. They had never seen a person with white skin and straight hair. It took me weeks to persuade them that I was a "Wari" too, that there was a "we" that included me. Above all, it took time to make them understand that I didn't belong to a race called "Tsabel." When white men showed up in those parts after I left, they were Tsabel as far as the Wari were concerned. I'd rather not say anything here about those whites who came after me, nor about the misfortune that meeting them meant to the Wari, and to myself. But I was talking about something else. About the few nouns. Water, air, hunger, death, bone, flesh, fire, sky, house, enemy, mother, children, sickness, corn. After the first days had passed, a few secondary things: laughter, sex, songs, hunting. All the rest was superfluous. I don't know how many thousands of words in my vocabulary became completely useless. They couldn't be translated into the language of the Wari. Of course, I was prepared for that. Not only because common sense had told me it would be the case, but also because I had encountered similar situations before. In Africa, in New Guinea. I spent a great deal of time getting rid of what was superfluous, reducing my nouns to the indispensable minimum. When you have few fictions, it's easier to use few nouns. That's why I was able to live with them. If you peel away the layers of an onion, looking for the center, you're in for a disappointment; the center is just another layer. If you peel away the fictions from life, much the same thing happens. Breathing and eating and sleeping are all that remain. Just a few verbs, a few nouns, almost as little as if you were dead. The borderline is only a heartbeat. That's why we create legends. That's why the Simóns and the Russian women exist. That's why I'm here, availing myself of death, of my false death; it allows me to make a life almost without nouns. I breathe, I eat, I float in the lake; at night, I listen to the frenzy of insects. It's only natural that others should think I'm dead, and yet I feel more alive than ever.

~~ TUESDAY ~~

Something's up with Alberto. If I know him as well as I think I do, it's something serious. There's no other explanation for the dogs in his face and the howling in his eyes. I hope I'm wrong and it's just a phase, but I'm not used to seeing him this way. His function in the family is to be the nice guy, to remain calm even when the worst happens. Performing this role has never been too much of an effort, because it's in his blood, like Papa, like Simón. It may be that he simply didn't get much sleep last night. I haven't exactly been sleeping soundly myself, and every five minutes I could hear him sighing and moving around. He didn't get up until ten o'clock, when the rest of us were already having breakfast. He sat down at the table without even so much as a "Good morning," and drank two cups of coffee. He didn't eat a thing. Maybe the best move would have been to ignore him, but Papa's not exactly attuned to such subtleties. Poor Papa, as his illness has progressed, he's developed extraordinary sensitivity to other people's states of mind and an absolute clumsiness when it comes to dealing with them.

"Does anyone know if Alberto's up yet?" he asked, addressing me. I could have stuck a napkin in his mouth. He has occasional moments of lucidity, but truth could have chosen a better moment to come shining through. "I don't remember hearing him say good morning."

"Let him be, Papa. He probably had trouble sleeping."

"All the same. It's just two words."

In Papa's view, a bad mood is no excuse. In this house, you got more of a reward for smiles than for good grades. Luckily, Alberto limited himself to grunting an enigmatic reply, and then took refuge in silence, looking sulky and sullen, his lips pressed together. I've never known him to be so tense, not even in his worst moments, when he was going through one of his separations, for example. Or the interminable months that Luis spent in a coma. That's when I realized that Alberto's determination, that shipwreck-victim's perseverance of his, could also be applied to anger. I watched him treat Luis's doctors like a despot talking to his underlings. But I never knew that he could entrench himself in silence so ferociously. For a while, all you could hear at the table was the sound of the coffee spoon as Papa unceasingly stirred his cup. We all looked at my brother, hoping for something to break the spell and retrieve the Alberto we'd always known, the good-natured, smiling Alberto, the man never at a loss for the right word at the right time. In the end, he exploded. "What's wrong?" he asked. "Do I have a bird on my head?"

"No, not a bird," Luis replied quickly, as little disposed as his father to let anything drop. "I'd say it's more like a nest of spiders."

"Then you'd better be careful they don't bite you."

I thought I saw a faint glimmer of hope, so I said, "Now, now, children, let's not spoil the party."

Somebody had to try. Besides, although I'm fond of arguing, like everyone in my family, I can't stand it when the atmosphere turns hostile and unpleasant, especially not since I've been pregnant. I don't have morning sickness, I don't feel confused, I'm not any hungrier than usual, but everything seems to get on my nerves.

"Party? What party? I thought this was a funeral."

"Come on, Alberto. For once, when we're all together—"

"Together? We're together?" His tone announced the irreparable collapse of my diplomatic mission. "All of us? Then how come I don't see your brother Pablo anywhere?"

"All right, Alberto, stop right there." I too, when pressed, can show some attitude. I had no problem exchanging my white flag for a weapon. "What do you mean, *my* brother Pablo? He's yours, too. What are you talking about? He said he'd come today and the day has only just begun. And not very well, at that."

"What time is he coming?"

"I have no idea."

"Why don't you call him?"

"I don't know where he is."

"On his cell phone, damn it."

"He doesn't have a cell phone."

"You don't mean to tell me he's lost the fucking thing again?"

"What do you think?"

"That's an artist for you. He doesn't even make enough money to buy a cell phone. How's he getting here?"

"How should I know?"

"Well, it's just a question of whether he's taking the bus or someone's giving him a lift. God forbid he should learn to drive. That would mean acting like an adult for once in his life, and we certainly couldn't have that."

"Let's not start, Alberto. Even if Pablo could drive, you know he doesn't have the money to buy a car."

"That's not a problem. If necessary, I'll pay for one myself."

"Right, and that would entitle you to continue saying he'll never grow up."

"Let's just drop the subject. Are you sure he'll get here today?"

"He said he'd come on Tuesday. Today's Tuesday, and unless I'm mistaken, it's only a little after ten. Do me a favor and calm down."

"You know, he's entirely capable of forgetting Mama's ashes."

"I don't think he will. He promised not to."

"What were you thinking, leaving the urn with him? You know how scatterbrained he is."

"Maybe you could try having a little more confidence—"

"It doesn't matter," Alberto said, cutting me off. "I don't want to argue anymore."

Alberto rose from the table, picking up his cup so clumsily he dripped coffee on the tablecloth. Then, without responding to Luis's murmured complaints, he shut himself up in his study. Several times I nearly went in to ask if anything was wrong, if he felt all right, but even without opening the door, I could hear him bellowing into the telephone. He came out of his study around noon, wearing a jacket and holding his car keys.

"Serena, I have to attend to a few matters. Do you mind taking care of Papa and Luis until I get back tonight?"

"You know I don't mind. Will you be home for dinner?"

"I'm not sure. Better not wait for me. Thanks."

And good-bye. Without even giving me time to ask him if I could help in any way, not that it makes much difference. I know what he'd say: "No, thanks, I'll manage." It's the same old story. Sometimes I wish Alberto were as good at asking for help as he is at offering it, but I can't change him now. It's just the way he is. And he's right: he'll manage. He always does.

It's eleven at night and he's still not back, and Pablo hasn't arrived either, but I'm not going to worry. They're both grown-ups, they know what they're doing. I'd just like to take advantage of the blessed solitude on this terrace for a little while longer, write a few more lines, and then go to bed. Tomorrow is another day. A better day, I hope, because I wouldn't wish a repeat of the tedious evening I've just spent on anybody.

Luis came up to see me. He gave me one of his bear hugs and said, "I've come to console you for your defeat."

"What defeat?"

"Crazies 2, Normals 1. Well, we actually won 3–1, because Dad came over to our side."

It's his favorite joke. According to Luis, Alberto and I are the Normals, the sane members of the family. He and my father make up the Crazies, and Pablo plays for one team or the other, depending on what day it is. I once asked Luis what team Mama was on and he answered, "Grandmother doesn't play. Someone has to be the referee."

Luis isn't crazy. In medical terms, he has something called "Transitory Disinhibition Syndrome." In plain language, it's as if fear, caution, respect, social conventions, and all the other mechanisms that usually restrain us from saying what we think have departed from his brain. To put it simply, Luis has a medical permit to say whatever he thinks at any given moment. In fact, it's not just that Luis is able to say what he thinks; he's often unable to stop himself from doing so, as though his mind were wired to a loudspeaker.

His condition may seem serious, but in reality it really isn't so bad. He doesn't go around all day talking nonsense to himself, for instance; it's nothing like that—in fact, he speaks less now than he did before his accident. But when he does, you have got to be prepared for a whole range of possibilities: a brilliant idea, an offensive question, a howl of inarticulate fear, an insult, words of praise doubly valuable because they are never calculated.

I don't want to slide into melodrama, but I have to say that seeing him alive and hearing him speak—even in salvos—makes up for any temporary annoyance his comments might cause. Luis should have died. He owes his life to a miracle, not brought about by divine intervention or the wonders of medical science, but by his father. If Alberto hadn't been so obstinate, Luis wouldn't be alive. Three cheers for Simón's legacy! For Alberto, there are no small matters in life, and defeat is unacceptable. He faces everything with the same resolute energy I imagine he has when he's defending cases in court. It's no surprise that he's considered one of the most important lawyers in the country.

Less than three years ago, Luis was involved in a horrible motorbike accident. There wasn't even a collision, just a simple skid. The road was wet, the rear wheel lost traction on a curve, and Luis was flung into the air. He wasn't wearing a helmet and his head bounced off the edge of the pavement. Three times. A triple cranial fracture. With the third blow, he landed against the base of a streetlight, and a protruding bolt perforated his skull and affected his frontoparietal lobe. He had a hole in his forehead, right above his temple. The traffic police notified Alberto by telephone at two in the morning. Alberto called me and Pablo and told us to go straight to the hospital. We spent the rest of the night in the waiting area outside the emergency room, but we didn't see Alberto. He was in the operating room. I don't know how he persuaded them to let him in there, nor did it occur to me to ask him at the time. That's what Alberto does in life: he finds out what he wants, and then he obtains it. The operation lasted five hours. When they finished, it was already day. Alberto left the operating room and summarized the situation for us in words that my memory brings back to me, syllable for syllable, every time I see Luis: "It looks very bad. He's lost a lot of blood. The doctors won't predict whether he'll live or how damaged he'll be if he does. Thanks for coming. I'll call you tomorrow. Please be sure to tell Mama. It would be better not to let Papa know anything just yet. I'm going to bed. I need to recover my strength, because Luis has to get better, whatever it takes."

Whatever it took: the best clinic and an army of neurologists, recruited from wherever Alberto could find them. Whatever it took: every kind of therapy, conventional and alternative. Whatever it took: obstinacy and patience. Luis was in a coma for fourteen months. After the first few weeks, the doctors declared his condition irreversible and tried to convince Alberto that his efforts were useless. His faith was what faith must be in order to merit its name: blind to the evidence and deaf to reason. While the rest of us were waiting for Luis's grip on life to loosen, while none of us could find enough courage to tell Alberto that his stubbornness was not merely futile, it was also beginning to seem cruel, he was visiting him every day with the same smile, as if Luis had been laid low by a bad cold instead of a deep coma. Every day, he repeated the same ritual: he threw everyone out of the room, doctors included, lay down beside his son, and lightly scratched his shoulders, all the while whispering into his ear an account of the events of the day. Nothing important: family news, things that had happened at work, memories of some friend or other, even the latest football scores, as though he were trying to ensure that Luis wouldn't be out of step when he returned to normal life. Then, with infinite patience, he massaged Luis's body. His whole body. He flexed one muscle after another, beginning at the fingers and going up to his neck and then from his shoulders to his lower back. He lifted Luis's legs and moved them around in a circle, as if the boy were pedaling an invisible bicycle in the void, a void from which he would eventually return one day out of gratitude to Alberto, who had taken charge of maintaining Luis's body during its owner's absence.

"He's going to make it," Alberto said to me once, when Luis had been unconscious for three or four months. "I really think he's going to make it." Although he was looking me in the eyes as he spoke, it was obvious that he was only using me as a witness to the conversation he was having with himself a dozen times a day. "The tricky part is going to be his rehabilitation, but we'll manage."

For the first time, I dared to contradict him. "But, Alberto," I said, "suppose he doesn't make it? Suppose all this only prolongs his suffering? One of these days, you're going to have to accept that some things are beyond your control—"

"I told you he's going to make it, goddammit." He was speaking like a man possessed, almost as though he were talking to himself. "Lay your head on his chest. I swear you can hear life running around in there. It's like listening to an underground river. In the end, he'll climb out on one side or the other. Besides, survival's in his blood. Remember Simón. Imagine that it's Luis floating out there, clinging to something, I don't know what, but clinging to something, because if he weren't he'd already be dead."

"That's what his doctors say: the real miracle is that he's still alive."

"Then it'll be one miracle on top of another. I tell you, he's going to make it."

After eight months, the neurologists asked Alberto to meet with the medical team to evaluate the situation. We all figured the result would be the decision to disconnect Luis from his life support, even if gradually, all the while maintaining his analgesic dosage to counteract pain he might not even feel; to withdraw his respiratory assistance, little by little, along with the whole battery of other devices that were supporting his vital functions. But just the opposite occurred. Alberto didn't even let the physicians speak. With consummate courtesy, he thanked them for giving him the opportunity to address all of them and proposed that they should keep on working, basing their efforts on the premise that Luis would eventually regain consciousness. Then, taking Luis's survival for granted, Alberto asked the doctors to explain to him in detail what state the boy would be in when his brain finally decided to reconnect to life. The terrifying list of possible outcomes included all sorts of dysfunction, from permanent paralysis to partial recuperation of his faculties.

The final words with which Alberto declared that conversation closed are famous in our family: "You do your work, and let me do mine." Then, with an ironic touch all his own, he added, "And if the fortune this is costing me doesn't bring him back, I trust it will at least make you stop looking at me as if I were crazy. I know what I'm doing, gentlemen. And I know that this is a question of faith. I can't demand that you share mine, but I hope you will at least concede that pretending to do so is rather profitable." Case closed.

On the following day, for the first time since the accident, Alberto didn't show up at the hospital. He drove to Malespina, called an emergency meeting of builders, painters, and plumbers, and charged them with immediately tearing down the shed where the fishing gear was stored, and building in its place a veritable gymnasium with all kinds of machines, wall bars, rooms for doctors, nurses, and physiotherapists, and even a small, heated indoor swimming pool that could be used for rehabilitation exercises.

At the beginning of the tenth month, Luis started opening his eyes every now and then. Opening them wide. He would lie there without closing them for hours, staring at the ceiling. The doctors insisted that this was an involuntary muscular reaction, that it meant nothing, that we see not with our eyes but with our brains. I spent a few evenings with Luis at the hospital. His eyes were open, but they were there to be seen, not to see, like a lighthouse. He scared me a little. Sometimes, during the rare moments of calm when the doctors and nurses vacated the room and we were left alone, I would try to get a reaction out of him. I'd wave my hand in front of his face, throw coins on the floor, or leap about to surprise him. Once I drew near to him and closed his eyes, the way people are said to do with the dead. When I drew my hand away, they opened immediately, as if there were springs in his eyelids. A few weeks later, Luis moved a hand. No one saw him do it, but when the nurses went to change him the next morning, they discovered that his fist was tightly clenched around one of the corners of the sheet. They had to tear it out of his hand by force. An automatic reflex, the doctors said again, a muscular contraction. The gesture of seizing is so innate we don't even need to learn it. That's why babies only a few weeks old will grab an adult's little finger and then won't know how to let it go. Letting go must be learned. Alberto told the doctors yes, yes, if they said so, a mere reflex, but he decided to take a leave of absence from his office until further notice so he wouldn't have to leave Luis's bedside, not even for a minute.

When we got the news about Luis and the sheet, Alberto said to me, "You see? Just like Simón."

"What do you mean, like Simón?"

"Didn't Papa tell you Simón was holding on to a chunk of bread when he woke up?"

"Yes."

"Well, then. Luis has the same blood. He knows how to hold on."

Another two or three months passed without further change. Then one day, as the nurses were about to give him an injection, the boy muttered a few words, almost without opening his mouth: "Too many people here."

A barely audible murmur, then he fled back to the shadows. His father made everyone leave the room, opened the windows wide, lay down next to Luis, and started scratching his shoulders one more time.

That was a year and a half ago. A year and a half of forced labor in what Alberto referred to, euphemistically, as "the facility" and Luis called "the torture chamber." Luis can walk almost normally now, except for a slight hesitation in his step that sometimes reminds me of a puppet, and he doesn't have complete freedom of movement in his right arm. As for the rest, he looks like a healthy boy. His body is working. His skull fractures have knit properly. His problem comes from that hole in his temple, and although the word appalls me, a lobotomy is all I can compare his injury to. His memory has been somewhat affected; at times, his mental archives suddenly empty. It usually involves minor, trivial things. At midnight, he can't remember what he had for dinner. One day not long ago, a song came on the radio and he started singing along with it, but then suddenly burst out laughing. He'd just remembered that he knows English, including the lyrics of the song. He could also forget them the following day. Therefore, although his life resembles in many ways the life of any other boy of his age, he can't study. Not at the moment, at least. He's not going to be a doctor, as his father wanted him to be, nor a lawyer, which is what he probably wanted for himself.

What's certain is that he's making great progress and getting better every day. No one can predict when he'll stop improving, when his recovery will have to be considered as over. According to what the neurologists tell us, the brain's ability to compensate is unpredictable. It can adapt even in cases of tumors that have required the removal of active cerebral tissue. It seems that the neurons reorganize and the brain redistributes its functions. I find this amazing. The triumph of necessity. It's as if a man who's had both legs amputated could learn to walk on his hands.

Then there's the Transitory Disinhibition Syndrome. "Transitory" doesn't mean that the condition will necessarily come to an end one day; it means that the condition is not necessarily definitive, which isn't the same thing. In the beginning, we took turns trying to reeducate Luis, trying to make him understand that his frank outbursts could strew his life's path with wounded people. It was useless. Little by little, we've become accustomed to it. In fact we're the ones who have been reeducated, who have learned to live with his frank talk. During the first year, we tried to keep Luis in the house as much as possible. If he went out, we did our best to accompany him. After all, you can't go slinging truths about like so many daggers without one or two of them coming back at your head. As time passed, Luis learned to explain his condition by way of defending himself. He's capable of saying to a mother with a child in her arms, "God, what an ugly little brat." But then, right away—if he realizes what he's done—he apologizes and explains that he has Transitory Disinhibition Syndrome. And if the person shows the slightest interest in him, he's liable to tell the story of his accident or go on about his year and a half in a coma. Maybe they should call it Absolute Brazenness Syndrome. I don't know whether people believe him or take him for a harmless madman. I imagine they can see in his eyes that he means well. At least, he has yet to return home with a bloody nose.

"I'm going to the torture chamber," he announced this afternoon after lunch. "I haven't done any rehab since Grandmother died. If you need help with the zombie, let me know."

The zombie is Papa, who was sitting in his easy chair with a blanket on his knees and the newspaper open, ready to spend the afternoon enveloped in the fog of oblivion. The zombie, the Crazy.

"Don't call him that, Luis. He'll hear you."

"Him? Come on, he's got less hearing than a mushroom." He went up to Papa to kiss him good-bye. "Wake up, Grandpa. That newspaper's from last week."

"Are you going? Well, well . . ." said Papa in a distracted voice. "So much for last week."

And so I spent the whole afternoon with Papa. Crazies 1, Normals 1. An honorable draw, arrived at by dint of a great effort on my part. I watched him the whole time. It's like looking at the blind eye of a lighthouse in the middle of the day; you intuit the presence of the light, you know it's there, but you're not going to see it. When he's like this, I don't know what to do. I stare at him fixedly, although I'm sure he doesn't even notice my presence.

I adore that man. When I see how he's fading, how he's approaching death without our being able to do anything about it, it splits my heart in two. Nevertheless, he often tries my patience. He spent half the afternoon in a trance, contemplating the portrait of the Russian woman. And when I say half, I mean half, maybe more. It's a lovely picture. We all like it because it's part of our family history, and Papa has more right than anyone to look at it as long as he likes. After all, he painted it, and he was the Russian woman's friend. He told us the story a thousand times. But the problem was he didn't even know what he was looking at. He was spellbound, so utterly transfixed that more than once I was tempted to get up and turn the painting around. He wouldn't even have noticed. We've played out this scene many times. Too many times. His mind retreats and sinks into some kind of impenetrable mire, but he always leaves a buoy on the surface that he can return to every now and then. Always the same buoy: a sentence, a fixation he goes back to again and again and again. This afternoon it was the Russian woman's portrait.

"And so . . ." he said, asking the same question every few minutes. "And so . . . this picture . . . whose is it?"

I believe I behaved well the first five times. By the sixth, I couldn't take it anymore. "Yours, Papa!" I exploded. "It's yours! You painted it. I told you it was yours five minutes ago, and it's still yours now. Well, actually it's not. It's Alberto's. You gave it to him when he got the house. Alberto, my brother. Your oldest son, remember? A-L-B-E-R-T-O." I spelled the name out letter by letter, as if I were talking to a small child. "You told him that since he was getting the house, he could also have everything in it, including that painting. And if you ask me one more time, I'm going to put tape over your mouth and lock you up in the garage, all right?"

"Well, well . . ." Luckily, it didn't seem as though my aggression had pierced his absent consciousness. "So it's Alberto's, eh? And who is that lady?"

"The Russian woman, Papa. That lady is the Russian woman." I sat down next to him and took his bony hands in mine. "You painted her. How can you not remember the Russian woman?"

I lifted his hands to my face. Sometimes I sniff them, looking for the scent they always used to have, but now I find only the smell of old age ensconced in his skin: a premonition of death. I don't want to cry. I've already spent too much time assimilating the fact of my father's old age, and I've even managed to digest the idea that his death is probably imminent. But what I refuse to accept is the devastation of his mind. It's as if time wanted to play a joke on him, by stealing away his memory and conveying him to his end dispossessed of the past. As if life, before abandoning him, insisted on toting up his outstanding charges and presenting him with a bill for the many times he availed himself of the advantages of forgetting.

"Don't you remember, Papa?" I gave it one more try. "The Russian woman. The one with the beach. And the castle, remember? The one with the botanical garden. How can you not remember the Russian woman?"

I sat on the arm of his chair and joined him in contemplating the portrait, as if it might offer some temporary comfort. The Russian woman, naked. How odd. After passing half her life as a near recluse, allowing—almost provoking—the entire population of Malespina to turn her into a legend, she suddenly agreed to pose in the nude for my father. I don't know how he persuaded her to do it. Charm, I suppose. That's the way he got almost everything: unadulterated charm.

When Papa painted her portrait, she was over sixty, and even though she did justice to her reputation for vanity right up to the end, by that time she'd stopped dyeing her hair and wore it in a long gray plait hanging halfway down her back. Time had been ruthless with her body; Papa's paintbrush was even more so. He posed her in profile and painted her against a dark background, delineating her soft flesh, shading in her fallen breasts, and making no effort to conceal the deathly patina that time had deposited on her skin. In contrast, her face—

slightly turned so that her eyes stare back at whoever contemplates the picture—exhibits a hypnotic vitality. Against the somber background, the only light in the portrait seems to come from inside it, as if emanating from the model's body. On the ground at her feet, a bed of pink flowers spreads out into the shadows. If there was a moment when my father approached artistic mastery, it was when he painted those flowers; he endowed them with a texture so real you're tempted to reach out and touch them. A confession: when I was a young girl, on more than one occasion I did slide my fingertips across the bottom of the canvas, and a few times I even went so far as to press my nose against the picture. I was surprised to find the penetrating odor of oil paint instead of the flowery fragrance I had expected. At the time, I thought the flowers were roses. I didn't know that Japanese jasmines are the same color.

Although the Russian woman's mouth remains serious, her eyes betray the hint of a sardonic smile. By posing nude at her age, she was making fun of her own legend; she was also making fun of those who had shaped it, the men who for years had dreamed of her naked body, frozen in an image of eternal youth that flew into pieces when it collided with the implacable, sagging reality the painting portrayed.

It is Papa's best portrait. Actually, there's no comparison at all between it and the rest of the portraits he painted. It's as if it were the work of another painter, as if every one of its brushstrokes had been produced by a hand with a much greater talent for authenticity than his. He was a respected artist, known and even praised by other painters, and his fees had climbed to a respectable level, certainly high enough to support his family, which was a pretty rare thing for a Spanish artist in those days. But he was still far from attaining the status of a great genius. He never attained it. The portrait of the Russian woman was his last work. In the twenty-eight years that have passed since then he's never once picked up a brush again; I'll never understand why, and it won't be because I haven't asked. Hundreds of times. He says . . . well, he doesn't say anything now. But he used to say it was pointless to talk about it; the past, he said, was the past. And if I grew indignant and rejected his assertions, if I refused to believe that he didn't want to paint again, that he didn't feel at least curiosity, or longing, or just a sudden impulse from time to time, he answered no, never, he wasn't interested in painting anymore, period. It was pointless to go on painting, he said, because the very instant he finished the portrait of the Russian woman, he'd realized that it was his best picture, the best he would ever be able to paint. He saw that he'd come to the end of the road.

Perhaps, if Mama had joined in our enthusiasm for his painting, he would have changed his mind. That's another of the things I'll never know. Mama didn't take part in the debate. More than once, I sought her cooperation, confident that between the two of us, we could persuade him to start painting again. She always replied that everyone is responsible for his own decisions, and that other people's autonomy must be respected even if they're making a mistake. Nonsense. I have no doubt that in the end she realized her error. That's why she eventually took the picture from where it lay forgotten in the lumber room and hung it where it hangs today. Too late. By that time, Papa hadn't touched a brush for nearly six years. He wasn't a painter anymore; he was a skipper, a boat captain, and remained one until he retired. He kept his boat in the harbor at Palamós, barely twenty minutes from Malespina, and between May and November, both boat and skipper were for hire, usually to tourist groups or the filthy rich. He took them on one- or two-week cruises up and down the Costa Brava and told them stories of the sea. If there was ever a perfect skipper, it was my father. The fact that I found working as a sailor much less interesting than a career as a brilliant artist was my problem, not his, as he often pointed out to me. And I have to admit that he was right. He forgot. Forgetting was his great strength. He never reproached anyone or complained. He simply locked away his painting gear and put his boat up for hire. The boat's name was the *Astor IV*: two masts, thirty-six feet long, a thousand square feet of canvas with a balloon sail. A real gem. Now we have the *Astor V*. Actually, Alberto has it, because it's his, but we go out on it every now and then. It's a double-deck motor yacht.

Every time he came back from one of his expeditions, Papa would glow with happiness: he'd recount adventures worthy of the greatest pirate, turning summer storms into hurricanes and gentle breezes into absolute calms. At their longest, these voyages might occasionally take him to the Balearic Islands, but he described them as if they were full of Caribs and galleys, as if the earrings old-time sailors used to wear as a distinguishing mark after successfully rounding Cape Horn should be dangling from his ears. In fact, I always thought people fought with one another to hire Papa and his boat not so much for his abilities as a captain, which were considerable, but for the entertainment he offered them with his stories. A question about the origin of the boat's name would be all the urging he needed to narrate the entire story of Simón's shipwreck, and the mere sight of the west coast of the bay would prompt Papa to start talking about the Russian woman, so vividly that all the passengers ended the cruise convinced they had seen her riding down to her beach on the back of her mule and swimming naked in the sea.

"Whose idea was it?" I asked him that afternoon, naïvely making an effort to conduct something resembling a conversation.

"What idea, sweetheart?"

"The idea of posing in the nude. Did you have to persuade her, or did she suggest it herself?"

He opened his mouth as though he were about to reply, but then he closed it, shrugged his shoulders, and returned to his world.

I said, "That's all right, Papa. Forget it. I don't know why I even try."

This is no way to talk to your father. We've all been very anxious in recent days. I'd never spoken to him like that, and I know I'd never forgive myself for saying those words if his mind were capable of registering them. It consoles me to see that he doesn't, just as he probably doesn't perceive the bitter tenderness in my voice as I say them.

It's weariness. The weariness of knowing what's going to happen before it happens. You know exactly when he's going to say he has to go to the bathroom. Urgently. You lift him out of his chair; it takes some effort, but there's no problem. Practice has enabled me to refine my technique: I stand in front of him, bend forward, and make him lock his fingers behind my neck. I take him by the arms, just above the elbows, and when I straighten up he comes with me, generally with a smile on his lips, a foolish smile, like a child who's just performed a magic trick.

We take three or four steps. Then he stops, casts his eyes around the room as though he's just been dropped into it and then asks, "So where are we going now?"

"To the bathroom, Papa. Didn't you want to go to the bathroom? Didn't you just say so? Well, that's where we're going."

Like a long-running theatrical production, we follow the same scenario word for word, act for act, day by day. The worst part is not that he'll do the same things over and over; it's that he causes me to do them, too. I try to persuade him to walk without dragging his feet and stumbling. He frowns a bit—it's his way of showing me he doesn't like taking orders. On a single trip to the bathroom, he'll ask me where we're going three or four times. Even when I've finally got him sitting on the toilet, he's perfectly capable of saying, "Well, now. What are we doing here?"

I don't usually lose patience. I'm often on the point of losing it, but generally I don't. I've known the text of this pathetic tragicomedy by heart for five years now. The doctor even took it upon himself to congratulate us. "It's not Alzheimer's," he said. "It's a milder variant of Parkinson's disease, slower, and the symptoms aren't as serious." In other words, we're in luck. The slow, gradual deterioration of his mental powers—announced the first time he forgot to take off his hat after entering the house and confirmed as incurable the day he had to be picked up at a police station because he was lost and couldn't remember his address—allowed us to grow accustomed, little by little, to a situation we would have found intolerable had it happened all at once.

Hard as it may be for us to accept, the only thing that remains for Papa is death. Maybe he'll forget to breathe one day, and then he'll forget himself. It would be the perfect culmination of his theory. Mark a date in the calendar. Move on. If everyone gets the death that's coming to him, this will be his: he'll forget to exist. Papa lived like a man in a hot-air balloon, dropping the ballast of his immediate past in order to gain altitude every time life started bearing down on him. I don't deny that the trick worked, but now that his fall is inevitable, he has no ballast left to jettison; all he has is this devastated present, and pulling him out of it would be abandoning the balloon, abandoning life.

There's a chance that the opposite is happening to me. I walk through life at ground level. I gladly take on the ballast of the past, I cherish it, I let it accompany me everywhere. What bothers me most is the present, with its fucked-up mania for meddling in everything.

Right now I'm in bed with my notebook because Pablo arrived a while ago, around one o'clock. I heard a car coming up the gravel road. Thinking it was Alberto, I went out onto the terrace to see if he'd come back in a better mood. A little black car had stopped under the cypress tree by the entrance. Pablo was standing outside, leaning in through the window, saying good-bye to whoever gave him the lift. Or, more accurately, kissing whoever gave him the lift. A long kiss, the kind where you have to come up for air. Long, loose blonde curls. If it weren't impossible, I'd swear it was Antonia. But it can't be. I don't usually meddle in other people's lives, but I confess I tried to get a closer look. The kiss came to an end. Just as Pablo turned around, the blonde mane put the car in reverse and pulled away before I had time to make sure it wasn't Antonia.

"Oh, good, Pablo, you're here."

Two kisses. Very calm. He smelled more than ever of tobacco. Or maybe I'm paying more attention to smells these days.

Despite the hour, the first thing Pablo did was to take off his clothes, put on the old rags he keeps in his closet here, throw a towel over his shoulder, and leave his room. He had to go swimming. At close to two in the morning, in the middle of October. The water was no doubt freezing, but he had to go down to the beach and jump in.

"Pablo, you're getting crazier by the day."

"What are you talking about? The crazy thing would be to come here and not go in the water. In fact, you should come down to the Russian woman's beach with me. You can't imagine how great the water is there at this time of night."

Naturally, I didn't go down to the beach with Pablo. It's a stroke of luck that he decided to be a musician and not a politician. He would have founded the Authenticity Party, and he would have been its most extreme and radical member. As far as Pablo is concerned, things that aren't "true"—that is, things that aren't what he considers "true"—simply don't exist: unless you're standing in the middle of the street right when the sky opens and the water comes down in torrents and soaks you to the skin, you can't say it's raining; unless you're losing sleep and sanity, you're not in love; unless you go skinny-dipping on nights when there's a full moon, don't you dare suggest that you like the sea; and naturally, if you're not capable of composing something obscure, incomprehensible, and impetuous, don't call yourself a musician. So he went swimming at the Russian woman's beach. Stark naked. The only way, he says.

Half an hour later, while Pablo was recounting the wonders of his moonlight swim, Alberto arrived. He seemed much calmer now, but judging by the look on his face, I'd say he's failed to resolve his problem, whatever it may be. It would be more accurate to say he seemed resigned.

"Well, if it isn't Beethoven."

"What's up, Rockefeller?"

Signs of affection. That's what men in families do; they demonstrate affection by way of reciprocal jabs. My brothers are very fond of each other.

"Shit, you're all wet. My shirt's soaked."

"So much the better. It'll help you remember what the sea smells like. You can't smell it on the bridge of your yacht."

"I don't want to hear about your mystical union with the sea. I'll beat you at anything you want—swimming, rowing, diving, you name it."

It was the first relaxed moment of the day. When those two start competing, it's a good sign. Unfortunately, it didn't last long, because Alberto suddenly thought to ask Pablo about Mama's ashes.

"Shit!" Pablo exclaimed, one hand on his forehead.

"Don't tell me you've forgotten them, because if you have, I'll kill you. I swear I'll kill you."

"I left them in the car," Pablo explained, calmly, as if he'd forgotten a pack of cigarettes. "Don't get angry. They're only ashes."

"Fuck, Pablo. They're your mother's ashes."

"Exactly: ashes."

"Give me your cell phone. I'll call her right now."

"Who?"

"The woman in the car, the one who brought Pablo here." As I spoke, I was getting my phone out of my bag. "A blonde with long, curly hair."

"Would you mind your own business?" I don't know anyone who protects his privacy as tenaciously as Pablo.

"A curly-haired blonde? Well, that sounds normal. I'll go and get the ashes myself if I have to," Alberto said. "But if this blonde is who I think she is, I'd better take my checkbook along. She's liable to try to sell them to me."

"Calm down. I'm the one who screwed up, so let me put things right. They'll be here tomorrow."

"Promise?"

"Promise."

I can hear voices, so they must still be having their discussion, although now and then there's a burst of laughter. Blessed normality. On the night table, as usual, I have a glass of water and my Orfidal. Recently, I've been trying not to take them. It's true that they help me get to sleep, but they also multiply my nightmares. And they're not good for the baby I'm carrying; should I decide to have it, I don't want to shoulder that particular guilt. I can't get used to this life that has opened inside my body. There's too much interference coming from the present to compound it with whatever the future's sending me. I don't want to think about that now, because if I do I won't get to sleep no matter how many pills I shovel in.

WITH LUIS

It's like having an illicit lover. I need to see Luis. To be alone with him. I need to talk to him. I go to his gymnasium in the middle of the afternoon, to see how he's doing, I say. He looks at me and smiles. He knows what I want. We don't talk about life or Mama. We don't waste time on preliminaries. As I've already said, it's what he's there for. I don't seek him out for what he can give me, but for what he can get from me. For what I want him to get from me—the truth.

You look all alone. It's the first thing he says when he sees me come in. I don't know why you're so alone. Nonsense, I tell him, I have plenty of friends. He stares at me: he doesn't have to say any more.

Truth is a bone and Luis is a dog. No: Luis is a dog, I'm a bone, and truth is the marrow. I can't believe you don't have a boyfriend, he says. I take a step back. Let's discuss what you mean by the word "boyfriend," I say. He interrupts me, Call it whatever you want: boyfriend, partner, mate, squeeze, lover. You don't have one. It's not so easy, I tell him. Demand is high, availability low. And most of them are faulty. Right, he agrees; but one, just one . . . I tell him about men who confuse passion with prodding. About athlete's foot, timid erections. The men of my generation don't measure up. They score low in mental health. Zero in commitment. Deficient in emotional intelligence. Half of them don't even pass the hygiene test.

He lets me talk for a while. Right, he says. But one, just one—even just to get laid from time to time. We're coming to the marrow. I think about the Syndrome. I think, if I tell him, if I talk to him about Ismael, if I reveal that I'm pregnant, he won't be able to stop himself from reporting it to the whole family. I'm frightened and I don't know if I'm turning red, but Luis notices. Oh-oh, he says, and bursts out laughing.

There's something you don't want to tell me. The dog has smelled the marrow, but suddenly he drops the bone. Starts talking about his exercises. Look, he says: I can straighten out my arm almost completely. That's terrific, Luis, I say; congratulations. I tell him I'm going to leave, because I don't want to interrupt his workout. He turns me loose, lets me go. We'll talk again, I say at the door. Whenever you want, he replies. Like an illicit lover. Not whenever I want; whenever I dare.

All you need is one night here to realize that the true voice of the jungle is the sound of its insects. Millions of bugs, each with its own distinctive sound. At sunset, the symphony is deafening. Sometimes it can last the whole night, and occasionally even a few birds join in, like the neighbor kept awake by the noise from a nearby party who sticks his head out the window and does a little shouting of his own. It's a phenomenon no one can properly describe. Serena would insist on finding metaphors: an orchestra being trampled on, metallic gods clearing their throats, things like that, words, both pretty and useless in equal measure. And they wouldn't suffice. You'd have to give a name to each element in the cacophony. The right person for the job would be a Linnaeus of sound, someone capable of dividing noises into classes and families and species. Linnaeus gave scientific names to tens of thousands of plants and animals, but toward the end of his life, a mental condition devastated his brain, and by the time he died, he couldn't even remember his own name. That's what names do: they proliferate to excess and destroy the place they occupy.

One night I dreamed I was sleeping, and in my dream an alarm clock went off. I opened my eyes and cursed, waving my hands in the air, looking for a night table that didn't exist. Of course, there was no clock at my bedside, but its unmistakable alarm continued to sound in the room. There's some bug around here that reproduces an identical version of my electric alarm clock in Barcelona. Another insect, which I imagine as smug and plump, sounds like someone scraping the strings of a cello with a razor blade.

What I mean to say is that you hear the most unlikely sounds in this place. That's why it took me a while to identify the distant drone and intermittent gargling I heard on the night Judith died. The sound was almost negligible in the midst of all the other racket, but after straining my ears, I realized that what I was hearing wasn't some bellicose insect, but a launch approaching on the river. I suppose I didn't react too slowly, all things considered, because it wasn't the first time I'd heard that sound, and only the fit of anxiety—not to say fear—that came over me had prevented me from recognizing it at once.

The problem was that it was nighttime. Almost dawn—probably past four o'clock—but still dark. I had a bad feeling; no sound brings good news at that hour. I thought about the groups of men who go around plundering ruins. They usually appear in the middle of the night, armed to the teeth with top-of-the-line automatic rifles and machine guns, and carry off the ruins in pieces under the frustrated eyes of the security guards, who have nothing to defend themselves with except dull, rusty machetes. They cut the ancient Mayan stelae up into crude fragments, using circular saws whose noise sounds almost obscene in the middle of the jungle. They dismember hieroglyphics as though they were pieces of a jigsaw puzzle. Later the pieces appear in private collections: someone sells them in St. Petersburg, someone buys them in Geneva.

Panic seized me. Panic. I don't know if the word alone can evoke the trembling knees, the dry mouth. But I do know that the state I was in made no sense: I bear some resemblance to a relic, but not so much that I should fear being carried off by thieves. And my age exempts me from the worst fears that assail a woman faced with a group of brutish men. My body doesn't awaken lust. But a rule of panic is that it obeys no logic. It was memory. I retreated thirty years into the abyss of time and saw myself harassed and threatened in another jungle. I remembered how my life had depended on the mercy of strangers. It was in Brazil, in 1971. Someone had set fire to the room where I was sleeping. It was no accident. They wanted to kill me. I believed I had overcome that fear, but that night, here in the Posada del Caribe, I knew I was wrong. It was as if that unexpected sound had gone down the well of my memory and found a deep terror waiting for the proper moment to claw its way back to the top. At the time I wasn't able to appreciate the irony contained in that fear: I came here, among other reasons, to re-create the setting of the greatest moments of my life; the rumble of a distant motor was all it took to evoke the worst ones as well. In Petexbatún, I found a substitute for the blessed tranquility of the Amazon, a tranquility I'd spent thirty years searching for; it was only logical that I'd also find the unbridled terror I'd spent thirty years running away from.

At first, I tried to block out the sound, to flee from it somehow, but that proved impossible. So I did the opposite; I concentrated on it, made it visible in my mind to convince myself that it was no more than what it seemed to be, the sound of a boat traveling at night, calmly moving from one place to another. Its occupants weren't even aware of my existence. They were just people going from here to there, delivering goods and picking up others. My breathing gradually slowed down. I even began to distinguish the silences that occasionally swallowed up the sound of the motor, as if it entered a glass bell for a few seconds from time to time. In and out. In and out. A launch passing through the islets: in and out. That was the only thing it could be.

After a long while, the vibration exploded into a howl pitched three or four octaves higher; then it fell silent. In light of what I've subsequently learned, it should have been easy to envision a wreck of some sort, the propeller screaming as it spun in the empty air for an instant before the boat capsized, but at that particular moment the idea didn't occur to me. Maybe it's a breakdown, I thought. Or perhaps the launch had simply arrived at its destination. I didn't think about an accident. Far from it: I welcomed the return of silence and tried to go back to sleep.

But I couldn't. For a couple of hours, I tossed and turned on my rickety old bed, which for the first time seemed uncomfortable, damp, and hard. When I can't fall asleep, I usually lie on my back with my eyes closed and my arms stretched out by my sides. Then I move my toes one by one, and count them, beginning with the little toe of my right foot. I move one toe and count one; I move the next toe and the next and the next, counting, two, three, four. It's important to move all the toes one by one, without skipping any or interrupting the count. When you reach the end, you start in the opposite direction: eleven toes, twelve, thirteen, and so on. This method almost never fails. I've never taken a sleeping pill. Never, not even valerian. Not during the worst nights at the hospital, the vigil at Luis's bedside. Julio took them with astonishing ease, a characteristic inherited by his children. Whenever sleep withholds itself for a few minutes, they summon it with a tablet of some kind. Not me—I like wrestling with sleep and taming it. Even when I went through a period of the most terrifying nightmares, the months following my encounter with the Wari, or even worse, after what happened in Africa with the Iraqw and I returned to Barcelona with the seed of guilt sending roots down deep inside me, I never took a pill. I always counted my toes, one by one. But that night, I was too nervous. And so I got up before sunrise and went to the lake. Putting so much as a foot into the lake before the sun showed its face seemed like an invitation to the great Towira, and I wasn't exactly in search of that sort of excitement, so I waited. I wanted an ancient, simple thing, a purifying swim, a little peaceful splashing that would wash away all the agitation of the night.

I found the peace I was looking for. It didn't last long, but I found it. When the sun appeared above the treetops, it was as if every drop of water came to life and paid homage. This is how the days begin here: a breath of air over the surface of the lake awakens a heavy mist, an almost solid fog that envelops everything for a few seconds and then disappears. I swam slowly, out to the middle of the lake, closing my eyes every now and then and taking deep breaths. On my back, arms flung out in a cross, legs straight. I felt a slight blow on the back of my neck; a piece of wood, no doubt. I stretched out an arm behind my head, not sure whether I should thrust the thing away or pull it closer so I could use it as a floating pillow, but it had hair, a head of short, thick hair, and I became blindly aware of something like a nose and a chin, I felt the touch of dead flesh, and I swallowed water and screamed and swallowed more water, a lot of water, and coughed and kicked and thought I was going to drown, I could practically see the great Towira and all his court, pulling me by my ankles, I imagined myself surrounded by the dead, the numberless dead, the dead *with arms like seaweed, the dead of ancient tribes, an obscene dance of the blank-eyed dead, and my head went under and I was running out of breath and my arms were thrashing the water like a turbine, shoving away the inert, stubborn corpse, which insisted on returning after every push, throwing itself on me as though my place in the water were its own, and little by little it stopped being merely a vague shape, the body had a face, a recognizable face, despite the open gash from its left temple to its chin, despite the purplish, water-swollen bruise, despite the absent light in the right eye, which stared at the sky and did not see the sky: Judith. Judith, dead. Her body, floating in the water. I cursed her name. I shouted out my curse like a cry of revenge. I'm not about to reveal this to anyone, but I gave her a good beating. I don't know exactly how it happened. Little by little, my anger gave way to hysteria, and my open hands, which had been flailing anxiously in the water, searching for support, turned into fists that I unleashed on her body, on her swollen chest, on her shoulders, I thrashed her with fistfuls of water in payment for her enormous crime of being dead, of being there, of floating up to me. When my anger was finally exhausted, I didn't know what to do. I didn't think I could make it back to the shore. I rested my head on Judith's body. It wasn't an embrace or a sign of grief; it was a surrender. I took in gulps of air. I don't know how long I stayed like that. Eventually, without detaching myself from Judith, I kicked out gently and began the slow return. I remember trying to breathe in great mouthfuls of air but succeeding only in swallowing water. Perhaps it might appear that I was struggling to save her body, to reclaim it from the water and grant it a dignified repose—even though everyone knows that as far as I'm concerned the only dignity in one's final repose is putrefaction—but the opposite was true: her body, dead though it was, saved mine. It was like a float, like a big piece of wood that allowed me to reach the shore.*

I have no idea how long it took. I had time to think about bad ways of dying. In every culture, there are good and bad ways to die. Dying at home is good; home is order. The forest is chaos, and the spirit of anyone who dies there runs the risk of not being able to find its way home. But the water is worse. In general, spirits can't swim, and so they drown along with the dead person. Drenched, restless souls, wandering forever. Among the Lugbara, nothing is considered more tragic than drowning, because it's taken for granted that the water in the lungs prevents the victim from pronouncing his last words. To die with them in your mouth, without ever managing to expel them, seems like the cruelest condemnation. I tried to imagine Judith's last words. A curse? Probably not. Perhaps only an exclamation of surprise.

I remember that my exhaustion brought in its wake a lucid calm that allowed me, for the first time, to connect the noises of the night and the horror of the day, the launch and the corpse, the last roar of the freespinning propeller and the awful gash in Judith's face. The absurd noises of the living and the absurd silence of the dead. I reached the shore. I was almost too weak to drag Judith's body out of the water and could do little more than lay her head and shoulders on the muddy sand, like Amkiel beaching Pampered Girl. *I looked for something to hold the body in place, but I couldn't find anything. It wasn't necessary—there's no current at the shoreline. I'm too old for rescue operations, or any other kind of heroics, for that matter. I remained on the beach, lying flat on my back by Judith's side. Had I known then what I know now, I would have realized that my situation summed up all the contradictions of this affair: Judith dead in my place, her body salvaged by me; Judith dead and wearing clothes, me alive and naked.*

Eventually, I gathered together enough strength to walk to the cabins. Before I connected the radio to the battery, I remember carefully drying my hands, as if Judith's mangled body had awakened my sense of impending danger. It wasn't easy to get a response to my call, but finally I reached the Boss. It was a strange conversation. It may be that people in these parts have caught their way of speaking over the radio from the military, because they always bark as though they're in the midst of a battle. The crackling static sounded like nothing so much as a roaring fire. I managed to describe, more or less, what had happened.

"Identify yourself. Over."

"*Isabel García, Posada del Caribe. Over.*"

"*The señora? Over.*"

"*The señora. Affirmative. Over.*"

"*What's wrong, señora? What's happened? Over.*"

I didn't know what to say.

"*I don't copy you. I repeat, what's happened? Over.*"

"*There's been an accident. Over.*"

"*Did you say an accident? Over.*"

"*Yes. Over.*"

"*Affirmative? Over.*"

"*Affirmative. Over.*"

"*What is it, señora? Have you hurt yourself? Over.*"

"*No. I'm not hurt. What happened was—*"

"*Was that a negative? Over.*"

"*Negative. I'm fine.*" *I was getting ready to tell him the whole story, but the jargon was making me feel vaguely hysterical.* "*Nothing has happened to me. But there was an accident last night. A launch sank.*"

Silence.

"*Can you hear me?*"

"*Say 'Over' when you finish, damn it. I beg your pardon, señora. What launch? I need to know the coordinates of the accident. Over.*"

"*Listen, let's stop all this nonsense. This is a serious matter. I'm fed up with 'overs' and 'affirmatives.' Stop asking questions and do something, for Christ's sake. I'm telling you that a launch went down last night and a body has landed here and I want you to be so kind as to send someone at once—*"

"*I don't copy you, señora. You said a corpse? Over.*"

"*Affirmative. Over.*"

"*Affirmative? Over.*"

"*Fuck! Affirmative! Over.*"

It took Amkiel a couple of hours to arrive. I had time to walk to the lake, make sure that Judith's body was still on the shore, return to the cabin, get dressed, and fill my backpack with various items in preparation for a move to Sayaxché. I don't know why I did it. No one there needed me. Maybe it would have been enough to turn the corpse over to Amkiel. It was curiosity, I guess. I imagined that someone would want to question me, so I put my identification papers in the backpack, along with some money, a change of clothes, and another pair of shoes, I also took a box of soap and a can of mosquito repellent. When I opened the toilet bag, my travel mirror fell into my hand. I opened it and looked at myself. I wasn't aware that it had been weeks since I'd last seen my face. I almost said hello.

Amkiel arrived accompanied by two boys as young as he was. They didn't come in Pampered Girl *but* Silent Girl, *a somewhat larger wooden vessel, as if the circumstances required a solemnity that the old aluminum boat could not provide. As they approached the bank, I signaled to them to go directly to the lake without landing to pick me up and set out overland to meet them. The four of us raised Judith's soaking body. We had to hold it up for a good while to allow the water to drain off, and it weighed so much that our feet sank into the mud. No one said a word. In the end, we deposited her in the bottom of the launch. Amkiel climbed in, unfolded one of those sheets of green waterproof canvas usually used to cover goods during sudden rainstorms, and spread it over Judith's body. He told us all to get in and began the maneuver that would dislodge the boat from the shore. The impression of Judith's body, surrounded by the eight deep holes our feet had made as we held it up in the air, still remained on the muddy shore. So did my backpack. We had to go back and get it. Amkiel used the motor to hold the launch steady while one of his companions, with the kind of agility that can't be learned, jumped onto the shore, tossed the backpack at our feet, and was back in the boat barely two seconds later. When he was sitting beside me again, he murmured, "Beg pardon, señora."*

"Not at all," I answered. "Thank you."

Then it occurred to me that he may have been apologizing, not to me, but to Judith, because the backpack had landed on her chest.

Amkiel turned the bow toward Sayaxché. I got up, stepping carefully so as not to unbalance the launch, and walked back to sit beside him in the stern. I started telling him what had happened, but it turned out that he had more information than I did. Apparently, my radio call for help had raised the alarm in Sayaxché, causing an urgent survey of launches and skippers: Cranky Girl *was found to be missing, along with her pilot, Armando. An elementary investigation had been enough to reveal that Armando, tempted by the offer of an extraordinary fee, had agreed to violate the skippers' code of never traveling by night and take three passengers to Aguateca: the gringa, a Frenchman, and a Guatemalan.*

"What gringa?" I asked.

Amkiel pointed at Judith's body.

"Her name was Judith," I explained. "And she wasn't a gringa. I think she was German."

He looked at me as if I were speaking Chinese. "Indeed, señora,"
he said. "A gringa from Germany."

Lies start eating our dead bodies even before the worms do. The gringa. The señora. If I should die in similar circumstances, I thought, the label "señora" would accompany my body back home, as if that absurd title could contain everything I had been in life and perhaps even things I had not. The señora died. She had an accident. The señora was nice, but a little strange. Nobody knew what she was doing here. The señora was half crazy—she swam naked in the lake. Simón, the shipwreck victim. The Russian woman. The Russian woman went swimming naked, too. The difference was that she was rich and so she bought herself a beach where she could swim alone and in peace. That's a lie; the real difference is that she didn't have to die before she turned into a myth.

Amkiel's voice interrupted my thoughts. "With any luck, we'll beat them there."

"Beat them?" Ever since I've known Amkiel, I've thought that his verbal frugality, his way of talking as if he were sending a message in cipher, was a great virtue. But this time it irritated me. "Beat whom?"

"The dead, of course."

The three fastest launches had left Sayaxché early in the morning, loaded with men. Amkiel had set out at the same time to pick me up. The

others had found Cranky Girl *near the beginning of the Río Petexbatún,*
a couple of miles beyond the point where it branches off from the Río
Pasión. The launch was capsized and empty, its bow stuck in an island of
reeds. Amkiel had passed by this spot half an hour later and found the men
from the other launches hard at work, sweeping the river for corpses.
They'd already found one, the Frenchman, but still had hopes of finding
survivors, despite the fact that the accident had occurred on the most dan-
gerous stretch of the river. Shortly after its separation from the main trunk
of the Río Pasión, the depth of the Petexbatún branch is reduced to
slightly more than three meters; in addition, its progressively narrowing
channel increases the velocity of the water. It's like what happens when you
squeeze the mouth of a hose. The state of Cranky Girl's *hull left little room*
for doubt: a hole in the bottom of the forward half was evidence of the blow
that had ended her career. According to Amkiel, the brownish gray color of
the water, which is particularly murky in this area because of the quantity
of earth carried along by the river, often masks the presence of floating tree
trunks. That's why the launch skippers don't usually travel at night.
Cranky Girl *had been pitilessly exploited over the course of many years*
and was in a terrible state of repair. She was also probably overloaded at
the time of the accident, and this fact, along with her sorry condition, had
contributed to the fatal outcome of what, in other circumstances, would
have caused nothing worse than a bad fright. However, on this stretch of
the Petexbatún there are no rocks and no solid obstacles that could hurt
you if you fell into the water. It seemed highly unlikely that none of the oc-
cupants of the launch knew how to swim or that all of them had succumbed
on impact. Therefore the rescue teams kept searching downriver, certain
that they would find someone still alive.

Our two companions remained silent while Amkiel and I talked. Even
so, with my memories of that trip still fresh, I'm struck by how little solem-
nity there was on board. It seems to me it would have been more appropri-
ate for us to travel up the river in complete silence, moved to pity by the
presence of the corpse at our feet, plunged into melancholy reflections on
the ephemeral nature of life. But our trip wasn't like that; I'd be lying

if I said it was. Not that the lack of seriousness surprised me, because I've frequently noted, in every corner of the earth, how the presence of the dead sometimes serves to mark the normality of the living. There are thousands of examples of ways humans invoke life when death appears among them: dancing, including rituals that depict unbridled sexuality; sham battles; grand banquets. In Southeast Asia, Berawan women spend the waiting period between death and interment playing games of chance. The gambling takes place in the doorways of their huts, and they mark the changing fortunes of the game with great shrieks. It's not that they have no regard for the dead; all they're doing is what they saw their mothers do, and what those mothers saw their own mothers do, in a generational chain whose origin is lost in the mists of time. Their behavior is merely an attempt, however unconscious, to represent the social chaos that death brings, to overcome that chaos with a game, and to pretend that chance is subject to order. To words. Conversation exorcises death. Whether carried on in the shade of a cabin in the African forest or in the kitchens of our homes, its function is the same. It's not unusual to hear jokes in a funeral parlor, told in a low voice, followed by suppressed laughter. Talking about the dead person is an excuse for talking about life.

I don't recall very well what Amkiel and I talked about before we arrived at Petexbatún. First he told me some details of the accident, and then I asked him about the origin of his name. He told me he would never trust a native who introduced himself as Miguel. Miguel is the same as Amkiel, just as Luis is usually Churi here. He's right. I've seen it all over Central and South America: Indians who can barely speak Spanish and nonetheless claim their name is, say, Cristóbal. There are Harrys and Williams, too. Amkiel uses his name with pride, chewing the two syllables that comprise it as if he were spitting in the eye of history. He couldn't tell me his age, and I don't think he was being coy. I would guess that he's less than twenty, but he told me he had two daughters who go to the grammar school in Flores.

As we passed the site of the accident, Amkiel slowed his motor to a minimum, stood up in the boat, and gazed into the distance. After a few seconds, he touched my shoulder and then pointed toward the shore. I squinted and managed to spot Cranky Girl's bow; she was capsized, abandoned, almost completely submerged beneath the water. I couldn't see the hole the accident was supposed to have ripped in her underside, but I did notice the cracks that scored the carbon-fiber hull like a spider's web. Amkiel's taciturn face suddenly became animated: if they'd called off the search without towing the damaged launch upriver, it had to mean that they'd found a survivor, perhaps injured and in need of urgent medical attention. Amkiel warned us to hold on tight and opened the throttle all the way, skillfully dodging the few reed islands that rose out of the river. We entered the broad channel of Río Pasión and Amkiel headed north, always on the lookout for the stretches where the current offered the least resistance.

The corpses were waiting for us on the wharf in Sayaxché, wrapped in canvas sheets like the one that covered Judith's body. There was a great hubbub of voices and a crowd of people milling about on the quay. We spotted the corpses before we docked. There were only two shapes lying there; the one we were bringing would make three. Since the launch had left with four occupants, one was unaccounted for. A survivor, or an unrecovered victim? As we were disembarking, people started telling Amkiel that Armando, the skipper of the wrecked launch, had been rescued. Someone had driven him in a car to Flores, where there was a better chance of finding emergency medical attention. Although he was in a bad way, with a huge gash in one leg and his lungs half full of water, he'd been able to talk before he left and had cleared up the few remaining questions about the accident. Judith had been the first victim. The violence of the collision raised the motor and propeller out of the water and Judith had had the bad luck of falling onto it, slicing open her face. Perhaps the blow didn't kill her instantly, but when she fell into the water it would have made breathing difficult and impeded her vision so that she couldn't find something to hold on to. The other two had died from a lack of judgment. Their heavy backpacks, still strapped to their backs, had dragged them to the bottom of the river.

Most of the men who were gathered around the bodies were launch *skippers, and among them the consensus was that the blame for the rash decision to travel at night did not rest with Armando, but with the foreigners who had persuaded him with the filthy argument of their dollars. The same could be said of the excessive cargo, however well intentioned, for the victims had apparently been bringing boxes of tools, medicine, and food to the Mayan enclaves of Aguateca. No one seemed to notice the paradox: a shipment of goods intended to save lives had, in the end, cut short the lives of those who were transporting it. Another point everyone agreed on was that the two men would have been able to swim to safety had they followed Armando's advice and stowed their backpacks in the bottom of the boat. It's not unusual for the dead to be blamed for anything that goes wrong, especially if they're foreigners.*

Amkiel related these details to me, translating the assiduous shouting of his comrades into comprehensible words, while someone collected Judith's body from the launch and laid it—stiff, covered, anonymous—alongside the others. I saw a few uniforms and somebody taking notes, but there was nothing official. From time to time, someone bent down and lifted the canvas sheets a few inches in order to see the faces of the dead, as though it were the only way they could believe what had happened. After a short while, a van arrived, the bodies were loaded onto it, and it left, bound for Flores. The departure of the van left a terrifying normality in its wake.

"And what is the señora going to do?" Amkiel asked me.

"What time is it?"

Neither of us was wearing a watch.

"Well, it must be around three, more or less. I think it's going to be too late to go back to the inn, señora."

"Could you take me there tomorrow?"

"Of course."

"Then let's find me a room and I'll stay here tonight. I need to buy a few things anyway. We'll leave at noon tomorrow, all right?"

"As the señora wishes."

There are three hotels in Sayaxché. Two of them are simple guesthouses frequented by the occasional government official who manages to turn up in these parts, and truckers who are willing to accept the minimal amenities in exchange for a night off the road. I chose the third one, the Hotel del Capitán, which is rather better equipped to receive the tourists who use Sayaxché as a base for excursions to the Mayan ruins of El Ceibal or, less frequently, to those of Dos Pilas and Aguateca. It didn't make sense to reject a real mattress and a hot shower for just one night. I asked Amkiel to come with me. It was only when I got to the reception desk and they asked for my papers that I realized I didn't have my backpack. It never occurred to me to consider the possible consequences of my forgetfulness; on the contrary, it seemed almost funny. I mentally retraced the movements of my backpack: from my shoulders to the mud; from the mud, through the air, to the bottom of the launch where it rested on Judith's chest and where it remained, transformed by my absentmindedness, into the property of the dead woman; and from there to the van that was taking the bodies of the accident victims to Flores. The crowd on the quay distracted me and I hadn't even noticed it was missing. Nevertheless, when I shut my eyes, I seem to see the backpack, as if my memory has recorded in detail, in slow motion, the moment when they carried it off on Judith's body. How deceptive memory is. I suppose it's tempting me now with this image of what I never saw because it would have been important to see it. To forget is to imagine that something didn't happen. To remember is to imagine that something happened. I don't know.

I wasn't too worried. The backpack contained only some clean underwear, two T-shirts, a few pairs of shorts, a pair of old canvas shoes. Not much money, either, only a couple of hundred dollars; the rest was back in a safe place at the Posada del Caribe. My papers were another matter. There's nothing more tiresome than losing your passport in a foreign country. It places you in an unpleasant bureaucratic labyrinth. I told Amkiel what had happened to my backpack, and he promised to recover it. "We'll pick it up tomorrow," he said. "I'll call them myself and take care of it."

I'm not going to make excuses. The backpack was mine, therefore the muddle was mine, so I won't be looking for anyone else to take the blame.

I don't feel guilty about how slowly I reacted. Of course, I could have found some driver and paid him to take me to Flores as soon as I realized the backpack was missing. But at that moment, it made no sense. Hiring someone to drive me to Flores would have cost almost as much as replacing the lost contents of my backpack in the general store in Sayaxché. My papers were important, but not urgent. I won't even say I had a blind confidence in Amkiel's ability to recover the backpack immediately, because that would be false. He's an intelligent man, and there's probably no one who knows the secrets of the river and the ins and outs of boats and motors as well as he does, but he's not the kind of person you'd send on a bureaucratic mission. The truth is I took it for granted that it would be a while before I got my things back, and it didn't seem to matter. All in all, the confusion was my fault, I'm very sorry about it, but if it were to happen again, I'd probably do the same thing.

What I do take the blame for is what happened the next day. Well, maybe "blame" is too harsh a word. Let's say that nothing I did—or better, none of the several things I neglected to do—was the result of any muddle or anyone else's intervention, nor was it in any way attributable to chance. It was a conscious, deliberate decision. This is the advantage of writing something I know will be read by no one but me. I can tell the truth, the pure, unadulterated truth, without any excuses. That night, I had dinner in the hotel, roast pork I thought was fabulous even though it came with black beans and white rice, which had been practically the only items in my diet for the past few weeks. I went to bed early, and fell into a deep sleep, despite the events of the day. The following morning, I got up early and had breakfast in the hotel before going down to the quay to find Amkiel. I asked him to lend me a hundred dollars, promising to pay him back as soon as we returned to the Posada del Caribe. I decided to walk around Sayaxché and look at the place through the eyes of a tourist, but it didn't take me long to change my mind. I discovered that wherever I went, the Myth of the Señora went with me, and even idle passersby insisted on giving me their opinions about my stay in Petexbatún and the events of the previous day, with the eagerness that tragic news usually provokes in remote places. I went back to the hotel and paid the nine dollars that gave me Internet access on one of the two computers set up in a little room off the reception area. I'm slightly ashamed to tell this part of the story, because I've always believed that a person intent on disappearing from the world should truly disappear. I wasn't even searching for news. A bit of nostalgia, maybe. I felt like looking at the weather page, as if learning the temperature in Barcelona could help me to picture the city and see what the members of my family were up to. It was practically a game. Here's the truth: when I saw the headline announcing the death of a Spanish woman in an accident in Guatemala, it never occurred to me to suspect that the dead person might be me. Nothing strange about that, considering I was very much alive. I moved the cursor and clicked on the headline to open the article, still without realizing what was happening. And then . . . then everything went very fast, from the instant my eyes caught, first of all, the name Pasión, followed by Sayaxché and Petexbatún, and then my name, my own name, Isabel García Luna. What a fuckup. There's no reason to call it anything else. What a giant fuckup, I saw it clearly right away, the van arriving in Flores just ahead of its little cloud of dust, my backpack resting on the canvas sheet on top of Judith's body, hatching an uproarious, impossible joke; the anonymous hands unloading the corpses, gently, perhaps, the way people unload fruit, other hands jotting down names and facts, unfastening a zipper with indolent curiosity, finding a passport—perhaps somewhat damp—belonging to Isabel García Luna, white female, medium height, fair hair, blue eyes, and then maybe an emergency autopsy, some Vernier calipers to measure the injuries, the amount of water in the lungs, the causes of death rigorously established and yet the corpse wrongly identified, because a name on paper gives more definite information than all the guts and organs put together. On the inside, we all look pretty much alike.

The truth? The truth is I found the mistake amusing. The truth is I thought it was terrible, but not so terribly serious. I'd be lying if I said I repressed an impulse to notify people at once and clear up the misunderstanding, because I felt no such impulse. In my mind, the mix-up was someone else's problem, as if my name didn't belong to me any more than Judith's body did. I thought that things would be sorted out quickly. I imagined Alberto becoming indignant when he learned of the mistake, presenting complaints and filing suits, demanding damages and costs, threatening an international scandal. I confess: I thought the error would be short-lived and enjoyable. Morbid? Prankish? I don't know what word would define exactly the way I felt. It never occurred to me that the mistakes would accumulate, one after the other, as if stupidity or blindness were contagious. At no point did I think there was any possibility that my children would also mistake someone else for me. I don't like thinking about that part. Children are supposed to be genetically predisposed to recognize their mother. Hell, even among the so-called lower animals, the newborn can recognize their mother with their eyes shut, by her smell, by her sound, by some innate instinct.

The truth is I didn't plan this series of fallacies, but I did welcome it.

That evening, when Amkiel apologized for not having been able to locate my backpack, I told him not to worry. I wasn't in a hurry, I said. He could bring it to me the following Tuesday when he came to deliver my provisions. I asked him to take me back to the Posada del Caribe as soon as possible. I didn't tell him what I had just discovered. I remember disconnecting the radio battery again as soon as I got back to the inn, but this time the smile on my face was less ingenuous. More mischievous. What can I say? I admit that silence is sometimes one of the most sophisticated forms of lying. I'm not frightened by either of the two possible punishments: imprisonment or exile. In fact, I welcome them. I already have them. I chose them myself. I chose them both because they're the same. This isn't a story. I'm not Li Po or Simón. Here, dead to all the world, I'm the little thing I am: I eat, I sleep, and I swim in the lake. I don't need impossible rescues on the open sea; I don't have to satisfy the emperor with a poem or fight victorious battles with enemy fleets. I don't need anyone to invent me. I'm no legend.

WEDNESDAY

It seems incredible, or at least contradictory, that Mama didn't clarify her last wishes while she was still alive. She left a will, of course, and we've executed it according to her instructions, which were as we expected: her estate is to be shared among the three children, although Papa can use or rent out the apartment in Barcelona as long as he lives. At one time, he was Mama's sole heir, but she changed her will when the seriousness of his illness became evident. Obviously, he's not going to want for anything. Alberto will see to that. The money will come in handy for both Pablo and me—not that it's a fortune. It's about 14,000 euros each, plus our share of the proceeds whenever we sell the apartment Mama used as an office. Alberto says it makes no sense for the three of us to hold on to such a small property, and he thinks we could ask more than 100,000 euros for the place. A tidy sum. We'll follow his advice, as we always do. The sooner, the better, he says. We could already have sold it by now, but first we have to clear it out. Or rather, I have to clear it out. In the division of labor, everything related to family history always falls under my charge. I'm not complaining, but I'm not in any great hurry, either. There are tons of documents in there—articles, photographs, professional archives. Fortunately, Mama kept them all in good order, and when the time comes for me to go through them, I'll probably enjoy myself. But not yet. At the moment, the mere idea of shutting myself up with that particular legacy terrifies me. The boxes I'd have to open, the catalogue of tears, memories, and intimacies each page, each card will present . . . I'm not ready for that just yet.

In any case, when I mentioned Mama's last wishes, I wasn't referring to her will. What surprises me is that Mama, who was so thoroughly familiar with all the rites the living use to honor the dead, who had expert knowledge about all kinds of funerals, cremations, lamentations, grieving, wakes, and bereavements, never told us what we should do with her body after her death. That's a lie: she always said we should eat her. Out of compassion. It was a joke, of course, relating to her travels in Brazil, and the frightful impression her sojourn among the Wari made on her. And not only because she witnessed their acts of ritual cannibalism. After all, however disagreeable that might have been, it was a rare privilege for someone in her profession. I think she was most affected by the violent controversy that broke out after her return, when she published the results of her research and stubbornly defended the need to preserve the Wari tradition. She was prohibited from entering Brazil again. Mama was used to seeing anthropologists from around the world systematically oppose her theories and her proposals, but this time the pressure was much greater. In all the previous controversies, her reaction had fallen somewhere between sadness and resignation. She may have been sad because she didn't have more resources at her disposal to defend her findings, but she resigned herself to waiting for the passage of time to show she had been right. This time, however, she was caught between indignation and fear. I don't know if it was fear, exactly, but I do remember her insisting that it was best not to talk about the subject, and although she continued to publish articles about the Wari, I could never get her to explain to me exactly what had happened there. As for her indignation, I suppose it was a normal reaction. That was the first time Mama had ever argued in support of any cause other than her own. She wasn't interested in demonstrating that she was right so much as defending the Wari from a form of moral persecution that she interpreted as an unmitigated assault on their customs. She always considered the cannibalism they practiced not as a form of barbaric cruelty, but as a sign of respect. It seems that certain interests did not find this theory of hers exactly convenient. Maybe the world wasn't ready to hear it, although there has been no lack of people who have dared to say she was right. The fact is that Mama declared the best thing we could do with her body would be to eat it, and we all kept up the joke: Luis opined that it would be preferable to eat her alive, because she'd be tastier that way; Alberto speculated about the best possible wine to accompany her, maybe a full-bodied Gran Reserva; Pablo proposed that we stew her; and even I joined in the fun, suggesting she should lose a little weight if she didn't want us to be obliged to invite the entire neighborhood to the feast.

All very well, but these pleasantries are no help now. We're not going to eat her ashes. They're here, and no one knows what to do with them. I'm not even certain how or when they arrived at the house. I don't know whether Alberto finally went to pick them up last night or Pablo made some kind of arrangement over the telephone. Since the unmentionable blonde is involved, I'd rather not ask. But whatever may have happened, the ashes are in the fireplace. That sounds like a joke, but it's not. The ashes are in a hideous urn, and it's standing on the mantel above the fireplace. I got up early this morning, while everyone else was still sleeping, and as I waited for the coffee to brew, I went into the living room to open the shutters. That's when I saw the ashes. Alberto will be outraged, and with good reason, by the urn Pablo and I chose. It's made of aluminum, but with various unforgivable polished bronze ornaments sprouting from the top and both sides, so that it looks like some pretentious piece of bric-a-brac. It was all they had. When I saw it on the mantel, its bad taste was apparent. But I suspect the ashes will stay on the chimneypiece until the day when we can finally scatter them in the sea. We were going to do it today, but the *Astor V* is in dry dock. Alberto says the algae spread so prolifically this year that the bottom of his boat has turned into a breeding ground for mollusks. It's being scraped and repainted. Pablo availed himself of the occasion to make fun of Alberto. If Alberto didn't have such a *pretentious* yacht, Pablo said, he'd be able to avoid such problems. Alberto replied that Pablo was just jealous, and tough shit. Et cetera. We agreed to try to find someone to rent us another boat, but it's not easy. It's the middle of October. Malespina has no port, nor can it have one—the water's too shallow. The hundreds of buoys that welcome launches carrying holidaymakers during the summer disappear with the arrival of the first autumn storms, which generally coincide with the feast of Santa Rosa in early September. The point is that there are no more than seven or eight boats in Malespina right now, and all are in the midst of repairs: October is the month for caulking, puttying, scraping, removing rust, repainting.

We could do it without a boat. We all agree that the most fitting place to scatter Mama's ashes is the Russian woman's beach. We could go down the cliff, taking the same path the Russian woman used when she rode her mule down to the shore and went for a swim. That wouldn't be bad, but scattering Mama's ashes into the sea seems so much better. I hope Alberto can find us a boat soon. I'm also a little afraid, because these kinds of things make me too emotional, but that's not what's important. What's important is to complete the process once and for all, for Mama's sake as well as our own. Wipe the slate clean and move on to something else, as Papa would say. I have the feeling the air in this house won't be clear again until we take that final step.

Although Mama didn't usually talk about her work, she taught us that the purpose of funeral rites is not to honor the dead, but to allow the living to restore order to their lives, and therefore it's best to perform the rites as soon as possible. But theory is one thing, practice another. It's not going to be easy. Recovering from a mother's death must be hard for everyone, but I think it's going to be even more difficult in our case because our mother was different—indeed the long list of peculiarities that made her a special person was one of the family's favorite topics of conversation, indispensable in any family gathering worthy of the name. Somewhere in this house, there's a postcard she wrote when she was three years old. It's usually trotted out as irrefutable proof of her genius, as if its mere existence were sufficient to demonstrate not only that Mama was different, but that she was destined to be different from birth. Because of his work, her father wasn't home for his birthday—I seem to remember he was in Majorca—and the little girl, no doubt instructed by her mother, wrote to him in red pencil:

"Best wishes on your birthday, dear Papa, from your daughter Isabel."
All in capital letters, produced with an unsteady but willful hand. Three
years old. She says she doesn't remember. (I mean, she said she didn't
remember; it's going to be an effort for me to get used to talking about
her in the past tense.) Mama was always like that. Whenever anyone reminded her that she was special and started to list her merits, she pretended she didn't know what they were talking about and changed the
subject at once. "Nonsense," she used to say. "That's just nonsense." I
don't think she was demurring out of false modesty; I imagine that the
virtues other people attributed to her were completely worthless as far
as she was concerned, and I think it may be that she died believing she'd
never accomplished anything of any real value, however much we all
believe the contrary.

The front of the postcard was a horrific Technicolor image of the
Church of the Holy Family in Barcelona, and every time someone in
the family resurrected it, its appearance would act as the catalyst for the
recital of a kind of virtuous résumé, repeated ad nauseam, detailing how
Mama was different: she's so smart, imagine, your mother, she was only
three years old, and look how well she could write, her letters are so clear,
I'm not surprised she was wearing trousers before any other woman of
her generation, and no wonder she went to university at a time when
higher education was usually reserved for men. She could speak foreign
languages from the age of fifteen and got her doctorate cum laude at the
age of twenty-three, and your father fell in love with her at first sight, not
that she was a great beauty, but she was smarter than everybody, bla bla,
et cetera. Maybe Mama was right to dismiss all that, to consider her ac-
complishments mere accidents of life, the result of having had, at best,
the common sense to find the most efficient and reasonable solutions. But
she was indeed special. She just didn't like to be told that. In fact, she
hated being the subject of conversation. I think what Mama liked most
was to be left in peace. And of all the narratives describing events in her
life, the one that made her most uncomfortable was the one about the origins of her university career. Because we repeated that account a thou-

sand times among ourselves, we probably turned it into a kind of story, but I still believe it's accurate in its details. We know that in the summer of 1953, her father, our grandfather Ernesto, urgently requested an interview with the mother superior of the Teresian convent school in Barcelona that Mama graduated from. No one else was present at that conversation, and yet we can all retell it using the exact same words, as if an invisible witness had taken the trouble to record them.

Once again, borrowed words. Once again, a story that someone said someone told someone else. It doesn't bother me as much as Simón's story does, for various reasons, the first of which is obvious: in this case, the present confirms the past, and the way one thing led to another is more or less clear. Maybe the conversation between Grandfather Ernesto and the nun didn't take place in exactly the terms we've always used when retelling it, but its consequences are demonstrated in what we know of Mama's life. Besides, it's only an anecdote. If Simón's shipwreck was, as Papa used to tell us, an inkblot in the manuscript of his life, a mark that stained all the following pages, you could say that the stain also spread beyond that manuscript, that the spilled ink soaked into our lives as well. Or mine, at least. In contrast, the story of Grandfather Ernesto and how he influenced Mama's decision to continue her studies has no greater significance.

"The thing is, Reverend Mother," Grandfather Ernesto said. This is the prologue we always attribute to him. He was famous for his moral rigor, his concise style, his desire to go immediately to the heart of any matter, and his disdain for any formalities that might prevent him from doing so. "I have a problem with my daughter."

"Good heavens, Don Ernesto." We all endow the mother superior with a stern, bony face and high-pitched voice, even though none of us ever met her. "Good heavens. I'm quite surprised. Isabel was always an exemplary student. Her academic results are truly—"

"I know, Reverend Mother, I know. She's intelligent, she's responsible, she works hard. There's no question about that."

"So?"

"The thing is, she's very obstinate."

"Ah, well, that. Of course, Don Ernesto. Although she's one of my favorite students, I won't deny that she's—if you'll permit me to speak frankly—as stubborn as a mule. And disrespectful too. Believe me, it's not that we didn't try to correct—"

"Yes, yes, Reverend Mother," Grandfather Ernesto said, interrupting her. "I know what an effort you've made. I'm not questioning your methods. It's just that I have to make a decision regarding her future, and since you and the other sisters know her so well . . ."

"Don't tell me, Don Ernesto, don't tell me that your daughter wants to join us and take the veil?"

The mother superior's face was shining, and the radiant happiness implicit in her remark convinced Grandfather that the conversational train had left the track for good. He decided to remedy the situation, even at the cost of a certain brusqueness. "No, certainly not. Who said anything about veils? Isabel wants to go to the university."

"Ah." Perhaps a shadow of disappointment passed over the nun's face. "So that's what it's about. The university. Then what's the problem? At the risk of sounding indiscreet, I assume you can afford it."

"Of course I can. That's not the problem. The problem is I had other plans for my daughter. There's a boy who's crazy about her. A fine lad, intelligent and hardworking. He'll be able to provide for her and he comes from a very respectable family."

"And what does Isabel say?"

"Isabel? She doesn't want to hear about it. You know my daughter: she's never shown much interest in boys. When the rest of the girls were learning to flirt, she always preferred to concentrate on her studies."

"And right she was, Don Ernesto."

"Precisely for that reason, and given that the young man in question has my complete trust, it occurred to me that maybe, if we could all make an effort to persuade her, if we could help her to look on him favorably . . ."

"Don Ernesto, are you suggesting I should act as matchmaker?"

"Not exactly," Grandfather said. "But you might perhaps offer a word of advice at the auspicious moment. After all, she trusts you. She's always said she feels admiration for you."

"Do stop, Don Ernesto, I'm going to blush," the nun said, breaking in on him with a false modesty bordering on coquetry.

An uncomfortable silence hovered over the conversation until the mother superior decided to get back to the point. "Well, well. She's an excellent student. So she wants to go to the university, does she?"

"Yes," Grandfather replied sadly. "I don't know what's got into her."

"Listen, I'm going to tell you something you may not want to hear." Now she was the one in a hurry to get down to specifics. "We apparently agree in our assessment of your daughter's obstinacy. To tell you the truth, I don't believe that either the wisest advice or the subtlest influence will incline her to give up her dream of a university education. So perhaps we should admit that she's right, to a certain degree. She has the qualifications to excel in any field."

"No one is questioning that. In fact, it's her enormous dedication to studying that worries me."

"I'm afraid I don't see what you mean, Don Ernesto."

"Look, it's quite simple. Nobody loves my daughter more than I do, but that doesn't prevent me from seeing the dangers ahead. Let's say that Isabel is not your average girl. I see that she spends too much time alone. She's obsessed with excelling at whatever she undertakes and knowing more than everyone about everything. I'm afraid that going to the university will exaggerate this tendency. I'm afraid the girl will turn into a bookworm, always in the library, spending her life shut up like a . . . like a . . ."

Grandfather's silence was eloquent. The mother superior finished his sentence for him: "Like a nun, you mean."

"Exactly. No offense intended."

"Please. But I don't see what we can do to discourage her."

"I could refuse to pay for her studies."

"Of course, you could refuse to pay. You could even force her to get married. It's been done before. But I think such measures would be counterproductive, not only in terms of Isabel's happiness. After all, she's hardly more than a girl, and she has the right to make mistakes, up to a certain point. But, beyond that, I feel that simply dictating to her would be a bad strategy."

"I don't see that I have any alternative."

"But you do. Maybe she'll find she likes this boy. Maybe he's destined, God willing, to become her husband. But if you force him on her, you'll guarantee that she'll never look kindly on him. You know how obstinate she is. Listen to me, Don Ernesto. You must be subtle. Let time sow its seeds. Stop putting up resistance and allow her to enroll at the university."

"And what about the marriage? She's the perfect age for marrying."

"She'll get married. Don't be in such a hurry."

"But she won't find a better husband."

When we reached this point in the story, we all looked at Papa. No more than a year and a half after the conversation between her father and the mother superior, Mama met Papa and decided to marry him almost overnight, even though her university career had barely begun. Their courtship lasted three months. And all the insistence that Grandfather had put into dissuading her from going to the university, all his interest in promoting a marriage for the apple of his eye, vanished as if by magic. He didn't refuse to accept Papa, nor did he punish her the way Simón's father would have done in similar circumstances, but he never considered Papa the ideal candidate for his daughter's hand. Naturally, this was something the nun could not have foreseen when she advised Grandfather to be patient.

"If she learns to moderate her tendency toward disobedience, there will be no lack of desirable suitors. Besides, your daughter's no fool, Don Ernesto. If this boy is as fine a lad as you say, she'll be able to recognize his good qualities. Find some excuse to bring them together, but let her discover his worth for herself. You never can tell. But it will never go any further unless she's convinced that he's not being forced on her, and that she's the one making the decision. Who knows, maybe then she'll be as determined to get married as she is to resist getting married now."

Grandfather thought for a while. It wasn't an unreasonable suggestion. This woman seemed to know his daughter even better than he did.

"Don't be impatient," the nun went on. "The Lord's purposes aren't always transparent. Grant your daughter the salt of her studies for now. Later, when the right moment comes, she'll turn to matrimony to slake her thirst."

"Perhaps you're right, Reverend Mother." The salt of her studies . . . slake her thirst . . . Grandfather arose and started to make preparations for his departure. He considered himself a well-bred man, and he was grateful for the advice he'd been given, but neither breeding nor gratitude meant that he was disposed to waste his time listening to gratuitous biblical parables. "If it's best for her, that's what we'll do."

The nun accompanied him to the door and bade him a courteous farewell. "May God be with you, Don Ernesto. I hope I've helped to relieve your worries."

"It's decided. She'll go to the university."

"God willing, Don Ernesto."

"But of course, God willing."

At that moment, the mother superior realized she'd forgotten to ask an important question. "By the way, what does the girl intend to study?"

"Philosophy and arts, it seems."

Although he said this in a sorrowful voice, as though he were admitting to her having some disease, Grandfather didn't seem to care what subject Mama chose; the dilemma of whether his daughter should or shouldn't go to the university had been resolved, and he was convinced that her desire for a degree would ultimately turn out to be a passing fancy. The mother superior, on the other hand, nearly had a seizure.

"Philosophy? Are you mad?" She lifted a hand to her mouth as though she had uttered a blasphemy. "I'm sorry, I didn't mean to offend you. But we have to talk about this, Don Ernesto. It would be a terrible mistake. Pure philosophy?"

"Why? What difference does it make?"

"Look, we've already discussed the fact that your daughter's rather stubborn."

"Yes, as a mule."

"Well, in addition, she's curious. Very curious."

"That may be true."

"But don't you see? Don't you know what sort of thoughts fill the heads of young people who study philosophy? I'm not saying your daughter's not a good Christian. As a matter of fact, she's always fulfilled her religious obligations flawlessly. But if we allow doubt to take up residence alongside her obstinacy, you may as well give her up for lost."

"Is it as bad as that?"

"Oh, and much worse. Look here, Don Ernesto, you must listen to me. I'm an authority in these matters." At this point, we assume that the nun's voice took on an emphatic tone. "Faith is a principle that one observes blindly. There's no reasoning about faith. If such a Cartesian intelligence as hers were to feed on the seeds of doubt, she would begin to lose everything we've worked to achieve all these years. I leave it to you to imagine the paths that curiosity such as hers would induce her to follow."

"Are you sure?"

"She wouldn't be the first student to be ruined by such trifles."

"What a mess." There seemed to be no end to Grandfather's problem, and his patience was wearing thin. "Let her get married, then."

"No, Don Ernesto. Let her study. Let her study and make the most of the intelligence God has given her. But philosophy and arts is not a suitable branch for her."

"What about sciences? I had thought that if she were to get a degree in pharmaceutics, maybe in the future she—"

"No!" the nun shrieked, as though admonishing Satan to get behind her. "Science is the graveyard of faith! Besides, scientific study is for men."

"Well, what, then?"

"It seems to me that the only option is to allow her to register in arts, but not to study pure philosophy. I recommend the least harmful of its derivations." Here, it seems, the nun began to smile again, as if she were pulling the last ace out of her sleeve. "History, Don Ernesto. And if she could specialize in prehistory, so much the better."

"You really think that's the most suitable field for her? Isn't it rather pointless to devote yourself to studying the past?"

"On the contrary. The study of the past imparts wisdom. History is full of atrocities, Don Ernesto. Wars and epidemics, betrayals and conspiracies, plagues and conquests. When one knows a little history, one learns to conform, to accept the destiny that the Lord has given us. And most important, contradictions are avoided. There's no way of arguing with history: it's all written down, and mastering it requires nothing but a good memory and disciplined study, virtues that Isabel already possesses in spades. And let's not deceive ourselves. Even if your daughter looks upon this undertaking as more than a pastime, in the end she'll accept marriage as what it is: inevitable. A female historian doesn't have much of a professional future in this country. Isabel could become a schoolteacher at best, but I don't believe she wants that particular vocation."

"Good, good." Grandfather, fearful that this woman might avail herself of the opportunity to bore him rigid with an entire theory of vocations, quickly put an end to the interview. "If it must be history, then history it will be."

"God willing, Don Ernesto."

"But of course, Reverend Mother. God willing."

And thus it was decided. Grandfather went back home and presented his daughter with his final judgment. Stubborn though she was, my mother understood that this was the only choice available to her, and in the autumn of that year, she enrolled in the University of Barcelona to study history. We're talking about 1953. Mama was born in 1932, so she was twenty-one years old. There were only nine female students in the entire degree course. The other eight got married after receiving their degrees and never practiced their profession. But she did. As usually happens in such cases, all Grandfather's carefully laid plans soon began to crumble, though it took Mama some time to overturn all his expectations. She didn't marry that boy—in fact she never saw him again after she began her university career—and as her knowledge of human history deepened, she grew more skeptical, a cynic in matters of religion, an atheist in regard to the gods. It's true that she specialized in prehistory and graduated with honors. But shortly thereafter, inspired by the published writings of foreign anthropologists, she began her battle for the recognition of anthropology as an independent science, and in 1967 she succeeded in establishing the first university chair in the new discipline.

I don't know whether this was all a deliberate strategy, or whether chance opened up a road and Mama simply traveled along it, spurred on by her iron will. In any case, the result was that, since she hadn't been allowed to choose her subject freely, she ended up inventing a field of study for herself. She became the dean of the anthropology faculty of Barcelona university; she was a pioneer in the publication of articles in scientific journals, some of them generating intense debate. The list of her achievements is long, illustrated by a series of certificates and diplomas, which (together with the birthday postcard to her father) come out of the old box at Christmas dinners and other family celebrations. It's not that Mama was famous. No scientist of her day was famous in this country. But she did acquire a certain degree of recognition, as the obituaries published after her death demonstrate. They all sing her praises, cite her books, point to her documentary films as proof of her contribution to the growth of public interest in anthropology. They lament her accidental death, which they unanimously declare premature and untimely.

Untimely? It's a lot more than untimely. Unnecessary, capricious, absurd, and, above all, preventable with even a modicum of common sense. What the devil was Mama doing in Guatemala? Field work? She was nearly seventy years old! She had at least ten or fifteen splendid years ahead of her, years when she could have enjoyed life in a manner befitting her age: that is, retired, respected by her professional colleagues, perhaps publishing the occasional article or memoir in specialized journals, or even dedicating to her family the time that all her goddamned traveling took away from us. And then she could have died a tranquil death in her bed, cared for by her children right up until the end. No one dies when they should. There's no such thing as a timely death. Though it pains me to say it, it would be best for Papa to die soon. Without drama, without protracting his suffering beyond measure; just fading out, little by little. Mama, on the other hand, was in the prime of her life. These days, nobody's considered old at seventy. All you need is to have a little common sense. You can't require your body to perform impossible feats. You can't believe you're Indiana Jones. It's pathetic.

My brothers shrug their shoulders and blame what happened on the vicissitudes of fate. I keep quiet, but I don't agree. I know I'm wounded and bitter. I know I'm groping in the dark, and all I can do is focus on my anger, at what I don't understand and can't accept. But it's more than that: I know that time will carry away all of this, the anger, the questions, the mistakes, the silence. Someday I'm going to die too, and nothing will remain of me, not even indignation. But let it at least be recorded that I was never in favor of that absurd trip. Never, not from the very first day forward. And I told her so, quite clearly. I should have insisted that after parents reach a certain age, the chain of command reverses itself and children become responsible for controlling their parents in certain respects. I tried, but I couldn't do it. Nor did she make it easy for me. One ordinary Sunday last June, she invited us all to share a family meal. She told Alberto there was something she wanted to explain to us, she asked me what my plans for the summer holiday were, and she revealed to Pablo—who has a sort of automatic solidarity with other people's states of mind—that she was feeling slightly dispirited and might need to take a break. To Luis, who sometimes has the urge to talk too much, she said not a word. Very clever. It was inevitable that her three children would worry, exchange these fragments of information, and arrive at the table predisposed to offer her some comfort. The first course came and went; so did the second; dessert and coffee were served. Nothing. All at once, a passing comment from Pablo while Alberto and I were transferring Papa to his easy chair gave Mama the opportunity to drop her bombshell.

The only thing Pablo said was "I can't believe how bad Papa is."

"Bad? He's terrible. Worse than ever. Every day I have to do more for him," Mama replied, and then there was no stopping her. "You are all going to have to take care of him for a while in the autumn, because I'm going away on a trip at the end of September and I don't know when I'm coming back."

Alberto asked, "What do you mean, you're going away?"

"Uh-oh, trouble ahead," Luis added.

Pablo hastened to make his position clear: "I'm going to be on tour, so I can't take care of anyone."

Then we all started talking at once. Since it's always up to me to ask questions, I believe I said, "What trip? Where? When are you leaving?"

"I'm going to Guatemala."

"Guatemala? You can't." Alberto was still processing the news. "You've always said the Mayan ruins were good for tourists, but they didn't interest you."

"Well, it's never too late to change your mind."

Pablo jumped as if he'd been pinched. "That goes without saying, Mama. You're free to go wherever you want, whenever you want." No one can beat him when it's a question of defending liberty—particularly his own. "And when did you say you were coming back?"

"I said I didn't know."

"How can you not know? Come on, Mama, you're not seventeen years old. You're not up to that sort of thing anymore. You haven't gone on a trip like that since you retired." I was incensed and spoke from my heart. "Look, if you announced you were going to Paris, then fine. But Guatemala?"

She made me stop talking; she didn't even have to raise her voice. She sat down at the table and spoke gently while I picked at a few crumbs remaining on the tablecloth. "Kids, it's all right," she said. "Precisely *because* I'm not seventeen but sixty-nine, I can do whatever I want with my life. You don't need me. All you have to do is figure out how to make sure your father's well looked after. Since that's just a question of paying someone, it's easily arranged." At this point, she raised her eyes and looked at Alberto. "Besides, it's not like I'm taking a trip to the ends of the earth or I'm going to disappear forever. I'll come back. I don't know whether I'll stay for a few weeks or months, but in any case it won't be a long time. I just need to rest and take some time for myself, time to think and be alone for a while."

My brothers thought this a fine explanation, but it didn't seem sufficient to me.

"No one's trying to meddle in your life or tell you what to do," I conceded, hoping to soothe her. "And don't worry about Papa. If necessary, we can move him into my house and get someone to look after him while I'm at work. But you must understand why we find your decision strange. In the past, you were obliged to travel for your work, but now things are different. You haven't traveled for a long time, and however much you may hate to hear it, you're not in a fit state for wild adventures anymore. Of course, you can go wherever you want. But how hard can it be for you to give us some kind of explanation?"

"You're right," she answered, meeting my eyes and smiling, as though we were talking about the weather. "It wouldn't be hard for me to give you an explanation if there was one. But there isn't. There's nothing to explain. I want to go away, and I'm going. I don't know why you're all so surprised. As you said, I've traveled all my life without it being a problem, and I don't see why this time has to be any different. Before long, you'll have to carry me from one place to another like a suitcase, the same way we carry your father now. When that moment comes, I'll be able to resign myself. But I want to take advantage of my freedom while I still can. Look at what happened to your father: one day he thought he was in top form, and the next day he couldn't even find his head. So thank you for your concern, but I'm going to make my own decisions as long as I'm able to. I'll spend a few days in London, and then I'm going to Guatemala. And when I grow tired of it, I'll come back. That's all. I won't stay too long. Maybe a couple of months. I just want to exchange this imprisonment for a little exile. I don't understand what all the fuss is about. You've always been free to make your own choices, haven't you? Don't worry—if I ever should need your permission to do something, I'll be sure to ask for it."

It makes me mad. I'm remembering that conversation, and it makes me mad. Not just because of Mama's attitude; it's mine that bothers me more, or rather ours, because my brothers were also involved in this affair. Maybe not Pablo so much, since he's always off in his own strange world, but Alberto . . . Wasn't he supposed to be the voice of authority in the family? Well then, let's see some authority, damn it. But no. Like me, he submitted to blackmail, because that's what it was, nothing other than vulgar blackmail. And on top of that, we couldn't say that Mama was lying. It's true that she never meddled in our decisions. It's true that she never judged us; she didn't even express an opinion. Which is precisely the problem, because that's what mothers are for: to meddle, to express opinions. It's a little late for reproaches, but it's clear that sort of thing simply didn't come naturally to Mama. At all the critical moments in our lives, she limited herself to her chosen means of intervention: silence. For many years I didn't think she was doing anything wrong. What am I saying? I thought she was fantastic. I was proud that my mother was different, that she didn't try to influence our choices. But now I know she was making a mistake. And I know that when I'm a mother—I mean, if I become a mother—I'll make mistakes too, but I certainly won't make that one.

And so off she went to Guatemala. With her backpack over her shoulder, like a teenager. She went away, and she came back as a mound of ashes in a ridiculous urn. That's the result of her blackmail. And of our cowardice in submitting to it. This silence is the payment for that one.

I'd like to relate what happened in detail, but that's impossible. We have no more than four separate pieces of information to decipher, four fragments of an unfinished puzzle whose only intact piece is the date of her death. She flew to London on September 21. She called Alberto a few times in the course of the following days, instructing him to tell the rest of us that she was fine and asking about Papa. On the tenth day, we received an e-mail from igarcialuna@hotmail.com. "I'm in Guatemala. Everything's perfect. Splendid weather. I'm writing to you from a cybercafé. There are several here. It's astonishing—soon there will be cybercafés in the heart of the jungle. But not yet, so you'll have to spend a few weeks without news from me, because tomorrow, at the crack of dawn, I'm going to the Mayan ruins of Ceibal, where there's not so much as a telephone line. When I'm back in Flores, I'll send you another e-mail. Kisses to all. Take good care of Papa."

I'm not sure those were her exact words. Maybe she wasn't so terse, but what she said came down to this: I'm fine, don't worry about me. So long. We didn't hear any more news of her until Saturday, October 14. The news was bad, and I was the one who received it. I was at home with Papa. We'd spent most of the morning cleaning and arranging his hat collection. I don't know why, because for years now he's worn only his favorite, a Borsalino felt hat, waterproof and so flexible you can carry it folded up in your pocket. Actually, the collection stopped when Papa quit painting, by which time it numbered thirty-seven hats. One, clearly identifiable as the oldest of the lot and two sizes smaller than the others, belonged to Simón. It's Papa's only legacy from his father. Grandmother Amparo presented it to Papa on his eighteenth birthday, but even then it was too small for him, so he never could wear it. All the other hats he bought for himself, except for the ones we gave him as presents. It used to be rare to see Papa on the street without a hat. But all at once, after the Russian woman's portrait, he announced that he was tired of his collection and asked us not to give him any more hats. He said that maintaining them in good condition required too much time and effort, and his pleasure was turning into a burden. Ever since then, the only hat he wears is the Borsalino. No other. Not even when he goes sailing.

As I was saying, the fourteenth of October. I remember I was holding the Borsalino in my hand when the telephone rang, trying to get Papa to tell me where the hat had come from.

"The Russian woman. The Russian woman gave it to me," he said.

"Damn, Papa, that's quite a present. Borsalinos cost a lot of money."

"It was for her portrait. When I gave the painting to her, she said she couldn't pay me. I told her that wasn't necessary, but then she offered to swap me the hat for it."

"That can't be. You must be wrong."

"Why?"

"Everybody knows the Russians were millionaires, right? Besides, you never gave her the picture. It's been in the house in Malespina since you painted it."

"Well, what happened was—"

At that moment, the telephone rang. "May I speak to Don Julio Azuera?"

It was a woman's voice. Solemn, heavy, mysterious, dramatic.

"Who's calling, please?"

"I'm calling from the Ministry of Foreign Affairs."

"Just a moment."

Maybe I shouldn't have passed the telephone to Papa. At least, not before asking what the call was about. That's what my brothers think. All I can say in my defense is that, judging from the conversation we'd been having, I thought Papa was in one of his lucid periods; that I had no way of even imagining the information the telephone call would contain and thought it must be connected with an exhibition of his paintings abroad. But I seriously regret the mistake, because I know for a fact that phone call pushed Papa one step farther down the slope of losing his mind.

Papa slowly approached the telephone and took the receiver without asking who was calling. "Yes," he said. And then, after a pause: "Yes, Isabel. García Luna, yes, of course she's my wife. Have I what? Do I know what? What are you talking about? But what are you talking about? Serena! Serenaaa!"—at the top of his voice, looking at me— "Serena, you take it, I don't understand a thing."

But he must have understood something, because pain had grooved his face like a knife, and while I took his place at the telephone, he remained absolutely still, shrunken. He kept giving low groans of distress, as if an alarm were sounding in some recess of his unconscious. It was a struggle to wrest the telephone out of his hands, because he was hanging on to it with such force that his knuckles were turning white.

When I finally managed to get the telephone to my ear, I said, "I'm sorry, my father's not feeling very well."

"I understand," the voice answered. "I regret the intrusion. Had I known, I would have spoken directly to you. News like this is never easy to—"

"What news? What are you talking about?"

"Sorry. Let me start over again. I don't know if you've heard about the accident in Guatemala involving a boat, on the Río Pasión, between Sayaxché and Lake Petexbatún."

My legs gave way as though the blood were being sucked from them. I sat down on the floor. I didn't want to keep listening. How stupid, I thought: Río Pasión. All those names sounded like gobbledygook to me, but I knew very well what she was talking about. I had barely enough voice left to ask, "When?"

"Yesterday. We would have liked to inform you earlier, but we had difficulty in finding your telephone number, and with the time difference . . ."

"But—but listen, inform us of what?"

"It appears that Doña Isabel García Luna was one of the passengers."

Don't tell me, don't tell me she's dead, not drowned, don't tell me that, tell me whatever you want but don't tell me that. "That's not possible."

"Well, unfortunately, it seems extremely likely that she was one of the victims, because her papers were found next to her body. Nevertheless, we can't be certain until the identification procedure is complete, and that is the reason we—"

"Listen, couldn't it be . . ." I said, interrupting her.

Couldn't it be what? Couldn't it be possible she's still alive? Like Simón? That she stayed afloat, hanging on to a big wooden plank? For three days?

"Please, we don't want to rush you. I know this is very difficult, but it would be best not to speculate about the facts until we know for certain. Unfortunately, Doña Isabel's papers don't leave much room for doubt, and it appears that the authorities were also able to recover a few personal items. In any case, in accordance with international legislation, and in the interests of your family, it's essential that at least one of you travel to Guatemala to identify the body. If you would be so kind as to take down this telephone number . . ."

I curse the fate that chose me to receive that phone call. And I curse it doubly, because the first person to find out bad news is then saddled with the task of communicating it to others. But before I did anything, I had to soothe Papa, who remained motionless at my side, like a dead man standing. Now that I think about it, his broken mind must have been sound enough to grasp what had happened, because I don't remember ever having to say the terrible words. I didn't say, "Mama's dead, Papa." In fact, I didn't say anything. I simply put my arms around him and cradled my father in silence.

I don't know how long we stayed like that. I remember that his moaning finally grew quieter, and then I remember taking his face in my hands and looking into his eyes and seeing that he wasn't there. He was stiff and far away, concealed inside a stony silence. I managed to make him walk to the sofa, sat him down, wrapped him up in a cotton blanket, and gave him the maximum dose of tranquilizers.

Then I called Alberto.

"Hello?"

"Alberto . . ."

"Serena. What's wrong?"

It's uncanny. He comes equipped with some kind of problem detector.

"Mama."

"What about Mama?"

"Mama . . ."

"Serena, you're crying. Calm down. Take a deep breath. You've got to tell me what happened. Take your time."

". . ." I couldn't speak.

"Can you hear me? Breathe. Say something. What's happened to Mama?"

His voice. Alberto's voice, more deliberate than ever, helped me.

"She's dead, Alberto. They called here. She died. A boat sank. In a river near some lake."

"Sweet Jesus."

He didn't subject me to an interrogation about the details. He didn't try to drag out the words that were stuck in my throat. He's always known the best way to handle any situation.

"Is Papa with you?"

"Yes."

"Does he know?"

"Yes. Well, I think he does. He got into a state. I've given him two Lexatins. Now he's asleep."

"Stay with him. Don't do anything else. I'm leaving right now. If you have to, take a Lexatin yourself. I'll see about getting in touch with Pablo."

"Love you, Alberto."

"Love you too, sister. I'll be right there."

I never used to tell my children very much about my trips. I tried to bring them back exotic gifts, and every now and then I'd recount one of my adventures, or repeat some of the legends I'd heard in those distant corners of the world. It didn't happen very often, because, after all, I saw little else besides the dead and the living who mourned them. Not exactly appropriate material for children. I felt I should protect them from such information, but it's possible I was mistaken. Maybe if I'd told them more of my stories back then they'd know who their mother is today. They'd be able to recognize her. But it's a little too late for that. A little late to tell them what I saw in Melpa. I explained to them that I'd been in New Guinea, and maybe I took the opportunity to teach them something about the Antipodes, but I don't believe I told them what I had seen there. That was in 1970, so the oldest one was only thirteen. Too young to begin to know his mother? I'm not sure.

Becoming aware of one's errors at this late date isn't very commendable. In fact, it's useless. It's as if I've made a film and realize only now that the script doesn't work. I can't even hope to correct my mistakes in the next film, because there won't be one.

The script of my life included a part for a character named Isabel García Luna, anthropologist. Halfway through the film, the script called for this character to travel to Melpa in the Papua New Guinea highlands, because there was a persistent rumor that this was where it was still possible to observe cannibalistic rituals in honor of the dead. There were all kinds of interpretations of cannibalism at the time, but none of them had succeeded in completely explaining the phenomenon. It was the great unresolved topic of anthropology. We had at least realized that it wasn't simply a savage act in which a group carried its anni-

hilation of the enemy to the extreme of literally devouring them. We already had proof that there were also many cases of cannibalism occurring among members of the same tribe as the deceased, including blood relatives, so a more sophisticated and nuanced explanation of the phenomenon was necessary. Everyone rushed to offer his theory. Many were psychoanalytic in origin: desire to possess the soul of the dead person and therefore the virtues he had demonstrated in life, multiplication of the self, and so forth. They were lovely literary theories, but I never gave them much credit. Bloch's analysis marked an advance. He established the concept of "negative predation": the idea that cannibals ate their enemies not so much for the direct benefits they obtained from consuming them as for the injury they inflicted on the rival tribe by depriving its members of the possibility of performing their funeral rites. Very clever, and perhaps true. But it still failed to explain the cannibalism practiced among the members of a single tribe. The technical, nutritional interpretations also sounded quite good. According to these, the communities in question had adapted their moral code to obtain essential proteins from the flesh of their deceased tribesmen. Yet today we know that, in the majority of cases, protein requirements were amply fulfilled by hunting and rudimentary farming.

I contributed to gathering this information in a wide variety of locations. It was very difficult—not to say impossible—to carry out a proper field investigation, because among other things, in those days the missionaries usually arrived ahead of the anthropologists. And the first thing the missionaries did was to persuade the local people that they should abandon the practice of cannibalism. "Persuade" isn't the appropriate verb in this context; perhaps it would be more accurate to say they blackmailed them, and in some cases they forced them. We arrived sometime afterward, and instead of facts, we found memories of facts; stories, not actual events. Then the rumors from New Guinea began to arrive. We heard about groups, above all groups of women, who practiced cannibalism in secret. According to these stories, some of the women of Melpa, under the guise of dogs at night, would steal the flesh *of the recent dead. It was taken for granted that they ate this flesh, but they also practiced acts of witchcraft with it, acts to which they gave the name* kum. *Apparently, they would dip the stolen flesh in springs, and then whoever drank from the water would develop a taste for human flesh. "A taste for human flesh": I remember those words in English. The phrase was rich and sonorous, the perfect title for the grandiose novel I would never be able to write, neither in English nor in any other tongue, because what has always eluded me is the language of fiction.*

These stories were believable in part, but it was advisable to distrust them. Frequently, the accusation that a tribe practiced cannibalism was made with ulterior motives and was fed by the greed of those who intended to obtain some profit from the tribal lands in the form of rubber, petroleum, or any other substance that couldn't be extracted as long as the natives lived there. One had to be careful. I know from experience. I let my guard down only once, in Brazil, and it nearly cost me my life.

I wanted to talk about what I saw in Melpa, not about cannibals, but since I'm on the subject I'll say just a few things more. It will be a distraction. I won't think about how furious and offended I am, and I won't feel the recurring urge to stay here in hiding and let my children weep as long as it takes for the tears to wash out their eyes so that they learn how to look. To distinguish what they should be able to recognize as their own, even with their eyes closed.

Let's return to 1970. I packed my bags and went to New Guinea, as the script required. To begin with, I needed no excuse to go wherever I felt like going. I've never needed one. Besides, to an anthropologist specializing in the way the living members of a human community treat their dead, cannibalism was like the philosopher's stone to an alchemist. In the end, other death rituals differ from one another in aesthetic nuances, in the length of the mourning period, the rhythms of lamentation, and the destiny of the body, but these differences aren't substantial. Everywhere the initial grief is followed by a relatively brief period of social chaos, of emptiness and readjustment, followed in its turn by a new order; death rites exist precisely for the sake of proclaiming and establishing that new order, which is frequently reaffirmed in a ceremony that takes place sometime after the death itself. The visit to the cemetery on the anniversary of the loved one's demise. All Saints' Day.

By 1970, many of the differences between East and West in this area had already been closely studied; there was a widespread notion that perhaps the East had succeeded better than the West at recognizing the interdependence between life and death and the certainty that either one loses its meaning in the absence of the other. We knew the extreme disdain that death provoked among many nomadic African hunting communities and the way they all but ignored its appearance, denying it any intervention in their lives that wasn't merely incidental and haphazard. When the old died off, the living would simply move their settlement a few dozen meters farther on, without so much as interring the body. At most they would cover it with a few palm leaves snatched from the roof of the nearest hut, without any show of reverence, without any kind of ceremony, and apparently with the sole purpose of postponing the arrival of the carrion eaters. Even for what seemed to be an absolute negation of grief, materialism offered an explanation: since the groups in question were nomadic hunters, it was understandable that their own dynamic would push them to continue on their way, abandoning their dead just as they abandoned the bones of the animals they killed and ate, without stopping to reorder their lives because their lives required not order but movement, a new displacement, another animal to hunt. The members of sedentary cultures need ceremonies to reaffirm the fact that they're still alive. All nomads have to do is keep moving.

All in all, we thought we knew the foundations of our discipline, but the existence of cultures in which the living ate the dead continued to pose a series of questions that none of our formulas of thought or theories could completely answer. We had to see.

In this sense, my trip to Melpa was one of the most frustrating I ever took. I didn't see anything. I heard things; people told me ambiguous stories that were perhaps their own invention, or perhaps had simply been repeated from generation to generation. I'm not saying that those stories were false; I'm only saying that I was never able to see such events actually taking place, and I couldn't afford the luxury of credulity in professional matters. I had enough trouble enduring the absurd polemics my theories stirred up even when they were corroborated by the evidence.

Nonetheless, the trip was not made in vain. In Melpa, I witnessed something beautiful, something that made up for the trip, the infernal heat, and all the other hardships. When a child is born there, the villagers plant a tree. They dig a hole to accommodate its roots, into which they place the newborn's placenta and umbilical cord. The tree is given the same name as the baby. Until the child is weaned, its excrement is used to fertilize the tree. If all goes well, this period lasts three years and when it's over, an initiation rite is celebrated. The father gives a banquet to which he invites the members of the mother's family. This is a way of showing gratitude not only for her fertility but also for her strength, which has been demonstrated by the long years of nursing. At this banquet, the child's hair is cut for the first time. The following day marks the beginning of the long apprenticeship that will teach the child to find nourishment from other sources and to deposit his excrement in the places designated for such use. It is believed that the child will live as long as the tree does, and that the tree has the ability to reflect the condition of its namesake. The leaves of the tree will wither when the grown man is sad, it will shine when he falls in love, its fruits will gleam when he reproduces, and it will even wilt and droop if the person becomes sick. This information had no professional value at all, but I did find it beautiful.

Planted human waste; a twisted, nourishing cord that must be cut in order to separate two bodies; a flow of milk that takes the place of the cord; life giving life. It's written in the most ancient books: blood of my blood, flesh of my flesh. You don't have to go to New Guinea to understand that. Almost as soon as animals—especially but not exclusively mammals—are born, they're able to recognize their mother. They're able to pick her out of a group composed of thousands of individuals. They carry this ability in their blood. Presumably, we all do.

There are still societies that lack what we would consider basic bio-

logical knowledge, people who attribute the birth of a child to the influence of the stars, to the opportune flight of a bird, to every kind of more or less esoteric phenomenon. The Wari consider it impossible to conceive a child in a single sexual act. They believe that the mother's womb contains a kind of bag where semen accumulates. The mother transmits blood to the child, and the father, by means of his semen, provides the child with its physical structure, its bones and flesh. Once the fetus has been conceived, the Wari believe that the parents must perform the sexual act with increased frequency, so that the child, having benefited from the steady contribution of paternal semen, will be stronger when it comes into the world. If a woman is widowed during her pregnancy, it's normal for her to take a lover, because if she doesn't do so, her child will be born weak or perhaps even dead. In short, I've heard the most outlandish theories—but never have I seen the unique, indissoluble bond denied. Children come out of their mother and they are hers, they recognize themselves in her, they recognize her until death.

I don't know what kind of atrophy, what blindness, what mutilation of the senses can justify a child's failure to recognize its mother. I can't comprehend it. My profession and my experience help me to understand not only some basic laws of humanity but also the errors that sometimes contravene those laws. But not this one. There's no room for any sort of excuse in this case. Of course, I could have prevented the confusion even before it occurred, the moment I noticed my backpack was gone. I could also have straightened everything out the next day, and I didn't. I won't say it didn't cross my mind; I considered the option, and I rejected it. All I'll say in my defense is that the other temptation was too strong. Fate dealt me a winning hand filled with fresh, new cards, right in the middle of my life. And so I dared to play them.

If I ever do go home again, the chief reason will be so that I can stand face-to-face with Alberto. Stand face-to-face with Alberto and say, look at me, because you're my son. Look me in the eye and tell me who I am. Tell me who your mother is. Touch me, if your eyes aren't enough. Smell me and tell me I'm not your mother.

The most unpardonable thing is that the mistake was his—I'm certain of that. He's the one who always takes charge in such situations. I might have expected the two younger ones, the impractical ones, the ones with heads full of music and stories and clouds, to screw up, or even to mistake an old shoe for their mother. But not Alberto. It's hard for me to forgive him now, and it will never be easy.

For the sake of a complete inventory, I'll admit guilt in one more area. It may serve to illuminate some of the finer details, just in case my children insist on knowing things like this, especially Serena. We attribute importance to such details in novels, but they are of no consequence to me, because we're not talking about fiction here, we're talking about life: what happened happened and it was horrible and I didn't like it at all and I don't feel like doing anything to clarify or diminish it. I do, however, make this concession: I took too long to react. I can't deny that the three days following my return to the Posada del Caribe were very different from the earlier ones, however similar they may have been in appearance. Those three days passed more slowly, swimming in the lake gave me no comfort, I made up any excuse to spend hours hovering around the radio, and I even breathed differently, because I had a crowd of butterflies fluttering wildly around my stomach. God, how dramatic—I sound like my daughter. It was nerves, sheer nerves. I was overwhelmed by the sensation that somewhere, in a place where I was supposed to be but wasn't, something had happened that shouldn't have happened, something contrary to what logic required. Because logic required that someone should say something, that the unknowns in the equation of chance should start solving themselves of their own accord.

I remember when I played hide-and-seek as a little girl. Sometimes I was afraid I'd hidden myself too well, I'd found a hiding place so inaccessible and remote that no one would discover me and I'd remain not just hidden but completely lost, even after the game was over. It would have been easy to come out of my hiding place, but I didn't. I shut my eyes tight and concentrated on wishing that they would find me, that a hand would point at the spot where I was hiding and a voice would call out my name.

That's very much like me, constantly looking for the most remote spot, the perfect hiding place, and carrying the feeling of not belonging, of being like a planet without gravity, floating outside the laws that govern the systems, always directionless and adrift, simultaneously fearing and hoping that the others would come to my rescue. During those three days, I experienced that feeling again. Maybe the silence of the first day could be explained by the time difference, I thought, the second day's by ticket availability and red tape, and the third's by the length of the flight. On the fourth day, I accepted that bad news could be the only explanation for such a long silence and that I alone, dead as I was, could break it. I didn't yet know exactly what the mistake was, but something had clearly gone wrong. And so I had to hook up the radio and send my oxidized voice out into thin air. Just as I was beginning to believe that no one was going to answer, the Boss's voice finally came through loud and clear.

"Hello. Please identify yourself. Over."

"Hello! At last!"

"Who's speaking and from where? Over."

Isabel García Luna *from the land of the dead, I should have answered, but I wasn't in the mood for jokes.*

"Isabel. Posada del Caribe. Over."

"My, my. The señora. Over."

"Yes, the señora. Over."

"It's an honor, señora. Is everything all right? What can I do for you? Over."

I didn't know what to say. The question was clear in my mind, but I couldn't find a way of putting it. Do you know anything about my children? Has anybody, by chance, talked to one of my . . . ? *No.*

"Listen, Boss, has my backpack turned up? Over."

"What backpack, señora? Over."

"No backpack. Over. Wait! I'm sorry, not over. Tell me, do you have any news? Over."

"News of what, señora? Over."

"I mean, what became of the dead people, the victims? Over."

"Ah, you're always so kind, señora. I didn't have time to thank you for all your help. Over."

"Right, fine, but what happened with them? Over."

"You have nothing to worry about, señora. That's all being taken care of by the authorities in Flores. They've got everything under control. Thanks anyway. Over."

"What about Judith? Over."

"Who's Judith? Over."

"The gringa. Over."

"No . . . but what gringa, señora? Her family came over to claim her remains, and it seems she was a Spanish lady like you, Spanish from the old country. Over."

"That can't be, Boss."

" . . . "

"I said that's impossible. Do you hear me?"

" . . . "

"Over, dammit! Answer me!"

"Well, look, señora, what can I say? The truth is I don't handle that sort of thing. It seems her papers were in order, and like I said, her family came over and they even buried her and all. Over."

Buried? Dead and buried? Her family?

"Listen, Boss. Send me Amkiel right away, today if possible. I want to go to Flores. Over."

"So you're leaving the Posada? You have two more weeks before the tourists start to arrive. Over."

"No. I'm not leaving anything." I spat those last words out, realizing, even as I spoke, that I should have considered my reply more carefully. Arguing with the Boss didn't make much sense, and I didn't have a clear idea of what I was going to do during the following days. "I just have some errands. I may come back here tomorrow. Over."

"Some what, señora? Over."

"Errands. Shopping. I want to buy a few things. Understand? Over."

"*Yes, señora.*"

Questions of blame were quickly resolved, one after another. The imaginary web of unavoidable circumstances and foreign incompetence I'd woven to deny the obvious quickly fell apart. It wasn't fair to blame the Boss; after all, his sole responsibility was the management of the minimal tourist services in Sayaxché. He was told a gringa had died, and then he'd heard she wasn't a gringa but a Spanish woman; then he learned that her children had arrived in Flores, and gone through the necessary formalities before identifying the body and taking charge of its destiny. But the Boss hadn't participated in those formalities, and he probably hadn't seen or heard my name assigned to the corpse. Over. Or rather, over and out. Nobody's to blame. Well, Amkiel is, but only partly. Amkiel might be accused of excessive indolence, of letting too much time pass before trying to recover my backpack. He probably delegated the chore to someone who then passed it on to someone else, who then forgot about it. . . . But it doesn't make sense. It doesn't make sense to blame the crime on Amkiel. He was just a cog in the machine, the drive belt in a motor. If on the first day, when I discovered that my backpack was missing, I'd said to him, "Let's go to Flores right now and pick it up," none of this would have happened. Be that as it may, Amkiel must have been feeling a little guilty, because almost immediately after my last conversation with the Boss, Amkiel presented himself at the Posada del Caribe, and as soon as he arrived, even before he greeted me, he launched into a stream of excuses for not appearing with my backpack in his hand, a discourse in which he explained how he'd given the job to X who in turn told Y and then on Wednesday in the afternoon he came back and said they said . . .

All right. Each of us must face up to his own responsibilities. I didn't care about the chain of carelessness and bureaucratic banalities that might explain the mistake. I didn't want anything to distract me from my only real concern, a phrase the Boss had used that kept resounding in my brain: a Spanish lady like you. Her family came over to claim her remains, and it seems she was a Spanish lady like you. A Spanish lady like you. Her family. Like you.

And so I made Amkiel calm down, telling him that the backpack hadn't contained anything important. Then I asked him to take me as fast as he could to Sayaxché, where I intended to stay only a few minutes before continuing on to Flores. I did my best to enjoy the trip one more time, trying to concentrate on the magic of the islets and the welcome coolness of the river breeze, augmented by the speed at which Amkiel drove us along. But there was no free space in my brain for breezes, reeds, or scenery. It was filled with only one name: Alberto. Alberto and the unforgivable mistake.

I exchanged hardly a word with Amkiel the whole trip, and as soon as we reached Sayaxché I jumped onto the landing dock. I asked him to have transportation to Flores ready for me in an hour and bade him farewell. I knew it wouldn't take more than an hour to confirm what had become clear, during my last conversation with the Boss. Centro Internet. Nine dollars. www.periodistadigital.com. El País, La Vanguardia, El Periódico, ABC, El Mundo, *all the Spanish newspapers. In each case, I went back to the day of the accident and found the same article I'd read then. There followed two days of silence, two days without any reference to "the Spanish anthropologist, killed in a boat accident on a river in Guatemala." On the third day, the obituaries appeared. My death was made official.*

In Uganda, the Lugbara use a form of singing called cere *to announce the news of someone's death. They gather around the door of the dead man's cabin and sing the* cere. *The music is a shrill, piercing falsetto that can be heard throughout the village and the nearby woodland, so that no one fails to learn the news. The text of the* cere, *which changes from one death to another, is made up of the words that the living identify with the dead person: house corn children land, if he was a farmer; rain nuts weather healing, if he was a fortune-teller; arrow forest bird moon for a hunter. They don't say his name. It's assumed that the choice of words is so precise that whoever hears them will be able to deduce who has died. If there's no corpse—if, for example, the dead person has been swallowed up by the river—they put some object that* represents him in his cabin and then they set it on fire. As the flames rise, the villagers start singing the cere. My own cere has no music but instead is a printed text; however, I'm not sure that the words from the obituaries represent me: pioneer professorship books documentaries controversy science three children dissemination jungle. If high-pitched voices had brought me those words in the forest, I don't think I would have thought that the dead person was me.

Flores. I didn't even check in to one of the five hotels in town. I knew I was going to leave Flores, but I didn't know whether I'd be returning from there to Spain or to the Posada del Caribe. Strange: the verb "return" applied in both cases. Yes, I knew I wasn't going to stay in Flores. I had nothing to do there, except to tie up a loose end: Alberto. La Esperanza Funeral Services. It's the only morgue in Flores, and you can spot it from many meters away, with its clinical appearance and its white marble façade, though you might mistake it for a hospital or a massage parlor. I was met at the entrance by a woman schooled in kindness.

"Please come in," she said. "How may I help you?"

"I'm a friend of Isabel's," I lied.

"Isabel? Do you know her last name?"

"Yes. García Luna."

"Ah, the Spanish woman."

"Exactly. The Spanish woman who died in the river."

"So she was your friend. What a shame. Please accept my sincere condolences. Accidents of that sort are quite unusual around here, señora. What happened was that—"

"Don't worry about it," I interrupted her. "I'm familiar with the details. I just want to know where she's buried and perhaps visit her grave."

"Of course, señora. The thing is, Doña Isabel wasn't buried. We cremated her yesterday."

"Ah, she was cremated. I was told she'd been buried."

"We usually recommend cremation in cases like this, because the red tape required to release the body for repatriation to Spain takes so long to get through, and then there's the complication of transport and so on."

"Right."

"For a cremation all we need is the signature of a member of the family."

"Ah, so someone from her family came here?"

"Yes. Two of her children, in fact."

"Her children?"

"Yes, a man and a woman. But the man was the only one present at the identification. It was obviously too painful for the daughter. Very understandable, of course. Many people refuse to contemplate that final image of the dead. They prefer to keep the memory of the living person."

"If I told you everything I know about the dead and their memory," I said. The words escaped me, but I spoke softly.

"I beg your pardon? What did you say?"

"Nothing, nothing. Just talking to myself."

Alberto and Serena. In the midst of all the confusion, this was the first piece of real information I'd heard. Alberto and Serena. Serena, refusing to look. Faced with a choice between reality and memory, Serena had chosen memory. Naturally. She made the effort to come here and then left her brother with the responsibility of seeing my dead face and signing his name on some document. It makes sense. Of course Alberto accepted the responsibility. He faces problems and solves them, unlike his father. His father prefers not to see them and his brother Pablo prefers not to solve them. His sister Serena prefers to remember them. Alberto looks, makes a decision, and acts in accordance with that decision. Except this time he made a mistake. I don't want to count how many times I've gone over this in my mind. Obviously, the cut from the propeller had disfigured Judith's face. But I recognized her, and I'd seen her only one other time in my life. My son Alberto didn't recognize me. He didn't realize it wasn't me. I still can't understand it.

Ashes. Dead and cremated. The definitive proof of the mistake didn't infuriate me. I wasn't angry, I was sad. A profound, swampy sadness, a tremendous urge to take on the lightness of those ashes that didn't represent me. And, above all, to write. To write my own obituary.

The only perfect autobiography, a unique tale of a whole life, because it would include the author's death.

Now, it would be easy to say that I returned to Petexbatún to get even with my children. To let them weep for me a little longer in payment for their mistake. But no. I didn't feel that kind of rage. On the contrary, I was almost relieved. I finally understood why I was there. I wasn't in the jungle for the sake of the jungle, or for the Wari, or for the river, the mosquitoes, the peace, the silence, the distance. I was in the jungle of Petén for death. The last voyage. Ever since I left Barcelona, even during the week I spent in London visiting newspaper archives, finding out a few things about the Russian woman and feigning a worldly interest I didn't feel, I was just searching for the last voyage.

I began writing that same night, after I returned to the Posada. I believed I was going to sing my own cere *by writing down, one by one, the words that represent me, so that when I really do die, someone will be able to recognize me. I wanted to leave in writing the story of who I am. Since that time, not a day has passed without my filling a number of pages. When I look over the first ones, I'm not surprised to see that in the beginning the only words I could find were words of surprise: Dead? Me, Isabel, dead?*

Today I spoke to the Boss and learned that the first group of tourists is going to arrive in three days. Obviously, I can't stay here, but I don't know what I'm going to do. Return home? I suppose I might. But it's still too soon. I have many things left to say. My cere *is incomplete. There are words I haven't even pronounced yet. Anxiety compassion solitude danger injustice cowardice happiness fear are words that represent me, and I haven't yet dared mention them. In some cases, I'm uncertain of their meaning. Return, for example. I'm not sure what the word "return" really means.*

THURSDAY

Simón's children. We're all Simón's children. I have to write this down while it's fresh in my memory, even though I have a throbbing, bandaged finger and it's hard to write with the blood welling up under my fingernail. It's nothing serious—just a clean cut that will close in four or five days—although it *was* rather dramatic. I was chopping onions for a potato omelet, and I almost sliced off half of my finger. It happened because I'm stupid, because I'm absentminded, because my mind's always on other things. The thing is, I can't see an onion without thinking about my grandfather, about his hands scrubbed with bleach; I see an onion, and my ears are practically filled with his powerful, velvety, squandered voice.

It's hard to find an onion in my house. Not in Mama's. She said onion was the indispensable basic ingredient and she didn't want to hear any Simón stories or other foolishness. My view of onions is different. I can't eat them in my house. It's a matter of principle, like not giving water to your enemy. This is my historical revenge, however small, a way of giving Simón's father a slap, of asking him, where's your son?

But Pablo bought onions. He said that a potato omelet without onions isn't authentic; it wouldn't hurt me to make an exception for him. And so this afternoon I had to deal with onions. I looked at them as though I were chopping up insects, and maybe that's why I cut myself. My fastidious fingers could barely bring themselves to touch the onions, as if the merest contact with them would expose me to Simón's curse, as if their smell brought with it a historical condemnation. And so it did: the condemnation of memory, the sour, stuffy smell of the fruit and vegetable shop, the thick, salty, murky smell of the shipwreck, the greasy, sooty, sticky smell of the oil lamps Simón studied by. And above all, the acrid smell of his frustrated dreams.

When the tears started to cloud my vision, I didn't know if they were genuine, that is, if they were just the effect of the onion I was slicing, or if they had something to do with the memory of my grandfather, with the memory of his life as I suddenly perceived it. Simón, ashamed of his hands, with his bleach and his sponge.

The knife went partway through the tip of my index finger and even chopped off a bit of the nail, but I was so far away, so spellbound, that it took me a few seconds to realize I'd cut myself. Even then I was unable to react, hypnotized as I was by the paths my blood was making among the onion slices. I stayed there in the middle of the kitchen, as if the entire history of my family were passing in front of my eyes, as if that blood contained not only the genes that explain me, not only the microscopic history of Simón and his father and mine, but also Alberto's stubbornness and Pablo's musical notes and my cloud collection, and I saw Simón swimming desperately against a current of blood and Alberto studying thick law books and Pablo renouncing everything for a piano, and I saw myself looking for a lighthouse on the night of a shipwreck and I thought, Simón's children, we're all Simón's children; I think I even said that out loud before I fainted. I leaned my back against the wall and bent my knees little by little, letting myself fall, and maybe I'd have stayed there if Luis hadn't come in, followed by Pablo and Alberto, all of them alarmed because it was amazing how much blood flowed out of such a small cut, and I don't know if I said there you go, there's your authentic omelet, but I remember thinking it.

It wasn't the first time this had happened to me. Whenever I see blood, I faint. When I need to have a blood test I go through a series of tricks: I look away, I close my eyes, I count to a hundred; once I even tried the opposite approach, staring at the blood and envisioning it as water. Useless. Whatever I try, I can bear it for only a few seconds before I feel a familiar numbness that starts in my feet and settles in the pit of my stomach, and then my shoulders sag, my neck gives way, and my jaw loosens like heated wax, and by the time it reaches my brain I'm no longer there. Blackout. It's not unpleasant. On the contrary, there's something delicious about that abandonment, that total disconnection of awareness. I'd like to sleep like that forever, adrift in a peaceful sea with all my moorings cut. A fainting fit is outside of time, in a dimension all its own, a state that seems eternal even if it lasts for no more than a few seconds. I don't know how long I lay on the kitchen floor today—a minute, maybe a minute and a half at most. Nevertheless, when I heard the voices, when I noticed that several strong hands were lifting me up by the shoulders, it seemed to me as if I were returning from some interminable voyage filled with the words of generation on generation. The onions and the blood were solely to blame, but I was in a place far away from here, and had my brothers not come into the kitchen, had my brothers left me on the floor for a few hours, they would have found me in an immense pool of words, all the words of Simón's story, spilled out through the tip of my index finger; the accusing finger, the one that points to lies and punishments and escapes.

The story continues more or less like this: Simon's imprisonment lasted no more than two long weeks, during which his father unlocked the door of his room three times a day to give him a plate of food and, when necessary, to allow him to go to the bathroom. The same treatment that prisoners receive, made worse by the demonstrations of affection for Simón that his father insisted on making, replacing his earlier blows with clumsy gestures meant to approximate fatherly love. These gestures were accompanied by paternal advice and admonitions about Simón's need to reflect on his ways and change them, and he rounded off his discourses with the usual observation that the boy's suffering was for his own good, and one day he'd appreciate that.

During this time, the lessons of the shipwreck were very useful to Simón: he'd learned that only passive resistance can work when the enemy is much stronger than you are. In the sea, he'd understood that every stroke he swam would bring him closer to death and that he must save his strength for the battle ahead; now, faced with his father's punishment, he had to lower his arms, breathe deeply, and concentrate all his strength on keeping himself afloat. Simón renounced quarreling, feigned a repentance he was thoroughly unable to feel, and even declared that he deserved the punishment his father was inflicting on him. If fortune had placed a wooden plank within his reach at sea, now his father's obstinacy required him to lash together a raft of lies.

But no punishment is eternal. Gradually, Simón's father relented and in the end offered him a deal. He would unlock Simón's door in return for the boy's promise, sworn upon the name of his dead mother, to confine his life to two areas: the family shop and the family home. As for university, they would talk about it when the new term began. No more theater, neither as actor nor as spectator. No more lies. No more going out, not even for a walk. "I want to know where you are at all times," his father said. Or that's what we suppose he said. And he didn't want to hear any of Simón's friends even mentioned. Signing the agreement, Simón accepted a state of permanent surveillance, a rigorous scrutiny of his every word and deed.

Ironies of fate: the more Simón's father prohibited him from exercising his talent as an actor, the more he pushed the boy to use those very talents on himself. Simón adopted the role of model son and exemplary student. For some months, he played his part so masterfully that not even his father, despite constant surveillance, could detect any flaw in the performance.

At this point in the story, Papa liked to leave open the possibility that Simón really did feel a certain amount of remorse or even resignation; as if on some level he might have been inclined to accept the destiny imposed on him—a future in the legal profession—and to renounce his artistic vocation. I don't agree with this view. For many years, I thought disagreeing with Papa was practically illicit, as if being Simón's son, he had more right to establish the truth. But that feeling left me some time ago. Both of us have only borrowed words to tell this story with, and mine are worth as much, or as little, as his.

I'm sure that my grandfather's apparent submission was only his way of gaining some time. Little by little, the hand that was suffocating him began to relax: his schedule became more flexible, his father's vigilance less strict. Then Simón asked for more time to study. Because of his two months of forced absence from classes, he'd missed his examination in Roman Law, but now he had the chance to sit for it again in November. Simón insisted that life was offering him a chance to correct his mistakes, but his father had his doubts. On the one hand, he looked upon his son's transformation with pride, but on the other, he understood that Simón's progress had been the result of threats and punishments, and he was afraid the progress would be reversed if Simón recovered his freedom. In the end, the boy was allotted four hours of study time daily, but he had to display the results of his efforts every night by submitting to a review of the day's material conducted by his father. His poor, unfortunate father. Those sessions must have been torture for him, since his knowledge of the written word was barely sufficient for him to deal with simple letters, notices, and posters.

Every night after dinner, Simón placed some hefty legal tome filled with impenetrable hieroglyphics in front of his father and recited passages from it like a cockatoo. His father, frequently interjecting demands that the boy recite more slowly, followed the lines in the book with his eyes and an index finger, struggling to determine whether the printed text matched the flood of words pouring out of Simón's mouth. From time to time, Simón would stumble and his delighted father would prod him to continue, inwardly relishing the opportunity to demonstrate that he hadn't been lost in the dark forest of letters. On other occasions, when the boy used the wrong word or changed the order of phrases in a sentence, his father would pounce to correct him, reminding him in severe tones of the virtues of exactitude. Sometimes the density of those legal texts, the lateness of the hour, and the recent meal combined to afflict Simón's father with a terrible drowsiness, but he fought to keep his eyes open and his back straight, continuing to move his finger over the page so that Simón wouldn't notice he'd lost his place. The boy, who was surely aware of his father's nightly struggle to stay awake, avenged himself by reciting in a steady sleep-inducing monotone. In the end his father would drift off, rocked into dreamland by a lullaby of laws and amendments, and Simón would take advantage of the opportunity to mock him. Careful not to wake him up, the boy substituted his recitation of legal texts with a string of insults, and derision and blasphemy, saying things to his father for which he would have been soundly thrashed had the old man been in any condition to hear them.

The remnants of what little respect Simón felt for his father had disintegrated under the pressure of his excessive and arbitrary authority. It is possible that during the few months of life that remained to him after he ran away, Simón didn't retain the memory of his father as the unjust, pitiless man who had kept him prisoner; it's more likely that he remembered him as a sad person capable of making an absurd effort to defend the few outdated principles that were lodged in his primitive mind.

He's easy to hate. Simón's father, my father's grandfather, my great-grandfather, is a man who's easy to hate. However, I don't believe that Simón hated him during that time. I don't even think he bore him a grudge. A grudge is an anchor that fixes us in the past, and those were precisely the two things Simón wanted escape from: anchors and the past. He was concerned about the future and nothing else.

The date of his freedom was set: August 12, 1922. Seven months and a day since his shipwreck. Nearly five months since his return home. Simón knew that if he wanted to reach the terra firma of his freedom, it was essential for him to accept the agenda that his father had laid out for him. The boy got out of bed at five in the morning, had breakfast with the old man, accompanied him on foot to the shop, and immediately devoted himself to the wearisome task of unloading the day's produce. Although his body was still bruised and aching from the beating he'd received weeks before, Simón diligently carried out the sacks of potatoes and onions—those damned onions—and arranged the fruit in perfectly aligned piles. And when his father criticized the inexact positioning of an apple, Simón obediently dismantled the entire pile and built it up again as many times as necessary to obtain his father's approval. Then, with perfect calligraphy, he wrote down the price of each item on the pieces of old scrap paper that his father hoarded for this purpose and proceeded to spend the rest of the morning pretending to pay careful attention to never-ending lectures on how to sell more, and better.

Simón never told his father that his business had no future and never pointed out that not even the most sophisticated sales techniques could ever make the minuscule, foul-smelling shop competitive with the stands inside the market. He remained silent, not because he didn't want to say such things, but because he no longer saw it as his problem. All that mattered to him was the successful execution of his escape plan, an indispensable part of which called for him to do whatever it took to retain his father's confidence. That was why he ate his lunches with his father in the rear of the shop—and why, having swept the whole place from one end to the other, he pretended to be too busy to disappear at the agreed hour, always waiting for his father to dismiss him.

The chief architect of the escape plan was Amparo. She had learned of Simón's return and found out about his punishment. She was smart, my grandmother. For days she resisted the temptation to go to the shop for fear that Simón's father would recognize her, even though he'd seen her only once. After some time had passed, she sent Simón a message through one of the stagehands attached to the Compañía del Corral whom Simón knew by sight. The stagehand entered the shop like any other customer and asked to buy some apples. He paid for them with a folded banknote and said, "Would you write down the price, please? The apples aren't for me." A piece of white paper was hidden in the folds of the bill. Simón cast a sidelong glance in his father's direction to make sure he wasn't looking, unfolded the paper, and saw that it contained only a question mark and Amparo's signature. Picking up the thick pencil he used to price merchandise, Simón turned the paper over and wrote, "Get me out of here." No signature. Two days later, Amparo's friend turned up in the shop again and asked for half a kilo of green beans. Using the same system, the friend and Simón exchanged notes. This time, Amparo had written, "How?" Simón scribbled a reply: "Theater."

Amparo couldn't take any more. With the help of some colleagues in the troupe, she prepared a disguise that made her unrecognizable: makeup, wig, and even some wads of cloth stuffed under her clothes to give her more bulk, including the full breasts that nature had denied her. She went to see Simón every Tuesday morning in this disguise, which was so perfect that not even Simón recognized her the first time until he heard her voice. "Young man," she said, "I'd like some of these San Juan pears. I haven't had any since last year."

Simón remained motionless for a few seconds, as if Amparo's voice had opened a window on his sad imprisonment and let in a blast of icy cold air. Finally, he answered her. "Yes, they are a little late this year. These are the first." As he spoke, he rummaged around in the heap of pears with trembling hands, pretending to choose the best ones. "Look at this one," he said, indicating a pear somewhat larger than the rest. "Big as a house." Simón's father was behind him, and the boy seized the opportunity to wink at Amparo. "How many would you like?"

"Not too many. Three or four," she answered. "They're for this evening."

"Then we'd better make it five. Wait till you see how good they are. I'm sure they won't stay in your house for long. You'll probably eat them all before you even reach the front door."

A miracle. Message transmitted: that very afternoon, at five sharp, in the doorway of Simón's apartment building. That was the only possible time and place, because Simón left the shop every afternoon at four-thirty and went home, supposedly to study. His father would finish tidying up, pull down the rolling shutter, and follow him half an hour later. The meeting between Simón and Amparo, therefore, was necessarily brief. There wasn't time for exchanging deferred kisses or making up for the missed opportunities of the past; it was more a question of resolving the future. Simón begged Amparo for help, asking her to do everything in her power to persuade the director of the Compañía del Corral to reserve some role for him in the summer tour. Some role.

Any role. And if that wasn't possible, Simón was prepared to accept anything—prompt, stagehand, whatever might be available. Amparo promised to try and implored him not to give up. He should trust her, she said, and in the meantime he should be careful not to do anything that might incur his father's anger.

On her next visit to the shop the following Tuesday, when Amparo feigned interest in the quality of some custard apples, Simón answered that they were as good as the pears she had bought the previous week. Every bit as good. Which was to say: same time, same place. Week after week, they found a way to arrange another meeting. Simón, more and more restless with each passing day, renewed his requests. Amparo tried to calm him down. One day she told him that she had to gain the director's trust before anything could be done; the next week, she announced that she'd managed to mention Simón's name in a conversation. Although it looked to Simón as though the days were passing and no progress was being made, every time they met, Amparo assured him they were moving closer to their goal.

Well, maybe the story didn't go exactly like that. I don't know that Papa ever in his life saw a San Juan pear that could be called as big as a house. They're green and hard and the size of plums. And as far as I know, you can't get custard apples in summer. Such facts made no difference to Papa. In fact, this was Papa's favorite part of the story, because it allowed him to play the different characters: he'd push up his chest to illustrate Amparo's disguise, pitch his voice high when he spoke her lines, and punctuate the story with winks to emphasize the hidden meanings of the conversations in the fruit and vegetable shop. Papa reveled in that sort of thing. And maybe he was right: what's the difference if they were pears or watermelons? The important thing is that after several of these afternoon visits, Amparo finally succeeded in fanning the flame of Simón's dwindling hopes.

As soon as she arrived at the door of the building that afternoon, Grandmother took from her bag a copy of *El burlador de Sevilla*, "The

Seducer of Seville," Tirso de Molina's play about Don Juan. "I think we're on the verge of success," she said, handing him the book. "Here, learn this, just in case."

"This?" Simón asked, holding the book in his hand. "This?"

"It's the next play on the company's schedule. We're opening in August. I'm not sure of the date yet. There may be a role for you."

"A role?" Simón covered her with kisses. "A role for me?"

"I don't know yet. The director told me we'd talk about it. He may let you audition for the part."

Amparo's visit had now grown too lengthy, so they said their good-byes. She had the door open and one foot in the street when Simón realized he'd forgotten something important. "Wait!" he said, catching her arm. "Which role?"

"What?"

"Which part am I supposed to learn?"

"I don't know, Simón. It's too soon to say."

"Then what should I do?"

"Learn the whole thing," Amparo said as the door closed behind her.

If there's anything in this story that's beyond doubt, it's that Simón had a truly prodigious memory, since every night from then on, after his father's ridiculous examination in Roman Law, he went to bed, waited until his father was sleeping, then got up again and memorized the entire text of *El burlador de Sevilla*. At the end of fifteen nights of such furtive vigils, he knew the play by heart from beginning to end, word for word, including Tirso de Molina's sporadic stage directions for entrances and exits. He was so immersed in the work, so imbued with its words, that in his few hours of sleep he would recite extensive portions of the text, muttering the lines between his teeth; even sometimes during the day he had to bite his tongue to keep himself from speaking in the play's padded verse, thus revealing the real cause of the rings under his eyes and his inadequately stifled yawns. His father naïvely attributed Simón's lack of sleep to the pangs of remorse.

During one of her subsequent visits, Amparo told Simón that the director was keeping the part of a fisherman open for him. All he had to do was pass the audition.

Simón, who knew the characters by heart, asked, "Which fisherman? Anfriso or Coridón?"

"I don't know," Amparo answered. "One of them. He said 'a fisherman.' He didn't give a name."

"That's all right," Simón said. "I know them both."

He went back up to the apartment, opened his copy of *El burlador*, and quickly turned to the last pages of the "First Day," where Anfriso and Coridón make their entrance. He read over their respective lines and concluded that they were of equal importance. He counted the number of times each of the fishermen appeared, and they turned out to be the same. Either of the two parts would more than fulfill his dreams; he hadn't imagined that a professional company would entrust such important roles to an actor making his debut on the stage.

The date for Simón's audition was fixed. He was to meet the director the following Monday at coffee time in the Can Soteras restaurant on San Juan Avenue. When Amparo gave Simón the news, his euphoria was so great that he forgot that if he prolonged his demonstrations of gratitude, his father might arrive and put a premature end to his hopes of freedom. Fortunately for both of them, Amparo kept her head. She extracted herself from his embraces and stepped to the door, bidding him farewell with a warning that sounded almost like a threat.

"Don't fail me, Simón. I've had to go through a lot to make this happen, and I've told the director good things about you. Now you have to prove you deserve it."

That Sunday, Simón pretended to feel ill. As the day went on, his feigned illness grew worse, until it finally compelled him to take to his bed. This was the prologue to the audition he was scheduled to undergo the following day, and the boy spared no effort to aid his cause: his body shook, his nose ran. In the end, after these symptoms were corroborated by a thermometer which Simón had surreptitiously rubbed against the leg of his flannel trousers, his father was convinced. Not only did he allow his suffering son to stay in bed for the rest of the day, he even treated him with poultices and syrups. Early on Monday morning, Simón dared to exhibit a certain willingness to get up despite his supposed fever, thus presenting his father with an opportunity to show his magnanimity, appeal to the boy's good sense, and demand that he stay in bed one more day.

Simón left the apartment at two o'clock and arrived at the restaurant fifteen minutes later. He had little difficulty recognizing the director as they had seen each other at one of the few premieres Simón had been able to attend. The boy approached the director's table but cursed his excessive punctuality when he realized that the man had a companion. He turned around, resolved to maintain a discreet distance. However, the director's imperious voice stopped him in his tracks:

"Simón! Simón! Come here, Simón, don't be shy."

"It wasn't shyness, señor. I didn't want to disturb you."

"Sit down. This is the company's producer. I was just talking about you."

My grandfather took a seat but turned down an invitation to join the other two in a cup of coffee. Then the director said, "I have a proposal that's going to interest you."

"Consider it accepted," Simón blurted out. "Anfriso or Coridón, either one is fine with me. And you have my sincere gratitude."

"Wait, let me finish. As you no doubt know, ours is not a theater company with abundant resources. Our season is hard; we travel great distances, usually not in comfort."

"None of that will be a problem for me," Simón interrupted him. "I'm prepared to—"

"Let me finish," the director repeated curtly. "We often give open-air performances, and so we're exposed to the inclemency of the weather. Summer storms usually bring a variety of maladies with them—colds, laryngitis, all sorts of things."

"I'm not afraid of that, señor. I'm young. I'm strong and healthy."

Simón's eagerness to obtain a role in the director's play so overcame him that it prevented him from listening to the very offer he so longed for. The director looked at him with an indulgent smile on his lips; so did the producer, but his look revealed a certain level of exasperation as well.

"What I'm trying to tell you," the director said, "is that our principal actors fall ill far too often. We can't afford the luxury of keeping a substitute for every one of them, and canceling a performance, no matter how extenuating the circumstances may be, not only costs us money but also exposes us to the wrath of people who are not characterized by an excess of civility. This being the case, we need someone who can learn all the male roles perfectly so he can replace any of the actors when the necessity arises. Amparo tells me you have a very good memory."

"Ah, I'll be a prompt."

"Not exactly. You'll be a stand-in, which isn't the same. And in order to help you lose any stage fright you might have, I've invented a character for you. You'll come on with Anfriso and Coridón when they gather around Tisbea on the beach. You already know the play, right? It's the scene when Don Juan appears after being saved from a shipwreck."

"I don't wish to seem immodest, señor, but if you'll allow me, I'll tell you why I may be able to contribute more to that scene than you think," Simón remarked. "It's not that I'm an expert in shipwrecks, but I do have some experience in that area, because not too long ago I myself—"

"How interesting," said the director, interrupting him. "Don't forget to tell me about it another time. But for now, the most important consideration is your knowledge of the text. Amparo says you have a fabulous memory. She says you could memorize the entire Bible if you had to. If that's true, then you can consider yourself hired. Here's something to think about: we'll go to many places where they don't even have a theater. We perform in town squares, in community centers, on improvised platforms built against garden walls. In short, wherever they pay us. Usually, there's no box for the prompt, and experience has taught me not to place too much trust in my actors' memories. You'll have to be close to them at all times in case someone needs you to whisper a line. We'll look for silent roles for you so you can always be on stage, but in the background. All you've got to do is show me you're capable of handling the job."

Simón wouldn't let such an opportunity pass. He immediately launched into a recitation of lines from *El burlador*, as effectively as when he recited legal texts to his father, except that instead of dipping his voice in the well of sleep, he modulated it with a variety of tones, and when he had to make it clear that a female character was speaking, he even went so far as to tighten his throat and squeeze out a suitable falsetto. Finally after almost fifteen minutes the producer, who was watching this display impassively, uttered a brief sentence, without even removing the cigar from his mouth: "That will do."

Then the director made the proposal official by saying, "Fine, Simón, fine. You're hired. You'll be our stand-in. We leave on the twelfth of August. Meet us at seven in the morning in front of the Teatro Goya. It's essential that you know the entire text like the back of your hand by the time we set out."

"Don't worry, señor. I'll justify your faith in me. Now, if you don't mind, I must leave you."

As Simón was rising to his feet, the producer leaned over to the director and spoke a few words in his ear. As if he had just remembered something important, the director stopped my grandfather. "Wait a moment, Simón."

"As long as necessary, señor," he answered, sitting down again.

"Don't forget, the car's important, too."

"The car?"

"I imagine Amparo explained it all to you?"

My grandfather didn't have the slightest idea what car the man was talking about, nor what he, Simón, could possibly have to do with it, and he had even less of a clue about what role Amparo might have played in this mysterious matter. Nevertheless, a sixth sense told him to trust her and not to ruin everything with an outburst of puzzled sincerity. So he answered, "Ah, the car. Of course, señor. Consider it done."

Obviously, once he'd left the restaurant and was on his way home, he spent some time going over that inexplicable reference to the car. A car? What kind of mess had Amparo got him into? Yet at the same time, he felt an overwhelming gratitude toward her, and he didn't forget that he had begged her to do everything in her power to get him an appointment with the director. He remembered having used those very words to her: everything in your power. If Amparo had been forced to make something up, blessings upon her imagination, there would be time enough to take care of whatever it was. Because they *had* succeeded! He floated down the street as though suspended above the ground.

Simón undeniably had a lot to think about during the twenty-three days until his definitive liberation. On the day following his meeting with the director, a Tuesday, Amparo arrived for their five o'clock appointment as she did every week, but this time she was happier than ever, because she'd already heard from the director that Simón had passed his audition. But she was also feeling remorseful, because the moment had arrived for her to come clean and explain the business about the car, which she'd been hiding from Simón for weeks. She started telling him about it as soon as she saw him. She explained that her frequent pleas on his behalf had met with more than one refusal, and that the director had given as his reason the fact that there wasn't enough room for Simón in the van the company used for traveling from town to town. She told Simón that she'd lied in his name, without thinking about the consequences, and she apologized for that. She also begged his pardon for not having told him before. "I didn't want to discourage you," she said. Apparently, after being refused for the third time, Amparo decided to overcome the director's resistance with the first lie that came to mind. "Simón has his own car," she said, almost biting her tongue as she said it. In any case, there was now no way of going back on the lie, so they had to find a way of sorting it out. Simón argued with none of this. Instead he told Amparo, "We'll find a way, don't worry about a thing. You only did what you had to do. Now leave the rest to me. I'll find a way."

But he didn't find a way. The days passed, one by one, and he didn't find a way. He kept postponing the problem, trusting his powers of imagination, convinced he'd be able to think of a solution; but, to his regret, he discovered that he didn't have enough time to think. He had to concentrate all his efforts on keeping his father in the dark about his plans. This deception required Simón to continue going to the shop every morning as though nothing had changed, to waste each desperate evening with his Roman Law textbooks, and to wait until even the ghosts were asleep before he could take out *El burlador de Sevilla* and improve his mastery of it. That was the only happy moment in his day. He had no other. He didn't even have his weekly appointments with Amparo, because they had agreed it was safer that way. But the effort Simón dedicated to the play had its rewards. Even though he knew the work by heart, he kept turning back to it every night to give free rein to his imagination, so much so that the lines seemed to give him a conspiratorial wink on every page. Where Tirso de Molina's stage direction reads, "Exit Don Juan," Simón added a marginal note, "I'm out of here too," and had to cover his mouth to stifle his laughter. No matter which page he opened, he found a verse he could apply to his own situation. "In absence there is peace," says Octavio. "I wish to sail for Spain, / And let my sorrows cease." Simón nodded as he read these words. The musicians sing in the streets of Seville: "He who awaits some future pleasure / Despairs as he hopes, in equal measure." Simón smiled. And whenever Don Juan defied fate with his famous line "Why, how much time you give me!" Grandfather nodded again, and counted the remaining days.

At times it was impossible for him to hide the smiles that crossed his face during the day, and his father would react as if he had seen the signs of fever in his son's flushed features. "What's wrong with you, Simón?" he asked. "Are you happy?"

"No, Father," the boy said, recovering himself. "I was thinking about the future."

"And it's going to bring you such good things they make you smile?"

"When I get my degree," Simón lied, "when I'm a lawyer, I'll take you out of this place and you won't have to work anymore."

"And what makes you think I want to leave this shop?" his father asked sharply. "Have you ever heard a single complaint from my lips? This is my place in the world, Simón. I neither have nor want anything else."

Simón often lay awake at night, pondering the problem of the car. In the end, he surrendered to exhaustion, thinking he'd take care of it the next day, and if not, the day after, but probably tomorrow, tomorrow . . . And so the night of August 10 arrived, the second to last night of his imprisonment. Seeing that it was after two in the morning and that three o'clock was taking a long time to arrive, he decided to give himself the final audition. He closed the book, got into bed, and, keeping his eyes shut, started to recite the whole play in a low murmur, starting from the first word, including the stage directions. *Hall in the palace of the King of Naples. Night. Enter Don Juan Tenorio and the Duchess Isabela.* I myself know that part by heart, and I know for a fact that Papa, before Parkinson's disease began snatching away pieces of his mind, knew many fragments of the play as well. But only fragments. Not like Simón. That night, he felt certain he could recite the text from beginning to end without looking at it even once. Murmuring through clenched teeth turned out to be quite appropriate for the whispered scene that begins the play: "Duke Octavio, this way / Will bring you safely out," says Duchess Isabela in a Neapolitan palace. "Duchess, have no doubt," Don Juan replies. "I shall my dear pledge keep." I don't remember exactly how the remaining lines in the first scene go. Obviously, Don Juan has just robbed Isabela of her honor while passing himself off as Duke Octavio. Robbed her of her honor. That's the way they said it then, meaning the two of them had been screwing. When she lights a candle, she realizes her mistake, and her indignant cries awaken the king. Don Juan flees. Simón would think me irreverent for saying this, but Don Juan does nothing in the play but fuck and run. However, we weren't talking about that; we were talking about Simón, lying in his bed, reciting softly. And thinking, once again, that the piece was an uncanny representation of his life: the nocturnal setting, the stealth, the character in disguise . . .

The more lines he spoke, the more trouble he had keeping his voice down. He managed to stifle the shouts of surprise that echo through the palace when Don Juan's treachery is detected, but the clamor of the subsequent duel was irrepressible. His father woke up and heard the distant voices; believing they came from the depths of his dreams, he rolled over and tried to go back to sleep. But the incomprehensible murmuring didn't stop. Finally, he got up, walked on tiptoe to his son's room, and took up a position in front of the door, unable to believe the voices he was hearing. Inside the room, Don Juan lay in Tisbea's embrace, crying out to her:

I need no longer fear
In hellish seas to drown,
For in your shining arms
I rise to heaven's crown.

The father stealthily opened the door and slipped inside, still walking on the tips of his toes. Simón was stretched out on the bed with his eyes closed, completely concentrated on his audition. The recitation continued:

The fierce and frightful storm
That struck my ship athwart
Has flung me at your feet,
My shelter and my port.

Seeing that Simón was enunciating these words with his eyes closed, the father believed that his son was talking in his sleep. He crouched down next to the bed, put out a hand, and shook Simón by the shoulder, giving him a mortal fright. Simón let out a terrified scream, as if he'd seen a ghost.

"Wake up, son," his father urged him. "You're talking in your sleep."

Without realizing it, he had just provided his son with the perfect excuse to keep his lie intact, and Simón latched on to the excuse immediately: "What was I saying?"

"I don't know. Foolishness. Something about the sea."

"Now I understand. I had a terrible nightmare, Father. I dreamed I was in another shipwreck. I don't even know how I lit the candle."

"It doesn't matter, son." His father's usual severity seemed mitigated by his concern. "It's over now. Go back to sleep. We're opening the shop in just a few hours."

With a grateful murmur, Simón closed his eyes, turned over on his side, and abandoned himself to the happy thought that only one more day stood between him and his freedom. But he was not destined to fall asleep that night. A car; he needed a car. If he didn't get one, the whole scheme would fall through.

I know that he did manage to get a car. Or to be more precise, we know that we were told he got a car. The problem is that there's no way of knowing how. This shouldn't surprise me, because the same remark applies to Simón's entire story. Death turned him into a specter. There are no photographs of him. There's not a single document. For years I thought that in some theater in some town in Spain I'd find a flyer or a leaflet with a cast list, and in it there would be at least a brief mention of his name. *A fisherman: Simón Azuera.* Perhaps even accompanied by a picture. Not a picture of him, because he never had sufficient standing in the company to merit that, but maybe a group shot. Impossible. The Compañía del Corral never performed in any theater worthy of the name. They went from village to village and worked in the village squares, with neither the press nor any camera to record their presence. So here, as before, the only reliable source we have is Grandmother Amparo. Borrowed words, once again.

WITH LUIS

I need to reach the end. I tell him the whole thing all at once, at least almost the whole thing: His name is Ismael, I met him at work. How many children does he have, he asks me. What do you mean? Look, if you haven't told anybody, it must mean he's married. No, he's not married. Then what's the problem? The problem is . . . I get confused. I bow my head. Luis doesn't pressure me. He knows I'm on the point of saying it: The problem is he's twenty-three.

He goes quiet for a moment and stares at the roof. He's doing a calculation. I give him a hand: Fifteen, Luis, I tell him. I'm fifteen years older than he is. So what, he says. He looks at me. So what. But I think he's talking just to talk. To say the right thing. That's not a problem, he says. Don't be ridiculous, Luis, I'm a mature woman. Ismael's a baby. Well, if you're in love with him . . . In love? You don't know what you're saying. It's on the tip of my tongue. I want to tell him: I'm not in love, what I am is pregnant.

He asks me why. He wants to know if it's for the sex. Yes, I say. That is, it's for the sex, too. What do you mean? I mean I suppose there are many reasons. I don't understand you, Serena. Speak clearly. I tell him once again that men my age are screwed up. Burned out from I don't know how many breakups and fed up with failing. Or just the opposite: totally innocent, despite the passage of so many years. Ismael's a virgin, I tell him. Virgin? He's shocked. You don't understand me, I mean that I can teach him things. He's curious. I can talk to him. I don't have to provide him with extensive therapy in order to fuck him. Luis wants to talk about that. I feel a little embarrassed.

after only three weeks. I told my children that I'd cut my trip short because the death rituals among these tribes were so meager they didn't merit a full-scale research project. I've already mentioned how certain nomadic hunting tribes abandon their dead. And it wasn't just the dead; they abandoned the old and the injured as well. They'd leave them enough food and water to last a few days, in the belief that, should they manage to recover, they'd rejoin the group farther on. If they didn't survive, it made no sense to stop and wait for them. Since people are always well disposed toward travel anecdotes, this was the sort of tale I told. There's always an audience for descriptions of men in loincloths and women adorned with stones, for stories featuring arrows and spears. I'd tell people about the two days I'd spent in the bush, accompanying two Hadza men on a hunting expedition, about their killing and skewering of birds. I told the story of the antelope that scoffed at arrows, limiting myself to the reasons for this behavior according to Hadza mythology. Death hardly has repercussions in their lives. We anthropologists have agreed to attribute this characteristic to the fact that they're hunters: they live with death on a daily basis. What's more, they live off it; they nourish themselves with death. Maybe that's why they accept it and have no need of liturgies to explain it. They weep for their dead, and if conditions are favorable, they perform some rudimentary dance in their honor, but they appear to forget them quickly.

There's only one particular circumstance in which this principle doesn't apply and death intervenes among the living: when a member of the tribe dies and another is in the forest hunting and hasn't heard the news. In this case, the hunter's arrows miss their target again and again, no matter how fine a shot he is, and the animal escapes his pursuit unharmed. I saw this myself. Of course, having seen it doesn't mean I believe it.

I'd been in Tanzania with the Hadza for more than ten days when two young men decided to break off from the group and go on a hunting expedition. They allowed me to accompany them, but not without first taking the necessary precautions, which chiefly consisted in extracting a *promise from me that I wasn't having my period and didn't expect to get it in the next few days. Among the Hadza, a menstruating woman is a hunter's worst enemy. Her presence cancels the killing power of the poison they dip the tips of their arrows in before they shoot them. An entire theory about the imposition of life upon death can be spun out of all this, but I'm not going off on that tangent now. In any case, they accepted my company, and during the first day I watched them hunt small game, especially birds, which they carried skewered on a stick. Although this wasn't the first time I'd gone along on a hunt in the forest, I admired the hunters' skills once again: among the top branches of the trees, or within the narrow spaces that separated them, the arrows of the Hadza archers struck down birds whose presence I hadn't even been able to distinguish. At sunrise on the second day, some wet, trampled tracks revealed to them the presence of an animal which I'm certain they called* mbema, *because that was the only word they spoke until we caught up with it. It was a relatively small antelope, but large enough so that even I could make it out when I saw my two companions take aim. The two bows vibrated in unison, and for a second it looked as though their arrows would find the prey. However, barely a meter or so from the antelope, the arrows strayed off target. I'd seen the hunters miss on other occasions—when they hurried their shots, or when the uncomfortable position the archer found himself in caused his shot to go astray—but this time was different. One arrow fell at the feet of the* mbema, *as if its strength had failed at the last moment; the other passed a few centimeters above the animal's head. The* mbema *ran away, and we had to follow its trail.*

It took us hours before we came across the little creature again. Once again, the arrows flew off course just as they were about to sink into the antelope's flesh, as if the air had protected it with an invisible shield. Two consecutive failures were enough to convince the hunters that there was no use in continuing their pursuit. We started to return to the settlement where the main group was. Until that point, I'd been struck by how stealthily and cautiously my companions moved through the forest, by their ability to turn themselves into shadows; when they lay in wait for their prey, these men were capable of literally melting into their surroundings. Now, by contrast, I was surprised at the speed of our return, the determination with which they fended off underbrush and dodged roots. They didn't care whether they scared off potential prey or not. On two occasions, I spotted birds of a respectable size, similar to the ones my two companions were carrying. Proud of having been the first to detect the birds, I alerted the hunters to their presence. The Hadza didn't even raise their bows. At first, they disdained my show of surprise at their attitude. Only after I insisted did they respond with a series of explanatory gestures, from which I deduced that the two tribesmen, after their failure to take the antelope, considered their arrows irredeemably cursed, and that they refused to waste time and effort shooting them at any other prey. Little by little, I was able to gather that their refusal to continue hunting had something to do with death.

Had I done my homework for the trip, I would have known in advance that when a Hadza hunter's arrow inexplicably veered away from its target a second before striking it, he interpreted this anomaly as a sign that he must return to the settlement as quickly as possible because a member of the tribe had just passed away. The strayed arrows were like church bells in European towns, tolling for the dead. In other cultures, we'd be talking about the soul of the deceased and its migration to the forest, where it placed itself between the animal and the arrows. But the Hadza have little belief in souls and spirits. A colleague of mine, a man named Woodburn, had spent four months with the Hadza the previous year and documented all of this, but at the time I knew nothing of his field work among the nomadic tribes of Africa. Had I been aware of his writings, things would have been quite different, because he describes one of the most remarkable customs of the Iraqw, a tribe that shared a common origin, language, and geography with the Hadza but had reached a different stage of development. They were, so to speak, the

Hadza's distant cousins, but in the previous decades the Iraqw had gradually abandoned the nomadic life and dedicated themselves to harvesting.

When we arrived at the settlement, the two hunters spoke with old people and women, and the consternation caused by the answers they received was visible on their faces. Nobody had died. They wandered around for hours, worried and restless, apparently unable to attribute the fact that their arrows had missed their mark to any cause other than someone's death. It was almost as if they wanted someone to have died, because the death would assure them that they hadn't lost their skill with a bow. The news came later that night. In a nearby settlement inhabited by the Iraqw, a young woman had died, carried off by fever.

Woodburn's work, which was published only after I'd been back in Barcelona for several months, described how the Iraqw, having become sedentary, had developed the need to bury their dead. They could no longer abandon them and move on, because they had nowhere to move on to. This brought them face-to-face with a new problem peculiar to the funeral rituals of sedentary peoples, a problem known among anthropologists as funeral pollution. Almost all cultures establish some practice by which relatives of the dead person purify themselves after handling the corpse, some method that allows them to get rid of the last traces of the dead person. These are usually simple rituals, often involving water. Among the Iraqw, who are monogamous, a new widow or widower is allowed to have sexual relations with a person from another tribe in the days immediately following the death of his or her spouse. Only after doing so is the survivor cleansed of the undesirable traces of the dead. To refer to "another tribe" is to refer to the Hadza, who are, geographically, the closest. It's not only that the survivors have permission to have sex with someone outside the tribe; they are urged to do so as quickly as possible. They won't be allowed to reintegrate themselves into the society until they have completed the purification ritual. The same person who cleanses the widow or widower from pollution by means of the sexual act completes the ritual by shaving the other's head, whether man or woman. In exchange for these services, the Hadʒa usually receive clothes and food, and no one is troubled if they take away some object that belonged to the dead person, as the Iraqw consider those objects contaminated, too, and therefore renounce all claim to them. This practice makes sense: the Iraqw cleanse themselves and since the Hadʒa don't believe in spirits, they can't be contaminated. The practice also makes evolutionary sense, because otherwise tribes with relatively few members would be condemned to endogamy.

I knew nothing of this. Nor much about anything else. I was young. If I remember correctly, I must have been thirty-six or thirty-eight at the time, more or less the same age as my daughter is now. I was like her: there were too many things I knew nothing about. But I was no beginner and I had done quite a bit of traveling. Always in a southerly direction, and each time farther south. First Morocco. Then Senegal, Mali, and Benin, which was called Dahomey at the time. But this was my first experience with nomadic hunting tribes, with their frugality, with the idea that the enclosure of your skin contains almost everything you're going to need in life. I knew so very little. Maybe that's why my obsession with knowing carried me all over the world.

As soon as I realized that there had been a death in the Iraqw settlement, I collected my tape recorder and my notebooks and asked for someone to take me there. I was more interested in the death than the hunt. We got to the settlement at sunrise. It was easy to locate the dead person's family. It always is: there's always grieving, fire, water, or dancing. Or a festival. Sometimes there's just a hut covered in a dark mantle.

It's going to be hard for me to tell this story. Many years have passed, but it still has a strange effect on me, which I can't describe as anything other than sheer embarrassment. I asked permission to see the widower. His relatives stopped me in front of the entrance to his hut and made me wait for a few hours, during which time they frequently went inside to confer with him; when they came out again, they looked at me strangely, or so I thought at the time. Finally, one of them indicated *that the widower was prepared to receive me. When I entered, I found a man sitting on the ground in the middle of the hut. With an enormous erection. I don't know how to describe it, it was throbbing, I wonder what Serena would say, what metaphors she would dream up for the web of swollen veins and the thick stalk of his reddened flesh. A lighthouse. Serena would surely speak in terms of lighthouses. But she knows nothing of this story.*

For a while I was paralyzed. I hadn't read Woodburn and I didn't have the slightest idea of the purifying role this poor wretch expected me to play. I took a step backward. He got up and gave me something resembling an embrace, with the plain intention of detaining me. I'd be lying if I said he was violent; abrupt, awkward, and eager, but not violent. He didn't want to hurt me, but I didn't know what to do. I suppressed an impulse to scream. Had I raised my voice, there's a good possibility that whoever responded would have come in with the intention of helping the widower, not me. A terrifying image of collective rape crossed my mind. I told him no. No, no, no. In a soft voice, almost whispering, again and again, and I kept on saying no even after I was sure that he understood me, even after his embrace, if not his erection, relaxed, even after he retreated to the middle of the hut and got down on his knees, as if he were expecting some punishment.

Tapping on his penis with one hand, the man picked up a rusty razor that lay on the ground in front of him. A safety razor. In societies like this, metal is an intrusion, an unmistakable signal to the anthropologist that someone has been there before him. We always exchange metal objects and mirrors for knowledge. Had I read Woodburn, had I known of his sojourn to that part of the world a short time before my own, I would have thought that the razor was his. Although I wasn't in a position to do much thinking. The man began to weep, and his lamentation was more terrifying than his earlier grunts. He made a sign to me with the razor and then raised it to his hair, which was long, coarse, and dirty, repeating the gesture several times and imploring me in his incomprehensible language to shave his head. I stepped over to him, took the razor, stationed myself behind him, and began to pull the rusty blade over his scalp.

At first I was afraid of cutting him and hopeful that what was required would be no more than a symbolic act, a question of shearing off a few locks of hair, but it didn't take me long to understand that I was expected to shave the whole lot. I felt the same pity for him that he'd probably felt for me a few seconds earlier, when I so roundly refused what he wanted. I concentrated my gaze on the clumps of hair that fell away from the razor, sometimes glistening with a few drops of blood, but it was impossible for me not to see the tears that kept spilling from his eyes and the swollen head of his still throbbing penis, which seemed to be staring up at me with cyclopean intensity. In the end, some drops of semen dotted the tangled clumps of hair on the ground. He didn't interfere with me in any way; the experience wasn't repulsive. No human conduct has ever repelled me as much as some of the theories invented to explain it. Perfect theories; insupportable lies. Woodburn had the good sense to limit himself to recording what he observed, but some who came after him wanted to explain it: they talked about the regeneration of life through the sexual act. Theoretical nonsense. I touched those blood-stained clumps of hair, I saw the semen fall more sorrowfully than the tears. Nothing regenerates anything. At most, we cleanse ourselves in whatever way we can. And we remove the traces: of persons, of things, of spirits. Of ourselves.

I remember that when I was about to leave the hut, I was tempted to bend down and collect one of those shaven clumps of hair. I didn't do it. That same night, when I returned to the Hadza settlement, it became clear to me that my trip had come to an end. The same men who during the two previous weeks had given me free entry into their cabins, the same people who had pointed out objects to me with a couple of gestures and a few scattered words, now refused even to look at me. I could have explained to them that nothing of what they imagined had taken place in the Iraqw widower's hut, but I didn't even try. Only silence could protect me from their disdain, which was more hurtful than the widower's *tearful erection. Even in Nairobi, as the plane carrying me back to Barcelona took off through the misty fog that only an African morning can bring, I knew I was taking that silence with me and would never be able to get rid of it.*

I didn't tell my children. I ended the story after our return to the settlement, at the moment when we learned that death had visited the small village nearby, thus providing an explanation for the arrows that had missed their mark and the subsequent abandonment of the hunt. I don't know how many times I must have repeated this story since then, at dinners and family gatherings, parties and conferences. But I had to suppress the rest, the truly important part. Actually, I don't know whether I had to or I chose to; I suppose I did what was most convenient. But it seemed to me that there were certain stories a mother should never tell.

It may be that my silence protected me, too. It helped me to turn those events almost into something that had happened to somebody else. Likewise, when I came back from Varanasi, I talked about ashes floating in the Ganges and about funeral pyres, I even mentioned the impression made on me by the smell of roasting hair and by the fibulas that occasionally showed through the flames, but I didn't say anything about my encounter with the Aghori ascetics. That's a lie; I did tell my children about it, I even wrote numerous articles about everything I'd seen. But I said nothing about myself. *Those tales necessarily had to be told in the third person: on the page, because the "I" does not exist in the scientific community; and in oral accounts, after-dinner tales, stories told to family and friends, because . . . well, because it was easier that way. It's hard to explain what you feel when you see a man—it was a man, after all, despite the long, matted hair and the furtive wild eyes— sitting next to a funeral pyre and drinking his own urine out of a bowl made from a human skull. The Aghori do that. And we anthropologists go to see them do it, if they allow us, and afterward we write about it. No one asks us to talk about ourselves. I watched the Bara divide into groups of men and women and perform frenzied dances and never stop crying, not even when the contest between the two groups grew heated, nor when winning meant possessing, nor when the duel turned into an orgy and the weeping was mingled with howls of pleasure before the very door of the dead man's hut. I saw that happen, and I told the story in great detail: I even showed photographs and distributed tapes. But I said nothing about myself. How do you explain to your children that you can feel fear in your vagina and excitement in the pit of your stomach, all mixed together. It's not easy. And not everything I kept quiet about was scatological or related to sex. I was also incapable of describing the flash that went through me when I witnessed what the Zulu did with the bodies of their dead. When a Zulu man dies, his widow turns him over to his heirs for burial. His body is bound so that it remains in the fetal position. Sometimes, if rigor mortis has stiffened his limbs, his bones must be broken to do the job. Once the corpse is properly tied, the widow brings it out of the cabin to deliver it to the dead man's children, who are waiting in the doorway. They bring the body out headfirst. It's a symbolic representation of a birth: pushed by the woman, a body folded in upon itself pokes its head out, as if it were not dead but being born.*

Describing all that isn't difficult for an anthropologist. Establishing a coherent, credible theory to explain it isn't hard, either, provided sufficient information is available. All funeral rituals share a common motive: to allow life to go on, as before. Societies are eternal, or at least long-lasting; the individuals who constitute a society are not. That's the universal law. And it's the contradiction that we humans, of whatever tribe, try to resolve with our rituals. Therefore we dispose of the dead in more or less theatrical ways, in ceremonies that ultimately serve only to help us get rid of the corpse. The individual has disappeared but the group remains. The dead person's inheritance is shared; the future of his land is decided, as well as that of his personal possessions, which, contrary to appearances, serve to remind us not that our loved one has died but that we're still alive.

What's difficult to explain are the twisty paths this information takes inside you as you go about accumulating it, especially when the information consists not of data but of corpses. I've seen too many corpses. That's probably what's the matter with me. Along with a certain amount of selfishness. My parents died in old age, and everyone praised my fortitude in coming to terms with my loss. A few people even said they envied me for knowing so much about death, perhaps assuming that my profession provided me with some kind of preparation for this fateful moment. Well, maybe it did prepare me for the passing of other people; but not for my own. Every day of my life I was less prepared to die. All the information accumulated during so many years began to shout two things at me: first, that I was daily approaching the moment when I could no longer be an observer of others' deaths and would become the protagonist of my own; and second, that when that moment came, life would go on. For other people. That's why I've wound up here; so that other people don't exist. And that's why, when chance made it seem that I was dead, I had no desire to contradict it. It was an absurd moral victory, my only possibility of affirming that life goes on even though I'm dead.

I envy Julio's enormous capacity for forgetting. I envy it because I don't have it. And I don't have it because in order to forget as he does you have to be able to invent as he does. Even now, when his mind is no longer able to construct the gigantic fortresses he used to build to protect himself from the truth, he's surely still erecting houses out of thin air. Julio could forget anything because he was capable of making up its opposite. Not me. I saw what I saw. Maybe I lack imagination. I have other flaws as well. For example, I have a hard time being frivolous. I possess a certain sense of humor, but I've never been good at the blindness required for joking. Because that's what death is, a huge, grotesque joke, to which humans respond with lesser jokes, with childish jests and pleasant laughter. I could never do that. I could never reduce the importance of things, as the majority of my colleagues did. I was amazed by the plastic skeletons some colleagues carried on their key chains and by the skulls others used as paperweights. I knew a Canadian who cleaned his desk with a duster made from genuine human hair, which he claimed to have gathered up from the ground after a funeral in Canton Province in China. The same hair with which the young female relatives of the dead man, on their knees at his feet, had rubbed his coffin to clean off the pollution. The Cantonese consider this pollution so contaminating that family members with newborn children are exempted from attending the funeral. Nevertheless, the women have to rub the coffin with their hair. And nevertheless, a Canadian anthropologist can collect that hair and make a duster out of it. Maybe laughing like that was the healthiest reaction, a defense mechanism of sorts. But I could never do it.

With forgetting denied me, joking impossible, and a faulty imagination, I watched everything shrink, little by little, until the only tools I had left were silence and renunciation. Silence, in whose refuge I have come to feel secure, withdrawn from life like someone watching a military parade from an open window, knowing he can close it as soon as the first salvo is fired. I couldn't say exactly when it was that I closed that symbolic window. I think I managed to keep the bridges open for many years, coming and going between the wild frenzy of life and the quiet certainty of death. No one can say I didn't try. I even went so far as to write seven books, as if I had something to say. Me, when the only language I've truly mastered is sign language. And then there were my children and the love I felt for them. The knowledge that they needed me—that helped, too. The duty of looking after other people makes you real. But that doesn't last very long either.

I don't know. I think about my friends from university days, and I realize we've grown old in contrary directions. Maybe we were all looking for the same thing, a few certainties, and surely each of us will have found the ones she deserved, or the ones that could illuminate her knowledge, but we've arrived at them by different paths. They've used addition; I've used subtraction. They've had their hectic daily routines, they take their grandchildren out for walks, pay their bills, and go to the dry cleaner's, as if such insignificant acts might serve to do anything other than fill up life; as if they might serve to explain it. I moved

toward the same goal, but in a contrary direction. That's where renunci-
ation comes in: you start off by doing without everything that seems
like an accessory, and you wind up with the frugality of the nomads.
Breathing, eating—in Chapacuran, the language of the Wari, the
verb wereme *means both "to breathe" and "to think." Poor Descartes.*
To breathe; to be. To think. Renouncing the rest, shedding it all. For
decades I disparaged the myth of the noble savage in print and in per-
son. But I won't let anyone deny the wisdom of the Wari. They count
their days differently from us: they go from sunset to sunset. This means
that their day begins at the end of the day. They're wise. Why mention
this here? All this has a great deal to do with my silence and my renun-
ciation, because it's likely that my sojourn among the Wari marked the
precise moment when the water demolished the bridges and showed me
the path. A path. The path that brought me here: to this jungle, this si-
lence, this distance. To this death, if anyone wants to call it that. To the
only truth that remains when you've dispossessed yourself of the rest.

FRIDAY

This morning I promised I'd write down the history of Li Po's exile. Alberto left the house at dawn, determined to find someone who'll rent us a boat. Luis proposed we take a short walk, and Pablo offered to stay with Papa because he has to practice. We left him sitting at the piano, with Papa installed in the easy chair by his side. Quite a luxury, rehearsing on a Steinway grand piano a hundred and fifty meters from the sea.

Sometimes I think we're not fair to Alberto. We ought to thank him for his generosity at least once a day, but we forget. We think it's easy to be generous when you have so much of everything, but we're wrong. Take that piano, for instance. When Pablo had been married to Antonia for a year and their problems began, the atmosphere in their house became tense and suffocating. She subjected him to round-the-clock emotional blackmail, told him she couldn't bear to live with those scales four hours a day, interrupted his practice sessions with sham headaches, and invited friends in for drinks during the very hours that Pablo usually devoted to playing. For months, he put up with it, but in the end he exploded and told us the whole story one night when we were having dinner at Alberto's. Alberto listened to his complaints and made a suggestion: "Why not come here tomorrow around noon? We might be able to arrange something." The following day, Pablo found the Steinway grand set up in Alberto's library; Alberto had had the good taste to exit the apartment several minutes earlier, so Pablo could practice undisturbed. Or maybe so as not to overwhelm him—I don't know. Alberto had left a note for Pablo on the keyboard cover: "I hope this is up to your level." When he finished playing, Pablo added a line to the same note, "No, my level's a little lower," and left it on the bench.

Not only are we ungrateful; we also like to make trouble. When

Pablo and Antonia finally broke up and he could go back to rehearsing on his old upright piano, Alberto moved the Steinway to Malespina so Pablo could practice here as well. He doesn't come often, but from time to time he settles in here for a few weeks of composing. And the first thing he does, upon arrival, is to complain that the piano has no soul because nobody plays it. He says the humidity in Malespina is softening the piano's wooden insides and making all the notes sound bland. A bunch of nonsense. And he's not alone. We all should learn not to complain so much. We'd be nothing without Alberto. We wouldn't even have this house. When Papa retired—in 1986, I think—he had to put it up for sale. He couldn't maintain it and he didn't have the nerve to tell us so. To him, it was much more than a place in the world, it was a place in history. He'd built it with his own hands. He chose its location in homage to his father and situated all its big windows so that they faced the sea in the direction where Simón fell off the ship. I can imagine what it must have meant for him to accept that he couldn't afford to maintain the house any longer. I say I can imagine, because he never wanted to talk about it. He limited himself to declaring that we had to look to the future, that the house was already part of the past, and that someday we'd find something else. What Papa didn't know at the time was that the buyer was his own son. If I remember correctly, Papa signed the contract in June, and Alberto kept his purchase a secret until Christmas. Until Christmas Eve, to be exact. When we sat down to dinner, each of us had a little gift-wrapped package lying on our plate. We all opened our packages at the same time. Inside were copies of the key to the big door of the garage in the Malespina house. At first, I thought it was a nostalgic gesture, a final souvenir of our childhood home, but then Alberto stood up and toasted the future with one of his characteristic speeches, imposing but full of style and tact. He said he had known about Papa's decision to sell the house right from the start, and the buyer was one of his emissaries. He asked Papa's pardon for his subterfuge. It was very touching. "You can't imagine how many qualms I had," he said. "At first, I thought about lending you the money or simply giving it to you, but that seemed like a terrible idea. I suppose you wouldn't have accepted. Although the house is in my name, it goes without saying that it's not mine; it's yours, all of you, it's ours, the same as always. I'm dying for everyone to go there and see it. I want you to tell me what you think about the improvements I've made."

Ah, the improvements. What can I say? The house is much better now than it was before: it's more comfortable and has lavish amenities everywhere. Nevertheless, I still have the effrontery to complain. I don't complain to him, I wouldn't dream of it, but I do complain, out of pure nostalgia. I miss the days when we had to draw straws for our turn in the only bathroom and the nights spent sleeping on the sofa, because there weren't enough beds. I miss the symphony of beetles tapping deep inside the beams at twilight in early March and the clanging tune of raindrops falling into a zinc bucket. I'm being unfair. I'll make a note and try to be more appreciative from now on.

It shouldn't be hard. All I have to do is think about what we'd be without this house, without this village. As the Russian woman said, it's the most beautiful place in the world, even more so at this time of year, on a weekday with no people around, in the precious autumn light. I don't know if there are many places where you can take a walk like the one Luis and I took this morning. At the end of it, we were sitting down on the low wall that separates the road from the beach, our feet dangling down almost to the sand. It was one of those glorious autumn days. A light but constant north wind had swept every cloud from the sky. The local experts say, correctly, that when the north wind rises this way— steadily, without any wild gusts—it brings with it a gift of fair weather that never lasts for fewer than three days. Barely three miles away, the modest Formigues Islands discreetly broke the line of the horizon. It's impossible to look at those rocks and not think about the good judgment of whoever gave them their name. I'm not certain who that person was, but I know for a fact they were already known as the "Ant Islands" in the Middle Ages. In any case, it must have been on a morning like this one, under the sway of this same light.

"It's a bird," Luis said in a whisper.

We couldn't even hear the sea. An offshore wind pushing it out like this, away from the land, seems to cocoon the water in silence. There wasn't a soul in sight. Not a single car. My mind was blank. This happens to me sometimes. In those rare moments of peace, I go far away. My hands settle on my stomach although it's much too soon to be able to notice anything. I just rest my hands there and feel the heat passing back and forth between us. I could spend hours like that.

After a long while, I asked, "What bird? What are you saying? There's no bird."

"The light," Luis explained. "The light's a bird."

"Ah."

He talks like that sometimes. Then he's silent again. A sentence was going through my mind: "Nothing new is known to have occurred in the vicinity of this station." The calm after the storm. Eventually, my sense of responsibility pulled me out of my reverie. "We should go back, Luis," I said. "Poor Pablo's been alone with Papa all morning. And there's lunch to prepare."

"Already? Shit, it's so nice here. You're always in such a hurry. At least you could tell me the story of the battle of the Formigues Islands."

"Are you crazy? That would take all afternoon."

"Was it that long?"

"It lasted an entire night. The night of August 28, 1285. But that's the least of it. The story's long because there were actually three battles, not one. And there are so many obscure details that not even the contemporary chronicles agree with one another."

"How many people were killed?"

"No one knows for sure. But thousands."

"Then I don't understand at all."

"What don't you understand?"

"Why Grandfather told me——"

"Ah, no, no," I said, hastening to interrupt him. "I know that tale. The story your grandfather told you was a lie."

"A lie? You're fucking kidding me."

"I'm not fucking kidding you."

"He made it all up?"

"I don't know. I don't think so. I imagine he heard it from some fisherman. Or maybe from one of the local people. Who knows? Do you remember the story?"

"More or less, I guess."

"Let's see. Tell it to me."

"Well, it goes something like this." He stood up. Like Papa. Like me, I suppose. Good stories should be told from a standing position. "Roger de Lloria, pursued by two French ships, took refuge in Malespina bay. It was late in the afternoon. The *garbí* was blowing, which as everyone knows is a southerly wind that suddenly disappears around five o'clock. Finding themselves becalmed, the three vessels struck their sails."

"Go on. You're doing very well." I admit that I became a little emotional listening to Papa's exact words in Luis's mouth: as everyone knows . . . becalmed . . . vessels . . . "And then?"

"The French didn't know that the *garbí* usually starts blowing again a few hours later, but Roger de Lloria was well aware of this fact. Barely five minutes before the wind rose again, he ordered the crew of his ship to hoist the sails as quickly as possible. When the wind arrived, it found him ready. The French didn't even have time to understand what was happening. Lloria maneuvered his ship between the two enemy ships and sank them both with cannon fire."

"Perfect. That's the history of the battle according to Papa. Suppose I told you the ships were galleys?"

"What difference does that make?"

"Although they carried a mast and sails, galleys were propelled by oars, especially when they were maneuvering. That's where the expression 'condemned to the galleys' comes from, because the oarsmen were usually prisoners and their work was laborious and exhausting. In other words, a change in the wind, no matter how familiar it was to Roger de

Lloria and how much he may have taken advantage of it, couldn't have had so much influence on the battle. A confrontation between galleys required a series of maneuvers that were necessarily executed by rowing."

"Fine, that's a detail. It may be important—who knows? But to go from there to denying . . ."

"And suppose I told you that galleys didn't carry cannons in those days?"

"Well, shit, that does change things."

"Then the only thing left to tell you is that there weren't three ships, but scores of them, more than a hundred in any case, so your grandfather's version is sunk, pun intended. Right off the coast here, in these same waters that look so calm today, there were thousands of men, howling, stabbing one another, and drowning."

"And how do you know all this?"

"Because it's written down. There are contemporary chronicles that record the history of the battle. They're full of lies, too, but their lies are less false than the story your grandfather tells."

"Then tell me the real story."

"No, not now. We really ought to get back to the house. The next time we have a chance, I'll tell you the story."

"You swear?"

"That's not necessary."

"Oh yes it is. The only person around here who doesn't need to swear is me, because I always tell the truth. There are advantages to being a Crazy."

While we were walking back to the house, Luis seemed to be pondering what we'd just talked about. Halfway home, he spoke up: "In other words, Grandfather's a liar. And then he comes round threatening people with that bullshit about imprisonment or exile. There were nights when I was punished and sent to bed without supper for a lie. What a bastard. As soon as I see him, I'm going to tell him so."

"Don't judge him, Luis. And don't even think about saying anything to him." I was worried that Luis's frankness could cause a row, and in my case, I really believe that Papa doesn't deserve to be judged for the liberties he took in his storytelling. "After all," I went on, "they were just stories. He was only trying to entertain us. Besides, he wouldn't understand you."

"You're right about that."

"You want to know something else?" Maybe I shouldn't have told him this, but the temptation was too strong. "The exile story was a lie, too."

Luis was stunned. He turned deathly pale, as if someone had knocked the wind out of him. I suspect that for him, as for all of us, the story of Li Po is sacrosanct. He said, "Oh, no. Not that."

"Yes. That."

"Li Po? He's a lie too?"

"A half lie."

"Like the battle."

"Like the battle, but the other way around."

"I don't understand."

"Well, look. In the case of the Battle of the Formigues Islands, Papa took a long, bloody, and complex history, a war that involved at least three countries plus the Vatican, with the economic stability of the Mediterranean at stake, and turned it into a simple anecdote that could be told in two minutes, as you demonstrated a little while ago. In the case of Li Po, he did just the opposite. He gathered up the few bare facts that are known about Li Po's life and built a gigantic legend out of them."

"It was beautiful. He told it to me so many times, but it always seemed new, and when it was over I wanted to hear it again and again."

"You're right. The same thing happened to me. But the story was false. Or rather, it's true that Li Po was the greatest poet of his time, that he drank too much, and that the emperor's son discovered him. Those are all facts. And it's also true that the emperor found Li Po's verses so moving that he installed the poet in his palace. It may be true as well that the court eunuch conspired against him out of envy, but Li Po's best biographers call this a possibility, not a certainty. And it's not clear whether or not he was a eunuch."

"And that's it?"

"That's it. There was no exile. Li Po may have taken to the woods, but he wasn't exiled. At most, he was running away. It's not even known how he died."

"Well, shit. I like Grandfather's story a lot better."

"So do I. I know it by heart."

"Then why not tell me that one?"

"I can't, Luis. Only Papa can tell the story of Li Po."

"Didn't you just say you know it by heart?"

"Yes. The words, yes. But what was magical about the story was much more than the words. It was Papa's voice. He'd start talking and all at once you felt you were in a palace in China, with silks and jewels and jade flutes everywhere. When he said, 'A bellow so powerful it made the palace's foundations shiver,' he made me want to hide under a table."

"I know what you mean. I remember being almost scared sometimes. And when he recited Li Po's poems . . ."

". . . which weren't by Li Po."

"No. Even the poems were fake?"

"Well, he always put four poems in the story. Two were by Li Po, the other two weren't. I imagine Papa made them up himself. The important thing is that he presented the story so well no one else can tell it. I tried it a few times, but my voice . . ."

"Maybe you could write it down?"

"Maybe so."

I thought about this possibility as we walked along. Luis was right. If nobody is ever going to tell this story the way Papa did, the right thing might be to write it down so that it'll be recorded in some way. Submitting myself to this test appeals to me, for various reasons. First of all, for the pure challenge of seeing whether I'm capable of doing it.

Second, so that the story will survive. So that in the future, I won't have to say, "Here's the story your grandfather told"; I can say, "Take this and read it for yourself." It doesn't matter to whom.

"You know what? You're right. I'll write it down one of these days."

"What do you mean, one of these days? Today."

"Okay. I'll try it tonight."

"You swear?"

"I swear, you pest."

And here I am. I turn the page and begin.

THE ~~TRUE~~ HISTORY OF LI PO

Many, many, very many years ago, there lived in the far-off Chinese Empire a poet named Li Po, a man so skilled in the use of words that neither the river's transparency nor the ephemeral abundance of the dew could elude his well-aimed metaphors. Raised in an impoverished rural village, he turned up at the imperial court in the year 742. At that time, the city of the emperors was Ch'ang-an, a gilded metropolis whose denizens were heavily engaged in enjoying the splendor and opulence resulting from two decades of peace and exceptional harvests. No one paid any attention to the good Li Po. The story is told that for seven nights running he recited his poems aloud in the dark streets of Ch'ang-an without anyone noticing the beauty of his verse, perhaps because of the poet's rustic appearance, or perhaps because of his shrill, piercing voice, which did not do justice to his words. In desperation, Li Po frequented taverns, where he drowned his sorrows with wine. However, on the eighth night, the emperor's firstborn son, whose name was Ho Chi Chang, happened to pass in front of the Inn of the Winged Dragon, where Li Po had just finished declaiming some verses. The place was closed, but it is said that the poet was on his knees outside, holding in his hands his only audience: the chipped, empty glass from which he had drunk to excess. He began to recite again:

> *O wretched glass, you'll never be a mirror.*
> *Nor can I see myself in you—that's no surprise:*
> *I raise my voice and no one listens either.*

Ho Chi Chang, perhaps moved by the verses or by their author's groveling, had Li Po brought to the palace. He ordered that the poet be bathed, given a meal, and put to bed, where he would be wrapped in sheets of the finest silk. For weeks he was the guest of the prince, who not only provided for his material needs, but also, and more important, lent an attentive ear to his poems. A month passed before Ho Chi Chang dared to disturb his father.

Finally, the prince approached the emperor and said, "Hsüan-tsung, lord of the earth and everything that breathes upon it, wise and just father: I have in my house the greatest poet in all our empire."

"Bring him to me immediately," the emperor ordered.

"I do not dare to, Father," answered the son. "Though his verses are pure as moonlight, the poet has a defect that might offend you."

"And what is this defect? What could be so important and so terrible that it would sully the beauty of his verses, if they are as pure as you say?"

"He drinks a great deal, Father. He drinks at all hours of the day and night, and when the spirit of the wine takes possession of his tongue, what he sings are not odes, but merciless satires."

It is said that the emperor considered for a few seconds before deciding: "Bring him to me all the same. I want to hear him."

The following day, Li Po appeared before the supreme ruler. So fearful were the courtiers that the drunken poet might allow some unseemly words to slip in among his verses that a crystalline silence reigned in the court. But Li Po was sober. He recited his poems and dazzled the emperor, who ordered him to change his quarters without delay. In his new situation, the poet enjoyed even better food, smoother, more refined wines, and finer, more beautifully woven silks. In exchange for this lavish hospitality, the poet's only obligation was to recite a poem every day. And so he did, throughout that winter. Concerned with maintaining his privileges, and determined to preserve his benefactor's favor at all costs, Li Po gradually changed the nature of his verses; the plum tree abloom in winter appeared less often, and the perfect white of the river sand was compared not so much to the best rice paper, but to the perfect complexion and the pure, extraordinary face of the princess Yu Chen, the emperor's favorite daughter.

Li Po was not in love with Yu Chen. He simply flattered her and did his best to delight her, hoping that he would continue to merit the approbation of her all-powerful father. This trick worked so effectively that the emperor, not content with doubling his favors to the poet, made up his mind to accompany Li Po's readings with the legendary music of his jade flute. Such behavior was unheard of. Everyone knew that the mighty emperor was capable of extracting from his instrument notes that made even nightingales die of envy, but nobody had ever known him to put his music at the service of one of his subjects. So rare a favor aroused disdain, which sowed its seed, put down deep, vigorous roots, and invaded every chamber in the palace.

Then Kao Li Hi appeared, a powerful eunuch, a dreadful poet, and a schemer of the worst sort, whose mission in the palace was none other than the care and preservation of Yu Chen's virginity. Chagrined by the oblivion to which he had found himself consigned ever since the emperor decided to hear no line of verse that did not proceed from Li Po's masterly pen, the eunuch, availing himself of his closeness to the royal family, undertook to awaken in the monarch the hidden, sleeping beast of suspicion.

"Do you not see, sire, that he is deceiving you?" he said to the emperor, between flattery and falsehoods, as the great man dined. "You, who are so just and wise, do you not discern how he exploits your kindness and seeks only his own advantage?"

"Nothing could be further from the truth, Kao Li. Li Po's verses extol the honor of my family."

"Does this not seem to you too much happenstance, sire?" the eunuch asked the following day. "Is it not a remarkable coincidence that none other than your daughter is the object of his praise?"

Thus, insidiously and astutely, the eunuch applied himself to his task day after day, until eventually he succeeded in troubling the emperor's conscience as well as his sleep. In the end, the monarch, by now incapable of determining whether the truth lay in the dark warnings of Kao Li Hi or in the flattering verses of Li Po, summoned the poet and subjected him to an interrogation before all the dignitaries of the court.

"Li Po, damnable verse maker, they say that you deceive me!" the emperor bellowed as soon as the poet entered the hall.

"How could I, sire? In what way could such a one as I, an insignificant servant, deceive your highness, whose wisdom is renowned throughout your empire?"

"Be done with your flattery. They say that you mock my daughter."

"But, sire, you yourself have heard—"

"Yes, I know. I have heard your verses. I have been a witness to your admiration. But I am told that you lie every time you recite. They say that when you compare her eyes to the purest crystal, you refer not to their transparency but to their lack of expression."

Dispirited and dejected, the poet was unable to answer.

"They say," the emperor continued, in a bellow so powerful it made the palace's foundations shiver, "that when you declare her waist to be slender and supple as a reed, you think not of her graceful movements but of her humble, rustic appearance."

Li Po still did not reply. The dignitaries of the court stirred in their seats, unable to contain the murmuring that was slowly but surely growing louder.

"You have nothing to say? Am I to interpret your silence as an admission of your guilt? Damnation, Li Po, say something! Speak in your defense now, while you still have time. Otherwise, I will understand that those who accuse you of lying speak the truth, and in that case I will not hesitate to take your life with my own hands."

"Sire," Li Po finally stammered, his shrill voice reduced to a barely audible whine. The court shuddered in suspense. Hunched over, fragile, struggling to control himself, the poet spoke without daring to look his sovereign in the eyes. "Sire, you command me to speak, but you take away my words."

"How so, poet?"

"My compliments to whoever is the author of these calumnies. He has drawn a perfect circle around me, a trap from which there is no escape."

"What are you saying, Li Po? I don't understand you. You must speak louder and more clearly. The wine is heavy on your tongue."

"It is not the wine, sire," the poet said, daring to differ. "It is the cunning of my enemies."

Exclamations erupted in the emperor's court, but Li Po lifted a hand to silence them and, his voice now a little stronger, made a speech in his own defense that has figured in books of oriental history ever since as a model of oratory and rhetorical construction.

"Sire," he began, bowing his head as though asking for forgiveness. "If you do not believe my verses, it is useless for me to try to convince you. You have said that you are prepared to kill me if I have lied. As you are generous, you grant me this opportunity—for which I am perforce grateful—to demonstrate the truth of my verses and in doing so save my life. But for such an undertaking, I have no tools other than my words. I can but praise your daughter's beauty again. I can but reaffirm my old words with new words. And since you have admitted that you doubt the former, for what reason will you believe the latter? Yu Chen's supple carriage reminds me of reeds swaying in the wind. I can demonstrate this only by saying that the suppleness of reeds swaying in the wind reminds me of Yu Chen." Some of those present dared to assent silently to these words, but then they immediately hid their faces, fearful of inviting the wrath of the emperor. "You will grant, sire, that the trap in which I find myself is a difficult one. However, it is even worse than it appears. Imagine, for a moment, that I convinced you. Would you then believe that only admiration inspires my verses? I doubt it, because to convince you I would have to put so much emphasis on the princess's incomparable beauty, so much ardor into describing the purity of her soul, that you would then think me foolish and believe that I aspired to obtain her love and win her hand. I know very well who I am, sire. I know that I do not deserve such an honor. I know that such an audacious desire, such mad temerity, would also be punished by death. Why then should I defend myself, if I must face the same punishment whether I win or lose? You are the one who must find the solution to this injustice, sire. Look at your daughter. Look at her face when the moonlight shines on it and rocks its reflection in the river; look at the shadow of her feet when she walks on a bed of jasmine. Let your eyes be the judge of this matter. To know whether a man is lying, to know whether his words betray his intentions, is a task so impossible that it must be undertaken not by poets, sire, but by emperors."

Li Po, the crafty one, the great poet, had once again reduced the room to silence. With one magisterial stroke, he had just placed the emperor in as tight a spot as his own. Hsüan-tsung, he of the steady hand, he whose voice of thunder never trembled when the moment came to send his armies in search of death, the master of destiny, accustomed from the cradle to interpreting and announcing the will of the gods, suddenly felt incapable of making a decision. Tormented by doubt, he sent the poet away, but not before ordering him to appear at a final meeting, which was to take place in private the following day.

This time when the poet arrived, the emperor greeted him with a compliment: "You are clever, Li Po. You are very clever. I demand answers from you and you give me questions, but you will not get away with it. I lay awake all night, for as you know, my greatest desire is to be generous and just. I concede that you are right: only you can know if you are lying or not. However deeply I ponder your words, determining the truth of them does not fall within the scope of my reason. Not even if I tore out your heart could I know the intentions it harbors. Therefore I demand a response from you, but not to the question I asked you yesterday. It is not important that I know whether you admire my daughter or mock her. The answer I want now is to the question you yourself asked, and I want to hear it answered from your lips: How can one know if a man is lying? See to it that you give me a convincing reply by sunset, because otherwise I will cut off your sorcerer's tongue with my own sword."

Li Po considered the matter for a few moments and then replied, "I accept the task you give me, sire. Just is the punishment, if it seems just to you, but such haste is not just. Anyone who claims he can answer your question in so short a period of time is a madman, and his response will surely be wrong. To my regret, I find myself obliged to request that you give me rather more time."

"How much time do you need?"

"Ten years, sire."

The legend does not relate whether the poet blushed when he made his request, nor does it say whether the emperor was offended at hearing it. The proverbial ability of the East to measure time in grand cycles may have something to do with this omission. On the other hand, the legend does tell us that Hsüan-tsung granted Li Po his extended delay, but on certain conditions. "You shall have the time you ask of me," the emperor is supposed to have said. "More, if necessary. When the fruit of waiting will be so precious, ten is the same as ten times ten. But you will lose my protection and the shelter of the palace. I have already decreed your exile. This very evening you shall go into the forest, from whence you may not emerge until you can bring me the solution to this enigma, written in your own hand. And you must solve it yourself. You may not, therefore, as long as your banishment lasts, speak with any other person. I will make this prohibition known in every corner of my empire. Should you dare to leave the forest you shall be met with the most impenetrable silence, because I intend to make certain that all my subjects, even the very least of them, know that whosoever exchanges a single word with you, be it nothing more than a courteous greeting, will lose his tongue and perhaps his head. And, since on more than one occasion I have heard you declare that you find inspiration and answers in wine, you shall be forbidden to taste it. The truth must come from no place other than your heart."

The emperor's will was done. Li Po went off into the forest, carrying nothing but a dagger to defend himself from wild animals and a small sheaf of papers whereon he could write, should inspiration favor him, his answer to the emperor's question. Nothing more was heard of him. After ten years had passed, the emperor, surprised at having received no news, sent a party of his best men to search for the poet. They did not find Li Po. However, they were surprised to discover, fastened to a tree with the poet's dagger, the sheaf of papers, covered to the margins with the words of what historians of Chinese literature consider the most important poetic work of his time.

There has been much speculation about Li Po's end. Some say that the solitude of the forest sent its roots down into his mind and drove him mad. To support this theory, they put forward the difference between the first poem and the last in the poet's sheaf. The first poem says this:

You ask me why I am here, in the blue mountains.
I make no reply but simply smile, and my heart is at peace.
The flowers fall, the water runs, all things pass without trace.
This is my universe, different from the world of men.

In the last poem, on the other hand, the poet declares,

Today is not today, I find,
And my old self, a stranger.
Beset by doubt and danger,
I may have lost my mind.

Others, who also subscribe to the theory that Li Po went mad during his sojourn in the forest, attribute his affliction to the lack of his beloved wine. As support for their position, they offer another poem:

A pot of wine among the flowers.
There is no comrade to drink with me,
But I invite the moon,
And, counting my shadow, we are three.
The moon, however, does not drink,
And my shadow is content to follow me.

No one knows how Li Po died, nor where, nor when. Some soft voices, speaking behind closed doors and windows, beyond the range of the mighty emperor's sensitive ears, said that one night in the forest, the poet, captivated by the moon's reflection on the surface of a river and yearning toward the light, stepped into the water and was carried away by the current. However, since his body was never found, we must suspect that this final scene in Li Po's life belongs to the distant, improbable world of legend.

Mission accomplished; that's Papa's version of the story, as far as it goes. I'd even be so bold as to say that those were his exact words. After the word "legend," he made a sort of bow, a slight inclination of the head, and declared the story over. He had a hell of an imagination. None of the various biographical notes I've been able to find on the subject of Li Po is more than two or three pages long. Maybe there's something longer in Chinese, but I have no way of knowing anything about that. In any case, it makes no difference, because Papa couldn't speak Chinese.

The more I compare this story with the indisputable facts I've managed to find, the more I admire the intelligence with which my father gave free rein to his imagination. It's very easy to indicate the elements in Papa's story that don't correspond to Li Po's biography, all those that owe their existence solely to his urge to create a convincing atmosphere and give his tale the sweep of a legend; however, it's also impossible to demonstrate that any of those elements is false. That's why Papa's story about Li Po's exile is almost perfect. And if I say "almost," if I harbor some little reservations, that's only because Papa didn't do the research he should have done. The obsession with rigorously correct information and the capacity for shutting oneself up in a library are not part of his character. If I have this virtue, I must have inherited it from my mother, not from him. Had Papa taken the trouble to consult a couple of respectable anthologies, had he paused to reflect upon the multiple meanings of Li Po's life instead of getting carried away, he would have improved his story in several fundamental aspects.

First of all, the poems. Obviously, the quatrain that starts, "Today is not today, I find," does not come from the pen of Li Po. It's impossible. Although he composed many songs, he never padded his verses with such facile rhymes, and even if he had once yielded to such temptation, it seems highly unlikely that the rhyme would have been maintained in the translation. Put simply, Papa needed some lines to illustrate the hypothesis of Li Po's madness, and out of laziness, or pure vanity, he made them up. It's a shame, because there are some real poems that do indeed hint at a certain derangement and come from the last years of his life—which goes to show that Papa's poetic invention, precisely because it was unnecessary, may well have been true.

The second reservation is more important. It's true that nothing is known about Li Po's death. Papa embellished it with the image of the moon reflected in the river, but there's not even a legend about how the poet died, just a few hypotheses. The most credible attributes his demise to cirrhosis of the liver. There are also theories that speak of poisoning due to inhalation of mercury; what makes this condition relatively probable is the fact that Li Po, like every poet influenced by Taoism, spent many hours performing alchemical experiments. But it's impossible to know the truth. My father was unable to perceive that this was the missing element needed to turn his story into a perfect history. Li Po's disappearance without a trace was a monument to poetic justice. He had been required to give a response to an unsolvable dilemma: truth and lies; life and legend. Because no more was heard of him, his contemporaries were able to build a legend around his life, and my father, thirteen hundred years later, could do with it as he wished. I can almost imagine Li Po going into hiding before he died. "You accuse me of lying, as if a poet could do anything else," he must have thought. "But to explain my absence you will construct a lie so perfect that not even time will be able to overcome it." It's too bad that Papa didn't realize this. Nor did he give much consideration to the role of the emperor, to the unbearable heaviness that must have descended on the palace in the absence of Li Po. I imagine how Papa's story might have gone had he understood the significance of this possible ending, and what he could have done with the deranged emperor, wandering up and down the corridors of power, perhaps requiring the imperial band to play at all hours in order to mask that merciless silence, perhaps blaming himself for having chosen the truth and realizing that his choice had left him with nothing, or perhaps slitting the eunuch's throat with his own hands, as if doing so could allow him to return to the moment of his mistake and rectify it.

The third and last reservation is the most serious, because it's true that after the poet vanished from court, a manuscript was found that contained his answer to the emperor's insidious question. Now, I know that in all probability the emperor never asked him anything, and that the poet's disappearance was not exile but flight. But Li Po did leave behind an answer. It didn't turn up in the forest, pinned to a tree with his dagger. Nothing like that. The discovery took place in 837, sometime after his disappearance, when neither the emperor nor his son was still alive. The work is called *The Seven Proverbs of Li Po*, although this title is a convention agreed upon by sinologists. It was a manuscript of just eight pages. I have a facsimile edition, which was included in issue 28 of the journal *Poesía*, published by Editora Nacional in 1997 and dedicated in its entirety to the poetry of the Far East. The first page of the manuscript contained a title, *Seven Proverbs of the Lie*, but the first character, the one corresponding to the word "lie," was crossed out. Under it was written *Seven Proverbs of the Truth*, also with the first character crossed out, as if the poet had hesitated between these two titles, ultimately deciding on neither of them. This was my inspiration for calling the present history *The ~~True~~ History of Li Po*. After the indecisive title, each page of the manuscript contains a proverb, without any crossings-out, indeed without a correction of any kind, as if the poet had written all his proverbs with the fanatical certainty of one who believed he had stumbled upon a universal law. The first proverb goes like this: "He who utters a lie seeks to benefit from it." The second says, "He who pursues the truth seeks to benefit from it."

I wish this situation of mine had resulted from a premeditated plan. I'd be lying on the shore of the lake right now, breathing deeply, declaring to myself that everything had worked out really well. If it were a film, we'd be about to have the final scene, a glorious close-up in which I take my leave of the audience, perhaps with a final wink at the camera. I've seen lots of films on this subject: someone fakes his own death and, from the impunity of his supposed demise, he keeps weaving the threads of the plot and bending the living to his will. There are a few differences though. For example, if this were a film, the last scene wouldn't be set here in this inhospitable place but in some Polynesian paradise, say, or in the gaming room of a casino in Monte Carlo. Furthermore, I'd probably be a man. All right, maybe these days there's a fair possibility that the protagonist of such a story would be a woman, but then, at the last moment, a man would appear by my side. A coup de théâtre for the audience: the secret, forbidden lover, the object of desires whose satisfaction would have been impossible in my former life, hence my disappearance. Or maybe the camera, in an apparently casual pan, would reveal the presence, at my feet, of a sack containing a stash of dollars, or perhaps, in the backseat of a convertible, a trunk full of jewels.

But this is real life and there's no final, well-rounded explanation capable of justifying all this confusion. If this is the end of the film, then here I am, with nothing and nobody, and the audience will leave the theater complaining the whole thing was a rip-off. I would join in their protests, because this muddle is not the result of a plot, but its origin. It didn't begin when I announced to my children my decision to go to Guatemala, or when an outboard motor sliced Judith's face in half, or when our bodies were floating together like corks on the water. And not when chance played a little game with my papers and won, thanks to my cooperative silence.

No, the confusion started earlier than that, and I brought it here, or it came with me, which isn't the same thing. It wasn't a twist of fate that turned this jungle into the precincts of the dead; I did it. I wanted to spend some time alone. I especially wanted to think in peace and quiet. Well, I've done it. I've thought a great deal, and now I'm suffering the consequences of knowing. Because I know several things. I know that my only reason for coming here was to stifle the monotonous whimpering with which every muscle in my body was announcing the irreparable deterioration of time. I was the one who brought death to this lake because I came here for that very reason: to die.

Maybe it's an exaggeration to say that. Perhaps it would be more accurate to say that I came here to prepare myself. This may seem like a contradiction, but I've spent my whole life trying to ignore this moment. It's as if a builder, always busy constructing houses for other people, should forget to repair the cracks in his own. To have seen death playing its joke on humankind in every possible language doesn't make me immune to its laughter.

My father, for example. My father died an old man. He was ninety-one. He spent barely two months in bed, and was only intermittently conscious; his lungs were flooded, but he wasn't in much pain. A few minutes before he died, he suffered an attack of coughing that sounded as though it were going to suffocate him. I was sitting at his bedside, and I pulled him up to a sitting position, gave him a few futile claps on the back, and also fed him a spoonful of cough syrup. When I realized that my efforts were in vain, I laid him back down on the bed and started to call the doctor. With the scant strength remaining in his hands, Papa held me back. He looked into my eyes, shook his head, and said to me, "There's no need." And then he died. It's good to die like that, but such a death wasn't enough for me. I wanted more than just that last-minute lucidity, that ability to lower my guard at the end and accept defeat. No, I wanted to win the battle. I wanted to say to death, "Don't try to surprise me; I know you too well. I've spent my whole life studying you."

Well, maybe the verb "wanted" is a bit grand for my purposes, especially in view of the results. What I felt was less than a wish; it was more like a low rumbling I was barely aware of, a notion stored in a remote corner of my brain. That's where all my knowledge of death was, hiding in the corner where you keep old treasures now rendered useless by time and disorder.

So that's why I came here, then. To establish the necessary order before the day comes to move. I've dedicated many hours to this over the past few weeks, and I'm not exactly proud of my success. Has my attempt, therefore, been a failure? Maybe so. Which means the order I was looking for won't be in my luggage when I go back; instead, I'll have a chaotic universe divided in two by the Río Pasión: on this side, a kingdom of the dead, to which I don't yet belong; and on the other, the great beyond, a kingdom of the living, where no one's waiting for me. They will be grieving for my absence, of course, and maybe they're striving to remember me without knowing how that striving condemns me to oblivion. What a state of affairs: for me alone, life, not death, is the great beyond.

If the faithful Amkiel knew the myths of my culture as well as I know his, every time he encountered those islets, he'd feel like a combination of Charon and the Phoenix; like a gravedigger when he went in, and like a midwife when he came out. In and out; in and out. It will be odd to pass through those islands again with this new perspective when I set out on my return journey. Because I know I'll go back in the end, and I know my return can't be postponed too much longer.

So I came here in order to arrive at the brilliant conclusion that I have to go back? Second meditation, second failure. Or maybe not. Maybe this is the only way to learn something, to establish that I was mistaken and perceive that I'll be mistaken again. In this case, to accept that dying is the last work of the living and that I can perform it only in *the land of the living. The jungle, the silence, and the distance may make this a good place to be dead, but not a good place to die.*

This is no revelation. I've had no epiphany, no secret wisdom has suddenly been visited upon me, nor any flash of knowledge. All it takes is adding up what I know, and I'm surprised I wasn't capable of doing that until now. Even though every culture I'm familiar with resists the notion that a "good" death is preferable to life, they all make a distinction between good deaths and bad ones. A good death takes place at home, no words are left unspoken, and the dying person is surrounded by the living. A bad death is what chance invented for me, with some assistance from my silence: a death by drowning in a remote place, alone, with no chance to say those final words that I may never be able to say, not even if I go back, because my return won't erase what I've learned here.

Lies. Maybe, if I had died in this jungle, "lies" would have been my final word. If the water had risen up in front of me one day, as it did to Judith. Lies. Simón's a lie, Julio and I and our children are lies, the love that made all this possible is a lie. The Russian woman's a lie; the stories are lies; this life is a necessary lie. I'd say, "Lies," and it would be the truth. Now my only hope is that life will show some consideration and grant me a little time. In exchange, I promise to make the most of that time by using it to choose my final words with great care. I want to deserve a good death, or as close to one as I can get, and therefore it's important that my final words should be constructive, should contribute to building something, even if it's precisely the house of cards I'd prefer to demolish with a sweep of my hand.

Dying well doesn't mean eluding pain; it means avoiding surprises. If you're a Hindu, you'll try to die in Varanasi, preferably during the winter solstice, amid hymns extolling the names of the gods. If not, people will say that you didn't die "your proper death." Like me, since I've died Judith's death, but not my own. Among Hindu ascetics, a case like mine would be odd, but they'd accept my return. They'd interpret it as part of the gods' plan and consider me a sort of lost soul, a ghost.

They'd have pity on me, and they'd even make an effort to console my spirit, which they would assume to be in torment. However, they'd refuse to eat with me. The logic is crushing: ghosts don't eat. It could be worse. If I belonged to the Dogon tribe, I'd be completely ignored after my return to the village. No one would address a word to me. Yet, after my eventual, real death, they'd finally acknowledge my existence and perform the necessary rites for my remains.

If I were a Lugbara, I'd have to die at home, lying on my bed, surrounded by my family, and only after uttering my last words. Then someone would intone the cere and recite in song the best known facts of my life. I believe I've already described this, but I don't know whether I mentioned that it would be of particular importance to the Lugbara only if I were a man. As a woman, I could die more or less any way I pleased, because no one would care too much.

In general, time and space define the quality of a death, as they do a life. A death is good only if it comes when and where it is fitting and proper. To die unexpectedly, whether from a sudden illness, an accident, or through an act of violence, is a curse. And to die where you shouldn't is an error. As simple as that. Obviously, the person who cares least about the possible goodness or badness of a death is the dead person in question. The dead are long gone, so they don't matter. Those who do matter are the living, with their obsession for maintaining the fiction that death is something that always happens to other people. For being immortal as long as they live.

With the exception of the Wari, all tribes, including our own, treat death as if it were the last lion left in an impoverished circus: they put chains around its neck, file down its sharp teeth, and put their heads in its mouth so the children will believe that the beast has been tamed. That's why funeral rites and the laws of transmission exist: to make something routine out of the only event in life that can't possibly be routine, because it happens only once. The Hindu Aghori and the Dinka witch doctors reach the limits of this misrepresentation in that they conduct their own funeral celebrations. As leaders of their respective communities, they're so powerful they manage to preside over the ceremonies attendant upon their own deaths while they're still alive. In the case of the Aghori, their control reaches such incredible extremes that they are capable of altering the nature of their bodies: they can go for many minutes without breathing and mentally control all their vital fluids, including their semen, whose flow they are even able—according to legend—to reverse; that is, they can reabsorb it into the penis after ejaculation. Through the use of some astonishing techniques, they enter a state they call samādhi, an existence suspended in space and time, identical to Brahma's when he created the world. In samādhi there are no living and no dead, because it's a state that precedes the rise of this duality. The Aghori claim to have control over when their death will take place. They put themselves on a level with the gods.

Control. That's why we want to die at home. No more arguments are necessary. The conclusion is clear: if I want to die well, I have to prepare for my return home. It makes no sense to keep going over it in my mind. And I can use my last few days here to resolve the two doubts that plague me. The first one may seem minor or even ridiculous, but I can't get it out of my head. What should I do? Or rather, how should I do it? I could go down to Sayaxché and send an e-mail. From: igarcialuna@limbo.com. To: my children. Subject: the mistake. Dear all, although this may strike you as impossible, I'm alive and . . . Ridiculous. Absolutely ridiculous. I could also telephone. I'd call Alberto, I suppose. And what would I say to him? Hello, son, I'm calling from beyond the grave to tell you I'm alive. I immediately eliminate this possibility and go back to thinking that an e-mail might be the best idea; it would be less of a shock. I could also go back and present myself in person, without warning. But what would I do? Appear in a white robe, trailing chains? I have to take that idea as a joke, because nothing else occurs to me.

Therefore, I'm doing what we all do when we don't know what to do: nothing. I haven't hooked up the radio transmitter for some time, *but I'm sure that as soon as I do, I'll hear the news that the tourists are about to arrive. I'm only stalling for a little more time so I can figure out the least harmful way to proceed. I think about my children all day long. That's all I do. And about Julio, too. I think about our reunion. Not about the beginning, not about the initial shock or the happiness or the wailing. I think about what must happen next. Does Julio even know I'm dead? Surely they've told him, and he probably took a shaky part in the rituals of my alleged demise. But who knows what goes on in his brain while his neurons are spinning out into space? It's impossible to predict his reaction: he may not recognize me, or he may give me an emotional welcome home, as if I were returning from a long trip, or he may greet me normally, calmly, as if only a few days had gone by.*

I don't know what's going to happen with Alberto, either. Maybe he'll die of shame. Or he could go crazy, for once in his life, when I say look at me, Alberto, look me in the face, smell me, tell me I'm not your mother. Will I say that? It's also possible that he'll be indignant and let himself get carried away by angry questions, like where the fuck were you, Mama, and what took you so long? I can't deny my children the right to interrogate me. Even Pablo—his questions will be bewildered, wordless; his questions will be in his eyes. Poor Pablo. And I don't even want to think about Serena.

I don't even want to think about her, but I can't help myself. Because that's my second worry, which may be less urgent than the first but is also more important. If my calculations are correct, I was declared dead more than three weeks ago. That means it's been at least ten days since Alberto and Serena left Flores with my ashes. Let's suppose they dedicated two or three days to completing the procedures necessary for getting rid of me and my memory: scattering my ashes, maybe spending time together in Malespina and sharing their recollections. And let's give them, say, two or three days more, for whatever reason: maybe Serena needed to rest after the trip and all the emotion, maybe it took them more time than it should have to make their way through all the bureaucratic red tape. However I do the math I'll be getting back too late. I have no doubt that Serena's already been in my office. If there's one thing I can say about my children, it's that they've learned to share our family duties. Order is Alberto's department. Therefore he took care of making all the official arrangements: the identification (if we can call it that) of the body, the cremation, and so forth. In the same way, history is Serena's affair. And since my death has turned me into history, I'm in her hands. The mere thought of Serena in my office, with all the drawers of my filing cabinets open, taking notes, filling boxes with papers, scribbling interminable lists of questions in some notebook, simply terrifies me. Poor Serena, I can just see her, avidly opening each folder. And, above all, I can imagine—fearfully—her intelligence, her tremendous ability to turn each new piece of information into a well-aimed query. She must have sharp, penetrating, hungry questions. The entire history of the family ends in a question mark. And I don't know what I'm going to do. For many years I pretended not to know the answers to many of the doubts tormenting my daughter. Now I will be obliged to respond to the information in Serena's hands. Truth is a lighthouse: I can use it to show that the coast is safe, or to illuminate rocks, or to give ships lost in the night the ability to see one another. I can also use its light to burn my daughter's eyes. Or even worse, I can use it in the manner of the old-time pirates who lit bonfires in the middle of reefs so that ships would be deceived by that false light of truth and run aground, irretrievably.

SATURDAY

"What would you say if I asked you to describe what Grandma was like?" Luis said to his father, when dinner was just about over. "Without making a speech, okay? In four words."

"Four words? Different. Intelligent." He paused. "A little mysterious."

"One more to go."

"Come on, it's not easy. I'm thinking. Clear-headed, maybe."

"How about you?" Luis said, looking at Pablo and inviting him to join in.

"Oof. Intelligent and different—I'll go along with those. And authentic, and . . . I don't know. Frail." He flashed one of his killer smiles.

Luis was in a playful mood. "What do you think?" he asked us. "Shall we try, Grandpa?"

"Leave him alone," I said at once. "He won't understand you."

"Go ahead and try," Pablo urged. "You don't need anyone's permission."

"Grandpa, what four words would you use to describe Grandma?"

Papa remained absorbed, staring at the bowl of strawberries in front of him.

"You see? I told you he—"

"She had adorable feet," Papa's voice suddenly rang out, loud and clear this time. "Reserved. Unique. Surprising."

"Told you so!" Pablo exclaimed, scolding me for being skeptical.

"Invalid answer," Alberto said, always meticulous about the rules of any game. "He used more than four words."

"Your turn, Serena. You're the only one left."

"You're going to have to excuse me; I pass." In order to avoid a good browbeating, I immediately stood up. "I'm going to water the plants. It hasn't rained for days. Will someone put on some coffee?"

It's only a game, I know that, and refusing to take part only gives it more importance than it deserves. But it tires me. We've spent decades playing this game, exchanging labels the way children exchange picture cards. We're family. Boats from the same shipyard, constructed out of the same wood. We've sailed together many miles. We're in different seas, but we're more than familiar with the routes and the ports. We recognize one another at a distance, the same way you recognize certain ships, whether the night is foggy or not. We know one another so well, we don't even need to talk. I mean *really* talk; I'm not referring to the good-natured banter we continually exchange.

Papa had an old spyglass with which he used to scour the horizon off Malespina from this very terrace. He was proud of his ability to recognize just about any vessel that hove into sight. "There goes the *Altazor*," he'd say after barely a glance through the telescope. "She's moving more slowly than usual." A little while later, he'd say, "Look, the *Pañacocha*. She's late." Another pause, and then: "That's the same cargo ship that went down to Barcelona yesterday. She's already on her way back to Genoa." Sometimes he'd hear the distant rumble of a motor and make some daring assertion, such as, "The *Salamandra*'s not bringing back much of a catch."

Recognition isn't knowing. To recognize someone is to confirm that she's the person you already knew she was. To consider her a given. Mama was different; everyone's in agreement about that. But what does "different" mean? Or "intelligent"? Papa says, "Surprising." Seems like a contradiction because someone surprising is necessarily impossible to define. To say that something is impossible to define is a way of defining it. The contradictions link up to form a chain but the links in the chain are void of meaning.

Four words? Forget about it. The four words I'd like to hear are the ones that no one will ever say. The ones that were swallowed up forever in the clammy mists of Papa's brain. Mama's words, maybe spoken in a language I don't know, in some tribal confab made up of gestures. And my words. Pablo's four words come only from a piano. Not when he practices, and not on the rare occasions when he consents to entertain us: a little Beethoven for Mama, or some popular songs so Papa can imitate Chet Baker singing "Everything Happens to Me." No, I mean when he plays for real: when he unleashes the pack of wolves that hide in his piano. Those wolves are his four words.

Poor Pablo, I don't know what's going to happen with his music. I often tell him that being successful isn't any sort of betrayal, that he has to pay more attention to his career, that he's full of neuroses, and that he's acting like a capricious diva. Still, I can't help admiring his courage. To say nothing of the sacrifices he's made. The hours of practicing, good God, the millions of hours, and the cramps in his fingers. He never missed a single day. Not even when Antonia attempted to persuade him that music was a wonderful hobby but no good for making a living. She set all sorts of traps for him, including spectacular offers to work in her father's real estate company. Antonia wanted to travel and have fun and dine out and enjoy herself and own a very large yacht and have fun and live better and have fun; in short, she had very legitimate aspirations, except that she used them to torment Pablo, who didn't even need to breathe as long as he had a piano. He was twenty-one and had just won his first laurels, and festival directors were calling him up and record companies were fighting over him and critics were saying that Barcelona had never produced a pianist of his caliber, with the possible exception of Tete Montoliu. And Pablo had to hide in Alberto's house to practice on the Steinway so Antonia wouldn't find out. For these reasons, I rejoiced when they separated. I don't know if I've ever told Pablo this, but the night they broke up, I opened a bottle of champagne.

Antonia was an idiot, a rich bitch, the kind they made in those days, the genuine article. God, she said "pliz" instead of "please." And "papi" instead of "papa." And she said, "you know what I mean," and she said, "and so on and so forth," and I'm sure she says "awesome" today, still in that same cloying, nasal voice. Dammit, Pablo was a musician, so he had to have good ears. How could he fall in love with someone like that? Granted, he had eyes, too, and Antonia was a beautiful blonde, but I still don't understand it. How an intelligent, sensitive, creative man could fall in love with such a person remains a mystery to me. He gave a whole series of excuses; he said there was no better encounter than the meeting of two opposites and talked about complementary worlds. What do I know? They say that love is blind, and experience has taught me it's foolish too, but there's no reason why it has to be quite so stupid.

The reason must be written in his four words, which would probably also explain why he always chooses the least viable option, the one that leads straight to a disaster. If he has a triumph with a jazz trio, he wants his next record to contain nothing but symphonic music; if the public applauds his versions of the classics, he decides to compose his own pieces; if he is praised for his technical complexity, he opts for minimalism. I could go on. Now he's got himself involved in a tremendous row. He told me about it on our trip to Guatemala. It seems his record company is putting pressure on him. They want him to make a new record, and according to the terms of the contract, he's obliged to go into their studio to record. Moreover, they want him to return to the kind of music he used to play back in his glory days, when he used to receive invitations to tour practically the whole world. But he refuses. He says his mistake isn't that he doesn't have a new record; it's that he signed a contract in the first place. He says no one, no lawyer, no judge, can force him to record anything he doesn't want to. When Pablo utters the word "lawyer," he grows fangs. He says that when he's ready his next record will be called *The End of the World*. He wants to have the piano mounted on the deck of a boat and go sailing in a storm one night while bashing the keys with a mallet in each hand. At first, I took this as a joke. I told him not to worry about getting the storm right, because I'd be able to give him plenty of notice when a good one was approaching. But then I realized he was serious. Pablo has lots of faults but nobody can touch him when it comes to being audacious.

We had a fine conversation. In fact, the entire flight to Guatemala was fantastic, because we talked for hours, the first time that had happened in a long while. Furthermore, we were in first class, comfortable and well looked after. Alberto took care of that; according to Pablo, it was our brother's way of assuaging his guilt for not having been able to make the trip with us. "I can't," he said when we tried to convince him that he was the right man for the job. "It's impossible. I'll see to all the arrangements, I'll talk with whoever needs talking to, I'll do everything I can from here. But you'll have to go by yourselves." He suggested that he had to take care of Luis and mentioned various pending judgments and shareholders' meetings. Of course, by the time we left, he'd seen to everything: we had a folder with the names and telephone numbers of the people we might have to contact, from the Spanish consul to the undertaker; with the receipt for the hotel room, paid in advance; and with our confirmed reservations on the connecting flight between Guatemala City and Flores. Everything in writing and highlighted in at least three different colors. Alberto-style. And that's exactly what Pablo and I were talking about when we took off, about how meticulous our brother is, about the place he occupies in the world. We agreed that he's the most generous person we've ever met. Pablo opined that all generosity implies some selfishness; we didn't agree much on that point, but I resisted the impulse to argue with him about it, because we've already had that discussion too many times.

Then we talked about me for a while. I held back. I didn't feel like telling him I was pregnant, and naturally I preferred not to mention Ismael. So we talked a bit about my work, about my apartment, innocuous subjects like that. But Mama's shadow was traveling with us, and, little by little, we went back to talking about her. I admitted that I was very afraid and very angry; that I'd never wanted Mama to make the trip; that death by drowning was one of the most horrible ways to die, second only to burning to death; that I wasn't at all looking forward to seeing her corpse; and that ever since we got the news of her death, I'd been having nightmares filled with seaweed. Pablo listened to me the way he always does, without interrupting, looking me in the eyes, giving a nod now and then, but not feeling obliged to produce a steady stream of comment. He let me finish, and then he said that he felt just the opposite; that he had to see Mama one last time, that he wouldn't rest easy until he saw her.

"If I can, I'll give her a butterfly kiss," he said, and I supposed he was saying it as a joke to calm me down. Butterfly kisses were what Mama gave us when we were little and she put us to bed. If she wasn't on a trip. First there was an Eskimo kiss, where we rubbed noses, followed by the butterfly kiss: she'd lay her forehead on ours so that we were eye to eye with her, and then we'd blink really fast so our eyelashes would touch. "And if I can't, at least I'll see her face for the last time."

"Don't. Imagine what it's going to be like. They say that people's heads swell up when they drown—"

"I don't care about that," Pablo said, interrupting me. "Swollen or not, it's still hers."

"Spare me the bravado," I said. "I can read you like a book. You're as nervous as I am."

"You really think so? Well, you're mistaken. I'll admit I'm a little nervous right now, but that's only because I can't smoke."

"So, Pablo," I said, imitating Mama's voice. "We didn't even know you smoked."

It was a joke. He understood it at once and laughed so hard he almost choked. I kept quiet for a bit, surprised by the memory of Antonia that lay hidden in those words. Antonia's been on my mind a lot recently—that is, ever since the woman with the big blonde hair drove Pablo to the house the other day. Before that, I hadn't thought about her in years. Pablo's laughter surprised me, too. Since he and Antonia separated, we never mentioned her, not even in passing. When they broke up, she disappeared almost overnight, as though she had died in combat. I don't think we kept quiet about Antonia to spare Pablo's feelings, because even when he wasn't around, the rest of us never even uttered her name. Now I wonder why. Were we following Papa's maxim, forgetting about it and moving on to something else? Were we silent out of respect? Admirable, but hardly likely. I'm afraid a sense of shame probably had something to do with it. Or lack of practice. In our family, each of us has always washed his dirty clothes in private.

It was a July night in 1986. Pablo had recently turned twenty-five, and in theory he was enjoying the most triumphant period of his life; barely a week before, he'd played his first solo concert at the Palau de la Música in Barcelona as part of the jazz festival, and for the first time the program had consisted entirely of his own compositions. They'd been received with tumultuous applause, he'd been called back for several encores, and in the following days his concert was hailed as the moment that defined him as a truly important artist. I have the article from *La Vanguardia* framed in the entrance hall of my apartment. Every time Pablo sees it, he gets annoyed and asks me to take it down. Out of the question. Fuck him if he doesn't like it. He gets that from Mama, that haughty false modesty. As if I'm not supposed to be proud of my own brother. I know the article almost by heart, at least the beginning of it: "Pablo Azuera is not only an exceptional pianist. His compositions are destined to become fundamental chapters in the history of jazz. Like Thelonious Monk in his day, like Chick Corea after that, and more recently Petrucciani, Azuera reinvents the piano; he searches its keyboard and discovers new, brilliant keys, but the sounds he produces are so coherent and logical, it seems monumentally surprising that no one has come up with them before." If those aren't the exact words, they're close, and they lead to a tremendous climax: "The concert of the night before last was an authoritative knock at the gates of music history, that is, music with a capital *M*, transcending all genres. Azuera's music is like life; it moves you when you listen to it, but you don't understand it until it ends." Sounds to me like a resounding success, no matter how much Pablo tries to diminish its importance.

Several days after the concert, Antonia invited the whole family to a surprise party, a kind of tribute to Pablo. Without his finding out, she'd managed to obtain a surprise videotape of the entire performance. What an awesome time we'll have, she said. The idiot. She was an idiot, and we were stupid. We all went over to Alberto's place because his television set had the best sound, and because that way Antonia could keep Pablo away from the preparations until the last moment. When he arrived, Pablo seemed genuinely surprised to see the whole family and accepted with good grace our wish to celebrate his success. We drank aperitifs, joking and raising our glasses. Then we sat down at the table, and after the first course had been served, Antonia put the video in the player and announced, "Now comes the surprise. Let's drink a toast to the artist."

If there really were such a thing as selective memory, I wish mine could erase that moment forever. I can still see Antonia as if she were standing in front of me, a bottle of wine in one hand, the remote control in the other. She was wearing a short black dress, a red coral necklace, and her big pearl earrings. I especially remember the light in her eyes, a perverse light, like a lighthouse searching the horizon for ships, not to guide them but to expose their fragility. She turned on the video, and still without sitting down, she encouraged us to watch the screen.

"A video?" Pablo protested. "You must be fucking kidding."

"No, actually, I'm not the one who's fucking anything," Antonia said, and now it seems incredible that none of us realized what was going to happen and that nobody did anything to stop it. "Shhh," she said, raising a finger to her lips. "A little silence, pliz. The beginning's rather difficult to hear."

The television screen was still black, and at first all our ears could pick out were a few unrecognizable sounds. Then, little by little, they became identifiable: the hinges of a door, perhaps a lift; a man's voice; a woman's laugh; muffled footsteps on a carpet. Suddenly, much clearer, the unmistakable sound of a key entering a lock. The screen was still black.

"Aren't we going to see the concert?" I asked. Naïvely.

"Ah, it's the concert?" Pablo seemed relieved.

The first images appeared as soon as the door opened. It was an impersonal room, the kind you find in thousands of hotels, with the bed in the center, flanked by two night tables, each with its own lamp. The unnatural foreshortening of the image made me think that the camera must be in a corner of the ceiling. You could see almost the entire room, but the focus was centered on the bed, leaving everything else in a kind of semidarkness. All at once, on the left side of the screen, you could make out the shapes of a man and a woman wrapped in an embrace, taking off their clothes with rough, jerky movements in a circular dance. They didn't stop until they came to one of the night tables, where they paused briefly, no more than a couple of seconds, on their way to the bed, but time enough for the man to take a few deep drags on a cigarette that they proceeded to share, smoking it between kisses until the man crushed it out in the ashtray.

Pablo dropped his silverware onto his plate with a loud clatter, but no one looked at him. Or rather, we were all looking at him, but not directly; we were staring at his image—the man was now unmistakably him—as he sat the woman down on the bed and began kneading her breasts like an eager baker. As soon as Papa realized that the protagonist of the video was his son, he muttered, "I don't have to see this"; then he rose to his feet, left the room, and shut himself up in the kitchen. To forget, I suppose. To move on to something else. Mama sat completely still, like a marble statue mounted on her chair.

After a few seconds, all of us started talking at once, with the exception of Pablo, who was giving Antonia a murderous look. Antonia still hadn't sat down, and it was clear she had no intention of doing so. Suddenly, just at the moment when Pablo, with his trousers around his ankles, penetrated the woman, Antonia raised the volume, and the dining room was invaded by a series of gasps and exclamations that I will not describe here, not so much out of modesty but because of the pain, the immense pain the sight of Pablo caused me. The woman was all legs, which she flung around him with great force, as if she were going to engulf him, as if the video were on the verge of turning into a sort of apocalyptic cartoon from which the two bodies would disappear in the end, leaving behind no trace. What a contradiction: when the pleasure radiating from those images was at its height, the pain they produced was deepest. I could glimpse Pablo out of the corner of my eye, sitting there still and speechless, but still clinging somehow to the remains of his dignity and pride. My eyes were darting around like wasps, from Antonia to Pablo, to the other Pablo, to Mama, and back to Antonia, until finally I blurted out, "Enough! Please!"

At the same time, Alberto, as always, swung into action. He got up and tore the TV plug out of its socket. Antonia didn't seem to care. Mission accomplished. In a last, dramatic gesture, she poured her glass of wine down the front of Pablo's shirt, turned on her heels, and left the apartment, slamming the front door. She's been gone ever since. Well, until last Tuesday, if my suspicions are correct. Her departure was followed by an enormous silence, broken only when Mama said, in a low, tremulous voice, "So, Pablo, we didn't even know you smoked."

In other circumstances, it would have been an excellent joke. Ever since the moment when Antonia pressed Play, Pablo had maintained absolute silence. "Don't worry, Mama," he said now, as if the scene we'd just witnessed had been a minor incident. "I hardly ever smoke. Just a joint every now and then."

Now we laugh about it. Or at least we did the other day, in the airplane. But at the time, it was terrible. I've never seen Pablo as upset as he was then. The odd thing is that he was telling the truth when he said he hardly ever smoked. It was only after the scene with Antonia that he started lighting up one cigarette after another, hardly pausing between drags. That wasn't the only change. He never had another serious relationship. He started expounding his lengthy theories about what's authentic and what isn't. He withdrew even further into his scores. It was also around this time that he began to show a kind of persecution complex, according to which all lawyers were earthly representatives of the devil himself. All of them, including his own brother, Alberto. These days they joke about it, but in the months immediately following the separation, Pablo's attitude caused more than one row. Antonia decided to make his life a living hell, and armed with the crushing evidence we'd all seen, she not only asked for the sale of all their common property, but also insisted on a degree of financial compensation that Pablo had no possibility of providing. He responded to her lawyer's demands with silence, and when Alberto told him he must negotiate some sort of compromise, Pablo curtly replied that he was too busy with his music to waste time with legalistic mumbo jumbo. He said, "Let her have me arrested. I'll have a lot of time to compose in jail. I don't even need a piano." The male genes passed on in this family carry a heavy load of obstinacy and melodrama.

In the end, Alberto solved the problem. He called up Antonia and arranged to meet her in a café. According to what he told me, the conversation was so brief that it was over before the waiter even had time to take their order.

"I don't want to see my brother in front of a judge," Alberto said. "And I don't intend to let you drive him insane."

"Darling, you don't need to worry about that," Antonia replied. I can picture her serpent's smile. "He can do the 'drive him insane' part all by himself."

"Which is exactly why I want you to leave him in peace."

"Well, there's a very simple way to get me to do that."

"How much?" Alberto asked brusquely.

"Forty million pesetas."

"You're mad. All you've got coming to you is half of the apartment and half of the car."

"Plus compensation for my mental health. I'm very depressed."

"I've seen your petition. You're very clever and your lawyer is good. I mean your daddy's lawyer. But you don't have any children to use for leverage, so you'll have to be satisfied with less."

"For example?"

"Ten."

"Ha, ha, ha. No way, pal. You're the one who's mad."

"Fifteen, and no higher."

"Sixteen. A banker's draft. By this evening."

"Give me twenty-four hours."

"You've got until two tomorrow afternoon. After that, time's up. And I'm doing you a favor."

"You have no idea how grateful I am."

"Don't be sarcastic, Alberto. Any way you look at it, I'm the victim in this sorry business."

"That may be. But you have to admit, when you reduce it all to a mere question of money, it becomes a little vulgar."

"I'll admit that tomorrow, after you pay me."

The following day, in the same place, Alberto handed her the check and had her sign a series of documents, in which she renounced any further claims. That same evening when Pablo learned of the settlement, he flew into a rage, accused Alberto of meddling in his personal affairs, and threatened to do something crazy, though he never specified the kind of crazy thing he was talking about.

"She's within her legal rights," Alberto explained, trying to placate him. "It was the best deal you could get."

"Well, it may be legal, but I don't think it's just. I suppose that little nuance is invisible to a lawyer."

Angered by this remark, Alberto reviewed the situation for Pablo, declaring that he, Pablo, had no right to talk about justice. He reminded him that the law was on Antonia's side and that she had conclusive proof of her claims. Pablo answered that no law could tell him where he could and could not put his dick, and furthermore, he said, the only thing the evidence proved was Antonia's resolve to make his life miserable. Alberto counterattacked, telling him no new evidence or detectives or hidden cameras had been required to accomplish that particular end, as we had all known it was inevitable since before they got married, all of us except him, and since he hadn't been capable of realizing in time that he was marrying a materialistic, unscrupulous woman, his only recourse now was to face the facts and accept the consequences. If there was any time in their lives when they were really close to coming to blows, that was it. Then Alberto, seeing that confrontation wasn't getting him anywhere, changed his strategy. "This is the best solution for you," he insisted. "It's over and done with. The price has been paid. Now you can forget the whole thing and concentrate on your music."

"I'm old enough to decide what's best for me," Pablo said. "And furthermore, you're mistaken. I may have a lot less cash than you do, but I've never been in debt. The mere thought of owing you that much money makes me feel demented. Who could compose in such a state? How do you expect me to concentrate? Besides, I don't know how I'll find the time. I'm going to have to work hard to pay you back."

"You don't have to pay me back."

"So I'll be in your debt for the rest of my life? No, thanks."

"Don't be so proud, Pablo. It's very simple: I have a lot of money, and you don't. That's what brothers are for, dammit. Look at it this way: it's as if I've made an investment."

"An investment? Like I'm some kind of racehorse?"

"No, jackass. You're a musician. A fucking musician. And I'm investing in your music. I settle the problem with Antonia, you dedicate yourself to composing, and you pay me back with your music."

"No, Alberto. My music isn't currency. I'll pay you back every peseta in cash, no matter how long it takes."

And he did. Not, of course, thanks to his revenues from the five compact discs he's put out since then. Despite the great admiration my brother's talent arouses among specialists, jazz doesn't pay all that well. Moreover, there's the fundamental change that came over him after the fiasco of his marriage. Little by little, his music became less amiable and turned darker and more personal. Or, to be completely frank, more incomprehensible. I suppose in some respects the change was a positive thing. Pablo's prestige increased until it transformed him into a "cult composer," admired and respected by his fellow professionals as one of the pioneers, but treated with caution by the audience. It became harder for him to fill a concert hall. Things have now reached the point where he can make a living from his music, but barely. I admire the way he's been able to remain faithful to two contradictory promises: one to his art, which he has kept free of all interference; and one to Alberto, whom he's been paying back through all sorts of odd jobs, for which he steals hours from his sleep, from his leisure time, from everything except his music. That's how he's spent the last few years: more chastened, more exhausted and sleep-deprived; but also happier, if by happiness we understand a certain aura that emanates from people who have succeeded in living according to their priorities.

"At least back then, you only smoked joints," I said on the airplane, keeping the joke alive. "And very few, at that."

"I smoked less, it's true," he answered, finally recovering from his laughing fit. For a moment, he looked as though he might be taking the matter seriously. "And I was bored more," he added.

We spent the rest of the trip critiquing Mama with great affection. We laughed a lot. It was a tribute to her. We recalled the fits she threw whenever Papa mentioned the Russian woman, and then there was no way of stopping the memory merry-go-round. "Poor Mama. The only one who fulfilled her expectations was Alberto," Pablo said when we were getting close to Guatemala. "I was supposed to have been a doctor. Can you imagine? Poor patients. And you were pegged for a lawyer or an architect or some other serious vocation. Instead you spend your life looking at the sky."

I spend my life looking at the sky; that's what Mama used to say about me. Counting clouds. Playing cyclones. But she never opposed my interest in any way. I said so to Pablo. I challenged him to remember a single occasion when Mama had burdened any decision of ours with her opinion or blackmailed us with her expectations. He said that a mother's silence isn't a declaration of peace; it's the bomb that puts an end to the war. He said that when a mother reserves her opinion, she's actually conveying it but in a way you can't answer. "No matter how quiet she kept, we always knew perfectly well what her opinion was," he said in an attempt to convince me. "If she had spoken out, at least she would've given us a chance to discuss it. When she said nothing, we were still conscious of her criticism, but we couldn't refute it. I imagine many mothers do the same thing."

"At least Papa's happy with you. He wanted to have an artist in the family. In fact, I think you became an artist partly because of him."

"I did? Don't be so sure. It's true that he always encouraged me, but it's also true that I was on the point of giving up more than once, and he was to blame. Well, maybe 'blame' isn't the right word. But I often felt that he was making me become an artist as if it were some kind of duty. As if the fact that Grandfather Simón hadn't been able to become an actor had established a historical debt, and one man in each subsequent generation had to avenge the injustice done to Simón; Papa through his painting; me with the piano . . . Well, that's come to an end, fortunately."

"What do you mean?"

"I mean Luis isn't going to pick up that particular baton, I'm very clear about not wanting children, and unless you hurry up—"

"Are you saying I'm old?"

" 'Are you saying I'm old?' That's a dirty trick! Changing the subject with a joke."

Suddenly the pilot announced that we were about to land in Guatemala. The laughter came to an end, and the prologue to tears began. The passengers are requested to fasten their seatbelts, raise the backs of their seats to an upright position, and prepare themselves to see their dead mother. It almost sounded like that to me. We kept our mouths shut from this point on.

While we were landing, Pablo dug his fingers into my thigh in a gesture he meant to be reassuring, but only someone who knew him very well would have realized that, because it was belied by his whole body. His feet trod on nonexistent pedals and his hand, the same hand that was supposed to be soothing me, left twenty-four of Bach's preludes, together with their accompanying fugues, marked on my thigh. The strength of his hands has always surprised me. They don't fit the popular idea of a pianist's hands; they're broad and meaty with rather short fingers, more like the hands of a seasoned farmhand.

We spent no more than an hour in the airport in Guatemala City, filling the uncomfortable silences by laughing at Alberto and the precision of the plans he'd made for us. When we left the airport in Flores we found a car waiting for us and went straight to the Hotel Petén. It was already night when we arrived. Pablo didn't want to have dinner, declaring that he was tired from the flight, so he went directly to bed. After having dinner, I spent half the night lying in bed with my eyes wide open and the other half pacing the room the way ghosts or caged beasts are said to do. It was four nights since I had received the news of Mama's death. Only the assistance of Papa's medical arsenal—his Lexatin, his Tranxilium—had allowed me to cheat the insomnia of the three previous nights and get a little sleep, a sleep broken into fits and starts, mean and treacherous. Although I still had more pills in my bag, that night in Flores I chose insomnia over nightmares. Only one who chooses is capable of making a mistake, and I made more than one on that trip, right from the very beginning. I should have balked at going, that was my first error: not being able to summon up sufficient courage to tell Alberto no, no way, I'm not any good at these things; if I see a single drop of blood I faint. I made another mistake that night in Flores, sleepless and undone as I was, with my eyelids wide open for fear of nightmares, as if insomnia could really do away with them, as if from then on they wouldn't pursue me anymore as they do now, even when I'm awake, because of my guilt over my final error, the most serious one, which I committed the following morning when I refused to look at Mama. Because I didn't look at her, I didn't see her dead. There it is. I've said it. I didn't see her. Four words.

My big mistake was saying to Pablo, in the doorway of the funeral home, that I couldn't, begging him to forgive me, saying no, I'm not capable of doing it, saying I know how I am and how I hold on to things and how much it costs me to forget them, and neither he nor Alberto could force me to carry around that indelible wound in my memory forever. Pablo put his arms around me and tried to dry my tears. He said don't worry, nobody's going to force you to do anything. I'll go in alone and give her a kiss from you, you silly ass. We stepped into the funeral home and my legs buckled. It was almost like what happened when I cut myself the other day: I found myself sliding down the wall, already far away, very far away. Pablo went in search of someone to look after me, completed the bureaucratic formalities, and while I was being given water and sympathy he was led away through a corridor, accompanied by two small gentlemen.

I wish Pablo had been capable of making me go in there. Yes, I do. I wish he'd carried me in his arms and brought me to where Mama's body was. I wish he'd told me I was too old to hide my face. The truth, not insomnia, was the only cure for my nightmares. But he didn't do any of that, and here I am, still having them. Except when I write. Another contradiction: invoking memory is the only way I have of escaping it.

I'm not sure what I was thinking while Pablo was identifying Mama. I know that everything seemed quite strange. La Esperanza Funeral Services. I was expecting the type of morgue you see in films. People in uniforms, refrigerated compartments made of aluminum, labels hanging down from big toes. Not a funeral home with a marble façade. I expected red tape and long explanations, but Pablo came back quickly—he'd been gone barely ten minutes—held Mama's backpack aloft, and said, "That's it. You have to sign a few papers over there at the counter. And then we can go."

"And Mama?" I asked.

And Mama? Like a little girl lost in the woods. As if Pablo might have said, "Safe and sound. She held on to a big piece of wood. An Italian steamer rescued her, and she's in Buenos Aires. She sent a telegram." As if a voice scrawled in ancient ink could have said, "Nothing new is known to have occurred in the vicinity of this station." And Mama? She's dead, of course. What's wrong with you?

"We'll come back this evening for the cremation. Sign this. I'll tell you everything later."

If I think about it, the whole trip was like a dream, and that's the way I remember it. Walking on the shore of the lake, listening to Pablo's explanations. The locals had suggested that we might want to go to the Río Petexbatún, to see the scene of the accident. "I think it happened on the Río Pasión," I said. "That's what they told me on the telephone."

"They're practically the same thing," Pablo explained. "The Petexbatún's a tributary of the Pasión that flows into a lake also called Petexbatún. They say it's not far, but getting there is a little complicated. You have to go somewhere in a car, and then you travel by canoe and—"

"I think I'll pass," I said, interrupting him. "If you want to go, I'll wait for you at the hotel."

It made no sense. Go there for what? Maybe the place was the same, but the water wasn't. Pablo didn't want to go either.

The people in the funeral home had explained the various formalities to Pablo. The option of bringing Mama's body back to Spain required a long and troublesome bureaucratic process, and, clearly, the most practical choice was to have her cremated, but a question occurred to me: "Shouldn't we call Alberto?"

"No. I've already decided. Everything's ready for this afternoon at three-thirty. That'll give us time to catch the last flight to Guatemala City, and maybe we'll even be able to connect with the one leaving tonight for Madrid."

"I don't know, Pablo. Maybe we shouldn't be too hasty. If I know Alberto, he'll already be planning to bury Mama in high style."

"In high style? Well, let him take her ashes to the Himalayas. Besides, I'm sure he'll understand. We're choosing the most practical option, and that's an argument that will always appeal to Alberto. And if it doesn't, he should have come himself. We'll call him from the hotel later and tell him everything."

And so the matter was resolved. Pablo assured me that they'd embalmed her and that her body hadn't deteriorated very much because it had been found just a few hours after she drowned. He refused outright to give me any details, arguing that if I hadn't wanted to go in and see her, it made no sense for us to talk about it now.

Poor guy, I'm sure he was keeping quiet about what he'd seen because he wanted to spare me. But I'm persistent. In the end, he had no choice but to give me some of the details, at first vague and imprecise, as if he'd seen only a photograph instead of his mother, but then, gradually, he got into his stride. I listened hard so I could engrave all those details in my memory, as if his account allowed me to erase my cowardice and convince myself I'd seen it all with my own eyes. When he said that Mama's face was split open from top to bottom, I asked him to stop, but it was too late. I already knew it had been a mistake not to go in and see her and now my imagination would take his words and create something even worse than reality.

Like a dream: having lunch in the hotel, on the terrace next to the pool, as if we were there to get some sun. Like a dream: the time I spent alone while Pablo talked to Alberto on the telephone. Like a dream: Lake Petén Itzá, and its damned water—in my imagination, it came from Río Pasión or Petexbatún—its water in my eyes again until Pablo came back. How crude he is at times, and yet how sensitively he helped me get through those days, what an effort he made to keep me entertained, how affectionate he was when he led me back to the funeral home that afternoon, talking about a thousand different things, as if we were out for a leisurely stroll, downplaying my cowardice, watching over me the whole time. An absurd dream, in which I was obliged to choose an urn and all of them looked ridiculous; a strange dream, in which a fire blazed for a few seconds in a great metal mouth and its breath struck us with an incredible roar and then it swallowed up the wood and the flesh and the bones. The ceremony, if this incineration deserves such a name, was accompanied throughout by sluggish, intrusive violin music from invisible loudspeakers, its drone in stark contrast to the *agitato, nervoso* movement of Pablo's fingers on my shoulder.

The flight home was a dream, too. But a real dream, induced by several pills, and interrupted only a couple of times by Pablo, who shook me awake to inform me that I was crying. When we arrived in Barcelona, Alberto was waiting for us at the airport. I stopped crying. On the way home, I listened to a precise account of all the details, demanded by Alberto and patiently furnished by Pablo. From the backseat of my brother's car, I listened to the whole thing in silence without butting in, even when I heard that the plural prevailed the whole way through, with "we arrived" and "we were told" followed by "we were brought" and "we saw her" and "we identified her." Pablo gave Alberto a folder with the documents, and our signatures at the end confirmed his well-intentioned plural, because from the beginning I understood that it wasn't a mistake or a mix-up or a slip of the tongue, it was a lie, a kindly, protective lie, because I didn't see or identify Mama, and now everybody thinks I did. My fault. My fault for refusing to see her and for not saying anything in the car, although it wouldn't have been easy, because it's never easy to expose a lie told by someone who's trying to protect you. I remember going over Li Po's proverbs again, but I didn't find any that seemed applicable, unless it's the seventh, the only one I don't understand very well: "Fear of the truth is the mother of the lie, as fear of the truth is the father of the truth."

WITH LUIS

I don't have to say anything. He looks me in the eyes and asks: So when did you say this future's coming? I pretend I don't understand. What are you saying? Fuck, Serena, I'm asking you when you're due. How do you know? What do you think? You come and see me because you want to tell me, but you're afraid. You talk to me about the future. I'm a Crazy, Serena, but I'm not a fool.

I wanted to tell you, Luis, but I didn't know how. It's very easy. You just say, I'm pregnant. Right, but I was afraid. Afraid of what? Afraid because I can't be sure you won't tell anybody. You're right, he admits. It's a risk you have to take. I can't promise you anything. As a general rule, I won't say anything unless someone asks me. Why would anyone ask you? No reason. What are you going to do? Are you going to have it? I'd like to have a cousin, even if he turns out to be a shitty little brat. Don't talk like that, Luis. Besides, I still don't know whether I'm going to keep it or not. I don't know why you're hesitating so much; it's your last chance. Nonsense, I'm not that old. Sure, you can wait a few more years and have a kid when you're eighty. That way, you might be able to get what you want. I don't understand. Well, if you wait long enough maybe you'll give birth to a father instead of a son. It seems to me that's what you'd like. To have a baby in your arms and call him Papa and tell him stories, the same stories your father told you. Closing the circle. Giving birth not to the future, but the past. That's morbid, Serena.

I go away. I like it when he tells the truth, but I don't like it when he says things like that.

Is it all that serious? Does it really matter so much if Serena rummages around in my office? "Matter" isn't the appropriate verb. It inconveniences me, it bothers me a little, because I've always guarded my privacy jealously. I've never written anything that could be considered a diary, but I've taken so many notes and kept so many papers that anyone capable of giving them some logical order could put together something akin to an autobiography. And if that one person is Serena, I have all the more cause for concern. I can see her, imagining nonexistent links between one document and the next, inventing theories in order to supplant chance with reason, constructing a biography propped up by her imagination, in which she'll make up events she can't know anything about and posit reasons that were never written down. Nevertheless, it won't be any more false than it would have been had I written it myself; I, too, invent when I don't understand my own life, and those inventions form a part of who I am.

It's not a problem if my daughter reads all that material. It's just a little early, perhaps. It would have been better to put off the revelations until I was well and truly dead. Serena won't uncover any unconfessable sins in my notes. Some little surprises, at most, and some intimations her imagination will lend wings to. She'll be most surprised by my travel notes, which I wrote down upon my return from each expedition, generally on the flight home, so they would have the warmth of immediacy. I'm referring to the personal notes, to all the impressions I never shared with anyone but put down in writing, maybe because I had to get rid of them somehow. Some of them will probably seem like cryptograms to her, coded messages that only I could understand. In other cases, they're more explicit, maybe because they relate to events that moved me. It doesn't matter. It's not a bad thing for those words to be released from the imprisonment of my silence. If Serena rescues them, all the better.

What really matters, then, is the blue folder.

The blue folder. It's in the third drawer of the second filing cabinet. It contains three objects, but only one of these could be called a document. The second object is attached to the inside cover of the folder with a bit of Scotch tape, and it's so small that it might be spotted only by someone who already knows it's there. In other words, me. It's a minuscule grain of sand. It comes from some beach in Morocco. Exactly forty-six years ago, Julio had that grain of sand with him when he returned home, when he broke his promise not to see me again, or call me, or love me, and after disappearing from my life for almost two months, showed up at my door one afternoon in such a state we had to go down to the street for fear that Papa would come in and find him there and all hell would break loose. Out in the street I asked him, what are you doing here, will you tell me why you've come, you swore we'd never see each other again. He covered my mouth with one hand, saying be quiet a second, please, just for a second, and he stopped in the middle of the pavement and took off a shoe while I scolded him for being there, for playing the clown with me once again, and as I didn't know whether to kill him or cover him with kisses, I kept pushing him, and he kept hopping backward on one foot, saying please, just wait a second, and he took off his sock, then shook it carefully over the cupped palm of his right hand as if determined to find the gold nugget hidden inside. But it wasn't gold, it was sand, a small grain of sand, and he said, look at me, look at me now and please don't say a word. I thought Julio had gone crazy, because his eyes were darting from my face to his hand, from my eyes to the grain of sand, and he looked frustrated, almost angry, and he turned around and shouted, shit, it can't be, it's impossible, and then he put the grain in his mouth, sucked it, and took it in his hand again, holding it lightly between two fingertips. He brought it close to my face and said, yes, now that's it, you see? That's it, he said, it's exactly the same color, I knew it, that's why I came back. What do you mean, came back? I asked, came back from where, where were you? In Morocco, he said, but that makes no differ-ence; I was on a beach, and I found this grain of sand with the same color as your eyes, and I thought I was going crazy, I saw you everywhere, even if I shut my eyes, and the more I tried to forget you, the more I saw you. But this grain of sand, it was so exactly right, and I said to myself I have to go back, now I have to go back. . . .

If the folder is in Serena's hands, if she's noticed the tiny object taped to its inside cover, I know what she'll do: she'll raise it to her lips, smell it, and remember me, she'll remember the color of my eyes. Be-cause she knows this story. I don't know if she understands its signifi-cance, but I know she knows it.

I lost my virginity that night. Actually, as far as "losing" is con-cerned, I didn't lose a thing. I won a man I've gone on loving my whole life and whose love I still believe in, despite his peculiarities. That's a lot. But I also gained a fear I've never completely lost: the fear that everything was a lie. Julio and I fell in love like two children, which was almost logical: I was indeed quite young; he was nine years older than I was, but he was still a teenager at heart. I know that time multiplies the effects of nostalgia, and I don't want to get carried away and magnify something that, after all, happens to everyone at least once in a lifetime. I fell in love, period. But at the same time, it doesn't seem fair to deny the importance of what hap-pened. It was like the end of the world. It was electric, and that's why it made me afraid. It was as if I were a light bulb, and I was afraid someone would turn it off and leave my filaments trembling in the dark. I wanted to die. I must not forget that. I wanted to die with him, and that night I begged him to kill me, to keep on killing me; I begged him for that while he—so sweet, so happy, so careful not to hurt me—was entering me for the first time. Then, sometime around dawn, I went home, furious, happy, and worn out, and my papa was waiting for me. What are you doing coming home at this hour? I'm going to get married. Are you crazy? I said I'm go-ing to get married. My poor papa, I almost scared him to death. He tried to oppose our marriage; he was filled with rage. Now that argument, which lasted well into the morning, strikes me as incidental and I can barely remember it. We terminated the discussion after it became clear that no reasoning was going to bend my stubborn will. I then went to my room, but instead of getting into bed I felt around under the mattress and pulled out the portrait of me that Julio had painted when we first met; under the mattress, where my sons, many years later, would hide their first pornographic magazines, where old people hide their miserable savings. And I looked at the portrait the way they look at those savings: with the sorrow of knowing they're all they have and the anxiety of thinking they may not last long enough. Before then, I'd never recognized anything of me in my portrait. That was the first time. I saw the marks on the paper and felt as if I were holding a mirror in my hands instead of a drawing.

That portrait is the second document contained in my Julio folder. Serena will certainly have pulled it out of the drawer by now; she may even be criticizing me for keeping it there. But I keep that portrait in that drawer precisely so I can pretend to have forgotten it. Well, the result is the same. Serena may even have it framed already and have it hanging on a wall in her apartment. I hope that whenever she looks at it, she thinks a little about her father as well as me. Because it was her father who told her the story of the portrait. At least a thousand times.

If Serena already knows the history of those two objects, I needn't worry. They're nothing new, just old lies, because both are false. The only resemblance between the color of my eyes and the color of that grain of sand existed in Julio's mind. The miracle is that both of us have been capable of maintaining this fiction our whole lives. It was an effort, of course, but we must have found it worthwhile. That's not the kind of lie that matters to me. The portrait is more complicated, because it's doubly false. It wasn't anything more than a sketch made in a few minutes, and when Julio gave it to me, I thought it didn't look like me at all. Then I didn't see Julio again for two months, and a month after he came back we got married, an act that was contrary not only to my father's wishes but also to any future I might have imagined for myself. I could write a few thousand pages in an attempt to explain my reasons, but they would be false: falling in love is simply an unreasonable act. Always, by definition. Marvelous, but unreasonable. Supposedly, throughout nature, females are endowed with virtually infallible systems for identifying the most suitable male, the candidate who can best guarantee the survival of the species. But we humans have invented love, an unpredictable mechanism, unreliable, capricious, and perishable. I suppose it worked in my case, and maybe my three children are proof of its success. Serena would become indignant if she heard me. She'd tell me that love demonstrates the human being's superior evolution, his ability to separate sex from its reproductive function. Well, I know what I'm talking about. Besides, in those days, the concept of choosing a mate and the concept of having a family were inextricably intertwined.

Even without taking into account all the things I've learned about Julio with the passage of time, I can safely assert that he was not the most suitable man to have a family with. He was the best man to fall in love with, but those are two different issues. He was the man capable of painting a portrait that resembled his desire more than it did me, the man capable of making me want to be like his idea of me. Perhaps in a different time he would have been the perfect lover. If we were as young now as we were then, if I could receive the gift of starting over, I'd take him as a lover. Never as the father of my children.

The blue folder. The third document. An old sheet of paper, handwritten with a scratchy pen and torn out of a notebook. At the top of the page, a date: January 11, 1922. I know the text by heart: "At approximately nine o'clock in the morning, a cumulonimbus cloud appeared, driven by strong gusts of wind blowing from a southerly direction. Some seven miles off the coast, this cloud collided with the warm front whose presence has been reported over the course of the last few days and unleashed a powerful electrical storm accompanied by abundant precipitation. The duration of this storm was approximately three hours. These being the days of the tuna harvest, the storm damaged fourteen small vessels, some of which were completely dismasted; nonetheless all eventually reached land and put ashore their crews intact, without exception. Nothing new is known to have occurred in the vicinity of this station."

Their crews intact, without exception. All put ashore their crews intact, without exception. If I thought that that document had fallen into Pablo's or Alberto's hands, I wouldn't worry too much. They probably wouldn't even notice the date. But Serena knows. For God's sake, she's visited the San Sebastián lighthouse countless times, and she's spent hours in every conceivable archive, searching for that very piece of paper. All she has to do is read those words once, and she'll jump to conclusions. That's clear to me. What's not clear is whether they'll be the right ones. And whether she'll realize their significance.

First possible conclusion: All the men who sailed out of Malespina in those fishing boats on January 11, 1922, returned to land. No one died. Nobody was shipwrecked. If Serena considers this, she'll be troubled, as I was troubled, by two pressing questions: Why does the story refer to eleven people dead? And why hadn't the lighthouse keeper heard about Simón's shipwreck? There's no answer to the first question. As for the second, there are a few possible responses, all of them conditional: maybe because no one knew him, or because no one knew his name, or maybe they knew him but preferred to say nothing, and so on.

All this is far from the truth—the questions, the answers, and the conclusion itself.

Second possible conclusion: Simón never boarded any of those fishing boats. In which case, where did the story of his shipwreck come from? Not only is this question more distressing than the others, but Serena won't find an answer to it anywhere, except in her imagination. Amparo and I could answer it for her, but we're both dead. And there's no point asking Julio.

This second conclusion is also far from the truth, but not so far as the first one.

Third possible conclusion: Simón didn't exist. Simón never existed. And that's the truth.

The page torn from the lighthouse keeper's log is one of the few papers that Julio ever kept, and it fell into my hands by pure chance. It happened a little more than four years ago, after the doctors confirmed that his illness was irreversible. As a permanent invalid, he could now receive a government pension, and obtaining it required updating and *presenting a series of official documents. This drove us all crazy, because Julio had an artist's inability to deal with any sort of bureaucracy. Down with papers. Long live invention. We'd ask him a question and he'd smile. We'd insist it was important and he'd answer, "Contributions? Come on, what do I know about contributions?" It fell to me to go rooting about in places I'd always steered clear of.*

It was a monumental mess. The piece of paper in question was stuck inside an old drawing tablet, one of those that usually contained nothing but sketches. Julio stopped painting in 1973. I found the page from the keeper's log in 1997. Now, I know my husband's work very well, and although none of the sketches was dated, I knew most of the people pictured in them, so the deduction was easy as well as painful: I worked out that Julio had been in possession of the document since about 1969. And there's more. In the mid-1970s, when Serena's curiosity became too dangerous, Julio told her about the lighthouse keeper's storm log and encouraged her to have a look at it, but at the same time he warned her that she wouldn't find the page for January 11, 1922, because he'd already looked for it himself. When I found out about their conversation, I asked him why he'd sent his daughter on a wild goose chase. "So she'll take a break," he said. It seemed logical enough. Send Serena down a dead end. Wear her out. Let her runaway train and its load of questions reach the end of the line. It worked. Shortly afterward, when Serena had exhausted every possibility of finding the page missing from the logbook, her war of questions about Simón was over. Or it went underground—I don't know. What I do know is that the reason Julio gave me was false. What he was really trying to do was to turn his daughter into an involuntary witness to the lie. That's why he sent her to the lighthouse. Because he himself had been there before her. Because the person who tore the page out of the logbook was Julio. And then, instead of reconstructing his life, he decided to leave things as they were. I assume he knew he was deciding for all of us.

That was one of the worst moments of my life. I've never had such a fight as Julio and I had over this. I asked him how long have you known about this and do you realize what you've done, didn't you ever think about your children, didn't it occur to you to think about what Simón means to them. . . . Julio was holding the old handwritten page and looking at it as if he didn't know how to read. Then he burst into tears, and to this day I haven't managed to work out if he was weeping over what he'd done or if those tears were only a response to my anger and the unaccustomed violence of my attack. It was infuriating. It was like when babies start crying in the middle of the night and you can't make them stop and you don't know what's wrong. His illness is very convenient. Or quite an astute move on the part of fate, revealing the evidence of the crime only after the criminal has turned mute.

I never said anything to anyone. Maybe it would have been better if I had: "Children, there were no deaths at sea and no shipwrecks off the coast of Malespina on January 11, 1922. It's all a lie. Simón never existed." I was on the verge of doing this, but then I imagined the reactions my revelation would provoke and the questions my children would ask, and I realized there weren't going to be any answers. Clues, yes, and suspicions, intuitions, even the odd certainty; but no answers. Therefore, I kept quiet. Did I do wrong? I sincerely believe I did not. I believe my sole error was not getting rid of that torn-out page. I should have burned it. Or thrown it into the sea. I held on to it because I knew my children had inherited my respect for others' privacy and not one of them would have dared to open a single drawer in my filing cabinet without asking my permission. But naturally, for people to ask your permission, you have to be alive.

I had other reasons for keeping the document. It represented Julio with the same precision as the other two objects—that's why I kept the three of them together. Everything in the blue folder represents a man who has the ability to invent the woman he loves. Why couldn't he, when he was so clearly able to invent himself?

When it comes to drawing conclusions, there's a fundamental difference between Serena and me. I'm sure she's blaming her father; I never did that. I cursed him, but I never blamed him. The episode with the Russian woman, many years before this discovery, had already taught me that my husband's world was made of froth and that it would dissolve in your hands if you tried to confine it.

Besides, it wasn't fair to blame him, at least not for everything, because he was only the carrier of that baroque story. I've gone over the dates again. Julio inherited the story of Simón the way one inherits the color of his skin, and when he found out the tale was false, he was already close to fifty, with a wife, three children, and an entire life constructed in homage to his absent father. Would it have been fair to blame him for not tearing it all down after he made his discovery? Would it have been fair even to disclose it? No, the real guilty party is Amparo. How I wish I could have known her better. If I remember correctly, Julio and I had been married for thirteen years when Amparo died. I suppose our relationship was what was considered "correct" in those days. She was never quite happy with my profession. She said it couldn't be a good thing to spend your whole life looking at the dead. I imagine the fact that I had any profession at all displeased her, but she was careful never to oppose me in a direct manner. She'd make some oblique allusion, and I'd let it slip away into thin air.

We didn't spend that much time together, especially since I was busy traveling. When I was in Barcelona, we had a family dinner every Sunday; from time to time, she'd spend a week with us in Malespina; and we also shared all the obligatory holidays. She never meddled in our decisions or tried to interfere in the way we brought up our children. She was a classic grandmother who wore her bluish gray hair in a bun and spent her afternoons in a rocking chair, wrapped in a black shawl, sewing or knitting clothes for the children. Every now and then, she'd tell one of her stories. Stories about Simón. That's what made me most suspicious of her when the wretched page from the lighthouse keeper's logbook appeared. Amparo never talked about herself; her stories were all about Simón. And she always told them using the same words, like someone repeating a traditional tale. The same words that Julio later repeated.

I'm not saying that Amparo made up the character of Simón in order to make our lives miserable. She did it more out of compassion than wickedness. She wanted to give her son a father. I'm convinced that Julio's real father must have been some actor, or someone attached to the theater troupe. Someone who passed through her life the way storms pass: making plenty of noise, but never inclined to stay. It makes perfect sense. And there's a compelling fact: Amparo knew nothing about the sea; she did know a great deal about the theater. That's why the shipwreck part of the story was full of abstractions, imperfectly described boats, nameless clouds, unsatisfactorily explained storms, unlikely rafts. (Julio, who does know all about the sea, had to be the one who, years later, called that raft a hatch and talked about tuna fishing with trap nets, without realizing that his contribution was helping to cement the lie. On the other hand, the final part of the story—everything that supposedly happened from the moment when Simón joined the theater company, or even before that, when he was preparing for his audition by learning El burlador de Sevilla—all that is perfectly realistic, full of precise names, dates, and places, specific verses and detailed descriptions.

Let's assume my theory is correct and take it further. Amparo invented Simón out of compassion or shame. She made up a father for her son Julio. She gave her character a history, and she needed a mountain of facts to back it up, because, as I know very well, children ask many, many questions. Maybe she'd heard about the storm off Malespina. We'll never know. However, my theory does shed light on one of the most surprising aspects of Amparo's creation. Why didn't Simón die in the shipwreck? If the objective of the whole farce was to justify his absence and she already had him swallowing water, why didn't she simply drag him down to the bottom? Because she was afraid of Julio's questions. Because she didn't feel capable of floating in the sea she had invented. Amparo knew nothing about the sea, and so she pulled Simón out of there and brought him into the theater, a world she was sufficiently familiar with to be able to improvise responses to any probing on the part of Julio. There, in the theater, she could give Simón what he needed: a voice, a good memory, a strong will, a sense of frustration.

She could even make him happy, at least once; she could invent the single occasion when Simón finally succeeded in stepping onto the stage as an actor in a leading role, as none other than Don Juan in El burlador, and she could give him a standing ovation from the audience. Then, at last, she could kill him.

Has Serena reached this point with me? Perhaps she hasn't come quite this far. When Amparo died, Serena was only five. I didn't know her grandmother very well, and Serena knew her even less. Assuming she's seen the page from the keeper's log, Serena must know that Simón is an invention, but I'm not sure she knows whose. Maybe that's the only question she'll have. In which case, why am I hesitating? Why am I afraid to see her face-to-face? Because I won't know how to explain to her why it's all right this way. I've never been very good at talking to my children. I think I brought them up properly. But I've never been able to tell them the things I know about me, the things that go far beyond biography. The things I think. It has a great deal to do with who I am, and whether it may be false or not isn't so important. Maybe the others will understand, but Serena won't. It will require a fiendish effort on her part to accept that Simón is an invention. And it will take even more for her to forgive her father for that invention. But she's wrong, because Julio really is Simón's son, because he carries him in his blood. Simón runs through his veins. In fact, he runs through all our veins, including mine.

At first, after I found the page from the San Sebastián lighthouse log and decided not to tell anyone, I worried about my decision. But two years later, after Luis's accident, I knew I'd done the right thing. When I watched Alberto, convinced that his son was a natural survivor, insist on keeping him alive, against the advice of his physicians; and when Luis himself, a few days after coming out of his coma, attributed the miracle of his recovery to the genes of his nonexistent grandfather. That's when I realized that depriving my children of Simón's story would be unforgivable. What would have been left had I stripped them of this lie? Nothing. And then they would have had no alternative but to do for themselves what Amparo had done for them long before they were *born: she invented who they were. Invented and believed, doing both with the same faith, the same cunning, the same blindness. Just as the legend of Simón had explained their origins, their lives, up to that point, so they would have wanted to explain themselves from that moment on, with the legend of the first legend's falsehood. Instead of Simón's heroism, Amparo's lie. Or Julio's perfidy.*

So I chose for them and I chose well. Serena has spent her life fighting fiction the way good soldiers fight—intent on detecting its presence, harassing it, suppressing it—but I have to find a way to show her she's mistaken her enemy, to explain to her that whoever suppresses fiction destroys life, and that everything disappears with it, all love, all desire. If the past is an invention, it's not such a big deal. After all, the future's an invention, too, and no one finds that hard to accept.

So that's the harm Serena may cause herself by destroying the family lie. Maybe I can still get back in time to stop her. If not, I can search out answers to mitigate the effect. I can tell her, for example, that her father never saw that piece of paper. That I found it and was afraid of the damage it could do. I can even tell her I was the one who tore the page out of the logbook, so that her father would never see it. And then I can ask her forgiveness. I know this will make me guilty of prolonging the life of an old lie with the blood of a new one, but not of inventing the method, which is older than humanity. I could also just keep quiet. The human brain, like computers, tends to work with binary systems: zero, one; yes, no; truth, lie. After Serena discovered the Simón lie, I don't doubt that her brain hastened to replace it with a truth, with anything that could fill the vacuum, because binary systems don't work if one of the parts is missing. I wonder what new truth my daughter has constructed. At least it will be her own. I have a feeling that's my task at this moment: to help my daughter invent herself, once and for all. To help her build her house, even if doing so requires the demolition of hereditary castles. To help her cross out her history with the stroke of a pen, and rewrite it. If I succeed in doing this with my final words, I'll count myself satisfied.

SUNDAY

Before we go to the market, I try to make a shopping list, and Pablo gets upset: it's fine for going to the local shop, but not to the market. The peasants get up at five in the morning and prepare the day's produce so that you'll come along later and look at it and smell it and touch it and pick what appeals to you at that exact moment. It's like having a garden. "If you want to go with a list in your hand, it would be better to call up the supermarket and order everything over the telephone. . . ."

Et cetera, et cetera, et cetera. He's right, but he doesn't know what he's talking about. In the Malespina market, there are maybe two or three "peasants" who remotely correspond to this nostalgic vision. Peasants: even the word sounds old-fashioned. The other vendors go into their coolers every morning and take out vegetables which, in many cases, they haven't even grown themselves.

"You're right," I say, giving in. I ball up the shopping list and send it rolling across the table. "I was just trying to save time."

"Well, we're not in any hurry."

I don't feel like arguing. That's why I take the old road. The new one's straight and shortens the trip by about ten minutes, but I don't even consider suggesting it. In Pablo's view, driving on the old road is obligatory because it's authentic, original, the only road that existed when we were little. The other road, the new one, is enemy territory, because it's the one the invaders use, the tourists, the rich kids, the out-siders. Papa pointedly ignored the construction of this new road. Those were the days of the Seat 1500, with its gear stick mounted in the hub of the steering wheel and a bench-style front seat. As we climbed the slope, which was flanked by cypresses on either side, Papa would negotiate the curves clumsily, impatient to get to where we'd be able to spot the first glint of the Mediterranean. Then, even though we still had three kilometers to go before we reached the house, he'd stop the car in the middle of the road, yank up the emergency brake, crank down the window, and, filling his lungs with the smell of the sea, declare, "Children, we're in Malespina." I too remember those moments with a certain nostalgia. I don't tell Pablo that nostalgia is, by definition, the least authentic of all feelings. I don't remind him that those cypresses are gone and in their place stands a discotheque made of concrete.

Suddenly, Pablo asks Luis, "Since your father's not here, would you please tell us what's wrong with him? He's impossible at the moment."

Luis thinks before answering. Sometimes when you ask him something, he stays quiet for a while, and there's no way of telling if he's thinking or if he hasn't understood the question. "Nothing," he replies a kilometer later. "That is, nothing new. It's the usual. I believe he's in love."

"No!" Pablo exclaims, clapping his hand to his forehead. "You're joking! Again?"

"Shut up! You've got no room to talk," Luis replies, taking the words out of my mouth.

"Maybe not, but at least I've only been married once."

He has a point. Alberto's total is four so far. He started when he was twenty-six with Clara. They had Luis a year later. Four more years passed, and then one fine day he called us together to announce that they were getting divorced. By mutual consent, with joint custody, although the child was going to live with him. He never mentioned what this agreement cost him, and I don't even want to think about it. He told us how much he loved Clara, trotted out various intangible reasons for their separation, spoke of the eternal debt of gratitude he owed her for having given him a son, and stressed the efforts that both of them were making to preserve their friendship despite their isolated differences. Isolated differences, that's how he put it. I think they hated each other's guts. I haven't seen Clara since then, and I know nothing about her life except what I occasionally hear from Luis, who has dinner with her once a week. I remember how Papa, more than happy to adopt the formal tone that Alberto had tried to lend the proceedings, closed with an emotional speech in which he declared that everyone is free to do as he pleases in this life, that the most important consideration was to protect the child, and that the family would all pull together to support Alberto. Mama said she never meddled in anyone's private life. All she wanted to know was whether some third party was involved. Alberto answered in the negative and looked offended.

Eight months later, he announced his intention to marry Esther, his former secretary, and to make it clear that Esther was the love of his life, he held an elaborate wedding, with more guests than the first one. He and Esther lasted four years. Alberto convoked another family meeting and made another speech, this time shorter and sadder. Love had blinded him. In reality, it wasn't ever love, but a dazzling illusion that was unable to withstand the difficulties of actual cohabitation. Esther was the biggest mistake he'd ever made; they were so different, they couldn't possibly live together. Et cetera. Papa said, "Well, son, there's no use prolonging the agony." Mama asked if there were third parties involved, and Alberto swore there weren't. He wished there had been, he said. He'd be glad to meet another woman, someone with whom building a life together would truly be worth the effort, someone who had projects of her own, a woman who wouldn't settle for climbing aboard the train of his life but would take her place beside him. That is to say, someone very like Mariana, the woman from Cádiz to whom he coincidentally became engaged two months later.

Mariana was lovely, funny, charming, clever, and affectionate. The best sister-in-law of the lot. But she wanted children, and she wanted them right away. The idea made Alberto uncomfortable, because he wasn't in such a hurry, but above all because it made Luis jealous. He was not quite seven, and although he apparently accepted the parade of surrogate mothers his father presented him with, he didn't seem inclined to allow any of them to put down long-lasting roots. Mariana put up with five years of postponed promises: Maybe next year, maybe a little later, let's wait until Luis matures a bit. Then Mariana packed her bags and went back to Cádiz. As with the others, I haven't heard from her since. I liked Mariana.

Susana, Alberto's fourth wife, asked him for a divorce in the fifth month of Luis's coma. She was seeing Alberto so seldom she had to use me as an emissary. She said she didn't want to break Alberto's balls at such a difficult moment, but she'd come to the conclusion that she didn't count for anything in his life. This time, nobody was hurt. I think they even still see each other from time to time.

Pablo's case is different. He fucked up once, when he married Antonia. Ever since then, Pablo has preferred promiscuity, and skepticism. He says it makes no sense to deny the sacred law of life, which is that everything must die. He says the hotter love burns, the sooner the flame goes out. He says a lot of things, Pablo does. He talks about authentic love.

As for me, so far I've never been married. And I don't think I ever will be married. I'm the family's last hope, Papa used to say, when his brain was still up to joking. I don't know.

It wouldn't bother me if Alberto fell in love again. He's been in mourning for more than two years now, so it's about time. Besides, when that man falls in love, it's a blessing for everybody. He becomes euphoric, amusing, expansive. And generous. Alberto's always generous, but when he's in love, he loses all restraint and spreads joie de vivre everywhere he goes. I'm already looking forward to seeing him like that again, in a state of permanent, bewildered, happy-faced excitement. And this is precisely what makes me think that Luis's suspicion isn't accurate. Alberto's on edge, yes, but not in a good way. He's sulky, he scowls and frowns almost all day long. He's not even sad.

"Sounds like we'll be having a wedding soon," Pablo says. "Poor Alberto, he's going to have to buy me a suit again."

"What a nerve. You have your concert outfit," I say, even though I already know what his reply will be.

"How dare you. It's called a concert outfit because it's for concerts."

"When I get married, I'm going to ask you to play at my wedding. That way, I won't have to buy you a suit."

This sets him off. "Not a chance," he says. "No fucking way. My music isn't—"

"It was a joke, Pablo," I say, interrupting him before he gets carried away. His music isn't background noise, not a pastime, not entertainment. His music is the sound of the river of life. I'm familiar with this speech. "I was just teasing you." I hasten to change the subject. It's the third argument I've dodged in less than fifteen minutes. I ask Luis, "Do you know the candidate?"

"No. Not yet. This time, he's being very secretive. But I'll find out."

This answer confirms my suspicions. When Alberto falls in love, he usually has the beloved's name etched on his forehead. However, as I have no better explanation for his current state, I keep my mouth shut.

We arrive at the market and commence the quest for the authentic vegetable. Artichokes? Impossible, says Pablo. Artichokes in October, who ever heard of that? They must be plastic. The local artichokes, the *authentic* artichokes, come in May, and their leaves are violet. Those tomatoes aren't any good, either; they're too round, too perfect; they must be factory tomatoes. Cauliflower. How is it possible that no one's selling cauliflower? This is the season for cauliflower and beets.

The upshot of all this is that an hour after arriving at the market, we've bought enough food for one exquisite but frugal dinner. In my mind, trumpets sound the retreat, because the battle promises to be long and tedious. With the excuse that my finger still hurts, I pass the tote bag to my brother and suggest to Luis that he come with me to buy bread. We leave Pablo in strenuous conversation with his supposed peasants, touching and sniffing each product before dropping it into the bag.

We go to a café. I assume that, like me, Luis has been thinking about his father's wives. Ex-wives. As soon as we sit down, he says, "Poor Mariana."

"Poor? Why?"

"I think I made her life impossible."

"You did, a little." He looks worried. I try to soothe him. "Don't blame yourself. It was a long time ago. Besides, they were the adults. You may have created the problem, but they didn't know how to solve it."

"Right, I've come up with that blather myself. Did you like Mariana?"

"Yes, we got on very well."

"I couldn't stand her."

"Well, everybody needs someone to hate."

"Oh, they do, do they? Who do you hate?"

We're about to play a game. Luis loves this kind of foolishness. He gets a rapt look on his face. When I was fourteen, my friends and I spent the summer playing the truth game. We'd go into the woods, a whole gang of us. The question was always the same, but disguised in different words: "Do you like so-and-so? Would you like what's-his-name to kiss you?" Pity the girl who blushed before answering, because that showed she was lying. By the following summer, boys came with us, so the new game became spin the bottle. Before each game began, the players stipulated the type of kiss in question: with tongue or without tongue; long or short; hands or no hands; standing up or lying down; eyes open or eyes shut. If you had to kiss someone you didn't like, you pressed your lips together and took a deep breath. We had abandoned the truth game for a game of lies; it was more fun. Strangely enough, there was no prize in the truth game. No one could win. You lost, or at best you broke even. There was a punishment for lying, but no reward for the truth. On the other hand, for purely mathematical reasons, when you played the game of lies, you always won. It was only a question of time. No matter how often the bottle aimed at the wrong person, in the end the laws of chance would bring you the kiss of your dreams. We played all afternoon and into the evening, so we could take our time. The bottle pointed in every direction, like a deranged compass. Sometimes I think we're all—Alberto and Pablo and I—still playing spin the bottle and studying mathematical probabilities, waiting for the prize.

"Me? I don't think there's anybody I really hate these days."

"Okay, then how about before?"

"I guess it would be Antonia. But that doesn't count. Antonia deserved it."

"And why did Grandma hate the Russian woman?"

"Grandma?"

"Yes, my grandmother, your mother. She said the Russian woman was a walking, talking lie. According to her, the Russian woman wasn't Russian, that stuff about the prettiest place in the world was just a con they used to ingratiate themselves with the fishermen, the castle didn't exist—"

"Wait a minute, wait a minute." He stops, and I go on. "I'm going to have to recite Li Po's third proverb for you: 'There is nothing more dangerous than the lie we use to controvert a lie.' "

"What's that supposed to mean?"

"It means, don't exaggerate, don't understate."

"Great, we're getting somewhere. We have time. It'll be a while before your pain-in-the-ass brother tracks down the authentic cauliflower."

"Hey, have a little respect."

"Don't be offended, I'm only telling the truth. Besides, you still owe me the history of the Battle of the Formigues."

"Well, I don't really know where to begin, because no one knows the truth. What do you want to know?"

"I've always been fascinated by how differently Grandpa and Grandma viewed the Russians. In his view, they were like a couple of heroes. Grandma, on the other hand—well, Grandma didn't like to talk about them, but if you pressed her, she'd say that they were impostors, pretentious mediocrities, fake millionaires—"

"You're right. They could never agree. And you hadn't even been born when Papa painted the Russian woman's portrait."

"What happened?"

"Well, Mama wasn't pleased."

"But it must have been a good commission. If they really were that rich—"

"Don't be so sure. That's one of the things that isn't completely clear. Remember, the portrait has always been in the house."

"What does that have to do with anything?"

"Use your head, young Luis. If Papa kept the picture, that means there was no commission. Or if there was, he didn't collect on it."

"Damn. You're right."

"Not long ago, I was on the point of solving this mystery," I tell him. "We were arranging Papa's hat collection, and he told me the Russian woman gave him the Borsalino in exchange for the portrait."

"That doesn't clear up anything. You just said yourself that the picture never left the house."

"I know. I told him so, but we couldn't go on talking."

"What a shame. Did he space out?"

"No. It wasn't that."

It still gives me a lump in my throat and I have to force the words out: "At that moment, the Ministry of Foreign Affairs called to say Mama had died."

"Son of a bitch. God knows how long it'll be before he gets the urge to talk again."

"Please speak properly, Luis." I know his condition gives him carte blanche, but it irks me when he uses his permit so flippantly. "It's not a matter of urges."

"I'm not so sure about that. Haven't you ever thought he might be a sly old fox, fooling us all and understanding more than he lets on? All right, that's another subject. We were talking about the portrait."

"Which he painted in the summer of 1973. It took him almost two months. Every afternoon after lunch, Papa would announce, 'I'm going to the castle to paint the Russian woman.' And Mama would jump as if someone had poked her. 'She's no Russian,' Mama would say. 'She's English. And that's no castle, either. Unless you think a castle is a few bricks and a badly installed window.' "

"Ooh, Grandma. What a bitch."

"No. She said it half-jokingly. I don't think Mama cared one way or another about the Russian woman. What bothered her was Papa's inclination to swallow fantasies whole."

"And what did he say?"

"Nothing. Papa never liked arguing. He gathered up his gear and went off to the castle. Sometimes you could hear him cursing under his breath, but he avoided any confrontation."

"What a coward."

"No, not at all. My father's never been a coward. Besides, he got his revenge. Every night during dinner, he'd tell us stories about the Russian woman. It was fantastic. He'd start by telling us what he'd done that day, his conversations with her, his tours of the castle and the botanical garden, and then he'd describe how the Russian couple had fled the Revolution and gone to London as refugees. Mama pretended she was listening only because she had no other choice, but she was as hooked as the rest of us. It was like a soap opera. Every day, a new episode. That's why I say Papa got his revenge. Instead of arguing with Mama, he tricked her. He thought arguing wasn't worth the trouble. He thought time would tell."

"And?"

"And what?"

"What did time say? It's been almost thirty years."

"Nothing, Luis. That was Papa's mistake. Time never clears things up. Time's good for stories, but not necessarily for the truth. And now that the Russians are dead, who knows—"

"Look, I don't want to hear about fucking ambiguities." If there's anyone who's neurologically incapable of accepting that truth may not exist, it's Luis. "Someone has to know the truth. There were a lot of people who knew them, right from the beginning, when they arrived in Malespina."

"It's not that easy," I explain resignedly. "To begin with, many years have passed. The Russians came to Malespina in 1928. If they weren't the first foreigners in these parts, they were close. You can imagine how surprised the locals were. And on top of that, the Russians didn't just come for a visit; they came to stay. Evidently, they arrived in a horse-drawn carriage, and then they spent an entire day walking around the outskirts of the village. They chose a spot on the summit of the hill, the spot with the best view, and announced their intention to buy, with cash, all the land that sloped down from that point to the sea. All of it, including the minuscule beach at the foot of the cliff."

"The Russian woman's famous bathtub."

"Exactly. The Russian woman's famous bathtub."

"So the Russians bought an entire hill?"

"More or less. And that's how the legend began. Don't forget, it was Malespina, in 1928; in other words, the backside of the world. To the people of the village the Russians must have seemed like extraterrestrials. From the day they started establishing contacts to broker the sale of the various pieces of land, their history was full of myths that were impossible to prove."

"For example?"

"For example, it's said that they went and talked to the owners one by one, agreeing the price of each property. And they say that when it was the turn of some fellow who considered his plot less valuable than the others because it was on the steepest part of the slope, the Russians themselves raised his asking price so he wouldn't come out too far behind."

"How generous."

"Or not."

"Here we go again."

"Look, it may have been an act of generosity. But you wouldn't be so sure about that if you looked at the hill from the sea. Ask your father to take you out in his yacht one day. Tell me if you see any way of getting down to the beach that doesn't pass over exactly that piece of land on the steepest part of the slope. Furthermore, paying that much had a dramatic effect, which they very much needed."

"Why?"

"Come on, use your imagination. Without the cooperation of the village, it would have been practically impossible to build a castle and a botanical garden on the edge of a precipice overlooking the sea. They needed help, manpower, materials. I can't even tell you how poverty-stricken the people around here were in those days. They risked their lives on fishing boats for incomes that scarcely covered the costs of subsistence. The Russians bought themselves a reputation for generosity that quickly paid for itself."

"So the people accepted them?"

"Of course. And if there was any remaining resistance, everybody was won over after the Russians had their first meeting with the mayor. It seems that was when they announced they didn't want to compete with the local cork industry."

"Stop, stop. What industry?"

"Naturally, you don't know about that, because the only industry that goes on around here now is tourism. But you must have noticed that there are cork trees in the few remaining patches of woodland. Haven't you?"

"Yes."

"Well, in those days, when the winter weather turned bad, the fishermen dedicated themselves to peeling the bark off those trees and selling it for making cork. Local craftsmen turned the bark into bottle stoppers."

"Good, good, let's get back to the Russians."

"They told the mayor they were prepared to cede the village the right to harvest cork on the lands they'd just bought, but on two conditions: that no one enter the Russians' botanical garden without their permission, and that the privacy of their beach be scrupulously respected."

"And how were they able to talk with the mayor?"

"Good question. According to the legend, they had brought an interpreter with them from Barcelona. A little mongrel French, a few hand gestures, and some paper for jotting down figures would have sufficed for negotiating the prices of the land, but if the story of their famous conversation with the mayor is true, there must surely have been some sort of mediator present, because—supposedly—they talked at great length."

"About what?"

"I don't know, but toward the end, it's said, the mayor could contain his curiosity no longer and asked the question on everyone's lips."

"I can imagine what it was."

"Let's hear it."

" 'What the fuck are you doing here?' "

"Bravo, Luis, although I don't think the mayor was as vulgar as you. In those days, the ownership of land made sense only insofar as you could extract some profit from it. And since the Russians had agreed to renounce their rights to the cork their trees produced, he must have suspected that they had access to privileged information, some secret that would multiply the value of the land. Who knows? Oil, maybe, or some valuable mineral—"

"All right, so what was the Russians' answer?"

"Their answer was simple and intelligent, and it laid the foundations for the legend that grew around them. They said they'd spent a year traveling around Europe in search of the prettiest and most isolated place they could find, and they were certain they'd found it here, in Malespina."

"Damn."

"Right. Damn. I don't know if this reply satisfied the mayor's curiosity, but imagine how it swelled his pride. By that night, the news had spread like wildfire. In every house in the community, people went to bed convinced that their village was the most beautiful place in the world."

"Well, they weren't so mistaken. We often say there's no prettier place than this."

"Right, but that's just a manner of speaking. Apparently, the people of Malespina took it as the literal truth. They probably liked the land the Russians bought, but I wouldn't think they spent very much time on it. It was on the outskirts of the village and difficult to get to. The locals made their way up there a couple of times a year, stripped the cork off the trees, and went back home. Until the Russians came, if the villagers thought in terms of beauty at all, they probably thought about a fishing net bursting with a fresh catch, not about the landscape. And then, suddenly, some foreigners arrive, well-traveled people, and they declare that the hill is the most beautiful place in the world. Even today, if you happen to ask those fishermen's grandchildren why the Russians picked this place, they'll look at you as if you've lost your mind. They'll tell you, 'Well, obviously, because it's the most beautiful place in the world.' "

"So the Russians made friends with everyone in the village."

"Ah, no. Nothing like that. People in Malespina respected them, but it would be going too far to say they were friends. They accepted them with a kind of reverence, which was enhanced by the fact that they hardly ever saw them."

"Didn't you say lots of people worked for the Russians?"

"Yes, but not directly. Before the work began, they appointed a foreman named Federico Albala. He must have been clever with his hands, and he had worked on various houses in the village as a bricklayer. Albala took care of the management of the castle and supervised the works, transmitting the Russians' instructions to the workers. As you can imagine, this position made him the most powerful man in the village."

"What did the Russians do?"

"Apparently, they worked in their botanical garden. From time to time, emissaries would arrive, bringing them seeds from all over the world: pink jasmines from Japan, Himalayan cedars, everything imaginable."

"And they never went out?"

"Only on Sunday afternoons. Every Sunday, they strolled through the village, as calmly as you please. If they passed other people on their way, they greeted them courteously, but always kept their distance. They never stopped to chat with anyone. These promenades made the fog of mystery that enveloped them even denser."

"Why? What's mysterious about a Sunday stroll?"

I don't try to explain it to him. Luis is from another era, the one that came after the birth of color television and the death of intimacy. It seems very long ago to me, too, but it's easier for me to understand, to imagine the rumors moving from door to door like cats, jumping over garden walls, slipping into patios, reproducing in the darkness. Behind each window, in the shadow of craftily parted curtains, dozens of eyes must have followed those promenades, watching, recording each movement in order to magnify it later by the warmth of a fireplace.

I tell Luis, "If you ask people around here what the Russians were like, you'll hear hundreds of different descriptions, but they'll all agree on one thing. They'll all say that their behavior was majestic."

"Grandmother said it was all nonsense. She said they were snooty and pretentious."

"Well, there you have two different ways of seeing the same thing."

"But not the same."

"Of course it's not the same. But it amounts to the same thing. Suppose your grandmother was right. Suppose that sort of thing could be measured scientifically and a perfectly neutral instrument confirmed her opinion. It wouldn't make any difference. People wanted to see the Russians as majestic aristocrats, and that's how they saw them. Would you like me to give you some evidence of how little reality had to do with it?"

"Sure."

"Have you ever been to the Russians' grave?"

"Yes, a couple of times, with Papa."

"Then you must have looked at their gravestones, right?"

"More or less."

"What was the Russian woman's name?"

"I have no idea."

"You see? You didn't really look at it. You've got to keep your eyes wide open."

"Come on, spare me the sermons. What was her name?"

"Margaret Baker."

"Shit. Some Russian."

"Exactly. Some Russian. She was English. From London, no less. And no one can say the people in the village didn't know that, because there's a stack of documents that record the names of both the Russians. His name was Teodor Korzeniowski, but I doubt that anyone even tried to pronounce it; in fact, they applied themselves to the task of finding a nickname for him. Teo seemed too familiar, too common for a Russian aristocrat. But Albala put a quick end to the speculations, because he always referred to his boss as 'the Colonel,' and even offered a few facts that lent the nickname credibility. One night in the tavern, he told the company that his boss had been a senior officer in the Russian army. He'd been gravely wounded defending the czar, Albala said, and he'd been compelled to seek refuge in London."

"So that's where he must have met his wife."

"Exactly. And so Korzeniowski was dubbed 'the Colonel' forever. As for her, she didn't even need a name. She was the Russian's wife, so it followed that she was 'the Russian woman.' Everyone called her that. But the Russian woman's beach should have been called 'the English-woman's beach.'"

"Right. Grandma liked to call it 'the non-Russian Russian woman's bathtub.'"

"You know what your grandmother thought about her?"

"Only what I told you: she hated her. But Grandpa found her fascinating. I wish I knew why."

"Well, I have my own theory. I think, in a symbolic sense, they were made for each other. The Russian woman was determined to turn herself into a legend and Papa was born to create legends, but the only ones he had were from the past—stories of knights and dragons, Simón's shipwreck, Li Po's exile, medieval battles. The Russian woman, on the other hand, was a contemporary legend. And on top of that, he knew her personally. For the first time, he wasn't repeating a story that he'd inherited but constructing one firsthand."

The Legend of the Russian Woman. Once again, in my memory, Papa's words, begging to come out. Borrowed words: "It must be said that . . ."

More or less like this: The Russian woman, despite her reluctance to show herself in public, drove all the men in the village mad. Every morning around eleven o'clock she went down to her beach, which was a shelf of smooth rocks lying at the foot of a cliff. She may have been the first person ever to swim in those waters, because the beach was accessible only to someone who had a boat, that is to say, only to the fishermen, who considered both sunbathing and sea bathing frivolous activities. The new bourgeoisie of the cities were gradually beginning to look upon bathing in the sea as healthy and even necessary, but for the people of the village, it was still an immoral eccentricity. The Russian woman, however, had bought that beach in order to use it, and she wasn't inclined to let the difficulties of the terrain stand in her way. She charged Albala with procuring her a sturdy mule, and every morning, sitting astride the animal, she'd risk splitting her head open on the rocks in exchange for the pleasure of bathing on her very own beach. Some fisherman well off the coast must have seen her on the beach or in the water, and word spread immediately: some said the Colonel had ordered a secret tunnel dug; others said an ingenious system of pulleys operated by a dozen servants deposited her directly in the water whenever she felt like bathing; and most people said she took advantage of the inaccessibility of the place by swimming in the nude.

The tale about the Russian woman's skinny-dipping never seemed credible to me, despite the fact that there were people ready to describe the most intimate details of her body. We're talking about 1928. I don't have the least doubt that the woman covered herself with one of the bathing costumes of the day, like a suit of medieval armor.

"Made for each other?" Luis's voice brought me back. "Do you think Grandpa had an affair with her?"

"No."

"You sound very sure of yourself."

"I am. My father adored my mother. Besides, the Russian woman was fifteen years older than he was."

"So?"

"You're right. That's not an impediment. But in those days, it was a huge barrier. Besides, Mama would have found out. It would have been a fine scandal. She wouldn't have forgiven an infidelity of that kind."

"Then why did he paint her in the nude?"

"Don't be such a philistine, Luis. If you're going to assume that every time a model posed in the nude for a painter it was because they were sexually involved, the entire history of art would become a continuous orgy. Besides, that portrait isn't exactly erotic."

"Oh, no? It looks erotic to me."

"That's because you're very young. To you, a naked body is erotic on principle."

"Not so. You're mistaken. The body's the least of it. If she was too old for Grandpa, how do you think she looks to me? Those flowers are what I find erotic. The flowers and the Russian woman's smile. When I was little, I liked to imagine that the flowers were brushing against the soles of her feet and tickling her, and that was why she had such a strange smile on her face."

"Well, she was a very odd person."

"Did you know her?"

"Not exactly. But I saw her on various occasions. I remember she made a big impression on me the first time. We were in Papa's boat. I was quite small—five or six, maybe—which means it must have been the *Astor III*, the little sailboat. It had a tiny outboard motor—eight horsepower, I think. I can't tell you exactly what year it was, but it had to be toward the end of the 1960s. Papa was directing the boat toward the cove where the Russian woman's beach was. It wasn't easy, because there are a lot of underwater rocks. Suddenly, we heard shouts from the beach. It was Albala. His position had changed over the years, from foreman to butler. He was standing on the shore, dressed in a uniform."

"What?"

"I swear to you. He was wearing livery. With all the trimmings. A blanket was spread out at his feet, and some plates and a couple of wicker baskets were on the blanket. He was shouting and making signs for us to go away. Even Papa needed a few minutes before he could grasp what was happening. He must have left the motor idling in neutral, because we stayed there for a while, not moving, until Mama spotted the Russian woman. She was coming down the cliff on the back of her famous mule."

"And what happened?"

"All this was a few years before the portrait. At this point, Papa had never spoken to her. He must have known her by sight, and he surely knew what was said about her in the village. Suddenly, there she was. The cliff was so sheer that the mule looked to be on the point of sliding down it, but the Russian woman remained erect, as if she were riding a thoroughbred mare across a plain. Mama and Papa stared at her for a while and then both spoke at the same time. Mama said, 'What a buffoon,' and Papa said, 'What a goddess.' I asked what a buffoon was and I remember getting angry because no one paid me any attention. There was a little tiff because Papa reversed the motor and started to leave the cove and Mama told him he was a coward. She said that beaches belonged to everybody, and Papa said that wasn't so. That particular beach was the Russian woman's property, he said, and she had every right to go swimming whenever she wanted to."

"It's a shame you didn't stay. You would have seen whether she swam naked or not."

"Of course she swam naked," says Pablo's voice behind me. I don't know how long he's been listening to the conversation. "That morning she was wearing a bathrobe. I remember it perfectly; it was light blue. I guess it can't be very pleasant to ride a mule when you don't have any clothes on. But I'm sure she swam in the raw."

"Goodness, Pablo, how unusual. There's something you're sure about."

"And furthermore, I'm sure she and Albala started humping on the beach as soon as we were out of sight. Like rabbits."

"Oh, sure. She and Albala, her butler?"

"One of many. The Russian woman screwed half the village of Malespina. That's why people talked about her so much."

"You too?"

"Me too what?"

"Luis is convinced she had an affair with Papa."

"Of course she did. I wouldn't doubt it for a minute."

"No one has ever been able to prove she had an affair with any-one. And for that reason you've created a sort of fantasy for your-selves—"

"You're the one who's fantasizing. Papa told you the story about how she was some kind of princess so many times that you need to be-lieve it. They clearly had an affair. No way they didn't."

"Pablo—"

"Don't Pablo me. When are you going to wake up? You're not a lit-tle girl anymore. Or do you also think that Mama was faithful her whole married life? What are we talking about—fifty years of fidelity? Not even a little fuck, a wild one-night stand? Come on, Serena, I mean, shit, don't be so naïve."

"I'm not being naïve. Times were different. Screwing was—"

"Screwing was a way of getting something. As it is now, as it will always be. How do you think Grandmother Amparo managed to get Simón accepted into the theater company?"

"What are you talking about? You're crazy. Do you remember our grandmother's face? She looked like butter wouldn't melt in her mouth."

"Exactly, like butter wouldn't melt in her mouth. That's just what I mean. How do you think she got Simón hired? By telling the director her boyfriend had an extraordinary voice? By telling him about this wonderful lad's prodigious memory? What's wrong with you? Do you believe everything people tell you?"

This argument is important to me, even valuable, but I don't have it straight in my head just yet. We went home in silence. By the new road. I didn't take it on purpose to fuck with Pablo, I was just distracted. Maybe Pablo's right, but it's hard for me to accept that. Ridiculous, almost childish, I know. Children couldn't exist without sex, and yet children consider their parents to be asexual beings.

The first time I asked where babies came from, Mama gave me a scientific answer: the sperm and the egg and fertilization and childbirth itself and the umbilical cord, the whole thing. And she did it right, "Your father and I made love. . . ." My imagination constructed a mental picture of the strange enigma that was being revealed to me, in which Papa's little thing fit into Mama's little thing with neat, geometrical precision, the way two pieces of wood fit together in construction sets. But this image didn't correspond to the truth. It doesn't correspond to the truth. The image of our parents in the act of procreation doesn't feature hair and sweat and an imperious prick on the point of exploding. And it's not only the image of our engendering that's false. The image of our being born is false as well. The bundle of moisture, the furious weeping, the blood and the tearing, the lumps of congealed matter sealing the eyelids, the cold, the weightlessness, and the sudden obligation to be, all that swamp of cells forced to unite into organs and grow and divide and multiply and find a way out. That's what being born is: the search for a way out, a groping, jerky, blood-blinded search. And after that, an entire lifetime spent looking for another way out, an exit out of the fix the previous exit put us in. And so, with our memory suspended, we manage to think we weren't born that way, we think we came into the world all tidy and wrapped up like a caramel, smelling like gauze and ointments. We want to be children of love, and we're children of sex.

Love can contain sex, the way barely perceptible springs contain immense rivers. I have little doubt that that's how it was in our case. But such a love is a question of mathematical possibilities, it's the bottle in spin the bottle, it's the deranged compass signaling who should kiss whom how. Or as my brother Pablo would say, who sticks it into whom, and makes a child who perhaps in time will forget what he's the child of. Because we're also the children of words, and that complicates everything.

"Is it true that Grandpa never painted another picture?" Luis interrupts my train of thought as we're about to turn into our driveway.

"It's true."

"Nothing? Didn't he even draw a single sketch? A doodle on a paper napkin?"

"Nothing."

"Why not? Shit, I never got to see him paint anything, and it pisses me off. Besides, of all the pictures I've seen, the Russian woman's portrait is his best. By far."

"I don't know, Luis. He said that was precisely the reason. He said he'd never paint a better picture than that one."

"Like I told you. It's not that Grandpa's gone nuts recently. He's always been nuts. What bullshit!"

"It's not bullshit," Pablo jumps in. "It's a half-truth, that's what it is. Think about it. Why is the portrait of the Russian woman the best of all his pictures? Coincidence? Come on. Papa was in love with her."

"So not only did they have a fling, but now he was in love with her," I say.

"You can call it what you want. How many portraits did Papa paint in his life?"

"I don't know. Hundreds."

"Or thousands. Some better, some worse, just like anyone else's work. There are only two that are special. The one he painted when he fell in love with Mama, and the portrait of the Russian woman."

"I don't follow you."

"Because you prefer not to. Papa fell head over heels in love with the Russian woman, the way he had fallen for Mama so many years before. He painted a picture of her. Then he realized he'd never paint another picture as good as that one. But it wasn't a matter of technique. What he realized was that he'd never feel another passion like that one. That's why he couldn't ever paint a picture as good as his picture of her. Now do you understand? If I could manage to compose something perfect, I'd never play another note."

"No question, Grandpa was off his rocker," Luis says, interrupting Pablo. "But you're worse."

"What do you know, young whippersnapper?" Pablo replies.

I'm surprised to hear him answer so mildly, without seizing the opportunity to pounce on Luis and reduce him to ashes with a fiery discourse about authentic music, authentic art, and the authentic life. I seek his face in the rearview mirror and find him looking totally absent, like some kind of zombie. His eyes are almost dreamy, as though instead of fearing the moment that he attributes to Papa—the moment when he hit the wall of perfection—Pablo yearns for it. As if he really would like to compose a single perfect piece and then stop playing.

"What do you know of moonless nights," I say, seeking him again with a furtive glance, trying to determine whether he's already fled away to his own country, the land of impossible music.

"What do you know of luckless love," Pablo replies, unable to suppress a smile.

That's known as sibling complicity: the ends of the bond that unites us are always tied to memory. What do you know of moonless nights; what do you know of luckless love. I think Lorca wrote those verses, but I'm not sure they're accurate word for word. When we were little and we asked Papa a question he didn't want to answer, he'd reply by reciting those lines. Mama had another favorite phrase she used when confronted with indiscreet questions or when we dared to give an opinion on a subject we knew nothing about. She'd say, "Who asked you to stick your nose in?" I know that if I become a mother, the moment will come when other people's words start streaming from my mouth. If I have this baby, I'll turn myself into an echo. I know this, and I'm resisting it.

I think about Li Po. Fifth proverb: "Not everything you don't know is a lie."

There's no such thing as a return trip. The place you return to is altered by your absence, and you're not the same person you were when you went away. I found that out years ago. Nevertheless I kept on using the verb "return"—when I return, I'll return tomorrow, now that I've returned. This time, I can't afford that luxury. I'm not returning; I'm going. I'm going to the place where they think I'm dead.

I still don't know when. Amkiel's picking me up tomorrow. Pampered Girl will carry me to Sayaxché; I'll get a lift to Flores in some truck; a light plane will take me to Guatemala City. I'll be in the capital by tomorrow night. Then I'll have to start saying I'm alive. At the embassy, for starters. I have several borders to cross on this trip, and I don't want some official stopping me with the argument that the dead can't travel. I don't even have a passport. If they tell me I'm dead, I'll do what good liars do: I'll stick to my story. Dead? Me, Isabel, dead? Not a chance. All I know is that I lost my passport. I was in the jungle. I just found out about it; you don't know how sorry I am; no, don't call my children. I'd prefer to tell them myself. My passport, thank you and good-bye.

There will still be one other matter pending: Judith. I'd be lying if I said I haven't thought about her these last few days. Well, not about her, but about her children. This confusion is much worse for them, because it's going to end badly. Who knows, they may still be looking for her, and it would be better for them to know the truth. Or not. I don't know. I must try to take care of this as soon as I get back to Barcelona. It's not as though I'll be able to do much, because the information I have about Judith is meager. I don't even know her last name. I suppose I could send the ambassador a letter from Barcelona and tell him I met someone called Judith and I'm certain she was in the same area as I was and perhaps she . . . In any case, I'll take care of it. Now all that matters are the frontiers. The first one I have to cross is right here, on the Río Pasión, the frontier between life and death; this time, into life.

I came here by way of London, and I bought a return ticket that follows the same route in reverse. But I don't want to go back through London, for many reasons. To begin with, there's no point. I did what I had to do there on the outward journey, and it left me with a bitter taste in my mouth. And to top it all, I did it for the kind of petty motives you should never give in to, because they cling to you and stain your hands. Jealousy? Is jealousy what I should call the impulse that took me to London to confirm something that I'd suspected for many years? How about revenge? Or maybe rancor? It makes no difference what it's called: it's still ugly.

I wanted to prove that the Russian woman was a fraud. Now, I didn't have to leave Barcelona to be sure of that. She was English, and she allowed people to say she was Russian all her life. In public, she called her husband "the Colonel," but no one could prove he'd ever fired a shot. Their whole story stank to high heaven. That pretentious castle, and their eagerness to tell everybody that Malespina was the most beautiful place in the world. The most beautiful place? No, that's always a relative judgment and they knew it, because they'd traveled all over Europe. The truth was that it was the only place. The only place in the world where they could live and where the legend they were running away from wouldn't hound them. Where they wouldn't be continually stoned by the truth.

Digging around in London to discover something about a deceased Englishwoman named Margaret Baker might seem like madness, but I'm good at that sort of thing. I may not have Serena's capacity for obsession, her morbid, painful fixation, but when it comes to searching for information, I know the tools of the trade. I bet everything on one card: the periodical collection in the British Library. This wasn't a stab in the dark. According to the legend, she was an aristocrat, and he was a senior officer in the czar's army who had fled the Bolshevik revolution. The press in those days would have been interested in such a couple. To tell the truth, I found much more than I was expecting to find. I thought there would be, perhaps, a photograph, or a mention in the society pages. I focused on the spring of 1927, from March to May, a year before the Russians appeared in Malespina.

Usually I'm slow at any sort of research because I tend to follow tangents. But on that occasion, my curiosity was concentrated and purposeful. My target was stationary and clearly visible; my rifle loaded and ready to fire. But I could never have imagined I'd find such a well-armed firing squad, such a scandal on a grand scale.

Early in March 1927, Margaret Baker was granted a divorce from one William Lingard, Duke of Worcester. This news took up entire pages in the daily papers, both because of the lineage of the protagonists and because in those days a divorce was no ordinary matter.

Even in England the laws were much less permissive, and the majority of situations now considered grounds for separation were kept secret. Perhaps by 1927 the marriage of convenience was an institution that had already become outdated, but many of its complicated stipulations remained in force. Having lovers was permitted, as long as they weren't flaunted in public; the couple was not an ideal of perfection, but a mechanism that ensured the survival of the species; no marriage aspired to the condition of permanent satisfaction that makes marriages impossible today. In short, a divorce between two aristocrats required another explanation. My hands were burning, and I didn't only read the words; I devoured them. The articles were illustrated with a photograph of the Russian woman, which allowed me to confirm something else I'd always suspected: although she'd been an attractive older woman, in her youth she was much more than that. Unique, spectacular. Perhaps not so much as in my husband's fantasies, but striking all the same. I tore myself away from her vivacious eyes, her strong face and tightly pursed lips, and read on. There was more copy dedicated to the past history of each spouse, to their family roots and the value of their properties, than to the divorce itself. Only at the end did I find the words I was looking for, almost hidden between the lines, as though covering their faces. It was the husband who had requested the divorce, and not only did his wife agree to it without demanding anything in return, she even granted him sole custody of the son who was their only child. For a woman of the aristocracy to consent, in 1927, to a separation from a millionaire without receiving any compensation, there must have been powerful reasons. I kept reading. I went over the following days and weeks. Nothing. Finally, as I looked through the newspapers from a month later, I was surprised to see the Russian woman's face again. She'd participated in a charity event, accompanied—for the first time in public—by Teodor Korzeniowski. The article covered half a page. I scoured the first paragraphs, which explained that he was the son of a Russian officer who had fled the Bolshevik revolution. The son. So his father was the colonel, not him. Although the couple stood arm in arm in the photograph, the article spoke only of a friend who had supported Margaret Baker after the recent breakup of her marriage. I drew my conclusions at once: Korzeniowski was the Russian woman's lover. Her husband had discovered their liaison. That's why she'd had no choice but to grant him an uncontested divorce; she wished to avoid being publicly denounced as an adulteress.

At that point, I could have considered the investigation closed. I hadn't found out much, but it was more than I had expected to find. However, I'd requested newspapers for the entire month of May, and there they were in front of me, bound into a single gigantic volume with heavy cardboard covers lined in blue cloth. So, luckily, I kept on leafing through the days. Suddenly I was struck by an image that seemed much less radiant than the previous ones. It was a posed photograph of the Duke of Worcester. He was holding a small child in his arms, a baby of six or seven months, its eyes turned away from the camera. At first, I thought the dark spots on the child's face were due to the poor condition of the newsprint. However, the article's first sentence quickly illuminated me: "My ex-wife beat our son."

There was another photograph in the following day's paper. Margaret Baker, now the ex-duchess of Worcester, announcing her imminent departure on a tour of Europe. She would be traveling for months, she said, and she hoped the trip would help her recover from the pain the separation process had caused her, while at the same time she categorically denied, and so forth. This explained everything. The duke had demanded a divorce with no payment of any kind because he had proof that she had mistreated their son. Probably in exchange for her complete surrender the Baker woman had made only one condition: silence. Her husband could keep his child and his fortune as long as he didn't expose her. However, she committed an error: she showed herself in public with the Russian too soon. In the duke's view, everyone would now conclude that Korzeniowski was the cause of their separation. Maybe that was precisely her intention; she wanted to have an alibi in case the duke should ever decide to talk. She wanted to be able to say no, she'd never laid a finger on her son, the duke was simply jealous. In any case, her conduct enraged the duke, who then displayed his son's bruises to the world. Her only recourse was to put some geography between them.

What disgusts me is the final act of cowardice: her appearance in Malespina and her eagerness to shroud herself in a ridiculous legend. The most beautiful place in the world? What a crock of shit. Maybe the most remote, or the most ingenuous. As far as the Russians were concerned, Malespina was the ends of the earth. In the weeks following her departure, the image of Margaret Baker continued to appear in the society pages: outside a Parisian jeweler's, in whose shop windows the reflection of an elegantly dressed Korzeniowski is barely visible; on the Promenade des Anglais in Nice, as he gallantly covers her with a parasol; in Provence, visiting the fields of lavender in bloom; in the Dolomites, enjoying the purifying air. Those images were generally accompanied by a text that always found room for an allusion to the duke's accusations, accompanied only occasionally by the Russian woman's denial. They had to find somewhere as remote as Malespina in order to be allowed to live in peace. Only exile, their imprisonment in the forest, allowed them to survive. Only the lie about its being the most beautiful place in the world silenced the accusing voices.

Not even that bothered me much. After all, it was her problem, not mine. I didn't invent that legend, nor did I ever wholly believe it. What affected me most was something else, something that explains the reasons behind my visit to London.

The piece of land where the Malespina house stands borders the forest that surrounds the Russians' castle. You could say we were neighbors, although the distance from one house to the other was almost two kilometers. Julio built his house on the property before he'd ever seen the Russian woman. It's possible that when he bought the land he'd never even seen the botanical garden, because the road leading to it was always closed. The Russians had promised to open the road after the work on the garden was completed, so that the whole village could enjoy it, but until then an iron chain blocked the way. When the workers' trucks entered and left, the foreman came and unlocked the chain. I think his last name was Albala. And I call him the foreman because I don't know what else to call him: the odd-job man, the foreman, the butler, and I suppose also the Russian woman's lover. Who cares? In order to reach the woods, their trucks had to pass behind our house. At first, when we heard them toiling up the road, we often ran outside to look at them, because one would occasionally pass that was carrying materials not for the castle, but for the garden: Japanese jasmines, the Russian woman's favorite flower, which announced their arrival with a train of fragrance; dwarf palm trees; cases with thousands of seeds from all over the world. Back then it fascinated me to watch them go by.

Sometimes we'd see the Russian woman out on one of her Sunday promenades, which were less frequent by then, probably because the Colonel, who was some years her senior, was not always in the mood for trotting about. I don't know exactly how old they were, but my London research confirmed more or less what I had already guessed. I think the Russian woman was born between 1908 and 1912. The Colonel died in 1968, which means that she became a widow around the age of sixty.

They say she never left the castle again. Perhaps that version is too faithful to the legend. Let's say we never saw her again.

All in all, I think I saw her face only six or seven times in my life, and always from a distance. What a character. She would mount that pitiful mule and go down to her beach for a swim, sending Albala ahead dressed in a butler's uniform to prepare a picnic for her on the sand. I don't even know how he got there, because the Russian woman was the only person who ever rode the mule. All the men in the village were crazy about her, constructing extravagant fantasies about her in their imaginations. Slavering, all of them; not least my husband. Once we saw her coming down the mountain just as we were about to cast anchor in the sea off her beach, and Julio reacted like a vassal in feudal times: he vanished in order to leave her ladyship in full possession of the land. Of course, it was much easier to keep the legend alive if we all closed our eyes. Because, naturally, the reality of this absurd woman was anything but legendary, with her hair lying across her shoulder in a childish, ridiculous braid as she tottered atop her mule, trying to keep her balance.

Maybe Julio saw her a few more times than I did. He had more contact with the people of the village; he often went out on his boat, and he talked with the fishermen. He gathered the tales that were told about her and pieced them all together, contributing to the glorification of a figure that the village of Malespina had already been distorting for decades. He turned her into the protagonist of one of his favorite stories; maybe only the one about Simón was more important to him. The Russian woman must have suspected that strange rumors were spread about her in the village, but I don't think she had the least intention of instigating them. She did the things she did because she was unusual, or because she was slightly insane, or because she had spent her life fleeing from her past—who knows? Of course, had the legend been premeditated on her part, she couldn't have found a better accomplice for its propagation than my husband. And to be fair, I liked his story, too, because it was eccentric, old-fashioned. Maybe because the Russian woman, digging the soil in a foreign land to plant her jasmines, reminded me of myself on my expeditions? It makes no difference.

The fact is that one day in early summer 1973, Julio came home euphoric. Beside himself. Out of control. He said that Albala had sent him a message to say that the Russian woman wanted him to paint her portrait. It was a unique opportunity, he said. Julio was to go to the castle every afternoon and work for three consecutive hours, and that's what he did. During the first two weeks, everything seemed normal, except for the unusual state of excitement Julio was in because of his commission. I could understand that painting the Russian woman was a thrill for him, with the privilege of seeing her up close at last and spending long hours amid the ongoing construction of the castle.

Julio was nervous, agitated. He had little appetite. Above all, he was losing interest in any conversation that didn't involve the Russian woman. It was her, morning, noon, and night. The Russian woman for breakfast, lunch, and dinner. It began to seem excessive. And the strangest thing of all was the way the canvas kept coming and going. Normally, if Julio was painting a portrait at his subject's house, he left his things there. It seemed only logical. As long as the process lasted, he would go each day, paint for an agreed period of time, and return home leaving his paint, palette, and brushes behind. Not so when he painted the Russian woman. During those first two weeks, Julio came home every evening with his easel, his canvas, and the little case with his painting things, all strapped to his pushcart, as if he'd gone out to the countryside to paint a landscape. He was even wearing the Borsalino hat I'd given him so he'd be able to cover his head when he painted out in the open.

The canvas was covered by an old white sheet. I never asked Julio to show me the picture, because he jealously guarded the secrecy of his creative process. He didn't like anyone to see a painting he was working on until he considered it finished. He used to say that he wouldn't even allow the subject of a portrait to take a peek at it before it was ready. I had countless opportunities to lift the sheet and have a look, but I didn't although I was surely tempted. As I've already said, I have a great deal of respect for the privacy of others. While Julio talked about the Russian woman, while he fed the family new stories each day, tales that began with a flight to safety in the midst of the Bolshevik revolution, I kept thinking, What can he be painting, what is it that's rendered him so thoroughly blind? Was I jealous? If only that had been the case—that and nothing more.

It was hard to imagine that Julio was having an affair with the Russian woman. Certainly a man can love a woman older than himself, but experience tells me that this happens more frequently when men are young, when an older woman embodies the fantasy of apprenticeship. Then, as they grow up, the opposite fantasy begins to take its place, the fantasy of the teacher: they dream of finding a young woman to whom they can impart all they think they know in return for the gift of youth and rejuvenation. No, Julio was only a little more than fifty years old, and it wasn't likely that he'd begin a liaison with a woman well past sixty. I'm not saying that it wouldn't have bothered me had it turned out to be true. I'm a bit old-fashioned in these matters, and I believe in the old theories about loyalty and commitment. History may have condemned them to oblivion, but that doesn't mean they were mistaken, at least not in my case. Had I had well-founded suspicions that my husband was having an affair, I wouldn't have stormed over to the castle, I wouldn't have played the role of the jealous hysteric, I wouldn't have engaged in hair-pulling contests with anyone. I would simply have had a talk with Julio so that everything was perfectly clear.

A talk? At that point talking was impossible. I'd tried to broach the subject with him more than once, to make him see that this time his stories were going too far. I told him I couldn't even have a normal conversation with my children anymore; I explained to him that even when he was out of the house, all they wanted to talk about were Russians and castles and exotic flowers. Look, I said to him, you haven't eaten in weeks. You spend your nights tossing and turning in bed. Or did you think I hadn't noticed? It was futile. The picture of his life, he said, he

was painting the picture of his life. The best, the one and only. Every-
thing else had been mere stages along the path to this unique opportu-
nity.

I stood this madness for one more week, thinking it would soon be
over. And all the while, as my impatience grew, so did my curiosity. I
knew that the solution to the mystery could be found in the picture itself;
that one look at it would be all I'd need to understand the labyrinth of
light in which Julio had lost his head. So one day, very early in the
morning, when Julio was still asleep, I got out of bed and went outside.
The picture was in the shed, casually left among the children's bicycles
and the fishing gear. I stood in front of it for a while, as if we were oppo-
nents, measuring each other's strength before a fight. Then I took a deep
breath, stretched out a hand, and started to lift the sheet, holding it
lightly between two fingers as if I were removing the blanket from a
sleeping giant. Little by little, a dark, dense background was revealed.
Then, as I lifted the sheet higher, I saw the mass of her hair, almost
merging with the dark, except for her gray-white braids. And suddenly,
an absolute contrast: the pale, luminous, living skin of her face. And
her eyes. Or rather, one eye, the left one, gazing out at me. The giant
awakened. I snapped the sheet back down and left the picture covered.

At the time, I thought my reaction had been caused by shame, as
if the indiscretion of looking upon something hidden had activated a
spring that made me turn away. However, as the morning went on, my
discomfort took shape. It wasn't guilt for having violated a secret, nor
could the picture itself explain what I felt: I'd barely seen it. It was her
gaze, then. That magnetic eye, rudely interrupted by my presence. I felt
as if my body had interposed itself between the painter and his model
as they gazed on each other. As if my presence in front of the canvas
might impede the painter's hand; as if Julio were behind me, cursing
my presence, waiting for me to get out of the way so he could finish his
picture.

That afternoon, when Julio got up from the table, leaving his food
practically untouched, I behaved like a sulky teenager. I made fun of his

*legend in front of the children. What castle? I asked him. It's just
a pile of stones. And why do you call her the Russian woman, when
everybody knows she's English? In short, I was deplorable. Julio declined the invitation to quarrel. He was very good at that.*

*That afternoon when Julio left the house, I already knew what I
was going to do. First, I was going to wait for an hour, then I was going
to go after him and present myself at the castle. A certain degree of rage
was obviously involved, because I didn't even think of preparing an excuse. I set off through the woods, my clothes sticking to my body. The
salty blast of the* garbí *loaded the air with moisture. All at once, I
thought I heard Julio's voice. It was barely a murmur, as though he were
softly humming a tune. Or better, as though he was talking to himself.
I stayed stock-still. His voice was unmistakable. I crept toward him on
tiptoe. Thirty meters or so farther on, there was Julio, standing before
his easel, muttering incoherently, and staring into space. His hand made
brief movements between the palette and the canvas with the precise skill
of a surgeon.*

*I kept walking toward him, making an effort not to step on any
branch or make the slightest sound, though I suspected that even an
earthquake would not have broken Julio's concentration. I looked for a
spot behind him that would allow me to contemplate the picture. The
Russian woman, full-length, naked, gazed up at Julio from the canvas.
Much prettier than in real life. Her eyes—both of them, this time—
ignored me completely. They were focused on Julio, hanging on his
every movement, on every gesture of the paintbrush that was inventing
them. Because the Russian woman wasn't there. I looked for her even in
the farthest shadows of the forest. Although Julio was facing away from
me, I tried to deduce what point his eyes were fixed on, to determine
where his model could be hidden. I even turned around, fearful of finding her behind me. And once again I felt as if the two of them had
enclosed me in their circle. It was just then that I saw the Borsalino,
hanging from the lowest branch of a tree. I snatched it and pressed it between my hands without knowing what to do, bit into it to repress the*

scream that was about to burst from me, and all the while I kept looking at the picture and waiting for the revelation, the moment when the key to the mystery would be revealed. For a while I told myself Julio was painting in the forest because he needed that unique, almost other-worldly, light; the Russian woman had withdrawn to take a rest or was walking nearby while he retouched some of her features from memory; or maybe the previous sessions had indeed taken place in the castle, with the Russian woman sitting for him, and only on that particular day, perhaps because he wanted to give the picture the final touches . . . All lies. Excuses. Julio was painting nothing but a ghost.

All the resolution I'd felt when I left the house had vanished. It was replaced by an almost childish terror, as if I were trying in vain to awaken a sleepwalker and feared that he'd remain plunged in his trance forever.

I left the forest without understanding a thing. Or rather without wanting to understand, because everything was clear. When I was halfway home, I realized I still had his hat in my hand. As I entered the house, I hung it on the hat rack, thinking that Julio would see it there and feel obliged to talk. And so he did; he came home, and he talked. The way he did every night. As naturally as you please, as if I hadn't seen what I'd seen, he started repeating what the Russian woman had told him that afternoon in the castle. I had to get up from the table, feigning a sudden bout of nausea. I left them all dining on his stories and went to bed, but that night I was the one who couldn't sleep.

I went over the list of lies again and again. Some of them were symbolic, and I tried not to pay too much attention to those. For example: the Russian woman wasn't as beautiful as she appeared in the portrait. She never had that light in her eyes. Even the portrait of me that Julio had painted when we first met resembled his imagination more than it did reality, but that didn't mean it was false. The forest was more of a worry, that and the absence of the Russian woman. Why did he say he was going to the castle to paint her when he had probably never set foot in it? And all those stories. Why did he talk about the Russian woman so much *if, in reality, he never spent a moment in her presence? After all, painting a portrait from memory is one of the many options an artist has. But to dissemble the absence of the model with that elaborate tissue of fantasies, repeated to the point of exhaustion . . . I spent the night wide awake, trying to come up with an explanation. I did what mothers do when their children lie too much. First, we exonerate them, convincing ourselves that there must be some mistake. Then I looked for a way to shift the blame onto myself. Maybe my rejection of Julio's exaggerated fantasies had caused . . . No. I could accept part of the blame, but that wouldn't change what I had seen. Especially since my husband could always have talked to me at his leisure. He could have said, "I want to paint the Russian woman in the nude, but I don't dare propose such a painting to her. I've studied her face carefully, so I'm going to invent the portrait. And since she's a legend, I want to do the painting in the forest, for that special light." Period. It wouldn't have been so hard. But Julio wasn't like that. Those words wouldn't have fit in his mouth, because his mouth was full of stories.*

Nearly thirty years have passed since then, and my opinion of the whole matter has undergone some changes. At first I considered his lies contemptible and repulsive, especially when I saw that the days were passing and everything remained the same. There were new stories every night. Julio declared that the Russian woman had worn a pair of antique earrings that afternoon, and when he asked about their origin, she'd told him that, in her hasty departure from Russia, she'd barely had time to wrap them up in a petticoat, and that later, after arriving in London, she'd been obliged by the exigencies of the expatriate life to pawn them. The next day, he'd relate how the Russian woman had ordered Albala to prepare an infusion of jasmine petals for her. And the day after that, he'd produce an entire saga about the war in which the Colonel was carried across various borders on a stretcher by his last faithful servants while his wife silently prayed that the wounds he'd suffered in defense of the czar would not end his life. In other words, he was the same Julio as always, and that was what frightened me the most. What enraged me. Because

I'd always had reasons for suspecting that many of his stories were the products of his excessively fertile imagination, but at that moment I knew that the distance between his words and reality was a mirror of the distance between sanity and madness. I can't say that his behavior toward me, toward us, changed in any basic way. His demonstrations of affection were continual, joyful, unquestionably genuine, but that made me all the more uneasy. How could he spend his afternoons lost in that non-existent kingdom of his and return to us as though nothing had happened? How could he talk to me after he saw the Borsalino hanging on the hat rack, after he knew that I knew? The eyes Julio looked at me with were the same eyes that invented the Russian woman in the forest; the mouth that declared his love for me was the same mouth that pretended to be a mere interpreter of her stories.

He finished the painting and showed it to us. He unveiled it in the living room and responded to our compliments with a huge smile. It's my best painting. He said that several times. His best painting. When he announced he wasn't going to paint anymore, everybody thought he'd gone mad. Our children, our friends, everybody. They begged me to convince him that it was absurd to quit just when he had found his best style, that it was a crime, that it was suicide. I, on the other hand, was happy for him. For him and for us. It was clear to me that his decision was the right one. It was as if he'd announced that he was going to stop using a drug, that he'd realized the danger his unfettered flights of fantasy posed for his mental health. So I was happy. I was even on the point of revealing that I'd seen him painting in the forest, but it was for his sake that I kept quiet; I wanted to do my part in consigning the whole affair to oblivion. No one reminds an ex-alcoholic of all the drinking he used to do before he quit.

From that moment, everything went back to normal. Julio's new profession as a sailor meant his stock of stories was refurbished. It was then that the account of the Battle of the Formigues Islands moved into first place in order of preference, higher even than the tale of Simón, although Julio solemnly seized every opportunity to mention that it was in

these same coordinates that his father had fallen off the ship. He dedi-
cated the same concentrated attention that he'd previously focused on his
art to the care of his boat and the entertainment of his clients. He drew a
line on the calendar: up to here, the past; from this day on, a new life.

I also took up my traveling again. They say that some liars wind up
believing their own inventions because they've repeated them so many
times. I wish the same mechanism worked for forgetting; when we choose
to keep something quiet, I wish we really could succeed in believing it
never existed. I tried and failed miserably. It was always there, waiting
for me. Useless, invisible, but active; like the land mine that blows up
in peacetime, stepped on by some innocent peasant.

Because it did blow up. It took twenty years, but it blew up. When
Julio's mind started to go, the doctors said it was a variant of Parkin-
son's disease. They subjected him to every kind of examination: mag-
netic resonance, scanners, reflex tests. They talked about problems with
his circulation. I pretended to believe them, but I knew that none of their
sophisticated machinery could trace the map of connections between the
Russian woman's woods and the impenetrable jungle of his estranged
mind.

Three years later, the page from the San Sebastián lighthouse ap-
peared. I've already told that story. I've already said it wasn't hard to
identify the steps of Julio's journey into madness. First, he found out
that Simón never existed. Next, he painted the Russian woman who
wasn't there. And after that, he stopped painting forever. That was the
sequence. When that page appeared, I understood my husband's life
with a clarity I wish I had in regard to my own. Julio had inherited a
heroic legend in which his father played the leading role. Over the course
of the years, the story was magnified, first in his memory, and later in
his imagination. The entry in the lighthouse keeper's logbook, the
crushing proof that Simón had never existed, smashed the legend into
smithereens. And after that, nothing remained. A few ephemeral leg-
ends: of passion, of perfection, of ideal and untouchable beauty. The
Russian woman. Medieval battles. Stories of Chinese poets. We convince

ourselves that these things are worth living for, even though living comes to an end. First we invent an immortality as fragile as an hourglass: time turns it over and over, and we watch the grains fall, knowing that at any moment fate might intervene and smash the glass, scattering the grains. Then we invent ideas, like a mechanical clock that we wind up every time it's on the point of running down, believing that not even death will be able to stop it, or hoping that at least memory will remain, like a pendulum suspended in midair, marking the two extremes of our existence.

But I know that nothing remains. Julio knew this too. The only difference is that he learned it before I did and resisted it with all his might. Everyone fights against the devastation of time with the best weapons he has. I've learned to oppose it, but barely, with the weapon of knowledge. I've seen death coming for me and taken refuge in this apparent but useless learning of mine, like someone trying to protect himself from a virus by striking it with a microscope. Julio didn't look for a place of refuge. He went out into the open field and stationed himself in the first line of fire, armed with his imagination. Can I blame him for any of this? What's his crime? Inventing himself? If that's the case, I'll climb up to the scaffold with him and present my neck to the hangman too. The Russian woman wasn't his greatest work. It approached perfection, but it was only an attempt. The definitive weapon, his absolute invention, is this sickness that allows him to take refuge in absence. Julio has invented his own nonexistence. When his eyes glaze over, when he's unable to remember his own name and my children sink into despair, I know where he is. I know what world he's dwelling in. An empty world. The self-portrait of his legend. That's the final victory: death arrives on the battlefield and finds it deserted.

Therefore, my investigations in London were petty and barren. Therefore, they left me with that bitter taste in my mouth. What was I trying to do? Conquer the past? Demystify the Russian woman? Shoot her memory? Shooting at shadows is a waste of ammunition.

MONDAY

All this, all the stories that have been told to me and that I tell in my turn, is a result of a tiny coincidence that took place in the spring of 1955 when my parents met on a tram. Three months later, they were married. I need to tell this particular story as if I believe it.

His name was Julio and he was thirty-two years old. He made his living painting portraits of the prominent ladies of Barcelona's bourgeoisie. To tell the truth, he did more than paint their portraits: he flattered them, provided them with conversation, and sometimes even seduced them. Naturally, his portraits made them look better than they really were. Prettier, of course, but also happier and wiser. He'd invent something mysterious in their gaze, as if they knew a secret. However, he did this judiciously, so that his portraits would not become offensive lies and so that the women would look upon them and believe this better version of themselves. His clients couldn't wait to tell their friends, the news spread fast, and so he made a steady income. He didn't care very much about money. He lived modestly and supported his mother, Amparo, paying for her small flat in the Sants district of Barcelona. His only luxury, a house in the coastal village of Malespina, barely deserved to be called that, since in those days it consisted only of a bathroom and another room that served as both bedroom and studio. Julio had been building it with his own hands for five years and intended it as a tribute to his father, who had been shipwrecked in the waters off that same coast. The house grew in fits and starts, according to no specific plan except for the requirement that the windows should face the sea. Whenever Julio received his fee for a commission, he'd hire two bricklayers for no more than two weeks to shore up a roof or install some plumbing and a drainpipe. When his funds ran out, he'd accept a new commission, and for the next two or three weeks he'd spend his afternoons in his new model's home.

She, Isabel, had recently turned twenty-three. She was a responsible young woman, a little shy, proper and well mannered. A middle-class girl; independent, perhaps obstinate, but prudent. Thanks to these virtues, she had successfully persuaded her father to allow her to enroll at the university and study history. She worked hard and didn't go out much, nor had she ever had a boyfriend beyond the hypothetical romances of adolescence. She was a small woman with a fine mop of dark brown curls, and although she wasn't especially vain, she did make an effort to straighten and subdue them. A few snapshots from the period show one of her typical gestures, a barely perceptible tic, which consisted of her pressing her lips together on the right side of her mouth, as though she were biting the tip of her tongue or, more probably, talking to herself.

He was handsome. Very handsome. He could have held his own against the film stars of his day; Cary Grant, or maybe Gary Cooper. A little over six feet of elegance with two burning black coals under a pair of thick eyebrows. The nose perfect, straight and even, but broad, a sign of an expansive personality. A wide, full-lipped mouth, always ready to break into a frank smile, that lit up his whole face. A light, flexible body. He was so elegant he seemed to float through the air.

I know little of their lives before they met. It's as if everything that had gone before was reduced to the status of a prologue. He was probably accustomed to relationships with experienced women. She, to her father's disgust, had rejected a marriage proposal about a year and a half previously, perhaps not so much because she found the candidate unsuitable as because marriage had not yet entered into her plans.

They weren't exactly made for each other. They came from quite different, not to say opposite, worlds; they lived more than a hundred kilometers apart; there was nine years' difference in their ages. In fact, she always said that she did as much as she could to ignore him during that first encounter. Ignoring him, however, wasn't so easy. Capturing eyes was my father's specialty, and he continued to exert this power for many years. He drew the eyes of others to himself almost without wanting to, the way a good pickpocket effortlessly steals away with other people's money. The same could not be said of her. She was used to being the center of attention because of her incisive remarks, and she was well respected at the university, even among the most sought-after women, who perhaps envied her intelligence and her common sense. Men came to her looking for advice, took her as a confidante, asked her help in preparing for exams, and predicted that she would have a brilliant future; but they didn't apply themselves to courting her. She didn't capture eyes. And if occasionally she did, it most likely occurred without her noticing it, because even in those days she went about the streets with her lips pressed together, in dialogue with herself, always busy seeking replies to the thousand questions that plagued her intelligence.

Chance brought them together one April day in the rear section of a tram. Perhaps I should explain that the trams had two driver's cabins, both exactly alike, at either end. These enabled them to be driven in both directions on any given street. When the tram was going in one direction, the controls at the other end were disconnected and passengers could occupy the empty cabin. Isabel was on her feet, leaning on the side of the cabin, imprisoned by the crowd and loaded down with an enormous bag in which she carried her university textbooks and various files. Julio was sitting on the driver's narrow seat, playing with the controls. He pretended to engage the power when the car accelerated and disengage it when they came to a stop, concentrating as if the safety of all the passengers depended on the precision of his movements. He overdid it a bit. He threw his shoulders back as he accelerated and hurled his whole body forward when he pretended to brake. He even punched the buttons that opened the doors and reproduced the sound they made by puffing out his cheeks and exhaling between his teeth. Like a child, except he was thirty-two years old. Mama used to declare that she'd found this strange man's performance puerile and pathetic, and that she'd forced herself not to reward him with a look. He, on the other hand, remembered not only that Isabel looked at him, but that she joined in the game to a certain extent, albeit with a shy smile. Perhaps encouraged by that very smile, he suddenly ended his performance and, like a little boy caught in the middle of some prank, arched his eyebrows, shrugged his shoulders, and tried to gauge the extent of her complicity. She blushed, fixed her gaze on the ceiling, and acted as though she hadn't seen him. Nevertheless, Julio persisted. He jumped to his feet and offered her the seat he'd just vacated with a gesture that was practically a bow. She accepted his invitation, although for years she maintained that she only did so to stop him from creating a spectacle in front of their fellow passengers. She pushed past a few people, took her seat, and murmured a few words of thanks; then she turned her back to him and stared out the rear window of the tram in silence.

He took up a standing position beside her. At the following stop, he suddenly took Isabel's left hand and, to her mute surprise, placed it on the power lever. "Now," he encouraged her. "Full speed ahead, because this next stretch doesn't have any bends."

She looked at him as if he were crazy, removed her hand and turned to face him. Addressing him formally, she spoke as curtly as she could without losing her composure: "Please behave yourself. And be so kind as to leave me alone."

Their faces were only a few inches from each other. On more than one occasion he later said he'd been on the point of stealing a kiss from her; if he didn't, it wasn't so much out of fear of getting slapped as the pleasure of prolonging the tension, which he found delicious. She always replied that she wished he'd tried it, not because she wanted him to kiss her, but because she really would have whacked him.

"As you wish," Julio said. "But don't be formal with me."

"I have no reason to be familiar," she protested. "We don't know each other."

"Not yet," he replied, perhaps encouraged by the flush that was spreading over Isabel's cheeks.

She turned her back on him and swore to ignore him completely, but he fixed his eyes on the back of her neck and the intense scrutiny made her uncomfortable. At last, seeing that her destination was only two stops away, she brusquely turned to one side, intending to spin her seat around, face her tormentor, and demand that he stop bothering her once and for all. But Julio was holding on to the back of the seat, and when it turned, he turned with it, so that in the end he was still behind her. He'd changed into her shadow. Isabel repeated this operation two times, and both times Julio guessed her intention and remained hidden behind her. The other passengers started nudging each other, whispering and clearing their throats, and Mama's flushed face instantly grew brighter at the thought that everyone in that tram was aware of her embarrassment. She thought about calling out for the driver and looked for the emergency alarm, but realized she couldn't get close to it without stumbling over this man. She closed her eyes, pressed her knees together, and swung the seat around again with all her strength. Opening her eyes, she discovered Julio's face in front of her, adorned with an amiable, almost dreamy smile. She clenched her fists, inflated her lungs and opened her mouth, but instead of the volley of insults she had intended, all that came out was a single question: "What!"

"I was just wondering if you would mind having a poor boyfriend," he answered in a whisper.

She hadn't counted on that voice, the legacy, apparently, of his father. It was a voice like water, a voice that could alternate between anger and tenderness in a single breath, overflow into threats, and grow still in a subterranean pool of secrets. We won't say that she became saturated with that voice, nor that she let herself be carried away on its current, but she did indeed yield to the temptation to dip a toe into it, like someone testing the water before bathing. "I already have one," she lied, thereby prolonging the conversation.

"I beg your pardon?"

"I said I have a boyfriend."

"Ah. Then he's not poor. He's the richest man in the world."

"If you don't mind, I'm getting off at the next stop," she said, lying again, because her destination was still two stops away. "Please let me pass."

"With great pleasure," he replied. Then he made a partial bow, and, in a voice loud enough for the people around them to hear, he added, "Make way for the queen."

She got off the tram and walked the five blocks to her home. On the way, she pondered the scene, chiding herself for the slowness of her reactions, for the bewilderment that had prevented her from making the witty, cutting retorts that were now rushing into her mind. She looked back only once, and felt a mixture of relief and disappointment when she saw that he wasn't following her. To tell the truth, that's not what she said. She said that she was happy she'd got rid of him, that she naturally thought she'd never see him again, and that she forgot about him immediately.

There is, of course, no way to be sure about what he was thinking at the time. We don't even know where he got off the tram, though we can be certain he had boarded it to go to the home of one of the ladies whose portraits he painted. Throughout the rest of her life, Isabel declared that she would have burst into helpless laughter had anyone told her it would not be long before that man became her husband. On the other hand, he maintained he'd never had the least doubt from that moment on. If he didn't propose to her on the spot, he said, it was because he realized there wasn't much chance she'd accept. There must have been some truth in what he said, because the next day he made sure to take the same tram at the same time and from the same stop, in front of the university. She arrived at the stop punctually too, as if it were a date. In the tram, he took up a position barely two meters away and gazed continually at her eyes, without blinking. Then he took out a pad of paper and a charcoal pencil and began to draw. She couldn't see what he was drawing but after he'd sketched ten or twelve lines, he approached her, tore the top page from his drawing pad, and gave it to her.

She accepted it reluctantly, glanced at it, then returned it. According to him, her hands were trembling.

"You don't like it?" he asked.

"It's pretty," she admitted. "But I'm not this person."

"You will be," he said. This time there were no exaggerated displays, no pretending. They were standing close to each other, swaying to the movements of the tram. "You'll look a lot like you someday."

I've seen this portrait. I can say, objectively, that it does bear a certain resemblance to Isabel, perhaps as if she and the woman in the portrait were distant relatives. Maybe she looks somewhat older, more marked by time and by all that time brings with it: desire and fear and pleasure and resignation. If it's true that her hands were trembling, maybe it was because all those things were visible together in the same face, but without contradicting one another.

"I don't know if I want to look like me," she said.

"That doesn't matter. It's not going to depend on what you want."

"That remains to be seen," she replied, apparently weakening.

Up to this point, it all seems believable. If you know who told this story, you can discount a large fraction of it as histrionics, yet still assume that it's more or less credible, as all love stories are up to a point. But then comes the part where he said, "Well, if it remains to be seen, then let's see it together," and she replied, "You're moving rather fast, don't you think?" He noticed that she'd addressed him with the familiar "you" for the first time, took this as an encouraging sign, and declared, "That must be because I know where I'm going," and with surprising self-confidence, she challenged him with, "Well, I shouldn't hold you back," and now her smile was no longer suppressed, and he took his eyes off hers for a moment, but only to gaze at her lips, and though she was gnawing at them, she succeeded only in increasing his desire to kiss them. He said, "No, I want us to go together," and it was hard for her to keep the conversation going, because that sentence came from a new world, a world impossible before she met this man and heard his voice.

If we were talking about ten, fifteen, or even thirty years ago, this story would end up in bed, and that would be that. However, we're talking about 1955, and in those days, it was the same ending, but it took longer, with more pauses and all the fancy footwork needed in between. What happened was that Julio wanted to go fast, and Isabel wanted to go slow. Some afternoons they'd have coffee; on others they'd go for a walk. They went dancing a couple of times, always unbeknownst to Isabel's father, because she couldn't imagine how she might even begin to tell him she was going out with a man nine years her senior, an artist and resident of a small fishing village, a man without a fixed income or a decent profession, the son of an unknown father; a man whose only living relative was his mother, a seamstress no less, with whom he didn't even live, in spite of his being a bachelor.

And so they continued to see each other in secret for a couple of weeks. He must certainly have found the progress of their romance irritating, or at least unnecessarily slow. It mustn't have been easy for her, either, going back to her father's house after each meeting, awash in guilt, convinced that it was the last time, promising herself she'd never see that man again or listen to his strange, intoxicating stories, trying in vain to concentrate all her attention on the studies she'd half abandoned despite the fact that her final exams were dangerously close.

Let's agree that chance and a barrage of Cupid's arrows are sufficient to explain the fever of those first encounters. Apparently, the bolts quickly struck home. Like two magnets whose poles attract and repel, they were pulled toward and pushed away from each other with equal force. This is not a suitable man for me, she thought continually, and he must have thought, This woman is driving me insane. They put the same passion into their fights as they had into those first delirious conversations. After they'd known each other for a month, he made a date with her to tell her that he was suffering too much, that it was better to break it off while there was still time, before anyone had to suffer too much, because their worlds were too different for this to turn out any way but badly, and there was nothing as important to him as his freedom, and nevertheless he would never stop loving her and he could only beg her to forgive him, and he hoped she'd at least believe him when he told her he'd never meant to cause her any pain. She interrupted him and said, me too, you too what, me too, I feel the same way, I can't bear the pain I'm causing myself and I don't want to harm you either, but when I see you I feel bad and when I'm not with you I feel worse, and this affair isn't right for either of us, and he said then we're in agreement, and she said well, yes, I think so, and for the first time in the conversation the two of them smiled. After a while he said maybe what we need is a little time to think things over, and she said maybe so, Julio, if we don't see each other for a while we might be able to think in peace and we'll be better able to find out what we really want, and surely she was thinking she'd rid herself of that passion, and he found some dignity in disguising a defeat as if it were a truce, and she said come here, idiot, come and give me one last kiss, and he kissed her as long as he could, and then she got up and went home. To think in peace. She was very fond of thinking in peace.

He shut himself up in his house in Malespina, to forget. Julio liked forgetting as much as Isabel liked thinking. But it was not to be. For the first and last time in his life, the little machine he used for moving on to something else broke down. I don't know how much time he spent in Malespina, two or three weeks, building walls to give his mind a routine that would distract it. The west wall of the outbuilding is still an irrefutable witness to the number of times, between one brick and the next, he said Isabel, Isabel, and of the nervous clumsiness that affected his hands as he worked. So he decided to put more space between them. "If you have to forget, you have to forget," he told himself. "And if it's a question of distance, a hundred kilometers isn't far enough."

It took him barely an hour to fill a bag with some clothes and a clumsy bundle of drawing paper and pencils and climb aboard a train that was passing through Barcelona. At each stop, he resisted the temptation to get off, because his intention was not to arrive anywhere, it was simply to go. To the south, to the border, to the last station on the map, which in this case was a metaphor for the new life that would begin as soon as he got off the train and boarded a boat to cross the straits, to land in another country and look for a beach where he could find a cheap room and spend as many days painting as might be necessary to bring back his lost serenity.

He spent interminable hours swimming and diving, holding his breath as he swam underwater, fighting against the permanent siege of memory as it prompted obvious comparisons between the protuberances of coral deposits and Isabel's body, which he had never yet seen and could only imagine. Or he sank into the embrace of rum, which only served to stir up more memories and confuse them, inventing the pleasures that had been denied him, the most treacherous form of remembering.

He persevered in contradiction. He convinced himself he was getting closer to his goal. Isabel's features were already blurred in his memory, and her voice, the voice he'd thought permanently lodged in his ears, no longer persecuted him. He interpreted this as a victory, rejoicing that the thick fog of oblivion was beginning to spread into the corners of his brain, thus succumbing to the most subtle of deceptions, since it is exactly there, in the mists, that the enemy can best prepare the final assault.

A few days were to pass before Julio grasped what was happening to him. He had spent an entire morning on the beach, lying on his stomach and rolling a grain of sand around in his hand. When he opened his eyes, the first thought that came to his mind was the absurd idea that the grain of sand was exactly the same color as Isabel's eyes. He stared into his palm for a while, and then a stampede of thoughts overwhelmed him: the notion that he was going crazy; the ridiculous sensation that none of his efforts would be of any avail; and the conviction that it made no sense to keep postponing the inevitable.

He returned that day to Barcelona. He crossed the straits in the opposite direction and then crossed the entire country, from bottom to top. The long walk from the station to Isabel's house seemed eternal, troubled as he was by the anxiety of not knowing if she would be waiting for him. But she was waiting for him, she'd done nothing else, so she answered the door with the promptness of someone who knows and fears and desires what's coming to her, and she was glad her father wasn't home; but she was afraid of tempting fate, and so she suggested they go wherever he wanted to take her, and they chose the nearest guesthouse. They used to pad this part of the story with details about all the things they thought and said that night, but I can imagine what happened. My brother Pablo would say they screwed like a pair of rabbits all night long.

I don't have any objections to raise. I've heard love stories more far-fetched than this one. So I believe everything my parents told me, even that they got married a month later. Even that Mama announced her intention to get married when she arrived home that same night, and her father made an enormous fuss and threatened to send her to a boarding school until she got over what he interpreted as an adolescent crush. She answered that there was going to be a wedding, with or without his consent, and that nowhere would be far enough to prevent her from keeping her promise, whereupon the story goes that he grew livid and blamed the nuns and the university and said it would have been better for her to get married a year earlier to a respectable suitor, instead of some dubious stranger. When he had no rational arguments left, he resorted to blackmail, promising his daughter that if she married this man she wouldn't see so much as a single peseta from him. Defiant and unwavering, she replied that he could stick his money wherever it fit, assuming that cultured people actually said such things to one another in those days. Because they were both cultured people, unlike Simón and his father, they were condemned to reason and negotiation.

The father's strength dwindled as the argument went on. He began to give ground and passed from an absolute negative to the search for a compromise. In the end he stated that he'd agree to their marriage if her fiancé found himself a job. She accepted this condition, but proposed that her father should be the one to find it by availing himself of his many contacts. He asked her what can this boy do, and she said he's not a boy, Papa, he's thirty-two years old. This information caused the conversation to heat up again, but finally the discussion ended with a proverbial I'll see what I can do.

What he could do was get Julio a job with Philips, with whose general director Isabel's father played bridge every Tuesday. When Julio learned of this, he answered calmly that if he was going to take a job, which he would do only because he loved her, it might as well be this one. Out of curiosity, he wanted to know what his duties would be, and she told him it wouldn't be too bad because his job would be drawing, and he said drawing what, and she cleared her throat and said, Well, those diagrams they use in the instruction manuals for household appliances, and when she saw him swallow hard, she begged him to be patient and promised that as soon as they were married, as soon as they were able to show her father they could support themselves, she'd be the first to release him from his work commitment. And they were married. He didn't stop painting, but kept at it despite the cost to his nights, and accepted commissions from anyone who could pay him, until it became evident even to Isabel's father that he could make a better living painting pictures than by drawing ridiculous diagrams.

And so they lived happily ever after, the end. Because from then on, they stopped being Julio and Isabel and turned into Papa and Mama: first for Alberto, who apparently pronounced those words early and with confidence; then for Pablo, who probably said them almost without wanting to; and finally for me, who has never stopped believing them. I mean, I believe all these things Papa told us because I don't have a better version. Was Papa lying when he told us this story? Yes, according to the criterion affirmed by Li Po. I refer to his fourth proverb: "Only the man who does not know he is lying can utter the perfect lie." A perfect lie; an old-fashioned love story. I believe the stuff about chance and Cupid's arrows and the comings and goings; I even believe the nonsense about grains of sand and portraits created by desire. From that time on, they lived together and were moderately happy for more than forty-six years. Forty-six years. They would have gone on even longer if Mama hadn't decided to board some stupid river launch when she was too old to do that sort of thing. In any case, it was a lifetime.

That's it, then. The story told as if I believed it.

I'm writing these words en route to Barcelona on Iberia flight 6112. If my calculations are correct, we'll arrive in a couple of hours. Limbo, transmigration, resurrection. I know all the names for this intermediate state. Yesterday I was dead in the jungle; today I'll be alive in Barcelona. Today or tomorrow, when my children see me, because only other people can certify that we're alive. They're certainly going to recognize me this time. I know what's waiting for me, and I'm prepared for it: a new order that excludes me, an organization imposed on the chaos caused by my death, enabling life to go on as before.

I didn't plan to do any more writing, because from now on the only words that are going to count will be the ones I say out loud or the ones I choose to repress. I've stuffed everything I wrote in the Posada del Caribe into my suitcase. Nevertheless, writing calms me down—that's one of the things I've learned on this trip. On paper I can cross out my mistakes and gather my ideas. I can have doubts; I can face the fact that I've died and nothing has happened. The world goes on and my absence from it means nothing. Of course, people will miss me, but if my children have complied with what the world expects of them, they must be tired of remembering me by now. They've probably already stopped finding an excuse to invoke my memory in every one of life's little trivialities.

I'm not saying I'd feel better if I returned and found that all my loved ones had committed suicide because they couldn't bear my absence. What I'm complaining about is that the world's the same, just the way a pearl necklace is still a pearl necklace after you remove a pearl.

I used to hope that death, when it came, would give my life some value: the exact minimum necessary for life to mean something. And if the world stays the same after I'm gone, that's because life means nothing. I'm sorry, but I just can't manage to reconcile myself to this idea. That's why I asked for writing paper, because ever since I stepped into the airplane, I've been thinking about the Wari. They eat their dead. Or rather, they used to eat them.

Let's be accurate: I didn't discover the Wari. The missionaries got to them first. The fucking missionaries, if you'll pardon the expression, and those pricks the rubber tappers. They're the ones who should fall to their knees and beg for pardon. From me and from the Wari. Because they may have been on the point of killing me, but they ruined the Wari's lives. I'm aware that things are better for the Wari these days, but for decades, every time a Wari saw a white man, he was looking into the face of death. Ever since 1919, when the first encounter took place. At that time, the Amazon region had been turned into a center for the extraction of rubber and latex. Work had begun on the construction of a railway line that was to link San Antonio do Madera to Guajara-Mirim, making it possible to transport rubber all the way to the port in Manaos. The railway workers came across a group of previously unknown natives and abducted a few with the idea of exhibiting them on their return to civilization. The Wari had to move deeper and deeper into the jungle, had to retreat toward the headwaters of several tributaries of the Río Pacaás Novos—the Lage, the Ouro Preto, the Ribeirão, the Formoso—whose banks they had inhabited from time immemorial. For two years there was no more contact with them. Then, in 1921, the demand for Amazonian rubber decreased in the face of competition from the forests of Malaya. The rubber tappers disappeared, and the Wari recovered their territory.

In the 1940s, during World War II, the Japanese occupied Malaya and the West needed Amazonian rubber again. The trains and the tappers came back, and this time they were determined not to let anyone ruin their business. Armed with tommy guns, they attacked the villages at dawn. Nothing could ever be proved, but it seems clear that in some instances entire hamlets were exterminated. The Wari took their revenge when they could. From time to time, a rubber tapper would be found rid-dled with their arrows. A few were eaten. The Brazilian government had to intervene, so in 1950 a plan to "pacify" the indigenous tribes was for-mulated. A government foundation answering to the name SPI directed the execution of this plan and was, as history has demonstrated, respon-sible for many atrocities before being replaced by the current entity, FU-NAI. The plan lasted almost twenty years. In 1956, the first peaceful contact was initiated, though in view of what took place, the term "peaceful contact" would appear to be a euphemism for "massacre." The Westerners established contact with the Wari by means of useful gifts. They sought out the paths the natives had made through the jun-gle and left bundles filled with attractive things: metal tools, machetes, clothes, mirrors. Once contact was established, the natives began to die like flies. That's the history not only of the Wari, but of almost all the tribes contacted by Westerners. Germs tend to go about their work with striking efficiency. Once they find their way into the natives' blood-stream, microbes that hardly provoke a sneeze in us turn into a source of deadly epidemics.

By 1969, the population of the Wari had declined by two-thirds. Even though we already had sufficient information about the devastat-ing effects of Western contact on other tribes to avoid the repetition of the same process with the Wari, the question of contact wasn't up to an-thropologists; it was in the hands of the rubber extractors and the mis-sionaries. Protestant missionaries. They're the ones responsible for an unforgivable vicious circle. They penetrated deep inside tribal territory, seduced the natives with their ridiculous gifts, infected them with all sorts of sickness, and then disappeared for a while. Not long—two or three weeks. Then they came back with the medicines the people needed to get well. It was as simple as that: the prey comes to depend on the predator; the murder victim on his murderer. Not only did the outsiders make the natives sick so they could cure them, but they convinced them that their illness was a result of their evil practices. Of course you get sick; you eat your dead.

At this point, the intruders were able to open negotiations with the tribesmen: tools in exchange for exploitable land; medicine in exchange for abandoning their customs. Above all, they were told that eating their own dead was a bestial practice. Better to dig a grave and top it off with a pair of crossed sticks. Better to maintain shrines to the memory of the dead and bring them flowers.

I don't want to get carried away. I'm only trying to explain why I went to Brazil and, in the last instance, why I'm thinking about the Wari now. By 1970, people had known who these natives were for more than twenty years, although they were still called Pacaás Novos because of their proximity to the river of the same name. Linguists were already busy studying the Chapacuran language family, and even such prominent anthropologists as Métraux and Lévi-Strauss dedicated numerous pages to the Wari, always grouping them under such broad categories as "Chapacuran Tribes" or "Populations of the Southeast Amazon and the Sources of the Madeira River."

Then the accusations of cannibalism began. Since I'd already decided that these populations were going to be my next project, I had been documenting the little that was known about them for some time. The accusations didn't surprise me; the accusers were playing a very old trick. Cannibalism was one of the excuses most often resorted to by the chroniclers of the conquest of Latin America to justify the extermination of the natives: in the eyes of the West, the practice of cannibalism dehumanized them and turned them into animals in urgent need of domestication. Back in 1503, barely ten years after the discovery of America, the massacre was so brutal that some voices were raised in protest. Queen Isabel was obliged to promulgate an edict in which the enslavement of natives was forbidden, except when they belonged to the tribes that practiced cannibalism. At the end of a few months, of course, there were very few tribes that hadn't been accused of it.

Now, all of this had already been written about, but it was remarkable to see the same mechanism being activated once again almost five hundred years later. And that's why I packed my bags for the Amazon even sooner than I had planned. I wanted to do things right. When I reached Brazil, I contacted the SPI. I did already have something of a name in academic circles, and I suppose it suited the SPI to pretend they were according me some attention. They placed a group of five men at my disposal and (after some money had changed hands) all the equipment I would need to penetrate the depths of the Amazon Basin: inflatable rubber boats, canoes, provisions, everything.

The first morning was enough to reveal to me that my traveling companions weren't exactly scientists. We all supposed that there were native subgroups that had, as yet, avoided contact with the outside world, and the others shared my curiosity about them. For me, however, this was to be the culmination of my career, and it quickly became apparent that I would fail if these louts were accompanying me. We went up the Pacaás Novos, entered the Mamoré, and came to its fork with the Lage. We weren't certain we'd find what we were looking for, but we weren't traveling blind. We knew that in 1961, some thirty Wari had survived the epidemic that decimated the Oro Mon subgroup and had gone off into the Mutum Paraná country, perhaps to join another group. In the two years preceding my trip, sightings had been relatively frequent. A few hundred acres separate the channels of the Lage and the Mutum Paraná. It wasn't unreasonable to suppose we'd find the Wari near the banks of one of those two rivers.

One night, I made the most daring decision of my life; it may also have been the most imprudent: I disappeared. It was easy. It's a simple matter to disappear into the jungle—fifteen paces, thirty paces—the trick is not to get lost. At the time, I thought I had made a clean getaway, but now I know it wasn't as clean as I thought; those five brutes were following me the whole time. Yes, I carry the guilt of having led five camouflaged rubber tappers to the last Wari subgroup that remained to be discovered.

This is my greatest problem when it comes to narrating what happened: Should I tell it as I lived it, with the naïveté of someone who thought she knew a lot and was basically ignorant? Or as I understand

*it now, when I do indeed know a lot and—for that very reason—con-
sider knowledge much less important?*

*Drums in the jungle. I hate that expression and the image it evokes,
when literature and films have reduced it to absurdity. Instead of drums,
I heard the sound of sticks striking tree bark, rhythmical, steady blows
whose human origin I failed to recognize at first and which I attributed
to monkeys; instead of tribal shrieks, I heard a confused murmur, which
grew loud enough to reach my ears only when the whole village joined
in. From that moment on, everything was simple. A three hours' walk
brought me to the village.*

*The first thing I saw when I arrived was a scattered group of men.
All lying on the ground on palm fronds, except for one, who was sitting
up in the midst of his fallen comrades, apparently awake. A little farther
on, a group of six women were mumbling something that sounded like a
song. Although the men lying on the ground remained perfectly still,
every now and then one of them would let out a piteous groan. It took
me a while to work out what was going on. I was assisted by the potent
aroma of* chicha, *the maize liquor that had overcome them all. It was
evident that some important celebration had come to an end. I later
learned that it was a* hüroroin, *which the Wari celebrate on special occasions, mainly when two groups that live apart are reunited. During
the course of successive days and nights, they stage mock battles and
obscene dances; rites of possession and surrender. And throughout the
festivities, they drink the fermented maize, until in the end they lose
consciousness. Literally: they fall down senseless, one after another.
That was the moment when I appeared, with all the men in the village
unconscious.*

*I've always wondered what would have happened had I arrived on
the scene at any other moment. I'd already had considerable experience
in dealing with native peoples, but I'd never actually been the first to
initiate contact. I knew about the hostility that had arisen in other first
encounters between whites and Wari, but I was convinced that it hadn't*

been provoked by the natives. In any case, I was greatly encouraged to see that my first contact would be with the women. I took a step forward.

The two kids who were beating on a tree trunk with stout wooden sticks spotted me first. They stopped their thumping, dropped their sticks, and ran away. Then the women stopped singing, rose to their feet, and approached me, talking among themselves. I stood still, showing my hands and endeavoring to maintain a smile that must have looked vaguely hysterical. They slowly walked up to me. We didn't sniff one another like dogs; there were no threats, no grunts, no aggressive gestures, nothing. In their wide-open eyes, as round as planets, there was only curiosity. They came and touched me: my white arms, my hair. They formed a circle around me and started walking, forcing me to keep step with them as we headed toward the first visible huts of the village. I think they wanted to wait until the following day, when the effects of the chicha would have worn off and the men could decide what to do with me.

I remember writing about my first night among the Wari while I was at the Posada del Caribe. Or rather, about my first night among the Wari women. About how I learned the meaning of the word "Wari" and decided to baptize them with it. The subsequent weeks I spent among the Wari were the happiest of my life, the dream of every anthropologist come true. To meet someone different and allow him to lead you by the hand into the corners of his existence. It's the only time in my life when I can remember spending as many hours writing as I have done during these past few weeks. They opened the doors of all their customs to me. I should have stayed and lived with them. I knew it wasn't possible, but I could at least make a conscious decision never to betray their kindness, to pay tribute to it with my silence, and not to publish anything about my encounter with them. I had some doubts. After all, I was there in the name of science, but giving it up didn't turn out to be so very hard. I took notes and thought that perhaps my children would publish them after my death. I even came up with a harebrained plan, which involved returning to the banks of the Lage after I'd gathered sufficient information and presenting myself in the area around my expedition's last campsite, pretending to have been lost and to have spent the previous five weeks nourishing myself on nothing but roots. If my companions had struck camp and returned to São Paulo to notify the authorities of my disappearance, I thought, it wouldn't be too difficult for me to run into other rubber tappers, because there were many working downriver. How naïve. They were probably right behind me the whole time, spying on me, rubbing their hands as they noted down every step I took. I'm sure of it.

At the beginning of the sixth week, an old man died in the village. The dead man lay inside a cabin for four days. There are all sorts of nonsensical theories according to which the Wari leave their dead exposed to the elements in order to facilitate their decomposition and make them more tender to eat. A lie. A cruel lie. I'm going to describe what I saw.

Several young men left the village and set out in canoes to notify other groups of the old man's death. Meanwhile, preparations for the ceremony kept the rest of the villagers in a constant state of activity. The reason the funeral rites weren't celebrated sooner was that it took the young men four days to return from the various subgroups, accompanied by representatives of each, who came to pay their respects. I watched while everyone present wept copious tears. Weeping is obligatory; not only to show generosity to the dead man's family, but also to grieve for one's own inevitable end. The lament that announces the death of a member of the tribe is exactly the same on every occasion; the same words are used, no matter what the age, the sex, the name, or the rank of the dead person. In this way, the news of the death of others is a reminder of one's own. For the Wari, death is a social event. We insist on believing that the individual dies and society goes on. Not them. In our world, the body defines and limits us. I extend as far as my extremities physically reach; beyond them, I don't exist. As far as the Wari are concerned, the body offers a flexible boundary, penetrable by fluids; so much so that couples, if they live together long enough, become blood relatives. When a villager dies, all the other inhabitants of the village die a little, too. They drown themselves in chicha until they lose consciousness, because in their culture the loss of consciousness represents a small death, and in this way they can claim to have accompanied the person who has passed away.

Right. I wanted to describe what I saw, not give an anthropological explanation for it. I saw them tear one reed off the roof of every hut in the village and light a fire with them. I saw the members of the dead man's family hauling in endless loads of wood to feed the fire. I saw the amount of wood necessary for cooking and eating a dead person. I saw that many of the logs, as well as the corpse itself, were painted with red vegetable dye. I saw the Wari chop up the body with bamboo arrowheads and place the parts on a huge grill. I saw the mighty effort being made by everyone present not to let fluids from the corpse touch the earth, because for the Wari, the earth—that same earth in which they are today compelled to bury their dead—has always been a dirty, contaminating place; so much so that adults never sit on the ground. I saw the descendants of the dead man divide themselves into two groups. One was made up of those who were his blood relatives: his children as well as his wife, because a man's wife is considered blood of his blood. His relatives by marriage constituted the other group: his brothers-in-law, his sisters-in-law, his parents-in-law, his children's parents-in-law. The members of the second group were in charge of keeping the fire going, while the others supervised their work. Each of them stood before the pyre and spoke a few words. If this was the first time they'd lost a family member, they said, "I never saw this fire before," or, if they'd already participated in a relative's funeral, they said, "I never want to see this fire again." I saw that they were pronouncing strange words and that some of them were threatening to hurl themselves into the flames, while others sought to restrain them, using heavy wooden sticks if all else failed. I saw how they cut up the organs. I saw them wrap the heart and the liver in the leaves of some tree. I saw them throw the genitals and the intestines into the fire.

All at once, the in-laws began to remove the body parts from the fire and set about preparing them. Although it may seem incredible, this wasn't a distressing sight. On the contrary, I shed tears, not of grief but of compassion. The enormous love, the immense tenderness with which they treated the dead man's limbs was so evident it cleared my mind of any thought of savagery. They did everything out of compassion, and I shared in it. They presented the dead man's widow and children with some fragments neatly laid out on mats covered with palm leaves. The children took charge of separating the flesh from the bones and cutting it into small pieces. Then they filed the bones down to powder, which they sprinkled on the flesh. Someone once told me that they mix the powder with honey at certain times of the year.

Then came the moment I couldn't comprehend. Just when it seemed that the children were about to eat the flesh that had been cut up and laid out so lovingly, the volume of their weeping rose to an unbearable level. They brought the flesh to the other group, the in-laws, who at first delicately refused it but then took it and began to eat. One group observed the other, the dead man's children throwing themselves into demonstrations of gratitude. The sisters-in-law, the nephews, and all the others ate with a degree of respect that drew my attention. I'd already seen how they devoured what they hunted: with their hands, tearing the flesh with their teeth, almost like hungry dogs. On this occasion, by contrast, they used small sticks, manipulating them with respectful gestures, making sure not to touch the flesh with their hands.

I couldn't comprehend this ritual while it was going on, but my later investigations allowed me some insight. For the Wari, eating flesh is a reason for celebration. Even if the kill is small game, they throw a party to consume it, for to eat is to celebrate life. The dead man's descendants need his body to be completely devoured so that all trace of grief will disappear with it; however, they can't eat it themselves, because doing so would be an offense to the deceased. By refusing to eat, they show that they're not in a festive mood, and therefore they turn to the dead man's in-laws. At first, as a demonstration of solidarity, the in-laws refuse the flesh. Their refusal signifies that they, too, are sad and little inclined to eat. But then they accept it as a favor to the dead man's children, thus helping them to forget their grief. One group eats, the other group looks on. Both groups weep without pause throughout this entire process.

By the time the ceremony ended, the night was well advanced. When I lay down in the hut they had erected for me, I was convinced I wouldn't be able to sleep. I was exhausted, yes, but also very excited. Images dashed around my brain, along with daring hypotheses that might explain them, doubts, and a frenetic review of my own reactions. Nevertheless, I slept like a baby.

The following day brought a major surprise, even more significant than the events of the previous night. I woke up at dawn, and when I stepped out of my hut I had the sensation that someone had taken advantage of my deep sleep to transport me somewhere else. I didn't recognize any of the nearby huts. And if any of them seemed familiar, it was only vaguely so, because their entrances weren't in the usual place. I walked through the village. The hut that the dead man and his family had occupied until the previous night no longer existed. I asked questions, although I avoided disturbing the family members. The Wari confirmed that this was their custom. After the funeral rites, the members of the dead man's family retired for the night, and several young men, chosen by the council of elders, were charged with changing the appearance of the village. I wanted to know why, and they gave me two different reasons, equally valid for anyone who knows anything about anthropology. One: if the dead man's spirit failed to find the way to the river, where the great Towira was waiting for him, and in his confusion he decided to return to the village with wicked intentions, he wouldn't be able to recognize it. Two: the family of the dead, when they awakened, would find the village so changed that they would no longer see in each corner, in each hut, a reminder of their grief. Not even the place where they had roasted and eaten the corpse was recognizable; the very ashes had disappeared. All the personal possessions of the dead man had been consigned to the flames. That same afternoon, I was given one of his machetes and requested to take it with me when I left the village, because they knew they couldn't make the metal disappear by burning it. They even burned the crops planted by the dead man, despite how vital they were to the community. According to what I've read in recent documents, when a Wari child dies nowadays, the members of his family—despite the fact that they're not allowed to eat their dead—request the schoolteacher to give them back the dead child's schoolwork so that it can be burned.

I wrote some years back, and believe to this day, that the Wari have understood the mechanisms of memory and knowledge better than any other tribe. In Chapacuran, the verb kerek means both "to see" and "to know." The Wari know that the only way to erase the memory of the dead is to alter the trace of life. In order to forget, they reinvent themselves. Against the chaos of death, we strive to reestablish order; they invent a new one. We rebuild the edifice of life; they allow it to fall apart, and then they build a different one. We say that life goes on; they recreate it. We conceive the memory of the dead as a form of homage to them; the Wari know the dangers of memory so well, they prefer to pay the dead the homage of oblivion. They've found the secret of active forgetting, which consists not in ceasing to think about something old but in inventing something new. Only when death visits the village again do they allow the memory of their dead to invade life for a few days. They can permit this exception; they know everything will start over as soon as the last breath of wind has scattered the ashes once more. The Wari can live with the certainty that nothing will continue in the same way after they die. They know their presence in the world is so important that it won't be the same after they're gone. I can conceive of no greater tribute to life than that.

The discovery of the enormous power of their compassion and their intelligence was accompanied by the consciousness of my own stupidity. Naturally, during the weeks I spent with them, I had almost forgotten my rubber tappers and São Paulo, even Barcelona and Malespina. I almost forgot myself. I spent the next five days gathering information, possessed by my own discovery. I learned that the dead man's family stopped pronouncing his name or referring to their relationship to him for a long time after his death. If they couldn't avoid speaking of him, they made their connection to him collective: instead of "my father," they would say "our father." I learned that after entering the underwater realm of the great Towira, the dead man could return to the world only in the form of a beneficent spirit, embodied in some animal that the inhabitants of the village would set about hunting and eating, certain in the knowledge that the spirit would automatically return to the river. I filled one notebook after another. I used up all the batteries for my tape recorder, and all my blank tapes as well. I took photographs of every nook and cranny.

On the last day, I found out that the dead man's family had gone into the forest to locate his usual hunting station, clear it, and burn the ground. As they were little more than a hundred meters from the village, I decided to walk to the spot alone and watch. While I was taking photographs, something whizzed past my head and buried itself in the trunk of a nearby tree. I ducked. It was an instinctive movement, but it saved my life. A second arrow crossed the space my body had occupied a moment before. I had no need to see my attackers to realize what was going on. The Wari use bamboo arrows for hunting. These weren't bamboo, they were made of hardwood, and they had metal tips. The rubber tappers. They were attempting to get rid of me the way you get rid of a tool you don't need anymore. My fault; I had led them to the Wari.

I returned to the village running and out of breath. I don't much like remembering this part. I still don't know whether I made a mistake, but I couldn't wait; I had to decide fast. I'd already committed the most serious error: I'd revealed the presence of the Wari in the area and shown the tappers the way to their village. If I stayed there, I thought, I'd be endangering something even more valuable than their independence: their lives.

I knew how cruel the rubber tappers were. I knew all too well that the SPI's supposed good will was a façade. It was clear that my ex-companions could have witnessed the same scenes of cannibalism that I had been present at a few days previously. It was also clear that they wouldn't interpret those scenes the way I did. I was sure that their account of the natives' bestial and inhuman practices had by now reached the ears of the appropriate authorities in São Paulo. If, on top of all this, I allowed them to kill me in the village, I'd be giving them the perfect excuse, because they would no doubt attribute my death to the savagery of the natives. I had to leave the Wari. I spent the rest of that day shut up in my hut and exited the village the following morning, but not before telling the women with whom I'd established the closest relations what had happened. I rejected the offer of a group of men who wanted to accompany me to the banks of the Lage and went alone.

I arrived at the river that afternoon. The camp was still there, and those five sons of bitches welcomed me back, as though I'd returned from the dead. Their performance wasn't very convincing, despite their pretending to believe my story about getting lost. That night in the camp, I experienced in their company a terror I'd never felt before, not even among people who belonged, supposedly, to the most hostile tribes in the world. What frightened me most were their cynical smiles and the open-mouthed guffaws that exposed their shiny gold teeth, the emblems of their greed. But when we turned in for the night, I saw that they weren't going to do me any harm: now that I'd abandoned the Wari village, it was no longer in the tappers' interest to kill me. The best thing for them to do, I reasoned, would be to avoid any scandal, take me back safe and sound to São Paulo, and make sure I returned to Spain. I was mistaken. Apparently, someone had decided that the best thing for them to do would be simply to postpone my death a little, to make it seem like an accident. We arrived in São Paulo, and I fulfilled my duty: I informed the SPI of what I'd found—hiding it made no sense now—but I tried to be as vague as possible when it came to specifying a location. I explained in writing, based on my personal experience, the new signifi-

cance of the Wari's rites. I earnestly recommended that all official contact with them should be avoided, and if this proved impossible, that their customs should be respected. I tried to make clear the enormous scientific value the preservation of those customs represented. The officials agreed with everything I said.

I returned to my hotel and went to bed, only to wake up a few hours later with the terrifying sensation that I was about to suffocate. I saw flames and thought I was dreaming about the Wari. Luckily, it didn't take me long to realize that I was indeed awake. Dazed, but awake. The room was filled with smoke so thick it looked solid, but I managed to get out. Somebody had soaked a few towels in fuel of some kind and ignited them inside my room. The result was more smoke than fire. The next day, I flew back to Barcelona. I published an account of what had happened, as is usually done in such cases, with the sensation of having been subjected to a form of blackmail whose consequences would be paid not by me but by the Wari. In other words, by those people whom I was endeavoring to protect. I avoided being too specific about any particular place. I spoke about governmental complicity but named no names. I did everything possible to correct my mistake.

For the next five years, I received all sorts of threats through the post: vulgar, despicable letters, packages containing bone fragments. None of that matters anymore. According to the last census, taken in 1991, a total of 1,930 Wari remain in the entire Amazon Basin. The SPI hasn't existed for many years, and an agency known as the FUNAI is now in charge of Indian affairs. Its intentions are better, but it's subject to the same speculative pressures and the same lack of resources. The Wari no longer eat their dead. That's something that does indeed matter to me. Now there's no place left in the world where dying is different, where when someone passes away, life pays itself the homage of a new beginning. All that's left are places like the one I'm headed for, places where we dead return to discover that nothing has changed, that everything goes on as before after we die. I'm almost there.

TUESDAY

If I were as bad at predicting changes in the weather as I am about foreseeing the vicissitudes of life, I'd quickly join the ranks of the unemployed. Yesterday I started thinking that this was going to end badly. I went to bed with a sensation something like a boat slowly entering a dead calm, all trace of movement being gradually erased. I came to Malespina convinced that these days of mourning would be good for all of us, and grateful to be able to spend them close to the sea. I believed they would pass slowly and offer me an opportunity to remember, to make notes, to investigate, and also to take my time doing the things that usually bring me some peace, such as looking at the sky or walking, even arguing with my brothers. But these days are dragging on too long. Yes, we're remembering Mama, and I suppose that's good, or necessary. But there's not much sense in staying here any longer. It's as if we've run out of tears and memories, and now all we have left are our anxieties. Especially Alberto. It was scary to see him pacing like a caged animal from one end of the house to the other. I really hope we're the cause of his mood, because if not, he's run into some problem that's too big for him, something capable of embittering his life forever.

That's what I thought yesterday. Today, everything's changed. Our faces were proof of that when we sat down at the table after spending the afternoon on the water. There's something very different about going out on a boat when you're pregnant. Your sensations are intensified: smells, especially, but also the strange physical sensation of floating while being aware that there's also something floating inside you. Or maybe it's paranoia; since I've been pregnant for so short a time I don't think anything is floating inside me yet. In any case, my fear of being seasick vanished as soon as I set foot on deck. At last, the salt on my lips.

At last, the euphoria of the wind in my face and the deck groaning under my feet. And the blessed words: close-hauled, tack and luff, tiller and sheet, centerboard, prow, helm, yard.

But even before we set out to sea we were alive again, up early in the morning, all of us scurrying about like ants. As always, a good part of the credit for this change goes to Alberto, who—contrary to my expectations—woke up today with a smile on his face. I repeat: I wish I were as good at forecasting people as I am at weather. One of his many telephone calls last night must have brought a solution to his problems, or perhaps just sufficient resignation to accept them.

Luis appeared in his pajamas and stationed himself in the middle of the dining room; then he stretched, walked over to the chimney, and picked up Mama's urn, balancing it in his hands like a paperweight. "Good thing she was cremated in Guatemala. Can you imagine if we still had her body to bury? Whew. No one would come near her."

And he was right. The wake was going on too long. After all, the only purpose that drew us all here was to scatter Mama's ashes in the Russian woman's bathtub. We could have done everything else in Barcelona.

Alberto was sitting beside me, and when I heard Luis's comment, I rested a hand on his leg, like someone stroking a nervous cat. I didn't want to start the day with a row, especially a row over Mama's ashes. But Alberto's reply confirmed my belief that all of today's omens were good. "That's exactly what I wanted to talk to you about," he said, gesturing to Luis to join us at the table. "I think I've found a boat. But it's a bit complicated. I'm supposed to call up and confirm, but before I do, I need your approval."

"It's about time," Pablo exclaimed. And then, adjusting his tone, he said, "I knew you wouldn't fail us, brother dear. And I'm impressed that you're even asking our opinion."

"Don't sing your victory song just yet; it's not that simple. Besides, I have other news. We're all going to have to pitch in a little."

"What's the problem?"

"She's a lateener."

"Well, well." This came from Papa, as if the mention of a lateen rig had penetrated the fog in his brain. "A lateener, eh?"

"So much the better," Pablo said. He looked enthused. "I don't see the problem."

"Well, she's a bit old."

"Like all of them."

"A little older than most. And she has no motor."

"Ah. No motor."

While my brothers were talking, I put two and two together. In Malespina, there are only five lateen-rigged boats. One of them is modern, made of carbon fiber. An abomination. A floating monument to bad taste but with a motor, of course. Then there are three old boats, authentic specimens from the 1940s, recovered in the 1980s by sailing fanatics who restored them with meticulous care. These were old fishing boats, and their new owners took advantage of the bilges, once used for the transport of fish, to install motors, thus assuring that they could get back home in unfavorable conditions. The fifth boat is the *Amen*, and she has spent nearly the last twenty-five years shut up in a garage with her mast dismounted. She doesn't have a motor. She never had one. She's the only original lateener that's still in one piece, which means she dates from the 1920s or earlier. She was probably one of the boats that participated in the tuna harvest of '22, when Simón was shipwrecked.

Alberto kept playing with Pablo, feeding him morsels of the information he wanted to swallow whole. I said the boat's name under my breath, partly because I could hardly believe it, and partly because just thinking about it scared me: "Amen."

Pablo jumped as if someone had pricked him. "What? The *Amen*?" He kept looking from Alberto to me and back, waiting for someone to tell him it was just a joke. "The *Amen*? I can't believe it! Alberto, tell me it's not true!"

"Well," Alberto said, maintaining his sunny smile. "I've already told you it wasn't confirmed. I've left a deposit, but they promised to return it to me if we decide not to use the boat."

"You mean to tell me you actually have to *pay* for that tub?"

"It's been caulked recently, and they've spent a fortune restoring it. They say they're looking for a buyer."

"I can't believe what I'm hearing. She's been out of the water for ages. We don't even know if she floats."

"My dear Uncle Pablo," Luis chimed in, gesturing theatrically, as if he were about to deliver a speech. "You spend your life talking about the authentic this and the genuine that and giving those deadly lectures of yours, and then suddenly, when you get the opportunity to do some serious sailing in an authentic, old-fashioned, motorless sailing boat, you shit your pants."

"You be quiet. You don't know what you're talking about. That's not serious sailing, that's risking your life."

"Don't exaggerate. We all know how to swim. Besides, you don't really think she's going to sink, do you?"

"It wouldn't be the first time."

"It makes no difference to me. I can swim even better than Simón."

They were both partly right. It's true that sailing in the *Amen* would be an homage to authenticity that Pablo ought to appreciate, despite whatever risks might be involved. No other boat around here can offer as pure a sailing experience as she can: an enormous, heavy, triangular sail, supported by a long spar high up on the mast and capable of displacing the tons of dead weight found in a vessel fifteen meters long. If the *Amen* were a land vehicle, she would be like one of those village tractors that are still running fifty years after leaving the factory. Maybe the truth is that Pablo's love of life is greater than his love of authenticity, and I'd be the last person to criticize him for that. After all, no one who knows the history of that boat can sail in her without feeling at least a shiver.

She wasn't always called the *Amen*. Until 1956, she was the *Carmen*.

That summer, the Santa Rosa storms came in early September and caused the usual havoc. The *Carmen* was lying in the bay, sheltered by the headland of Cabo San Sebastián and double-anchored. The wind buffeted her, but seeing that it couldn't destroy her, it went off in search of other, less obstinate victims and delegated its task of destruction to the sea, because the sea is much more lethal than the wind. Only the sea has the annihilating tenacity of time. It didn't manage to split the *Carmen*'s timbers, but eventually so much water flowed into her bilges that she sank from the sheer weight of it. Fortunately the bottom wasn't rocky, so her hull rested unharmed on a bed of seaweed for the duration of the storm. Her owner, Marcelino, had inherited her from his father but no longer devoted himself to the toil of the fisherman's life; instead he offered excursions in the *Carmen* to the first tourists who began to turn up on this part of the coast. Marcelino realized that refloating her would cost him less than buying a new boat, so four divers tied large inflated balloons to her and hoisted her up using a block and tackle. The refloating of the *Carmen* was a spectacular sight watched by everyone who was in the village at the time, my father among them. After hours of struggle, the port side of the prow appeared, and then the whole ship came up sideways, vomiting the foaming sea out of one side and breathing in air on the other. When the stern showed itself, everyone could see that the name had lost two letters, the *C* and the *r*, so it now read *a men*. Changing the name of a ship is supposed to bring bad luck. According to the tales fishermen tell, when you change a boat's name, the sea reacts by treating her like a stranger; that is, by attacking her or defending itself against her, which is even worse. Nevertheless, our Marcelino must have thought that in this case fate had spoken, and that if the sea had sunk the *Carmen* in order to turn her into the *Amen*, he would not be the one to deny it. And time showed that he was right, because twenty years later, when Marcelino died, the *Amen* was still sailing and in fine shape. His children tried to continue the family tradition, but it wasn't long before they gave up. Maintaining an old lateen-rigged vessel is an expensive business, and sailing in her requires not only skill and experience, but also a level of discipline that can be doubly vexing for someone who's not making any profit from it. Therefore, when the owners were unable to find a buyer willing to pay the price they were asking, they decided to keep the boat in a garage and wait for a better time.

"I have other news for you too," I said, determined to throw in a bad omen in case there was anyone who didn't think the boat's history was enough. "The weather forecast isn't exactly promising."

"Don't fucking start," said Alberto.

"That's all we need," said Pablo.

"I can't be sure, but I think a storm's heading our way."

"So what? If it rains, we put on waterproofs." A glance at Luis's face revealed that not even a cyclone would curb his enthusiasm for this adventure.

"Well, Luis, if I'm not mistaken, it's going to be more than just a little rain."

"Is it that serious?" When Alberto starts calculating risks, it usually means he's already made a decision. "We could still take her out, couldn't we?"

"I don't think it's going to be too severe. Besides, I'm not even sure. An east wind's been blowing since yesterday, and it'll stay that way for a few more days. Probably force five or six, and as I said, the wind will bring some rain. We had a few days of *garbí* right before this, so the atmosphere is saturated with humidity, and that means there will probably be localized storms sometime during the next few days. Nothing serious, but maybe gusts up to twenty-four knots."

"And what does that mean in my language?"

"In your language, more than forty kilometers an hour."

"Piece of cake."

"And what would you know?" Luis's insolence is starting to irritate Pablo. "It seems like madness to me. Besides, what are we going to do with Papa—"

Alberto interrupted him. "Wait," he said. "There's something else. We have to go to Barcelona tomorrow."

"To Barcelona? But if we haven't scattered the ashes yet—"

"Hold on, Luis. Don't get ahead of yourself." Alberto has a kind of natural talent for giving orders. "Serena and Pablo have to come with me, and someone's got to stay with Papa, namely you. So do me a favor and stop arguing. It's important."

"May we know why we're going to Barcelona?" I asked.

"To see the solicitor. I've sold Mama's office."

"Damn! When do we get the money?" Although we didn't know the amount yet, Pablo could already see himself happily playing the piano on a ship's deck in the midst of a storm.

"But Alberto . . . what's the rush?" The potential problems filled my head, and I didn't know which one to start with. "I still have to clear it out, and that may take me at least a couple of weeks, and—"

"Take it easy, Serena. I'm not in any hurry, but the buyers are. Let me explain." I know my brother very well. I know that "let me explain" really means it's all wrapped up, and there's no use going over it anymore. "I met a couple who wants the flat just as it is, because they're going to use it as an office too. They're prepared to pay more than the place is worth and they've offered me 190,000 euros, provided we agree that at least half will be paid under the table. It's a great deal."

"But—"

"Let me finish. They wanted everything signed and sealed right away, so they've given me until tomorrow. After that, they'll withdraw their offer. I had to accept it. Now, of course, this is a decision we should make together," he added, as if it were true. "So if you don't like it, I can always back out, because they haven't paid the deposit yet. But we're not going to get a better offer. And in return for signing the deal tomorrow, they've agreed to give us three weeks before we have to hand over the keys. In other words, you'll have plenty of time to clear the place out."

"I don't know, Alberto." I've never been good at quick decisions. "It's all a bit sudden. The boat, Mama's office—"

"Well, let's make some plans and see what's feasible. There are other possibilities."

We quickly came to an agreement. That is, we accepted Alberto's proposal, which included taking out the *Amen* this very afternoon, sailing her to the Formigues for a trial run, and then, if we're satisfied, reserving her for the day after tomorrow. We're going to see the solicitor early tomorrow morning to sign the act of sale for Mama's office; then we'll come back here in time to make the final preparations. Everything's in order. Everything's provided for.

Pablo's the one who resisted most. The plan seemed fine to him, he said, but he'd have to be nuts to go on board the *Amen* before he knew for sure it could float, and besides, someone had to stay with Papa, so the best idea was for him, Pablo, to stay behind, and if we all went under, there'd be no cremations and no ashes; he'd organize a cannibal banquet instead. All I said was I'd like to go to Mama's office, if only for a moment, before we saw the solicitor. I don't know why; to bid farewell to Mama's things, I suppose. Luis said he had no conditions to impose, called Pablo a pussy, and declared that as long as we were going to the Formigues, I might as well tell him the story of the battle once and for all, goddamnit. Alberto replied that the story was so short and simple he could tell it in a minute, flat. I gave a start but it must have been nerves, because what difference does it make to me what my brother thinks about the Battle of the Formigues Islands?

Of course, Alberto had taken for granted that we'd approve his plan, so he'd already hired a trailer to pull the *Amen* to the seashore and engaged two Moroccans to help us push her across the beach, rolling the ship down to the water on inflated rubber cylinders. When we were little, we used to call them "beach sausages," and if the sea was rough, we'd borrow them from the fishermen and ride the breaking waves as though those sausages were stallions.

So there we were, all of us, on the beach. Papa gave no sign of recognizing the boat, but he had such a gleam in his eyes, and started giving orders about who should push and who should pull so fast, that I would swear he saw himself as a captain again, standing on his bridge. After a great deal of shoving, the bow struck the water and immediately all the timbers began to sing, as if greeting the sea for the first time.

I wouldn't have thought there would be so many people in the village on an ordinary Tuesday in the middle of October. We had pushed the *Amen* out of the garage shortly before noon, and it had taken us almost three hours to get her ready to weigh anchor. During those three hours, people continued to appear in ever-increasing numbers, as if we were parading a patron saint through the streets. In the end, when we managed to set sail, about forty people were gathered on the shore to bid us farewell. You would have thought we were setting out on a transoceanic voyage. Papa waved his arms in the air; from a distance, it seemed to me he was crying. Pablo was hovering around him, but when we got back, I was so excited I forgot to ask him.

We reached two conclusions. The first was that the *Amen* floats. Her hull seems so solid, I'd take my chances on her in the face of any storm. She responds to the helm obediently if somewhat slowly, as if she has to process orders before complying with them. I've never sailed in a boat with so much personality. And then there's the rigging, the masts and the spars. If anyone were to commit the romantic folly of building such a boat nowadays, he'd be sure to install a more flexible mast and support it with thicker shrouds, and he'd probably reduce the canvas by half, because she has too much sail.

The second conclusion is that three people aren't enough to handle her. Once she's out to sea with her sail hoisted, three can do it, but the problem is reaching that point. Hoisting the sail is a job for titans. You've got more than twenty square meters of old canvas rolled around a solid oak spar that weighs I don't know how many kilos, and to hoist it, all you have is a thick rope and a double block and tackle. Even when all of us pulled on the line together we could lift it only a few inches. We started thinking we'd have to stay where we were, five meters offshore, with the sail at half mast, as if the *Amen* were in mourning. I remembered Simón, naturally. I mean Papa. I remembered Papa when he said that they needed four strong men to hoist a lateen sail, and so they let Simón go aboard one of those boats. We would have been glad of his help today. We did it, but I believe part of me is still there, lying in pieces on the deck. I talk about the blessing of salt in my face because I'd rather not recall the shooting pains in my back and the muscle cramps crawling like ants all over my body.

It's not important. I'd go aboard the *Amen* again tomorrow, even if all the muscles in my body were protesting. I regret having to go down to Barcelona tomorrow, because the *Amen*, from its mooring off the pier at Port Bou, is going to be calling to me all day long.

This afternoon, a refractory but benign east wind was blowing. When the sail was finally set, the wind filled it, but the *Amen*'s hull remained motionless for a few seconds, as though fastened by a chain to the bottom of the sea. Then Alberto started barking out orders that Luis and I followed like robots, and finally the hull announced our departure with a loud groan. The three of us began jumping about and shouting from pure emotion. We would have sailed straight to the Formigues, but Alberto wanted to test the boat in all possible variations: when she was close-hauled, she sailed arrogantly, as if too proud to heel over, and when we ran before the wind, her sail gulped the air with swollen cheeks.

At last we arrived at our goal, and Alberto decided to anchor in the lee of the islands. There we'd be protected from the east wind without striking the sail, as we didn't think we'd be strong enough to hoist it again. We didn't dare go for a swim; the water was too cold, and we worried about leaving the *Amen* by itself. From this side of the Formigues you can make out the plaque that the town council had fastened to the rock in 1985: SEVENTH CENTENARY OF THE BATTLE OF THE FORMIGUES ISLANDS. After reading these words aloud, Alberto said to Luis, "You see? Your aunt doesn't need to tell you her war stories. Everything's in writing right here."

"Nonsense. Not even the date is definite."

"Good. That means you can begin." Luis wanted to make me keep my promise. "Start off by telling me what they were fighting about."

"Well, no one even knows that for sure. The cause may become apparent at the end of a story, but never at the beginning. Unless you assume that they were fighting about power. In that case, you're probably right."

"Tell me at least what the French were doing here."

"Let's set the scene. We're in the year 1282, all right? The story begins in Sicily."

"Why Sicily?" Luis interrupted.

"Because the pope, Martin IV, had recently named Charles of Valois king of Sicily. But the Sicilian feudal lords rebelled and sought help from the king of Catalonia and Aragón, Peter the Great."

"Why?"

"Because the new French king denied them a number of the prerogatives they held as feudal lords. Power was being taken from them, so they looked for a foreign king who could protect them. In exchange, they granted him sovereignty over the land, as long as their privileges remained intact. The historical roots of the Mafia can be traced to this situation. Sounds incredible, doesn't it? Anyway, Peter the Great granted his protection to the Sicilians and sent them a fleet under the command of Roger de Lloria—his name was Hispanicized during Franco's time and became Lauria, but whatever you call him, he's the same guy. I call him Lloria because that's the way they refer to him in the chronicles of the time. When he arrived in Sicily—"

"Just a minute. What the fuck did the king of Aragón and Catalonia want with Sicily? What did he stand to win?"

"Good question. I imagine he'd obtain power and territory, which was no small thing in a period when the boundaries of the Mediterranean region were yet to be drawn. But there might have been a simpler reason. After Roger de Lloria had conquered Sicily and subjected it to the throne of Aragón, the king sent him an urgent letter by special emissary. In the letter, the king told Roger that the scarcity of grain in Catalonia was so great it endangered not only the public supply but also the provisioning of the royal household. As the wheat harvest in Sicily had been excellent, the king asked Roger to make sure that no one offered any resistance to the merchants who were traveling in the same ship as the emissary. Their mission was to secure an abundant provision of grain and return home immediately, under the protection of the fleet if necessary."

"For someone so obsessed with historical truth, this sounds a bit far-fetched," Alberto protested. "A private letter from the king almost eight hundred years ago?"

"But the letter still exists. The original is kept in the Archive of the Crown of Aragón in Barcelona."

"All right," Alberto said, still slightly skeptical. "So what started the whole thing was a little grain."

"A little or a lot, I don't know. But it set off a monumental row. The pope excommunicated Peter the Great. Now, I'm not sure if the pope wanted land or if he needed grain too, but in any case he called out a crusade against the kingdom of Catalonia and Aragón."

"A crusade? I thought crusades were only against Muslims."

"Actually, crusades were wars fought against the enemy, whoever that might be. And in this case, the role of 'the enemy' fell to Peter the Great. To give you an idea, whoever participated in the war against him obtained the same privileges as someone who collaborated in the Holy War to recover the Holy Sepulchre."

"Papal bulls, that sort of thing?"

"Papal bulls. Forgiveness of sins. Eternal salvation. This war ended with the retreat of the French. The chronicles of the time say that some soldiers who hadn't even had time to join the battle stood on the border and threw rocks into the forest just so they could say they had attacked enemy territory and therefore deserved a papal bull. Now, let's skip forward a little to 1285. Following the pope's instructions, the troops of the king of France, Philip the Bold, cross the Pyrenees and take Girona.

Their next objective is Barcelona. Peter the Great manages to put up decent resistance on land, but since the bulk of his fleet is still in Sicily, he's unable to stop the French advance by sea. The French fleet, which is the most powerful in the Mediterranean at this time, takes the port of Roses and sends a large force ahead to Sant Feliu."

"A large force?" There's nothing like numbers to arouse Alberto's interest. "How many ships are we talking about?"

"It's impossible to know for sure. The reason we lack reliable numbers isn't that there's a shortage of information, but there's too much. There are five contemporary chronicles, two of which are Sicilian, written in macaronic Latin; one's French, or to be exact, Provençal; and two are Catalan. The five of them never agree about quantities, which is rather suspicious."

"Suspicious in what way?"

"Well, it's impossible that such a large fleet could be mobilized without generating a series of official records that would have stated how many ships there were and how many people they carried."

"Then why didn't the chroniclers know this?"

"Of course they knew it. That's why I say their disagreement is suspicious. Consider this: the chronicles were written after the events took place—in some cases immediately afterward, and in others ten or twenty years later. And they weren't written to reveal the truth; they were produced to flatter power and instruct the masses. Each chronicler exaggerates the number of the enemy's ships. The losers do so in order to make their defeat seem more comprehensible and therefore forgivable. The winners want their victory to appear more heroic."

"So we don't know how many ships there were."

"We can calculate an average, and that's what I've done. I think there were about 160 ships in the French fleet: seventy anchored in the harbor in Roses, twenty or so in Sant Feliu harbor, and another seventy that were always moving from one port to another. As I said, Peter the Great's fleet was in Sicily, so he had no way of defending himself against such numbers. During the spring of 1285, the king sent various missives to Lloria, informing him of the French threat and asking him to be ready to come to his aid. In one of these missives, Peter asks Lloria's advice on how to defend the port of Barcelona should the French attack before he can return. King Peter may have been great, but the French king, Philip, was very rich. Peter, on the other hand, seems to have been running out of resources."

"There's something new—a story about the rich and the poor."

"Well, money plays a role, but it's not the most important thing. In the Archive of the Crown of Aragón, there are two extremely valuable documents. One's a note from the king himself, in which he extols the merits of two wealthy Barcelonan merchants named Marquet and Mallol. He even quantifies their contribution to the kingdom in a kind of inventory: so many silver *tournesols*, so many *carlins d'or*."

"What does this have to do with the king's fleet?"

"Who do you think the king charged with the defense of Barcelona? Marquet and Mallol, that's who. But here's where we turn to the second document, which is even better. In order to command the city's defenses, they had to receive appointments as admirals; in order to be admirals, they had to be noblemen, which they weren't. If the king named them admirals, he stood to alienate the entire aristocracy. So the king wrote a letter granting the two merchants permission to fit out a small defensive fleet and assemble it on the beach in Barcelona, but he did everything he could to avoid using the term 'admirals,' only granting them 'the power to exercise admiralship.' History's not always a collection of lies, but it's usually full of plays on words."

"What I'd like to know," said Luis, "is what this has to do with the Formigues."

"We're getting there. Marquet and Mallol gathered enough money to fit out a few galleys and kept them ready in Barcelona. Eleven, according to Montaner's chronicle; twelve, according to Desclot's. So small a force obviously couldn't have resisted a single enemy attack. Yet the two commanders insisted that the king grant them permission to move their galleys north and attack the French."

The clouds weren't yet visible over Cabo San Sebastián, but I had already begun to detect their presence in the humidity of the air. I said, "Aren't you surprised? I'm telling you that they didn't even have enough forces to defend themselves and they wanted to attack?"

"Now that you say it, yes."

"If you tried to find the explanation for this in the medieval chronicles, they'd tell you the men were heroes, so valiant that they knew no fear. But if you read between the lines, you'll realize that piracy was quite a profitable industry in those days. No matter how mighty the French were, it was unlikely that one of their ships wouldn't be left unprotected every now and again. And when that happened, the corsairs could pounce on the vessel and seize it. If it was a supply ship, they requisitioned it, divided up the provisions it was transporting, and later sold it. And if it was only carrying soldiers, they killed them all, except for the commanders, who were noblemen."

"What bastards! Why?"

"Why do you think? For money, of course. Marquet and Mallol wanted to attack so they could recover at least part of the money they'd spent in fitting out their small fleet. So on three separate occasions, they sailed out of Barcelona with two galleys, but instead of finding some lone French ship separated from the rest on the open sea, they came upon the bulk of the enemy fleet and didn't dare approach it. Of course, the Barcelonans didn't like this much. Rumors about the men charged with defending the city began to spread: that they were a pair of cowards, or, even worse, that they were swindlers who had deceived the king. Eventually the rumors reached the ears of Marquet and Mallol themselves. The two understood that their only recourse was to confront the French in a life-or-death battle. Fear, like money, is one of the great engines of history. Marquet and Mallol feared the enemy, but the idea that the population of Barcelona might turn against them filled them with even greater concern. And so, on the night of July 28, they decided to head north with their eleven galleys, and at daybreak they came upon a French force of more than thirty galleys."

"So what happened? They were wiped out?"

"Not at all. The Catalans won."

"Eleven against thirty?"

"Yes, indeed. They had a trick up their sleeves."

"What trick?"

"They were the best shots in the whole Mediterranean. They won not because God was on their side, as the Catalan chroniclers declared, nor because they were more numerous, as the French chroniclers claimed. It was simply that the Catalan galleys were better organized. They had invented something they called *ballesters en taula*. Remember, when galleys went into battle, they were rowed. And they had no cannons or anything like that. To defeat the enemy, you had to crash into his galley, board it, and fight hand-to-hand on his ship's deck. The galleys' prows were reinforced with metal plates, and when they rammed an enemy ship, they caused serious damage to her structure."

"And what about the *ballesters en taula*?"

"When the ships drew close together, but before they were close enough for boarding, their crews shot arrows at one another. The idea was to decimate the enemy before the final collision. In other fleets, the rowers themselves were the crossbowmen. They rowed like crazy to get close to the enemy ship, and when the moment came, they dropped their oars and loaded their crossbows. The Catalans, on the other hand, kept the functions distinct. The oarsmen rowed; the crossbowmen sat at ease so that they'd be fresh when the time came for them to shoot, and above all, their wrists would be steady, so they could aim their weapons with much more accuracy. Furthermore, behind the classic double file of rowers, the Catalans held a third file in reserve, ready to take the places of those who fell. Their organization was perfect. When the moment came to board the enemy ship, the Catalan arrows had already destroyed its crew."

"What happened to the losers?"

"The usual. The Catalans held on to Guillem de Lodera, who was the commander of the French fleet in Roses and must have been worth a fortune. You know what happened to the rest."

"How did they kill them?"

"How do you think? They tied them up and left them on the decks of the ships that were most heavily damaged, which they then sank."

"Sounds like torture."

"It was considered normal in those days. But let's return to the battle. One French galley had managed to escape. Mallol pursued it for several kilometers, but since he was towing the four or five galleys he'd requisitioned, he couldn't catch up with it."

"Listen, Serena, what does this have to do with the Formigues?" Luis sounded impatient. "Didn't you say they were near Roses?"

"The other day, you didn't believe me when I said this would be a long story, but I told you there were three battles, not just one. The ship that got away reached land and reported the French defeat. Within a few hours, men on horseback brought the news to Philip the Bold, who flew into a rage. Then he decided—"

"Then he decided you were right about the rain," Alberto interrupted me. "We ought to start going back."

"Relax. When the first clouds show up over Cabo San Sebastián, we'll weigh anchor. Where were we?"

"Eleven Catalo-Aragonian galleys defeat thirty French galleys, but one of them manages to escape and the French king learns the news."

"Perfect. Two weeks pass. Where do you suppose the victors were?"

"In Barcelona, drinking like fish and spending their booty on whores and banquets."

"It seems only logical, right? The French must have thought the same thing, and therefore they didn't set out in pursuit right away. But they were wrong, just like you. Precisely in order to prevent their crews from celebrating a victory, Marquet and Mallol looked for a port that was small but at the same time sufficiently equipped to repair the damage their fleet had suffered in the battle. They anchored in Sant Pol de Mar. And according to Desclot's chronicle, the prior of the monastery of Sant Pol informed the French."

"A priest and a traitor!"

"Traitor? Why? A prior's homeland is the Church, isn't it? Remember the papal bulls. Rome had turned Peter the Great into Satan himself. The prior probably thought it was his duty to announce the presence of the fleet in Sant Pol. When Philip the Bold learned that Marquet and Mallol were anchored there, he immediately issued orders: his commanders were to organize a force of twenty-five galleys, set off in search of the enemy, and avenge the recent defeat. At the same time, and without having received any news of the French expedition, Peter the Great joined up with Marquet, Mallol, and Roger de Lloria, who had recently arrived from Sicily with his entire fleet, except for four galleys that had been left behind and had taken refuge in the port of Barcelona. On August 27, all the parties began to move, but none of them had the least idea of the others' whereabouts. The French, hugging the coast, approached Sant Pol. Lloria's fleet left Sant Pol and headed for the open sea. The four stragglers, plus another galley that had joined them in Barcelona, sailed north along the coast, believing that Lloria was still in Sant Pol."

"My kingdom for a mobile phone!"

"Exactly. They were all sailing blind. In the midmorning, the five ships that were trying to join Lloria's fleet spotted a forest of masts in the distance. As they drew near, they realized it was the French."

"The twenty-five avenging galleys."

"The very same. Five against twenty-five. Imagine the fear. No matter how well organized and efficient they were, they couldn't hope for victory."

"So they surrendered?"

"Are you crazy? Surrendering was the same as committing suicide. They did the only thing they could do: they turned around and ran, under full sail and with the wind at their back. The French went after them, but when they realized they couldn't catch them, they called off the pursuit and left in search of reinforcements. For their part, the five escaping ships were able to meet up with Lloria on the open sea and join his fleet. This failed encounter would be the second battle, but we're counting it as a half because the two sides never came to blows."

"Shit, one disappointment after another."

"Don't worry. In only a few hours, these same waters would be filled with the blood of several thousand men. Because now we come to the third combat, which was the bloodiest naval battle fought in the western Mediterranean during the entire Middle Ages. And here's where the chroniclers diverge. According to Desclot, on the night of August 28 the two fleets finally collided head-on in some indeterminate place more or less near here, and all hell broke loose. The historians say that his version is the most faithful to what really happened, but Montaner was from this area, and so I think we should presume he was more accurate when it came to specifying locations. According to him, the battle occurred exactly here, right where we're anchored."

"Then the choice is clear."

"Not completely. Montaner goes on to declare that Roger de Lloria disembarked on the Formigues and used them as a platform for planning the battle. You've gone diving a few times in these waters, and you know what the bottom's like. So tell me if it seems credible to you that a fleet of eighty galleys, with their immense keels, could get so close to this cluster of rocks?"

"Impossible."

"You see? Besides, according to Montaner, the eighty ships waited behind the Formigues so they could surprise the French. Look over to starboard. Do you think there's enough space for even ten or fifteen smaller boats to hide without being seen from the other side?"

"So we're back to the usual problem. Since you say Montaner was from here, he must have known these islands. Why did he lie?"

"The usual reason. If he said King Peter's forces took refuge in the bay, then he wouldn't be attributing anything more than common sense to them. But if he portrayed them as hiding behind the Formigues, he would turn them into grand strategists. And should this strike anyone as impossible, the author could always resort to asserting that divine assistance had rendered them invisible."

I looked at Alberto to see if he would respond to this provocation, but he was too focused on the clouds, which were now coming toward us at full speed, swept along by the east wind.

"Let's go, if you want, but there's nothing to worry about. When the rain comes, the wind will die down."

With the anchor on board, some slight pressure on the tiller from Alberto, and a yank on the sail, the *Amen* took the wind and got under way. Sailing with the wind abeam, we wouldn't need to tack even once before we reached the beach, so that except for the possible annoyance of the rain, there was no reason to worry.

"So, Luis," I said, taking up the story again. "If you look to starboard, you'll see that practically the whole bay is sheltered by Cabo San Sebastián. Lloria's ships were stationed there. It's said that one of his men disembarked and went to the edge of the cape to serve as a lookout. His mission was to warn Lloria's fleet of the arrival of the French ships so they could be taken by surprise, but I don't know which side got the bigger fright. The French were looking either for the five straggling galleys they'd spotted that morning or, at most, for Marquet and Mallol's force of eleven galleys that had humiliated them a month before. They didn't yet know that the bulk of Lloria's fleet had returned from Sicily. When they rounded the cape, they found eighty well-armed ships."

"What a fright."

"Just imagine. But the surprise was mutual. The Catalo-Aragonians were expecting the twenty-five French galleys they'd spied that same morning. And then more than a hundred of them hove into view. Imagine ducking your head under the boom right now and seeing the prow of a battle galley rounding the cape. And then another one. And another. And behind that one, five, twelve, twenty more, all the way to a hundred. With hundreds of men armed to the teeth in each galley, all of them prepared to take suicidal risks rather than suffer defeat, because they're certain that if they lose the battle, they can expect an even worse punishment from their own king."

Luis stared into space and shivered. "I can imagine it," he said at last. "Gruesome."

"And it must have been even worse, because all of this happened at night. Can you imagine the terror those soldiers must have felt? The great majority of the men on both sides were there against their will. Most were convicts or outcasts, and in many cases they were being punished for nonviolent crimes. Hardly any of them could swim. And suddenly, they're in the middle of the sea, shaking with a fear so terrible that I'm sure more than one of them succumbed to panic and jumped into the water to avoid a worse fate."

"But you just told us what efficient fighters they were. So they must have been good at remaining calm under pressure."

"What do you think? Do you believe they were doing battle for the glory of the fatherland? They were fighting for their lives."

"Well, however it may have been, they won."

"They won. Or Roger de Lloria won, and that's why his name's in the chronicles. The truth is that he was a son of a bitch, but he must have been a great strategist, I can't deny it. A good liar."

"Why?"

"Because in those days, when the numbers on each side were more or less equal, the winner was the one who was better at fooling his adversary. Better at hiding, or at faking a withdrawal, or at feigning weakness in his moments of greatest strength. There was a moment at the beginning of the battle that must have seemed almost beautiful. At a certain point, Lloria had all his ships form a group and light three beacons each: one in the bow, another one amidships, and the third in the stern."

"And what was this supposed to do?"

"According to one version, Lloria's men hurled themselves on the French, crying out 'Aragón! Aragón!' The French, seeing that their ships were suddenly in the midst of a battle, tried to take refuge in confusion by crying out 'Aragón!' as well. Apparently, Lloria ordered the beacons to be lit so that his men would recognize their own ships and avoid attacking one another. But I don't believe this version."

"Why not?"

"Look, there's a battle going on. How can you holler out to eighty ships and give each of them the order to light three beacons? Besides, why three beacons? If they were trying only to identify their own ships, one beacon would have been sufficient. The other version seems much more logical. It says that Lloria had the beacons lit much earlier, so that the French, when they rounded the cape, would believe they were coming up against a fleet of almost three hundred ships."

"Such a clever fellow."

"Such a savage brute. And now I'm going to ask you to activate your imagination one more time. You know what splitting wood sounds like, don't you?"

"Yes."

"Then multiply that sound by a hundred, by a thousand. Remember, they had to ram an enemy ship, stick their prow into its belly, leap onto its deck, and throw themselves into hand-to-hand combat. Imagine a herd of elephants fighting and butting heads. Add in the whirring of the crossbows. Thousands of arrows flying from ship to ship. And listen to the giant roar coming from fifteen thousand men bursting their lungs to frighten the enemy. From this day on, when you hear the expression 'the din of battle,' you'll know what it means. Making all that noise must have helped the men stave off fear, but I imagine it also meant they were less likely to notice what was happening around them, the thousands of men who were dying."

"Thousands? How many thousands?"

"I don't know. Desclot talks about six thousand. But he probably inflated his figures to exalt the ferocity of the victors. Whether there were six thousand or double that or half that, it all came down to the same thing. At your side, three comrades suddenly fall, struck down by arrows; a few meters away, a man punctures another's lungs with the point of his sword, yanks it out and stabs someone else. Another adversary pounces on his back, dagger in hand, and slits his throat. When you come under attack, you try to take a step backward, but something is blocking your way. With a little luck, the great danger you're in prevents you from looking down and discovering that you're treading on a carpet of the dead and dying and that the deck is littered with the hacked-off limbs of wounded men. Everywhere, men writhing in their last agony—"

"That's enough!"

"What? I thought you wanted blood." I was so carried away, I didn't notice that Luis was the color of wax and had been for some time. "What's wrong? Since when have you had trouble with the dead?"

"I don't give a flying fuck about the dead. What I can't bear are the dying."

"How so?" I wasn't very quick on the uptake here. "What's that to you?"

"What's that to me? How can you possibly not understand?" He fell face down onto the deck and then cried out, "Look at me! Do I remind you of anything?"

"Shit!" Suddenly, I understood.

"Shit indeed. Fourteen months in a coma. That is shit."

"Forgive me, Luis. I'm sorry." I stooped down, but didn't know what else to say. "I'm really sorry."

"Don't worry," he said as he got up. "It's not so serious. Besides, I'm the one who asked you to tell the story. Fortunately, we're through with the dead and dying. All that remain are the survivors, if there were any."

"There were indeed, but don't think we're out of the woods yet. Let's take a break. I'll tell you the rest when we get to the beach, because that's where the survivors stopped being survivors."

I'd thought that Alberto hadn't been following the conversation, but then I saw that he hadn't missed a word.

"Since you're taking a break, I have an announcement to make," he said. "Ladies and gentlemen, the *Amen*, having successfully completed its day's run, is about to dock."

Immediately after mooring at the wharf, we lowered the sail. Luis and I jumped onto land, but Alberto stayed on board a few minutes longer, making sure that everything was well stowed. While we were waiting for him, Luis insisted that I tell him what happened to the survivors of the battle. It was just about then that the first drops of rain began to fall.

"I don't know, Luis. It's not a pleasant tale. Maybe it would be better for me to tell you the end of it another day."

"No, let's get it over with."

"All right, I'll summarize it for you. The chronicler who paid most attention to the final details of the battle was Desclot. According to him, there were some six hundred French prisoners of war. He explains in his chronicle that Roger de Lloria kept fifty of them in custody because they were 'good and honorable men,' meaning that they were nobles and he could demand a ransom for them." Luis was listening to me attentively, but as I anticipated the words I was about to say, I felt that they might be too harsh. I stopped for a moment. "Are you sure you want me to go on?"

"Go on, go on. Shit, there can't be much more, can there?"

"That depends on how you look at it. Anyway, five hundred and fifty men remained. Lloria gave orders that three hundred of them should be lined up in single file on the sand, right here where we're standing. When they were lined up, he ordered that they should all be tied with a single long rope, the end of which was then fastened to the stern of a galley."

"Holy shit! I can imagine what comes next."

"Then I'll spare you the details. Lloria gave the order, and the galley got under way, pulling these three hundred unfortunates in her wake. The admiral didn't allow the galley back until well after nightfall, at least twelve hours later. Obviously, somebody untied the rope from the stern before they returned to the beach."

"So we've got two hundred and fifty survivors left."

"If you want to call them that. In their case, the admiral's order was even more horrifying than the first. If you'd like, I'll say it to you just as it's written in Desclot's chronicle."

"Go ahead."

" '*Feu-los trer abdós los ulls e enfilá'ls en una corda.*' Literally translated, it means, 'He had their eyes put out and tied them all on one rope.' The first man, the one at the head of the line of prisoners, had only one of his eyes gouged out, so he could guide the rest."

"Guide them where?"

"To the border. To France. To see the king. Lloria wanted to be sure that Philip the Bold would hear his defeat narrated in the first person. And so he ordered that this line of blind men and their one-eyed leader be escorted to the border."

"What a son of a bitch."

"Not at all. A national hero. A few days later, some emissaries from the king of France appeared to negotiate with him. Since the French had lost the naval battle, their overland advance was thwarted, because they couldn't count on the Roses fleet for the transport of troops and supplies. It wouldn't be long before the French withdrew, but the emissaries were trying to gain time, and so they requested a truce. Lloria refused. They threatened him, informing him that their king had gathered together enough funds to equip more than three hundred galleys and that the following year he would return to avenge their defeat. But Lloria would not be intimidated."

"The man was crazy."

"Actually, he was brave. Do you know what his answer was? He told them he was convinced that from that moment on, no ship or vessel would dare to sail in these waters unless the standard of Aragón were flying from her masts. And he ended with a sentence that history has made famous: 'I believe that not even a fish will be so bold as to show itself on the sea without the king of Aragón's coat of arms stamped on its tail.' "

Luis listened to me in silence.

"What do you think?"

"I think I won't be swimming off this beach anymore."

On the way home in the car, Luis told his father the end of the story and the fate of the prisoners, but he did it in his own way, as if he were relating the plot of a novel. I pointed this out to him, but Alberto sprang to his defense, saying, "Look who's talking."

"Why do you say that?"

"Because you do the same thing. You always tell stories as if you're just stating facts, but your words betray you, Serena. I'm not saying you're lying, but the older the story you're telling, the more you inflate your words."

"Oh, yes? For example?"

"For example, if you had to describe how Pablo and I were arguing yesterday, you'd say we were both 'pissed off,' or that we had a 'huge fight,' something like that. But when your subject is a king from the thirteenth century, you don't say he was pissed off, you say he 'flew into a rage.' I can cite you hundreds of examples: your merchants don't load their ships with grain, they 'secure an abundant provision' of it."

"Maybe you're right," I admitted. "I guess it's inevitable. I don't know. When I talk about such things, I feel a little the way Papa must have felt when he used to tell us the story of Li Po. As if I were a kind of channel to other times."

"I'm not criticizing you. I enjoy your stories more when you tell them that way. You probably inherited the tendency from Papa. Papa's St. George didn't cut off the dragon's head, he dealt the dragon a mortal blow, remember?"

I thought about that. Of course I remember, but there's no possible comparison. When St. George dealt the dragon a mortal blow with his weapon's deadly blade—those were Papa's exact words—I could see the blood flow without his mentioning it. His words echoed in my mind and became huge and powerful, so that I could see the purplish red spilling out of the dragon's throat, I could even hear the rasping rush of its breath as it spouted air bubbles mixed with blood, and I waited expectantly for the beast's final bellow before it collapsed and died. Those words were like a spell, the open sesame that unlocked the doors to a mythical land where everything was possible and dramatic.

I don't want to imitate him. I once heard him declare that if the perfect story existed, it would consist solely of the word "life," at whose mention the planets and mankind would come forth out of nothing and all the things that followed would be made tangible. It was his version of the Book of Genesis: let there be light, let there be life. A Creator of all things through the power of the word. Papa wanted to be like that, but I know it's not possible. So when I refer to six thousand dead and I see that Luis doesn't flinch, I insist on relating their deaths one by one, and I talk about the noise, and I mention the blood and the wounds. But that's easier to do when you're talking about the past. Or when you talk about something that never existed. The future is also useful in this way. If you begin by saying, "There will come a time," you don't need to make much of an effort to finish the sentence, as dramatic, elegant words spill out almost of their own accord. On the other hand, the immediate present is almost always full of tiny words. Mine is, at any rate. I'm going, I'm coming. I think, I say, I said. I sleep, I do. A glance back over the pages of this very notebook is all it takes to prove my point. It's full of phrases like "Today we went to the market," "while we were having breakfast," "we go for a walk." How unheroic the present is. How small the truth. Unless you invent it for yourself, as Papa did. Or unless you invent a world where it doesn't exist, as he's doing now.

WITH LUIS

Don't even think about it, I tell him. Don't even think about saying such a thing again. I can't help it, Serena, I always tell the truth. Don't give me that. Once and for all, we're going to get this story straight: you always say what you think. That's not the same as telling the truth. All right, call it what you want, but don't get cross about it. I said what I think.

What he thinks is that we all wanted him to die. All of us, except his father. I went to see how he was doing because I was worried by the way he reacted yesterday on the *Amen*, when we talked about the dying. I asked if those fourteen months in a coma had made such a deep mark on him. It was a demonstration of affection, but he answered it with a bite: What do you care. How can you say that, Luis. Well, you all wanted them to unplug me. Don't say that, Luis. I only say what I'm thinking; you know, it's a disease. No, Luis, you're wrong. Your problem isn't that you say what you think. Your problem is that you've lost the ability to think. Thinking isn't knowing things; it's learning to compare them, I tell him. It's not choosing between two things; it's discovering all the nuances that separate them from each other. That's the reason why the development of intelligence is accompanied by an increase in vocabulary. Knowing more words doesn't mean we're more educated; it means we're better able to compare their meanings. Good, don't get carried away, he interrupts me. I'm not getting carried away, Luis. You say we wanted to unplug you. You could say we wanted to spare you all the suffering. You could say we were compelled to choose. You could say you might have thought the same thing in our place. Okay, okay, don't defend yourself. All I said was you wanted to unplug me. I dare you to deny that's the truth.

WEDNESDAY

How strange to be writing here, in Barcelona, sitting in this café. I'm amazed by the number of pages I've filled in little more than a week. So many that I'll have to buy another notebook before we leave to go back to Malespina. How strange. When I started, I was convinced I wouldn't find much to write about. Now that I think about it, I suppose I was a little frightened. I've spent so many years asking questions and trying to refute the answers people give me; it's like those cross-examinations you see in films. Seated in the dock, my father and mother, and with them the family's entire past. For the past five years, Papa's mental state has made him incapable of participating in the trial. It was a little difficult for me to accept this change, because I still had a great many questions to ask him. Nevertheless, I saw that the loss he represented wasn't grave; Papa was one of those unreliable witnesses who speak from hearsay. Mama remained: the silent accomplice. The only person who successfully avoided all my interrogations. Her sudden death left the courtroom empty. Or rather, it left me alone there, obliged to take all the roles, including that of the judge. I guess being pregnant also helped a little.

I can't claim to have made any colossal discovery, but I feel proud of a few small advances. On the subject of Simón, for example. Thinking about him for so many days has allowed me to perceive the principal flaw in his legend, and I even feel able to explain it: Papa based the weight of his account on the wrong scene. An understandable error, because not everyone survives a shipwreck after spending three days adrift on a piece of wood in the open sea. For me, the most important moment of Simón's life is his death. Because it explains his absence, obviously; but also because it defines him better than anything else. Simón's death—crushed behind the wheel of the car he had stolen two months previously—shows him to have been a coward, a victim not only of circumstances but also of his own lies. It seems incredible that this never occurred to me before, that so many years of indignation failed to uncover this contradiction. I owe this discovery to chance. The other day, as I was writing down the history of Li Po, I was struck by the excess of coincidences: if you consider the Chinese poet's exile and take away all its exotic trappings, the jade flutes and the reeds, the palaces and the silks, you're left with a story that closely resembles Simón's flight and death. That was the real track. I don't know what my brothers will think when I tell them that our grandfather was nothing more than a poor wretch, a fourth-class thief and a coward. I haven't told them yet, because I hate to break the peace that has reigned ever since yesterday, when we went out on the *Amen*. But tomorrow evening at dinner, I'll bring them up to date.

I've made other progress, perhaps less tangible and more difficult to explain, but equally important to me. For example, I think I know my father much better now. I've also realized many things about myself. All that anxiety I felt, that fixation on Papa's stories, on knowing whether what he was telling us was true—I always saw that as an act of justice, as if the family had handed me a torch and closed me up in the cellar of the past with the mission of remaining there until I could rescue hidden treasures from the darkness. It never occurred to me that the torchlight illuminated me more than it did the things hidden there. Why this obsession? Why this blindness? I now know why: I needed to be worthy of my father's legends, to appear in them somehow, even to take the leading role. Maybe he shared some of the blame for this, because he always gave me the feeling that only the legendary was worthy of his attention. If he went so far as to look down on his own life, periodically and systematically consigning it to oblivion, how was I going to be so deserving that he would grant the least bit of importance to mine? How could I turn myself into a legend? What was I going to do, get in a shipwreck and survive? Scribble down some poems in a letter and leave it nailed to the trunk of a tree? Sink French ships? I couldn't construct a legend out of my life that would be equal to any of his; and therefore I dedicated myself to destroying them. In a war, there's no better way to save your army than by destroying your opponent's.

I've made a third discovery that also gives me comfort: I *like* to write. I like the mere physical activity of it, the routine of sitting on the terrace in Malespina every evening, when everyone else has gone to bed. The other night, just as I turned a page, something green and shiny fell onto my notebook with a little click. I thought it was a leaf. When I tried to brush it away, it jumped and disappeared into the darkness. I didn't have time to see what it was—a grasshopper, I suppose—but it was as if it had come to tell me something. I left that page blank.

But it's not only that. It's as if the lines I've written somehow represent the ball of thread I was so concerned about unraveling when I started. Maybe I haven't achieved complete success, but at least, now that ball of thread is mine; I've been able to make the borrowed words my own. I feel as if I'll never stop writing, and even though I'm a little ashamed to say so, I may even, at some point in the future, try my hand at a novel; I feel that whatever I invent will be as much mine as this journal. Anyone who disagrees should ask my father.

Last night, after the interminable story of the Battle of Formigues, I went to bed too late. This morning we got up at seven and spent the whole day running from one place to another like squirrels, as if we were being pursued. That's what usually happens when Alberto takes command. Things are achieved. Many things, one after another. And quickly. He didn't even let us drink a cup of coffee in Malespina before we left this morning. I thought I'd avail myself of the opportunity to have a doze in the car, but Alberto took the first two curves at such speed that he managed to accelerate the sleep right out of my head. And once we reached the motorway, I was positively afraid.

Finally, I told him, "If you always drive so fast, you're going to wind up like Simón. You're going to have such a bad crash they'll have to suck you out of the car with a vacuum cleaner."

"Simón didn't know how to drive, kiddo," he said. "Besides, it wasn't here that he crashed."

"What does it matter, here or somewhere else?"

"Look, when you consider that this was a goat path at the time, that they were drunk, the kind of car they made back then—"

"That's not the difference, Alberto. The difference is that Simón was running away and you aren't. Nobody's chasing you."

"Running away from what? What are you talking about? Besides, what do you care?"

"I feel sick and this is making it worse."

"Your problem is you're nervous about the solicitor. God knows why. It's not like you're rich, you know. But instead of being glad, you're pissed off. Look, it's just a formality."

"I don't give a fuck about the formality, Alberto. It's the big rush that's bothering me."

It may seem contradictory. I've been complaining that nothing's happening, and then when everything starts going fast I can't accept it. This process is coming to an end. Everything's now a question of formalities, as Alberto says, formalities that eventually are complied with, no matter how hard you try to resist. Today, in Barcelona, we dealt with some of the formalities of life. Tomorrow, aboard the *Amen*, we'll observe the last formality of death, the one that brought us all together in Malespina. Afterward, there won't be any sense in prolonging our stay there.

It will be up to me to clear out Mama's office. I'm not looking forward to it, but I'm not complaining, because if my brothers did the job, the results would be disastrous. Pablo would never finish. He'd spend hours pondering the most insignificant documents and pass over the fundamental ones without a thought. Alberto would wind up the job too fast and be too indiscriminate. I can just see him, making piles on the floor as if he had to sell all the material by weight: this is for you, this is for me, we'll put those parcels over there in the attic in Malespina, just as they are, and the rest we'll throw away, and then we'll call somebody to give the place a thorough cleaning and that will be the end of it. Bang, bang. I'm sure he'd be finished by noon. It's going to take me longer—a lot longer.

The time flew by today, and I hadn't even begun to look at any of the papers seriously. I only opened a few drawers in the first filing cabinet and found three or four thick notebooks, the kind with square-ruled paper, bound together with a rubber band and bearing a label with the single word TRIPS. I went so far as to remove the rubber band and open the first notebook, but I didn't read anything. My heart sinks at the thought, to tell the truth. I don't know how many thousands of papers there must be in that office. Obviously, I'm not going to read them all—that would be madness. It will be enough to put them in order, to discard whatever isn't worth keeping, and to find a place where the rest can be stored, probably in Malespina. That is to say, I'll do just what Alberto would do, but more slowly and methodically. I'm not expecting any dazzling revelations. Mama never had secrets, and she wasn't fond of melodrama.

No, I know what I'm going to find there, and it's going to be largely shock-free. I'm just worried about the quantity. Maybe that's the problem: I don't know where to begin. Those enormous mahogany chests of drawers, with their contents preestablished and codified and labeled—they're a little scary. Trip-related materials go here, official university correspondence goes there, photographs in this drawer, all published articles in that one, drafts in the one after that. I even spotted a blue folder with Papa's name on the cover—probably filled with papers relating to his disability pension. I don't know what it is about the place that makes me so uncomfortable. Too much order, perhaps. Not that I dislike order, in and of itself. Order is a necessary part of life. Maybe that's what's wrong—this dead order, order where no continuity is possible.

I told my brothers about this shortly afterward, when we were on our way to the solicitor's office. Alberto told me that if I needed help, I shouldn't hesitate to ask for it. Help? What kind of help? He probably thinks this can be taken care of by paying a horde of librarians to go through Mama's office and turn it upside down. Pablo chose to favor me with one of his lectures, saying I haven't yet come to terms with Mama's death. My mind has barely begun to process the full significance of her absence, and therefore I reject any sign that confirms it. He all but told me this wouldn't be happening to me if I'd had the nerve to look at Mama's body. Give me a fucking break. Cheap philosophy and pocket psychology. It's a tiny bit more complex than that. I have indeed "come to terms" with Mama's death, thank you. The problem lies elsewhere.

Earlier today, when I was sitting at Mama's desk in the semidarkness, I was struck by something. It was the walls. The walls are practically bare. When it came to interior decoration, Mama was an exponent of what is now called minimalism, not only in her office but even at home, including the house in Malespina; although there, since it was more Papa's territory, she had to accept a few objects that were, as far as she was concerned, pure junk. The *Astor III*'s helm, hanging on the wall; the curtain made from old fishing nets that you step through to get to the terrace . . . She always made fun of those things. But the nakedness of her office is sad, and moreover it's illogical. One of Papa's paintings is in the entrance hall, a seascape with the Formigues in the foreground and the coastline of Malespina barely hinted at in the background. It's not especially beautiful, but it is exceptional, because Papa usually only painted portraits. There are two photographs on the desk. In one of them, Papa and Mama are dancing barefoot on the beach in Malespina. It's an old picture and they look very beautiful, both of them. When Papa dies, I suppose this will be the couple's official portrait. In the other photograph, we're all on the terrace. From the bulges in my bathing suit, I'd say I was still wearing diapers. We're all in the foreground, and in the background there's Grandmother Amparo, sitting in her rocking chair with her knitting needles in her lap. She's the only one who's not looking at the camera; she's looking at us with an enigmatic half smile on her face. A little farther down the hall, next to the bathroom, there's a reproduction of an old woodcut, a group of women with their arms raised to their mouths, as if they were biting their own elbows. There's no text, just an inscription: WARBURG, 1557. I imagine it has something to do with cannibals, because the women's gestures are quite evocative; they seem to be devouring themselves. I suppose I could trace the inscription and find out where this woodcut came from, but I don't find it all that interesting.

There's nothing else. Everything has been filed away. Ah, yes, there's a map of the world on the desk. Maybe it was the map that set me off on that particular train of thought. If a stranger walked into Mama's office, nothing else would reveal anything about her public life. Not one miserable African mask, not one tapestry, not one exotic hanging—a classic Indian sari, or a bright cloth covering some old piece of furniture. Nothing. I remember that she always came back from her trips with her bags full of these kinds of things. She gave large dinners at which she'd tell a few anecdotes from her recent trip and distribute exotic articles to relatives and friends. When we were little, those dinners seemed like banquets. It was as if the Three Magi had arrived from the East. Or from Africa, or South America, or even, on a few occasions, from Australia. What happened to all that stuff? Did she give it all away? Didn't she keep anything for herself? Wasn't there even one single object whose beauty or whose documentary value deserved to be displayed on a wall?

I don't understand. Actually, what bothers me is knowing that I will understand in the end. When I've opened all the drawers. I know that when I've opened them all, when a comprehensive, systematic review of the order of an entire life has allowed me to see the invisible links between all the documents that shape that order, I'll begin to understand. Every file reproduces the mental order of the person who maintains it. That's the only new insight I'll find in Mama's office: the logical scheme that life sketches out for each one of us; the moment when chance stops being chance and turns into cause.

None of the objects that really represent my mother is in sight. This befits her character. She spent her life hidden behind the opaque glass of her silence, her trips, her respect for privacy and the right of each individual to make his own decisions. If I want to see anything, I'll have to look for it.

Formalities. The solicitor. Diagonal, number 571, penthouse suite. We've been there once already, a few weeks ago, when we had to open Mama's will. The solicitor is a pleasant man and the buyers were a young couple. They smiled a great deal and appeared quite content. They said they'd never been in a solicitor's office before. I felt the urge to tell them a few things about Mama's office. Nothing important— maybe that it wasn't always an office, because my parents bought it when they were first married and lived there for a few years. But in the end, I told them nothing. I was there to sell the past; they were buying the future. They seemed so young and modern that I closed my eyes and imagined what the space will look like within a few months, after they've decorated it to their taste. I saw color, a great deal of color. Exotic masks, fabrics, lamps. You don't have to go to Africa to get an African mask anymore—you can buy one around the corner.

I felt rather sad when we left the solicitor's office, but Alberto did his best to cheer me up. He's back to his old self. Euphoric, invincibly cheerful, more delightful than ever. He said he needed an hour to take care of a few things. Luis might be right when he says his father's in love, and at this very moment Alberto may be with the person in question, whoever she may be. That's a good reason to be happy. Pablo said he wanted to take advantage of the opportunity to see someone. I didn't ask him if that someone had a mass of blonde curls.

I'm sure the two of them will arrive soon, because Alberto was very insistent on leaving here at one-thirty so we can return to Malespina in time to have lunch with Papa and Luis. After we eat, we'll go down to the beach and get the *Amen* ready for tomorrow. They're preoccupied with the boat, but I'm more concerned about the sky. The east wind smelled violent this morning. Nothing serious will happen if the wind doesn't change. But just now the *garbí* has started to blow from the south, so we're going to encounter some heavy seas. I don't suppose it will be too bad. Let the storm come, if it brings peace in its wake. Someday I'll learn not to distress myself about things I have no control over, so that if they happen, I'll limit myself to noting them down; and if everything turns out all right, I'll be able to end my report with the lighthouse keepers' incantation: "Nothing new is known to have occurred in the vicinity of this station." But until that day arrives, I have every right in the world to feel uneasy, because if my suspicions are correct, the sky's about to fall in on us.

If I still felt like making jokes and plays on words, I'd say that I'm dead. Dead tired. Confused to death. Distressed to death. Scared to death? Maybe so. I've spent many days thinking about Julio and my children, about the unforgivable fright I'm going to give them, but I haven't dedicated enough time to thinking about how I'm going to feel when I see them again. The thought of such intensity scares me. At least I've rid myself of the distress of not knowing how to tell them I'm alive. After much twisting and turning, I've concluded that the telephone is the only way. This decision wasn't easy. Soon it will be twenty-four hours since I left Guatemala, nearly sixty since Amkiel picked me up at the Posada del Caribe, and I've spent a good part of the time imagining the impossible conversation I'm going to have, grinding it between the millstones of my brain.

I'm here. I can't think of any other way to say it. I could shout it out, the way I remember doing the first time I went swimming in Lake Petexbatún. I could shout it out and wait for the jungle of life to send me back an echo. Or I could write it. One of the things that has always fascinated me about the great novels of the nineteenth century is the facility with which people exchange urgent notes carried by messengers. Dickens uses this device effectively. It makes no difference whether the exchange does no more than set up an appointment to have tea that afternoon, or whether it brings news of some terrible incident somewhere in the South Seas. The messenger leaves with a note and returns with an appropriate response, and meanwhile life goes on. Love notes, secret assignations, threats, wedding announcements, death notices. There are even times when someone sends a note with a brief announcement of some news that he promises to relate in detail under separate cover.

"*Your father is dead. Letter with details follows.*" Nowadays, things are different. All our means of communication have an immediate effect, like a cut to the jugular.

But the telephone is the tool of the times I live in, so I have no choice but to use it. I've made my decision. Getting up the nerve to carry it out is another matter. I've been in my office for two hours now, sitting next to the telephone, shivering with cold despite the lovely Barcelona sun. I've lifted the receiver three or four times. I even managed to dial the first few numbers, but didn't dare continue. Cowardice? Yes. I'm very much afraid. In fact, as soon as I arrived here today, a little after noon, I had a brutal preview of what it will feel like when at last I talk to my children. The only way to get into my office was to ask the portress for the keys. I arrived at the front door of my building, suitcase in hand, and just as I was pushing the handle, it occurred to me that maybe the good woman had heard the news of my death. The thought was like an electric current running through me, such a strange sensation. I'm alive, yet suddenly I felt ghostly, transparent, as if people could see right through me. I was afraid that if I called the portress, she'd look in my direction without seeing me. Or, even worse, maybe she'd see me and say, "I beg your pardon, but aren't you dead?" I found the idea ridiculous; it even made me feel guilty, though I don't know why. And then there was the tachycardia. My heart was in my throat. I couldn't do anything except close the door, beat a retreat, and take refuge in the café on the corner.

It took me half an hour to summon up enough courage to go back. Obviously, the portress doesn't know anything, because it wasn't my presence here that surprised her, it was my absence during these last few weeks. She even seemed glad to see me and launched into a long conversation, to which I didn't contribute much. Then she said, "Your daughter was here early this morning. Obviously, she was waiting for you, but she mustn't have had much time, because she left again after an hour."

The elevator felt like a cage. Serena. The blue folder, my note-

books, the office, my office. I imagined it empty and sterile. Or, worse, full of cardboard boxes, my whole life divided up into stacks on the floor. And yet what struck me most when I finally entered was that it was the same as ever.

No one would think I've been gone for so many weeks. Everything is just as I left it. That should please me, because there's no other place in the world where I've spent so much time as this; it was always my unique, immutable space. If I were to go blind, I'd come to live here. I could walk through the entire flat with my eyes closed, and I wouldn't run into anything, not even once. It's mine. We know each other. Nevertheless, as soon as I came in, when I discovered that Serena has not yet begun the work of demolishing my past, I felt that the place needed a radical change. A good coat of paint, not to preserve it as it is, but rather to change it from top to bottom. Color. The place needs color everywhere. It looks inhospitable, strict, too stern, as if the very walls are frowning at me.

It's well known that the places we live in end up resembling us. So I'm like this? Like this office? Has my life been so austere, so unadorned? I imagine strangers coming in here, people who know nothing about me. What would they think? When they saw the seascape in the entrance hall, they'd infer that I like the sea, but they probably wouldn't know it was off the coast of Malespina, and they wouldn't be able to guess the importance the place has had in my life and the lives of my family. Nor would they have any way of finding out that the painter of the seascape was my husband, much less that I chose this one because it's the only one of his paintings that doesn't represent an invention. Having passed through the hall, the strangers would approach my study. White walls. Two photographs. In one of them, I'm on the beach, dancing with Julio. I suppose they'd think this a handsome picture; everyone says so. That's because it shows Julio, whereas I'm mostly visible from the back. When the strangers looked at the second photograph, they'd say, "Well, she had three children. And that must be the grandmother." Period. No one could imagine the meaning of Amparo's gaze, fixed on her son Julio and her grandchildren. No one. A map of the world on the desk. So a person who travels, or daydreams. Good. Nothing else.

To interpret the engraving on the wall, the strangers would have to know the story of Hans Staden, which is unlikely, because it happened almost five hundred years ago. Staden was a German gunnery expert in the employ of the Spanish, who sent him to America in 1552. The ship he was traveling in was wrecked off the coast of what is now Rio de Janeiro. He survived the wreck and was rescued by the Portuguese, who had established a settlement on a small island nearby. Because of his knowledge of artillery, they charged him with the defense of their enclave, but it must not have been very valuable to them, because they left him there alone. A few weeks later, a tribe of Tupinambá Indians captured him. The Tupinambá were cannibals. They put him into a canoe, wounded but still alive, and took him to their village.

As they approached their landing place, the men in the canoes began to shout and beat their oars together so that the women in the village would be aware of their arrival. Although Staden was gravely wounded and in danger of bleeding to death, one of his captors forced him to stand up. Then he started striking the nape of Staden's neck with an open hand, repeating, over and over, the words "Ajú ne xé peé remiurama." Eventually, Staden understood what was wanted of him: he had to repeat those words. He did so, but when the blows became harder, he deduced that he had to speak louder so that he could be heard by the women, who were already assembled on the shore. He gathered his remaining strength and shouted, "Ajú ne xé peé remiurama." When the women heard him, they lifted their arms to their mouths and pretended to bite themselves. What's most surprising of all is that Staden lived with the Tupinambá for two years after this and avoided being eaten by deceiving them with all sorts of tricks. When he eventually learned the fundamentals of their language, he discovered that those first words meant, "I'm your food; I've come so you may eat me."

At last Staden succeeded in escaping, returned to Europe in a Portuguese ship, and was reunited with his family in Warburg, where *everyone had given him up for dead. He sought out a wood engraver, who made a fascinating series of woodcuts from Stader's drawings of everything he had seen during his captivity. Today, those woodcuts constitute an anthropological document of inestimable value.*

Naturally, no stranger could have any idea what this image from Staden's life has to do with mine, but now it's more pertinent than ever: shipwreck, rescue, cannibalism. I don't think even my own children would know enough to be able to establish the connection. That's too bad, because there's no other. Nothing visible. Nothing that says anything about me, about who I am, unless the visitor should start opening the filing cabinets. But that fact alone, the fact that all the information about my life is hidden, is eloquent. It speaks of the silence I've always maintained. The silence which, if my inference is correct and Serena hasn't yet put her hand into these drawers, I may have to keep maintaining. But that will be later. My voice should be enough to convey the message that I'm alive, whatever my words may be. "Ajú ne xé peé remiurama": I'm your food; I've come so you may eat me. Maybe that's what I should say.

WEDNESDAY NIGHT

I don't know what to say or what to think. My hands are shaking so much I can hardly write. Mama's alive. There, I said it. Or rather, Luis says that Mama's alive, but I'm not going to believe it until I see her. He says the telephone rang and he picked it up and she told him she's alive. Actually, she didn't say I'm alive, she said Luis, it's Grandmother. He said he hung up because it scared him so much he nearly shit his pants. Those were his words. I nearly shit, I'm telling you, I nearly shit my pants. The telephone rang again, and Luis said whoever you are, you can put your telephone where . . . No, Luis, it's Grandmother. She's alive. In Barcelona. Luis says she was speaking so softly, he asked her if she was calling from Guatemala. No, Barcelona; I arrived today. She asked him where we were.

I'd love to find a phrase worthy of the circumstances. Something grand, about life and death and frontiers and surprises. Obviously, I'm happy. But very nervous. We all are. Hysterical. No one understands a thing. I took a pill, but if I want to go to sleep, I'll have to take another one, or at least a half, because nobody could fall asleep in this state. I suppose "dazed" is the word for me.

We don't know anything else. It can't be. That's what Luis said, poor thing: Grandma, it can't be you, Grandma. He told her everything: the call from the Ministry, our trip to Guatemala, the corpse, the ashes, everything. He even told her about the *Amen*. He says she didn't want to tell him anything. Luis explained that he was alone with his grandfather; I'll put him on, he said to her, so you can tell him yourself. No, Luis, not over the telephone. She sounded nervous, he says, but she said she's all right and we shouldn't worry. She said she'll come tomorrow, and we'll talk about everything. Luis told her we were returning from Barcelona as they spoke and suggested she call Alberto on his cell phone. No, she said. She wanted him to tell us. She said we shouldn't even think about looking for her. She said she needed to sleep and she'd come tomorrow. We peppered Luis with questions, but I suppose I know the only detail that really matters: Mama's alive, and she's coming here tomorrow.

I've known this since three o'clock this afternoon, but until now, I haven't felt capable of writing it down. The last thing I want to do is blame poor Luis, but the truth is he's not the right person to receive this sort of news, much less give it. We were hardly through the door when he blurted it out, without warning, without waiting for an appropriate moment. Anyone else would have said, Sit down, I have some news for you. It's good news, but it's going to come as a surprise. Not Luis. When we came in, he was sitting on the bench in the entrance hall, right next to the door. He'd probably heard the car and was waiting for us with his mouth open. Hey, Grandma's alive. What are you saying, Luis, what in the world are you saying? I'm saying Grandma's alive. What? He says his grandmother's alive. What do you mean? What the hell is going on here? I swear to you. She called.

Alberto was worried. He thought his son had gone insane once and for all. Luis, calm down. No, I'm already calm. Well, all right, I'm hysterical, but I swear to you she called. You have to believe me. Look me in the eyes, Luis. Tell me everything. Once more, he began: Well, the phone rang, and I answered it. . . . And then the questions started again, everybody shouting at once. What did she say to you, what did you say to her? But she knows? You told her? Of course I told her. What did she say? It doesn't matter. What do you mean, it doesn't matter? She said it doesn't matter; that's what she said. It was all a misunderstanding. A confusion, she says.

I don't think I'll be able to sleep, with or without a tablet. I close my eyes and my whole body tenses. My bones feel rusty. According to Mama, when you can't sleep, you have to count your toes, but the mere thought of moving mine gives me cramps. I started writing to see if it would relax me, but I'm afraid this therapy is useless tonight. I'm in bed, just in case sleep creeps up on me, but it seems unlikely. No one in this house is asleep, except for Papa. I wonder how I'm going to explain all this to him. Alberto and Pablo are still in the dining room. I can hear the murmur of their voices, occasionally interrupted by Pablo's sobbing. Every now and then he bursts into tears, as if the emotion were surging over him in waves, surprising him every time. I hope the truth has a soothing effect on him, as it does on me. Because when Luis finished telling us about his conversation with Mama, when we had no other choice but to believe him, Alberto stared at us and said it couldn't be, someone had better explain what's going on, because it wasn't possible that both of us could have been mistaken, I'm prepared for anything from Pablo, because he doesn't live in this world, but you, Serena, it's not possible, you'd recognize your mother with your eyes shut. And then I couldn't bear it any longer and I dropped my bag on the floor and almost without my realizing it the words came out of my mouth: I didn't see Mama when she was dead. What? You heard me, Alberto; I didn't see Mama's body.

What a relief. I haven't felt anything like this since I was little. The weight of the truth, unloaded from my conscience: I didn't see Mama. I didn't look at her it's my fault I don't know what happened to me it made me so sad and I was so afraid I wanted to remember her as she was the nightmares terrified me I swear I tried I lay awake the whole night but when we got to the funeral home I couldn't do it I couldn't even take a step and don't ask me why I haven't said anything until now; I really wanted to but I felt bad for you, Pablo, I'm sorry, I know you did it for me, to protect me, but since you saw her I thought it made no difference, all right, there it is, I've said it, so now you know. Finally, just like that, everything pouring out at once like a flood. And Alberto sat next to me and took my hand, it's all right, Serena, it's all right, stop crying, come on, girl, I said stop crying, Mama's alive, damn it, we should all be happy, what does it matter who made a mistake and why. And I said no, that's exactly why I'm crying, I'm crying for joy, can't you tell? Well, I don't know.

No lightning bolt struck me, nor did the earth open and swallow me up. There was no exile and no prison. And then came the strangest and most uncomfortable moment, because we were all looking at Pablo. At first he was defensive with Alberto, don't look at me, I did what I could, and if you're not satisfied you should have gone yourself, I told you I wasn't any good at things like that, and don't blame Serena, she didn't want to go either, I don't know what was so fucking important you couldn't go yourself. Then he shifted to another excuse, time, the problem was too much time had passed and the corpse was unrecognizable. Alberto saw how worked up he was and said forget it, Pablo, no one's accusing you of anything, you don't have to defend yourself, I'm going to open a bottle of champagne and we'll drink a toast because we're happy, damn it, Mama's alive. Besides, you're right. That's what I get for staying home.

Pablo sat down next to me, between the two of us, and said no, Alberto, wait, I have something to say. There was a moment of silence as he searched for his voice. I was afraid, too. I lay awake the night before, shit, I even composed a requiem for Mama, but I've never dared play it. I didn't want to see her either, but someone had to go in. So I did the manly man bit. I'm sorry. I wasn't trying to fool anyone. Before I went into the room, they told me that in the accident the motor, the propeller, had split her whole face open. I thought I was going to be able to take it, but when they told me that, I was scared. Then they gave me the backpack. It was hers. Her passport and a few other things were in it. I recognized her gym shoes. I asked them to let me go in alone. She was laid out on a stretcher, covered with a sheet. All you could see were the soles of her feet. They were a little purplish, swollen and wrinkled at the same time, I don't know. I put my hand under the sheet and touched a foot. It wasn't a very pleasant sensation. I didn't lift the sheet. I saw neither the body nor the face; because her papers were there. It didn't occur to me for a moment that it could have been another person.

Fucking hell, Pablo, you could have told me. Instead of being brave, you could have told me. It would have been easy: Serena, I need you. See how easy? We could have done it together.

All that time I spent suffering, calling myself a coward every night, all the nightmares I had because I didn't go in and see Mama, and now it turns out that he, my own brother, didn't do it either. And all the details he told me afterward, as if he'd really seen her, almost as if he'd spoken with her. Butterfly kisses, give me a break. Now I'm sorry I told him off like that; who am I to judge? Fortunately, Alberto interrupted me, on about the third or fourth try, because I wouldn't let him talk, you shut up, you shut up, this has nothing to do with you, this is between Pablo and me.

In the end, Alberto grabbed me by the shoulders and gave me a shake, and then he made me look him in the eye and he started saying don't give me that shit, Serena, don't say this has nothing to do with me, because it does, we're all in it, because the first mistake was mine, I should have been there, I'm the one who should have gone, but I had reasons for not going, ridiculous reasons that seemed important at the time. You didn't go in and see her and no one's going to blame you, but at least Pablo tried, he was the bravest, he was the one who got the farthest, even though in the end, he didn't dare look. You know why? Because there was no need to. Because it was a bloody formality. The only thing they wanted you to do was sign the papers. Mama was dead. They told you so over the telephone. They had the backpack with her passport and everything. Pablo saw just enough to confirm what he already took for granted. The way we all would. Everybody but you. Sometimes you have to take things as given. Sometimes you have to stop asking questions and doubting everything.

In short, he gave me a real earful. He said I didn't want to go in because I refused to accept what had happened. He said that it was my way of making it clear that I had opposed her trip from the beginning. My way of punishing myself for not having been able to stop her. And besides, he said, what the hell does it matter now, why do you need to blame someone, why do you always need someone to blame. Our mother will be here tomorrow, Serena. Alive.

After that, we just sat there as though we'd all received a good thrashing. Pablo put his arms around me and I wanted to squeeze him and tell him I love you, you big dope, but I couldn't find the strength to do anything more than give him a kiss. Alberto looked at Pablo and me and said nothing. I believe the three of us would have stayed like that all night long, if it hadn't been for Luis, who was the first to recover his sense of humor. "Well, as Grandpa would say, now it's time to move on. So please stop the soap opera, because all we need is for me to start crying too." He said that he too had once risen from the dead, so now he's going to suggest to Mama that they found a zombie club. Club Simón, he wants to call it. He says the game ended with an avalanche of goals: Crazies 6, Normals 0.

I'm not sure how Alberto is feeling. It's always hard to tell with him. He looks all right, and I think he means it when he says it's the best news of his life. But you never know. When I got up to go to bed, Alberto had his Mont Blanc in one hand and a calculator in the other. I asked him what he was doing, and he answered that he was going over all the legal issues, because the red tape in cases like this is fiendishly complicated.

No one was hungry. We'd had tea and toast in the afternoon. The boys had insisted on opening the champagne, and we made a toast to life, but it seemed to me that the glasses remained full. We kept Papa out on the terrace all afternoon. Poor Papa, he was so happy, stuffed with Lexatins. Alberto took care of him. I barely went out to give him a kiss, because I didn't know how to look at him.

Tomorrow's going to be a strange day. If I were to start making a list of the questions I have for Mama, all the pages in the new notebooks

I bought this morning wouldn't be enough. I'm sure she has a few queries of her own. Before she comes, I have to decide how and when to tell Papa. As far as my brothers are concerned, telling him is clearly my job. One thing's for sure: I have to talk about this with Luis. It's urgent. Tomorrow, without fail. I would have liked to bring it up earlier, but we'd already had too much emotion for one day. The thing is I'm upset, because I've discovered that little bastard is a liar. Yes, we all lie; that was made quite clear today. But Luis, Luis . . . Maybe I misunderstood him, but I don't think so. He said, keep your voices down, because I decided not to tell Grandpa anything yet. Very good, it seems like a sensible decision, but something doesn't fit. Transitory Disinhibition Syndrome. Luis is not supposed to be capable of making such a decision. Supposedly he cannot choose not to say something, even more so when it's something as serious as Mama being alive. Or am I mistaken? It may be that the news made such an impression on him that his brain reacted by momentarily taking control. I don't know. I don't want to draw hasty conclusions, but I have to clear this up tomorrow.

It's going to be a strange day, but the most remarkable thing about it, the thing that fascinates me the most, is that in the end it will pass, just like all the rest. At some point I'll be able to write that nothing new has occurred in the vicinity of this station. I understand the old lighthouse keepers. It's not true that the calm always follows the storm, as people believe. The truth is that no matter what follows the storm, we take it as calm. Even if Mama really had died. We haven't been here two weeks, and already I was prepared to affirm that life goes on. Tomorrow we would have gone out on the *Amen*, and once the ashes were scattered, the end would have come for this journal I've been keeping. But my doubts will keep on piling up and getting entangled with one another until the wind of life blows them around and the storm knocks them over, and then I shall reconstruct them, shift them about, give them fresh names, and store them in my memory for a time, so that I'll be able to declare that nothing new has occurred in the vicinity of this station.

And that's how I'll go on spending my days, learning to recognize peace by the absence of storms. And when I die, someone will say it's nothing new, life goes on even if I don't, because the station will remain, as will the storms that assail it, as long as there's a keeper to take note of them.

THURSDAY

I woke up early today, thinking about my father. About what I had to say to him. I got up and had breakfast on the terrace, almost completely wrapped up in Papa's coat, because the east wind was disagreeably cold. I waited a good while for the sunrise, thinking that it would be the last time I'd see it for a while. We'll leave tomorrow, or the day after at the latest. When I went back inside, I paused in front of the urn with Mama's ashes. With Judith's ashes. Then, resolved to tell Papa the truth, I went to wake him up.

"Papa. Papa."

The poor man was sound asleep, with the covers up over his ears.

"Wake up, Papa."

"Mmhmmhmm?"

"Good morning." A kiss. "We have to talk. Are you awake?"

"Mmhmmhmm. What is it?"

"It's nothing, but we have to talk. Do you know where Mama is?"

"Guatemala."

Like a child who's memorized his lesson. Disheveled and bleary-eyed, he sat up in the bed. I was afraid I might damage him somehow.

"The Sex Platoon."

"What?"

"A river in Guatemala. Its name is the Sex Platoon."

"Petexbatún, Papa. Its name is Petexbatún."

"Yes. In Guatemala."

"Exactly. But she's coming back today."

"That can't be, she's dead."

"No, Papa. As a matter of fact—"

"Yes, dead." He said it calmly, looking me in the eye, without any distress, but quite certain. "In Guatemala."

"Papa. Mama's alive. She's going to come here today."

"She's back already?"

"Yes. She's in Barcelona now and she's coming to Malespina later today. You have to get up. I'm going to give you a nice shower and then I'm going to dress you so you'll be more handsome than ever when Mama arrives."

"Isabel?" A sparkle in his eyes. "She's back?"

It's easier to give Papa a shower here than in Barcelona. When Luis first left the hospital, Alberto had the small bathroom adapted to accommodate the boy's disabilities, so there's a metal bar on each wall. There's also a fold-up bench inside the shower in case Papa gets tired. He stands under the jet of water, holding on to a bar with each hand. I lathered soap on him from his head to his toes and scoured him until he gleamed.

Then I sat him down on the bench and shaved him. I wanted him to wear his best white shirt, and I had to iron it beforehand so it would be impeccable. Mama taught me how to iron when I was fifteen. "I'm teaching you this so you can do it for yourself," she explained. "Not so you can spend your life ironing someone else's underpants." Thanks, Mama.

The morning was the worst. No, the worst was not knowing what time Mama was going to arrive. It gave us too much time to think. We all sat together in the living room until noon, trying to initiate conversations that had nothing to do with Guatemala, but inevitably ended in speculative discussions about every possible explanation for the whole fiasco. We didn't yet know about the woman named Judith, so we spent most of the time thinking about whose ashes they might be. We even had a few laughs at their expense. After twelve o'clock, the silences grew longer. We asked Pablo to play something, but he wouldn't. Papa barely talked, but every time he opened his mouth he dropped a pearl.

"What's all this silence?" he suddenly said after we'd been quiet for a while. "Has somebody died?" A little later, surprised because nobody was budging from the living room, he said, "Will someone tell me who it is we're waiting for?"

Twelve-thirty. One. Gradually, each of us found an excuse to withdraw to their bedroom. Suddenly, at one-twenty, the telephone rang. Collective shudder. I picked up the receiver.

"Yes?"

"Good afternoon." An unfamiliar voice. "I'm calling from the Costa Brava Radio Taxi Company. We were asked to let you know that our number 112 is on its way to you from the bus stop."

Well done, Mama. How thoughtful. We nearly went into hysterics when the telephone rang; I don't even want to think about what would have happened if it had been the doorbell.

Company, fall in. Single file. Forward, march. Everyone out onto the driveway. Everyone standing at ease, except for Papa, who was sitting on a folding chair. All of us silent, watching the drive as if we were awaiting the Second Coming.

We heard the cab when it turned onto the driveway, but instead of rolling all the way to the door, the driver stopped down where the gravel begins, between the cypresses. About ten meters or so from where we stood.

Then the miracle happened. Papa stood up and started walking toward the taxi. He took three steps, clumsy but steady, with his back tensed and his eyes fixed on the car. Elegant. The light seemed to shimmer off his white shirt. I moved toward him to hold him back, but Alberto understood what was happening much sooner than I did and said, "Let him go, Serena." All of us motionless, except Papa. He took three more steps, and the door of the taxi opened. Two more steps, and one of Mama's legs appeared. The butterflies in my stomach were now in a frenzy. Three more steps, and there was Mama's face, her whole body, and then another step and they were clutching each other in an intense embrace, and that was when I started to cry, and I haven't stopped all day long, but I don't want to waste time on that because if I had to count all the tears and the hugs and the kisses and the shouts of laughter, there wouldn't be enough pages in any notebook. The old bastard—there's really no other word—seemed years younger. We couldn't make him turn Mama loose. They stood there embracing for so long that Alberto even had time to pay the taxi driver and see him off. They didn't speak, they hardly moved, and their eyes were shut. Mama was running one hand up and down his back, like someone calming a wild animal. And then, without completely letting her go, still holding her by an arm, he started walking her toward the house. The rest of us followed along behind, including Mama, with a dazed smile on her face, not knowing what to do and unable to say anything, because he kept talking the whole time, telling her all sorts of things: Guatemala certainly is far away, I can't tell you how much I missed you this time, I don't want you to go away anymore, we even thought the cannibals might have eaten you. He entered the house, holding her hand, and led her into the living room. Mama walked behind him, devouring him with her eyes, as if she didn't want to miss so much as a second of his amazing resurrection. And then, to top it all, I'll be damned if he didn't sit on the sofa, not in his easy chair, but right in the middle of the sofa, and he told her to sit down here next to me and tell me everything and give me a kiss and how happy I am that you're here, we've been talking about you for days.

Mama couldn't believe her eyes. She kept looking at us as though to say, what is this, a miracle, what have you given this man? But it was no miracle. I think the emotion of seeing her was so strong it dispersed the fog for a while and not only the fog; it even gave him more physical strength than he'd had in years. He held on to Mama's hand as though it were the last branch of a tree on the edge of a cliff. And in the end, he fell. Little by little, he lost his grip, sinking down as if those five minutes of lucidity had required him to expend such an uncommon amount of energy that the only way for him to recover it was to disappear into the darkness. He spent the rest of the day there.

Well. Each of us took a turn, hugging and kissing and not speaking much at first, as if no one knew what to say, or didn't know where to begin. Nothing important. Uncomfortable silences. Alberto had even prepared a speech. I'm sure he was up all night thinking about the exact words he would use in order to keep everything under control, to bring this matter to a close without having to count the victims. At the third silence, he cleared his throat and started in.

"Well, Mama, we have so many things to tell you. First of all, I want to say that we're all—"

"No, Alberto."

"Pardon?"

"I said no, not yet. Of course you have lots of things to tell me, but there'll be time. We need to do this slowly and carefully." It seems that she, too, had rehearsed a speech, because every word seemed meticulously measured. "I have things to tell you as well but there'll be time for everything. Now, let me look at you, all of you."

She gave everyone a thorough going-over. More affectionate than ever. She seemed different in many ways. Changed. She spent the afternoon hugging us, which I suppose was normal, given the circumstances, but she was also more talkative. Much more. And she was funnier too. She seemed to find everything amusing, and kept saying she was dead or dying. She was dying of cold in the afternoon, when she asked me to lend her a jacket, starving to death earlier tonight, when we realized that all the excitement had made us forget about eating, and dead tired a little while ago, when we were on our way home after dinner in the lighthouse restaurant. We were all in the car, no one saying a word, and then she came out with it: "I just realized, I'm dead." Absolute silence. "Dead tired, I mean."

Every time she said such a thing, her eyes would sparkle as if she was about to burst out laughing. As if she could die laughing, presumably.

After she'd given us the once-over, Mama asked Alberto to let her speak. "This is all my fault," she said. "I owe you more explanations than you owe me. Of course I have questions, too, but first I want to tell you everything."

Not everything; almost everything. For example, she didn't explain why she went to Guatemala, which is something I intend to ask her tomorrow. Without badgering her, without making demands, but I think I have a right to know. She also failed to tell us what she was doing in London, though I suppose that's less important. At her age, it's more normal to go to London than to vanish into a jungle. When the story she told us began, she was already in Guatemala. She gave us all the details: how she met Judith on the airplane, her arrival in Flores, the motorized canoes, the river, all of it. Those floating islands. And then the Posada del Caribe. Fabulous name. That's when the first laughs started. But it was also a little chilling—that image of Mama swimming naked in the lake, alone, in some godforsaken spot on the other side of the world. It gives me the creeps, not because of her, but because of the water, I suppose. If we'd been talking about the sea, it wouldn't have seemed so strange. But there, in the lake, those are dead waters. And the encounter with Judith's corpse. It frightened her to death, she said. This time, nobody laughed.

Poor Judith, whoever she was. At one point, Luis got up, took down the urn, and gave it to Mama. We all held our breath, waiting to see what she would say, and then she started laughing, so hard she seemed about to choke. It was a joy to behold. I don't remember ever having seen her laugh so openly, and when she finally could speak, she said the urn was ridiculous, good God, poor Judith, what awful taste. Then she told us about what happened with her backpack, and at that point we all interrupted her, all of us asking questions, because nobody understood. She told the story over again. At first, I didn't want to believe it. I mean, I believed the part about losing her backpack. That could happen to anyone. But the part where she realizes her backpack's missing that same night, when she's checking into the hotel . . . If her story was that she went back into the jungle that same day and didn't need anything in the backpack and therefore didn't notice its absence until it was too late, that would sound more normal to me. But to do nothing, to notice and do nothing, that's a bit hard to accept. She says she never thought she'd be declared dead because she didn't look much like Judith and she was sure someone would look at her passport photo and realize that. She thought that in any case there would be some procedure for identifying the body and that everything would be sorted out then if not before.

Alberto tried to break in on her here, telling her we all had something to confess with regard to the identification of the body, and he most of all.

"No, Alberto," she said. "We'll talk about that later. But first, let me finish. I had a lot of time to think. I imagine you all did too, but I had more than anybody, twenty-four hours a day for I don't know how many weeks. And now I know that I've always kept too many things quiet, that many times I've failed to tell you things I really should have told you. I don't want that to happen again. I want to tell you that I took so long to come back because I was angry with you, because I couldn't bear the idea that you weren't capable of recognizing me, but then I realized I was making a mistake. A very serious mistake. I want to apologize to all of you. I want to tell you all . . . damn, I have so many things to tell you, it's going to take years and years before I can die for real."

How about that? Mama, discovering the medicinal value of the truth at the age of sixty-nine. It's never too late. Just when I was thinking of giving up, she appears with stories to tell. This seems fine to me.

Around nine o'clock, when Mama said she was starving to death, I suggested we have dinner at the lighthouse restaurant. Luis stood up immediately. "We'll have to take Grandpa with us," he said, looking at his father. "Because if you're counting on me to stay here and watch him, you can forget it. I wouldn't miss this dinner even if I were dead. Right, Grandma?"

"Not a chance, my boy. Tonight we're all going together."

So we had to take both cars. With the excuse of going ahead to reserve a table, I suggested that the others ride in Alberto's BMW, while I took off first in my old banger. I was able to enjoy the lighthouse alone for almost twenty minutes. My God, what a spot. High up on the cape, and down below the roaring sea. The restaurant sits a little higher than the lighthouse tower, so you can see the lamp from above. You see where the two revolving bundles of light begin, and how they lose themselves out on the sea. In the old days, the flash would have blinded you. But when they restored the hermitage and opened the restaurant, someone had the fine idea of installing a sheet of iron about six inches wide on the land side of the light platform, so that the light is blocked for a few seconds as it swings past the restaurant and the eyes of those watching are spared. As I was looking at the lighthouse I thought: the truth is a light so strong it burns anyone who dares to look at it; the lie that covers up a truth makes it visible; et cetera. There are thousands of possible combinations. When the others arrived, I was thinking about Li Po's sixth proverb: "The intercourse between the truth and a lie is voluptuous and fecund. First they dissolve into a single body; then they produce millions of progeny."

At dinner I overdid it with the wine, and I'll apologize tomorrow to whoever wakes up with a hangover. I hope everyone agrees it was necessary. We all needed to loosen our tongues a little. It's fine that we're all being so civilized, but really, it was too much. I don't know, sometimes there are things that have to be said and that's all there is to it. And if they have to be provoked, then you have to provoke them.

I hope everyone will grant that I did it in the best possible way. Making sure everyone has wine is not enough; there's a whole strategy of pacing and rhythm, of waiting for the right moment. It's not easy. For example, in order to create a conducive atmosphere, there's nothing better than putting the first truth on the table yourself. But not just any truth. An intimate revelation, but one that can be shared. Pablo handed me my opportunity almost as soon as we sat down at the table: "So, Serena, tell us what you were thinking about out there."

"You won't believe me."

"Try me."

"I was thinking about the first time I made love. It was down there, right next to the lighthouse. Twenty-one years ago this past summer."

Everyone knew with whom, because he was the first serious

boyfriend I ever had, but I'd never told them how or where. In those days, the scenic viewpoint that overlooked the bay from the foot of the lighthouse was Malespina's unofficial love nest. Every night, starting around one o'clock, there seemed to be an acoustic competition going on between the crickets and the shock absorbers of the cars parked there. When you left, you had to drive down the lighthouse road with your head sticking out the window, because the windshield was usually so steamed up you couldn't see a thing. The poor unfortunate who had no car was out of luck. We talked about that for a while. A confession on the table, because one truth calls forth others. And steadily pouring the wine is essential. You have to do it progressively, topping up the glasses while they're still half full, never giving anyone time to empty his glass completely. That way, no one can tell how many glasses he's had. White wine is ideal for this purpose, because you can continue to serve it out in small amounts with the excuse of not letting it get warm.

The results surpassed all my expectations. That wine would be dangerous in the hands of an unscrupulous person. Of course, they couldn't count, as I could, on Luis's help: "So, Grandma, I've got a question I've been wanting to ask you since this morning."

"Fire away."

"What's that perfume you're wearing?"

"Why do you want to know?"

"Because it's very unusual. I don't know what it smells like."

"You'll never guess."

And then Pablo, who was sitting next to her, leaned over, put his face against her neck and said, "Holy shit! It's mosquito repellent."

"I just put on a few drops," Mama said as though defending herself. "I like it. It reminds me of Brazil."

"Well, well," Papa intervened, not exactly continuing the conversation. "This wine is really good. It goes down like water." We'd been sitting at the table for about twenty minutes, and it was the third time he'd said that.

"Mama." Alberto was still serious. It seemed as though the speech he'd had to swallow this afternoon had gone down the wrong way. "Mama, this afternoon you asked me to let you talk, and that was fine with me, but at some point we have to—"

"Stop, Alberto." Pablo jumped in, unusually fierce. "This one's mine." Then he looked at Mama and added, all in one breath, "Alberto wants to apologize to you for the fuck-up of having confused you with someone else and he doesn't know how to do it because the truth is, it was me."

"What do you mean, it was you?"

"The only person who went into the room where they'd laid out your body, that is, Judith's body, was me." Bull's-eye, first time. Blessed wine. "They said it was you and they showed me your backpack and your passport. They said your face had been split open from top to bottom and . . ."

"And what?" Mama was calm. I could almost believe that nothing we said mattered to her in the slightest. "It's all right, Pablo. Say what you have to say."

"And I was scared. I didn't lift the sheet to see your face."

"And that's what you're so worried about?"

"Yes, because on top of that, I didn't tell anyone. That's why it never occurred to us that—"

"That's not important, Pablo. What I'd like to know is why you were the one who had to do it."

She was looking at Pablo when she said this, but it was clear that her remark was directed toward Alberto. The eldest. The one who resolves things. The one who does everything right. The one who should have been there.

"Well, what happened was—" Pablo began to explain, but Alberto practically pounced on him.

"Jesus fucking Christ," he said, enunciating every syllable. "I'd really like to know why the hell no one wants to let me talk today. It's like a conspiracy. I've spent the whole day trying to tell you that I feel awful about not going. It was my job to go. I know what my role in this family is. I don't have a valid excuse, but you picked a bad moment to die, or not to die, however you want to say it. I couldn't leave Barcelona. I had a lot of problems at work and if I had taken off, everything could have gone to hell."

"Fine, Alberto. We agreed that it wasn't important."

"But it's important to me—"

"Then you're wrong." Now it was Mama who looked impatient. "You're all wrong."

"Delicious, this wine. It goes down like water."

"Yes, my love. Like water."

Another of Mama's changes. Before, when Papa would repeat himself like that, Mama couldn't stand it. She'd always treat him with respect and affection. But you could see her clenching up inside. Now she smiles every time he does it, as though they've just met.

"As I was saying, you're all wrong. All I have to do is look at you. You're falling all over one another to defend yourselves. Each of you wants to excuse the others and that's great, I'm proud of you. But there's no need. I could admit guilt too. I already did so this afternoon, but apparently none of you heard me. I'm as much to blame as you, or even more, because I could have eliminated all the confusion by means of a simple telephone call. We're using guilt like some sort of shield. You're the only exception, Serena."

Yielding the floor, however briefly.

"I have my share, like everyone else. I went to the undertaker's with Pablo, but I got cold feet before he did. I was on the verge of fainting, and that's why poor Pablo didn't tell me he hadn't seen you, because he knew that I'd—"

"See what I mean? You've made a ball out of guilt so you can pass it around. You all did something wrong. Alberto, I don't need to tell you; you should have been there. Serena, you've got more of an excuse, because everybody knows you faint at the sight of blood, but someday, somewhere, you're going to have to find the strength to stand it. Because eventually I'm going to die for real, and I'd like to know that you're going to be by my side. And as far as you're concerned," she said, turning to Pablo, "you have to learn that when you get to the end, you get to the end. And if you can't, then you can't. And that's it. Those are your mistakes. But you must remember one thing: none of you deceived anyone and I did. Because you all didn't know I was alive. Whereas I knew you thought I was dead. That's the difference. I've already asked you to forgive me and I'll do it again, as often as necessary."

"In other words, the ball is yours," Alberto concluded. "And you decide who gets to play."

"All right, already." Luis was getting fed up. "Let's talk about something else. The ashes, for example. What are we going to do with them now?"

Pablo suggested that we go out on the *Amen*, just as we'd planned, and throw the ashes into the sea. Mama said she thought the idea of taking the boat out was fantastic, but no one was going to lay a hand on Judith's ashes. She wants to send them to the Spanish ambassador in Guatemala with a letter, in the hope that he can do something about finding Judith's family. Sounds good to me, though I suspect that this is the ball of guilt that's burning Mama's hands.

"Incidentally, where were you thinking about scattering the ashes?"

"In the Russian woman's bathtub," Pablo, Luis, and I answered together.

"The Russian woman's bathtub? Are you all crazy? Out of the question. What's wrong with you?"

She turned red with rage. She said she'd never liked the Russian woman and we all knew it. And she said that scattering her ashes there would have been like spreading them in enemy territory. All that was impressive, but I was thinking about other reasons I didn't dare mention. My dear Luis was the one to fill the gap.

"Well, Uncle Pablo says you couldn't stand the Russian woman because Grandpa had an affair with her."

"Luis!" In his horror, Alberto almost knocked over his glass. "Apologize to your grandmother this instant."

But Mama seemed almost amused. "Do you want to know the truth? For a while, I believed that too. Not when he painted her portrait, because by then she was quite old. I suspected it was before, since he always talked about her in such a way. . . . Isn't that right, Julio?"

"Of course, my love."

Papa had no clue about the conversation, but the way he looked at Mama made it impossible to think that any other woman had ever existed for him.

"I went so far as to accuse him once. He swore it wasn't so, and then I felt bad for having thought it. I believed him then, and I still believe him now. But if what you want is definitive proof, I don't have any. What I do know is how much this man loved me"—she stroked his face—"so who cares about the Russian woman? And incidentally, why the *Amen*?"

"You think it's not good enough?" Luis, excited again. "It's an old fishing boat that was present when Simón's ship was wrecked."

"Ah, Simón," Mama said, cutting him short and raising her eyes to the ceiling. "I wasn't referring to that. I'm asking why we aren't going out on the *Astor*."

"Because Papa's having her fixed."

"That's a lie," Alberto said curtly.

"Shit, Papa, you're being strange tonight. You said—"

"There's no need to remind me of what I said. It was a lie. I'm not fixing anything. I sold the *Astor*."

"What?"

All of us. Like an echo. What what what what.

"I sold her a month ago. I needed the cash. I'm ruined. That's what I've been trying to tell you."

Christ. What a surprise. He gave us all sorts of explanations, but there are still things I don't understand. I'm not referring to the money, because the figures are clear. No matter how much Alberto makes, if you add up his lifestyle, his divorces, what it costs to give Papa his care, what he had to pay for the house, plus Luis's recovery and all the improvements in Malespina, not to mention the gifts he's given all of us . . . No amount of income could cover all that. What I don't understand is why he waited until now to say something. It can't be so hard to ask for help. That's what siblings are for. But it's a lie. And it's a lie when I say I don't understand. That's not what his siblings are for. His siblings are for everything continuing just as it is, for him to go on forever being the generous one and for us to remain the beneficiaries of his generosity, because that's how the roles are distributed in this play. And if Alberto told us his problem today, it wasn't because of the wine or the atmosphere or any such nonsense; he told us because he had no other choice. The house in Malespina is mortgaged, and he's months behind on his payments. If he doesn't catch up before the end of the year, they'll seize the house. To bring things full circle, Mama put the damn ball back into play again.

"It's my fault, Alberto."

"Mama—"

"Say it."

"No, we had an agreement."

"Agreement my foot. Don't you see? Don't you understand that playing the secrets game accomplishes nothing? Don't you realize your father isn't going to understand what you're talking about?"

Then Mama went ahead and told us that the idea of buying the house had been hers. Papa would never have accepted it otherwise. What I didn't like was the fact that they kept it a secret. After all, it was Papa they needed to deceive, not us.

Then Mama had a brilliant idea: how about selling her office? You're a bit late, it's already sold. Alberto explained that he wasn't keeping his share but using it to pay his debts. That was why he was in such a hurry when we left the solicitor's the other day. We took advantage of his inebriated state to drag some figures out of him. I think we'll be able to keep the house in the end, but it won't be easy. Pablo and I promised to contribute our part of the inheritance to the mortgage, but then Mama will be left without a euro, because that money is hers. Once again, Luis did his best to raise the spirits of the company. "Damn, Papa," he said. "So that's why you've been so nervous. We all thought you were in love."

Alberto seemed to smile, but it was more like a grimace of defeat. Then Luis started on me, and I could have killed him. Him and his fucking syndrome. "All right, Serena," he said, "since we're making confessions, don't you have anything to say?"

"Me? I don't know what you're talking about."

"Yes you do." He looked at my stomach.

I had no desire to play this particular game. "No. All I have are questions. For example, since we've been talking about liaisons, there's another one I'm curious about. Pablo's convinced that our grandmother must have gone to bed with the director so he'd give Simón a role in the play. I'm not so sure, but it does make sense."

"You're still going on about all that?" Mama seemed genuinely surprised. "Aren't you ever going to forget about Simón?"

But Luis was still in the mood for confessions. "Grandma, did Amparo screw the director? Guilty or not guilty?"

"I have no idea, Luis. I think there are many things about Simón and Amparo that we don't know and never will know."

"Well, I think I know a few."

Mama stared at me, and for a moment she looked almost frightened. "Like what?"

"Well, I think the famous car he was in was stolen, and that's why he was running away and that's how he was killed."

"Absolutely right," Alberto said, apparently still maintaining the remnants of his sense of humor. "Just what we need. Me ruined, my grandfather a common thief . . ."

But no one paid any attention to him. We were all concentrating on Mama. She thought for a while and said, "You may be right, Serena. I've sometimes thought so myself."

"I don't want to hear it." Now Alberto was serious. "Really. Let's ask for the bill. You can tell us tomorrow, Serena. There've been enough surprises for one day. Besides, I'm dead tired, and . . ."

". . . I've only enough strength to go to bed," Pablo, Luis, and I said in unison.

"Now you'll have to go to your room and we'll lock you in," Pablo went on.

"The one we're going to shut up is you, Pablo," Luis suddenly said. "For lying."

"Me? Lying?"

"All right, for keeping secrets."

"Let's hear it, Luis," Mama prompted him. "One more confession won't matter."

"Pablo's gone back to Antonia."

What an asshole. What a pair of assholes: Luis for saying it, and Pablo for doing it. We let him have it. Even Alberto, who seemed to have abandoned the conversation after confessing his financial ruin, jumped on Pablo with both feet. We hit him with everything imaginable. He was making a mistake. A giant fuck-up, as he himself would say. Pablo remained calm throughout. He said we were right. He said he would never be so mad as to marry her again, but as a lover, she was priceless. And then Mama said he was right. A very sensible decision, she said. Congratulations, Pablo, it's about time you grew up. Was it the wine?

In the end, we all decided that we'd take the *Amen* out tomorrow and sail to the place where Simón was shipwrecked, and there I could tell the story of the stolen car. Proposal accepted unanimously.

Since nobody else felt capable of driving, I left my car at the lighthouse, everyone crammed into Alberto's car, and I drove home. We were so silent on the drive it seemed we would all go straight to bed, but when we got home we collapsed in the living room, as if nobody dared bring the day to an end. Mama lay down on the sofa, covered with Papa's coat and with her head in his lap. Pablo went over to her, put a hand under the coat, and touched her feet. He kissed her forehead. Then he sat down at the piano, lifted the lid, and said, "This is what I composed that night in Flores. It's called 'Isabel and the Water.' "

And he started playing. I was terrified, because I was expecting one of those colossal things of his, a mighty funeral dirge. But it was the complete opposite; it was the music of moving water, overflowing, powerful, but almost joyous, like a dance. This son of a bitch, I thought, this son of a bitch. His mother dies, and he can think of nothing better to compose for her than a dance. I didn't know whether to laugh or cry. Mama got up and took Papa's hands and raised him to his feet, slowly, saying come, Julio, come on, and she embraced him as she had this morning, but moving a little, while Pablo kept playing, and it was as though they were doing the last steps of a dance that had begun many years ago.

WITH LUIS

He admits it at once. He doesn't even try to make an excuse. Of course, he says. For a long time now. How long, I ask him. I'm angry. I don't know, he says; weeks, maybe a couple of months. It's like I've got one of those flickering neon lights in my brain, a short circuit. Sometimes the light comes on. It only happens every now and then. Yesterday, for example, when I saw that I shouldn't tell Grandpa that Grandma was alive.

And why didn't you tell us anything, I ask him. This is important news. Well, you don't seem very happy about it, he answers. What do you mean? You're always asking me what I mean. I mean what I say: you don't seem very happy about it. I just would have liked to know sooner. Now I have the feeling you were playing a game with me.

Then he comes out with it. Of course I was playing, he says. So were you. The thing with you is that you want to have a sexual relationship with the truth. A perverse relationship. Danger makes you horny. You come to talk to me, you come to tell me truths, but you hide them and need me to drag them out of you. You need it to be a bit of a struggle. You need to feel the correct amount of fear. You need to know that you'll hesitate, but you'll end up telling me, and you need to know I might tell everyone else. You're going too far, Luis. It's a metaphor, Serena, a manner of speaking; you understand what I mean. All right, but you've gone too far. Then get dressed.

Swear you won't tell anyone what I told you, I say. I can't swear anything, Serena. When you told me you were pregnant, you knew I might say it to anyone I felt like telling. That was part of the perversity. I'm telling you, it was pure sex. You arrive dressed, you take off your clothes, you do what you have to do, you get dressed again, and you leave. But you're not the same person you were when you arrived. Neither am I. Now I have your truths. I don't know what I'm going to do with them. That's not a manner of speaking. I truly don't know. It depends on the neon light. It goes on and off.

FRIDAY

Latitude 41°36' N, longitude 3°15' W. These are the coordinates of Simón's shipwreck. There's no member of our family who doesn't know them by heart. Obviously, this location is only a supposition. All we know is that the wreck took place about seven miles off the coast. And not even that. When Papa was teaching us how to sail, he used to take us there so he could tell us the story in the appropriate setting. As he spoke, he would spread out his arms: the cloud came from over there, the boats were here, the first squall scattered some of them in this direction, the others drew together more or less here. Then Simón, clinging to his raft, went floating off that way. And so on. After we arrived home, I'd go out onto the terrace and stare at the view until my eyes hurt.

In those days, we didn't know the exact coordinates. That came later, when Alberto bought the *Astor IV*, with GPS and modern devices that were perfectly useless in a boat which was destined only for coastal navigation. Naturally, he wanted to sail to the shipwreck site on her first voyage, and we all went with him. We sat on the bridge next to the helm and noted down all the pertinent numbers, beginning with the ridiculous twelve minutes it took the boat's 280-horsepower engine to reach the spot and continuing with the 78-meter depth indicated on the sonar. As we approached, Alberto reduced the speed. Papa rose to his feet, sniffed the air like a clairvoyant, waited a few seconds, and said: "Here." Then Alberto turned on the GPS, and I made a note of the coordinates: 41°36' N, 3°15' W. No one argued the point, and the coordinates were officially established once and for all. The choice of the site was like naming a child: totally arbitrary, but irreversible.

I don't know if we were at precisely the right spot today, because the *Amen* doesn't carry a GPS. The plan was to set out very early, because according to my predictions, the east wind was going to start blowing hard in the midmorning, and when that happened, the chances were that it might rain. We got up early, but it proved impossible to weigh anchor before eleven o'clock. The blame for our slowness was divided equally between Papa and myself. I received my share because of this morning's hangover, which didn't dissipate until we were on the *Amen*'s deck. And Papa . . . well, it wasn't really Papa's fault. The fact is he was so ungainly it was impossible to get him on the boat. Nobody wanted to take him home and stay with him. In the end, Mama said she thought we should leave him alone in the house. We were astonished. "He can't go anywhere," she said. "We'll settle him in his comfy chair and leave him. It will be my responsibility."

Finally, we managed to get under way. The *Amen* sailed exactly as she had the first time, as if she didn't deign to notice the additional crew. When we reached the shipwreck site, Alberto turned the bow directly into the wind, we loosened the sail, and the *Amen* grew still, with a slight roll like the breathing of dogs after a run. Absolute silence, except for the water lapping in the bilge. When I saw that everyone was looking at me, I had a strange feeling, as if the roles had been reversed and I was to assume Papa's. If we looked at him like that, if we listened to his stories with the same anxiety I saw on my brothers' faces, I'm not surprised he let himself get carried away. Mama, who had never shown much interest in the stories before, seemed the most eager to hear them today. They wanted to listen to me as if I were a ventriloquist's dummy. As if Papa's incapacity had turned my mouth into a tool for repeating the old stories, the borrowed words. What was staged on the *Amen* wasn't a truth ceremony; it was the counterfeit of a legend.

In case I hadn't understood, Luis sought to clarify things right from the beginning, as soon as it became evident that I intended to go straight to the new conclusions I'd reached in the past few days. He protested at once, insisting that Simón's story, just as Papa told it, was interesting in itself, even if it happened to be false. He assured the others that I knew it word for word and didn't hesitate to reveal that I had written down the story of Li Po for him the other day. When he read it, he said, he thought he was hearing Papa's voice. Very clever, that boy. His last argument was that since there were no witnesses and no objective way of confirming the truth, the only way to know if my version of the story was credible would be to compare it with the other one.

I protested. "Simón's whole story? Are you crazy? We'll be here past midnight."

"Skip the shipwreck if you like," Mama proposed. "We all know that part. You could begin when he ran away from home."

"All right. We know that he left his house at dusk, and—"

"No, not like that, Serena," Luis interrupted me. "If you're going to tell it like that, I'm going to jump in the water and swim back to land. 'At eight in the evening on the eleventh day of August, 1922, Simón determined . . .' That's how Grandpa told it. And please don't skip anything. I want the card houses, the crumbling copy of *El burlador de Sevilla*, the three lessons, all of it. Please."

Please. Well, it wasn't so hard.

"At eight in the evening on the eleventh day of August, 1922, Simón determined that the success of his plan depended on the alacrity with which he set it in motion. In other words, he saw that the time for action had arrived. Just as caution and dissembling had been his chief allies thus far, from this point forward he had to count on determination and daring. His appointment with the troupe was for seven o'clock the following morning in front of the Teatro Goya. As his father generally got up shortly after five, Simón had planned to maintain the semblance of normalcy until an hour beforehand, or four in the morning, at which time, without making the slightest sound, without so much as lighting a candle, he would leave the paternal home forever. However, for the first time, seated before his heavy volume of Roman Law and assailed by nerves, he felt incapable of memorizing a single line. By now he'd already spent more than two hours lost in thought, weighing all the possible alternatives in regard to the matter of the car. He didn't know what to do. Admit the truth? Present himself at the appointment without a car and trust the director to keep his promise anyway? Too risky; it had not escaped Simón's notice that of all the contributions he could make, the one the company most prized was the idea that he had a vehicle at his disposal.

"More and more, he wanted to turn back time; to return to the moment when he had lied to the director for the first time. That is, when he corroborated Amparo's lie. But such a thing is never possible. The only thing we can do is correct the truth, and this was the task to which Grandfather Simón dedicated his mental powers that evening. As usually happens, his imagination refused to cooperate until the last moment, and only then did it dazzle him with a solution so perfect, so clear and obvious, that he would have wasted a great deal of time upbraiding himself for not having thought of it earlier had he not been spurred on by the thought of his father's imminent arrival. Now there was no time to lose. His new plan required the utmost haste.

"Aloft on the wings of euphoria, Simón put into a suitcase the few belongings he considered indispensable: two or three changes of clothes, two new decks of cards, and his copy of *El burlador de Sevilla*, which was so worn it seemed to be on the point of falling apart. Before leaving his home forever, he put his equally battered Roman Law textbook on his father's bed. At the page corresponding to the lesson he was supposed to review with his father that night, Simón stuck a note with the following text: 'Today, Father, it's your turn to learn a lesson. I ask only three things of you: that you don't forget it, that you take care of yourself, and that you waste no time in looking for me.'

"Simón never told anyone what happened between the moment when the door of his father's house closed behind him and the following morning. Not anyone, not even Amparo. All we know for certain is that a little before the appointed time, when the first members of the

Compañía del Corral started to arrive at the meeting place in front of the Teatro Goya, they found Simón asleep in a car parked by the pavement. No one realized who he was until Amparo arrived, and even she did not recognize him at first, because it would never have occurred to her that the driver of so luxurious a vehicle could be her boyfriend. It wasn't just any old car; it was a Hispano-Suiza, which, even in the dull light of early morning, gleamed with all the splendor of its silver-plated molding. Amparo knocked on the car window softly with the back of her hand, trusting that the metallic tap of her rings on the glass would be enough to rouse Simón from his slumber. When he failed to react, she opened the door and got into the car. Before she spoke, she reached out a hand to stroke the walnut door of the glove compartment and palpated the sumptuous leather seats with her fingertips, afraid that any sudden word or movement might, as in a fairy tale, cause all that beauty to disappear. At last, she whispered her boyfriend's name: 'Simón.'

"But Grandfather was deeply asleep.

" 'Simón, Simón.'

"She grabbed the lapels of his jacket and shook him until he began to open his eyes. Instead of throwing herself into his arms, Amparo drew back a little and inquired in an apprehensive voice, 'Where did you get this car?'

" 'Bought it from Alfonso,' Simón replied, his voice still thick with sleep. Amparo said nothing, but she knew perfectly well that there was no way Simón could have gathered enough money to pay for so much as a tire for a vehicle like this. She also knew that if she confronted him, if she openly demonstrated her lack of trust, she would get nothing in reply but obstinate denials. Therefore, she preferred to wait until they were on the road, where Simón would decide to tell her of his own volition."

I told my brothers this story just the way I'm writing it here. Up to this point, everyone had listened to me in silence, drinking like lambs from the trough of legend. It was very flattering, to tell the truth, but it also angered me. It's all right for children to listen to Daddy like that, with the ears of their imagination, not their intelligence. But we're all grown-ups, damn it. Even if we don't care for the truth, even if our interest is purely nostalgic, the story has enormous holes that cry out for explanation. He bought a car? Simón bought a car from his friend Alfonso? A deluxe Hispano-Suiza made in France? Don't make me laugh. It must have been obvious even to Papa that no one was going to believe that. Therefore, when he came to this part of the story, he asserted that Simón refused to answer Amparo's questions. In Papa's words: "We know only that Simón left his father's house before dinner that night and presented himself at the appointment the following morning, driving his friend's car and claiming to have bought it. Our only recourse is to imagine what took place between those two moments." And after he said that, he added, "I said imagine, not invent; those are two different things."

Pretty damn different, I say. We invent in order to make certain that the result more or less suits us; we imagine in order to approach a possible truth. Papa invented. Or rather, Amparo invented, and Papa did everything in his power to conceal the flaws in her invention. I encouraged my brothers to imagine with me. To apply, for the first time in their lives, a little logic to Simón's story.

"What difference does it make if he bought it, stole it, or found it abandoned on the street?" Alberto asked. "The important thing is that he needed a car and he got himself one. Without a car, there would be no theater, and the theater was his dream. It doesn't seem so bad to me if—"

"Bad?" I interrupted. "Who said anything about bad? I'm not judging Simón. The person I . . ." No, I couldn't say, "The person I'm judging is Papa." I started over. "I'm not saying it was right or wrong. I'm saying it was a lie."

The discussion went on unbearably long, and as usually happens, determining who was right became more important than determining what the truth might be. Alberto, Pablo, and Luis attacked my version of the story from every side. As I was preparing to beat a retreat, the bugle call of my unexpected ally sounded across the field, and Mama joined the battle.

"Let me make a proposal," she said with a broad smile, as if she found the discussion amusing. "Let her finish. Let Serena tell her version of the story. After all, that was the plan to begin with."

Thanks, Mama. Many, many thanks. Because in that moment, I understood that if my arguments weren't going to make a dent in the defenses of the entire family, I had to change my plan of attack from that point on; my objective was no longer to try to convince my brothers, but to crush the impossible legend of poor Simón.

"Does anyone know where Alfonso lived? Does anyone know what Alfonso's name was? Because even that's a lie. But in any case, let's suppose that Simón went to see him at his home. An address at the upper part of town, for example. It doesn't matter, does it, Alberto? After all, we don't even know exactly where Simón himself lived. He probably walked across the entire city. As we know, or as we believe we know, he left the flat around eight in the evening. . . ."

A miracle. Once again, they were all hanging on my every word. Especially Mama, who stared at me with such fierce intensity, it was as if she wanted to be sure I didn't squander the opportunity she'd given me. She seemed almost proud of me. Every now and then, she would nod or smile, encouraging me to go on. And so I did.

It's amusing to imagine this part in words like those my own father would have chosen. For example: Whatever Alfonso's address may have been, it seems clear that Simón arrived at his building around nine. His friend's family had gathered for dinner. We're talking about a home of the very rich here, so when Simón entered, he found himself confronted by a porter dressed in blue. The man looked him over, as one often does with people who are out of place; it's even possible that the porter sniffed at Simón, catching the scent of onions that betrayed his origins.

"Where does the gentleman wish to go?" the porter asked, proud of his double sarcasm, because he neither considered Simón a gentleman nor intended to let the young man go anywhere if he could stop him.

"I've come to see Alfonso."

"Who may I say is calling?"

"Simón Azuera."

"Please wait here. I'll tell him at once."

The porter made a show of dallying over some trifle in order to demonstrate to Simón that for all his nervous pacing up and down in front of the porter's lodge, he, the porter, was not about to act upon the young man's request with any sense of urgency. At last, Alfonso came down. The last time they'd seen each other was in Malespina as Simón headed out on a fishing boat on his way to a shipwreck that Alfonso, eager to return to Barcelona, had not stayed to witness. Maybe news of the storm had never reached him. Or maybe it had; it doesn't matter. Alfonso couldn't possibly have thought that Simón's surprise visit meant anything like good news, and it makes sense to suppose that he decided against inviting Simón up, which would surely have provoked his family's curiosity and a subsequent interrogation; instead he chose to go downstairs, receive Simón in the entrance hall, and find out his intentions. "I'm in a jam, Alfonso." Grandfather Simón's voice was shaking. "I've come so you can pay me back."

"Pay you back for what?" Alfonso asked, genuinely surprised.

"Our bet."

"What bet?"

"You owe me six hundred pesetas."

"Have you lost your mind?"

"No. I have witnesses. I bet three hundred and you doubled it."

"Fuck, Simón. Why are you springing this on me now? It was only a joke."

"No, it wasn't. To me, bets are sacred. If you were bluffing, I'm very sorry, but you lost."

"But Simón, we were drunk."

"Drunk? So who drove to Malespina?"

"It was a crazy thing to do, Simón. We could have been killed."

"But the fact is we're still alive. And you still owe me six hundred pesetas."

"That's a lot of money."

"Then you shouldn't have bet so much."

"You're right, but in any case, I don't have it."

"Then ask your father for it."

"My father? But I never told him about that night."

"That's not a problem. I'll tell him myself."

"Great idea! You don't even know my father. If he finds out, he'll punish me for the rest of my life. And you'll be in deep shit too. He's liable to call the police."

"Is that a threat?"

"No, I'm serious. My father's a very strict man."

"Don't tell me how hard your life is, Alfonso. I'd trade you for mine in a second."

The conversation had already gone on too long for both of them. I imagine Alfonso rummaged in his pockets and perhaps made a mental calculation of how much cash he had available upstairs.

"Calm down, my friend. We'll find a solution. Suppose I give you what I have on me, which is fifty, and I pay you the rest next week?"

"Impossible."

"Tomorrow, then."

"That's no good, Alfonso. I need it now."

"Shit, is it that urgent?"

"Yes."

"What kind of mess have you got yourself into?"

"It's a long story. The important thing is that I need the money right now. My life's at stake."

If Simón said this, it wouldn't be completely fair to accuse him of lying. Because, although his life may not have been physically at stake, the life he'd dreamed of for himself certainly hung in the balance.

"Well, I'm sorry, but I can't pay you. There's nothing more to say."

Although neither had intended this, their conversation probably began to resemble one of their card games. Good hand, bad hand; give and take; bluff and counterbluff.

"Either you ask your father for the money, or I'll go upstairs and ask him myself."

I imagine Alfonso standing at the foot of the staircase, trying to block the way and no doubt realizing that his body wouldn't be able to withstand an attack from Simón, a powerful young man whose strength had been honed by his physical labor in his father's shop. Perhaps there was the beginning of a struggle.

"Wait!" Alfonso was racking his brains. "I've got it! Take my watch," he offered, removing it with shaking hands. "Take it. And my cigarette case."

"Why would I want them?"

"You could pawn them."

"Not a chance. The pawn shop won't be open until tomorrow morning. . . ."

If my suspicions are correct, not only had Simón turned up at Alfonso's address knowing full well he couldn't cover the bet; he didn't even really want the cash. Six hundred pesetas were not going to solve his problem. The only solution to his problem was a car. That's why he drew out the conversation. That's why he insisted and threatened. That was his bluff. For some time now, he'd been waiting until the cord became tight enough for him to pull the ace out of his sleeve: "But now that I think about it, I can see another solution."

"What solution?" Alfonso asked, unable to hide a sigh of relief.

"Lend me the car."

"The car?"

"Just for tonight and tomorrow. With the car, I can take care of my problem. I'll bring it back to you this time tomorrow."

"Simón, that's even more difficult."

"Why?"

"Because it's not mine."

"What do you mean, not yours? You said you bought it."

"It's my father's. Sometimes he lets me use it. But that night, he didn't even know I took it out, much less that we went to Malespina."

"Goodness, Alfonsito. What a little liar you are." At this point, Simón must have thought that his plan was beginning to work. Maybe he tried to clinch the deal by tightening the screws on his opponent a little. "I don't know what your father's going to think when I tell him."

"Will you stop that? If he finds out, he'll kill me."

"Then you tell me how we're going to work this out, because I'm not leaving here without my money, or your car."

"But what can I do?"

"It's very easy. Tell your father it's being repaired. Make up some minor problem. Tell him the spark plugs are dirty, or say it got a little scratch. Tell him you're going to pick it up on Monday. After all, I'll be bringing it back tomorrow, right?"

"All right." Alfonso gave in. Since he had to face his father in any case, given a choice between the minor annoyance a fictitious mishap might cause him and the monumental row he'd have should the story of the bet emerge, he didn't hesitate to choose the first. "Take it. But treat it as if it were your child. And I want it back here tomorrow evening without fail. I'll give you the key to the garage, and you can take it out yourself; that way my father won't find out."

"I promise."

Before Alfonso bade Simón farewell, I have no doubt that he uttered something like this: "One more thing, Simón. You've never deceived me, and I have no reason to doubt you, but if you're not here with the car intact by seven tomorrow evening, I'm going to come to your place with the police."

"It's a deal. Give my best to my father," Simón replied with a grin.

I imagine he spent a large part of the night driving aimlessly around the city. He needed to. Simón had no driver's license and owed his rudimentary driving skills to the many times when he had been allowed to climb into the trucks that came to the store, to park delivery vans or move them a few dozen meters. In other words, it isn't far-fetched to suppose that he taught himself to drive that night, and we may also assume that, at least for a few hours, he was accompanied by the excitement of his triumph, by the feeling that now nothing, absolutely nothing, stood between him and the only dream that had ever truly mattered.

Similarly, I assume that at some point, euphoria gave way to weariness and Simón pulled over to take a nap. Perhaps he went straight to the Teatro Goya and slept there, which would explain why Amparo found him asleep in the car the next morning.

When I reached this part of the story, they were all listening to me as if their lives depended on it. As I looked at their faces, I realized that I'd brought them to a level of attention that allowed me to do whatever I felt like doing, to run into as many contradictions as I wished, to invent the secondary characters I needed to support my story. I could even invent the fact that Simón had never existed. What immense power. Now I truly do understand how Papa felt. Now I know what it means to tell a story when you know the people listening to you are going to swallow every grain of your imagination, provided you administer it with the appropriate words.

But that power is frightening too. I had to stop the story, let my feet touch the ground for a moment. The truth is arrived at slowly. Step by step.

"So what do you think?" I asked, to the disappointment of the entire family; they wanted stories, not opinions. "Is my version more believable? You might prefer the idea that Simón broke the piggy bank containing his impossible savings and bought himself a car at nine o'clock at night. Or that Alfonso was such a fool that he lent Simón the car to pay off their bet."

White flags everywhere. Even Alberto conceded. "Maybe you're right," he said. "But I still don't understand why that changes the cause of his death. As I told you before, what's important is that he got hold of a car and was able to leave with the theater company the following day. From then on, nothing changes."

"On the contrary; everything changes. Do you remember the story well?"

"Yes, but not as well as you. I mean, I don't remember Papa's exact words."

"Why don't you continue from where I left off?"

"No. I'm no good at telling stories. I have enough trouble with real life."

"It won't matter if you tell it badly. This isn't an exam, Alberto— no one's going to give you a grade. If you finish telling the story yourself, I feel certain you'll realize it can't be true. Please do this for me."

"Come on, Papa," Luis chimed in, coming to my aid. "Give it a try."

"Well, presumably by eight o'clock, the whole company had gathered." Alberto spoke slowly, testing the ground. "They left by the Tarragona highway. If I remember correctly, they all traveled in the van except for the director and Amparo, who went in Simón's car."

"The director, Amparo, and Andrés Salgado," Pablo corrected him, "the troupe's principal actor."

"Very good," I said. "Alberto, I want to propose something. Let's skip directly to the night before Simón's death."

"Just like that? It seems rather brutal."

"Not if you're going to decide you like storytelling so much. We can do without everything that happened between the departure from Barcelona and the night before he died. It doesn't have anything to do with the truth we're looking for."

Alberto hesitated. I guess he suspected I was laying a trap for him, and I can't criticize him for that, so I had to give him a little push.

"Let's say it's true, then, if you prefer. Let's assume that everything Papa told us was true. I'll even summarize it for you. As we know, they spent several weeks going from town to town. This was the longest part of the story: all those fascinating details about life in a traveling theater company. How the members of the troupe ate, where they slept, even how they went about giving their clothes a wash from time to time. And how Grandmother Amparo, with her miserable needle and thread, proved capable of getting them out of any tight spot. All that."

"All right."

"And if you want, let's pass over the long conversations Simón had with the director in the car, where he eventually managed to gain the director's trust. Because of that, he was told he would make his debut as soon as the occasion presented itself. Are we in agreement up to this point? Can we go directly to Teruel?"

"Wait." Alberto wasn't quite satisfied. "We've skipped something else that's fundamentally important."

"What's that?"

"The fact that Amparo got pregnant, of course. Don't you consider that essential? If she hadn't, Papa wouldn't exist."

"Nor you, nor me. Granted. Besides, that part was lovely. How did it go? 'Love found but few occasions to bring Simón and Amparo together, and since the company was numerous and their living space limited—' "

"Get out, Serena. What a memory you have."

"Wait, wait. '. . . they were often obliged to repress the ardor natural to their youth.' "

" 'But love knows no barriers,' " Pablo continued. "When I was a child, that line always fascinated me."

"Exactly: 'But love knows no barriers and respects them even less. It sets about removing them, undermining their foundations, if necessary, with the patience of water.' The truth is that this was pure romantic claptrap. You all agree, don't you? And then came 'One night—' "

" '. . . veiled by the new moon . . .' " Even Luis knew this part.

" 'One night, veiled by the new moon, they succeeded in slipping away from their colleagues—' "

"Wait, Luis. This is a really good passage, and you left out the walk. 'Veiled by the new moon, and with the excuse of stretching their legs, the two finally succeeded in slipping away from their colleagues, thus eluding their vigilance, their jokes, and their jealousy.' In other words, they went out into a field and had a good screw. Not for the first time, I should think."

"Serena, please." Mama raised her first objection since we began the story.

"Well, call it what you want. The fact is that Amparo got pregnant. Or, if you prefer to be more refined, 'She began giving the calendar sidelong glances and often checked her pulse, trying to attribute her increasingly frequent bouts of nausea to any cause but the obvious one.' "

"That's better."

"All right. Now we're in Teruel."

"You're still leaving out two important facts," said Alberto. "The first is that our grandfather hadn't been able to make his acting debut yet, because none of the actors ever fell sick."

"Right, and so he was frustrated. His role was limited to being alert to the many memory lapses suffered by the principal actor, Andrés Salgado. Simón often had to whisper his lines to him."

"That's the second fact. It seems that this Salgado was so forgetful that Simón was obliged to come to his aid several times during the course of each performance. This is important for understanding the end. Salgado was an actor with a great deal of experience. In previous tours, he'd been able to cover the gaps in his memory by ad-libbing. And now for the director—we've hardly spoken about him. He was a real son of a bitch, and the only reason he agreed to hire Simón was because he wanted to travel more comfortably in Simón's car."

"Or he was also a shameless jerk who just wanted to bang Amparo."

"Whatever. In any case, he was probably a carpe diem kind of guy. He didn't give a damn about the company or the theater except as a way of earning a living. That's why he'd never called Salgado's attention to all the mistakes he was making. Maybe he hadn't even noticed them. But that year, thanks to Simón's constant prompting, the director was forced to recognize the facts."

"Very good, Alberto."

"The upshot was that Salgado turned on Simón and accused him of trying to show him up. He called Simón jealous and said he was just trying to usurp his position."

"Now, right?"

"Now what?"

"Now we're in Teruel, at last, right? On the night before."

"Now, yes."

"Well, we all know this part. They had a huge row in Teruel because, for the first time, Simón dared to challenge Salgado. He told him he was sick of listening to his nasty remarks. He said he was only performing the function assigned to him by the director, and if Salgado wasn't capable of remembering such a well-known text as *El burlador de Sevilla*, the best thing he could do was retire."

"And they came to blows."

"That's an understatement. They gave each other a thrashing. It was so bad that Salgado lost some of his teeth and Simón was practically lame in one leg."

"The right leg," Pablo stipulated. I'm amazed at the number of details he remembers.

"Perfect." I took over the conversational reins, because we were getting close to the point that interested me. "So the commotion attracted the director's attention, and he beseeched them to resolve their differences amicably, for the mutual good. In the end, they decided to play cards for the role of Don Juan. That's rather surprising, isn't it?"

"If you say it like that. But in his version, Papa made it clear that they played long games for high stakes every night."

"You're right. He even told the story that one night one of the actors lost his girlfriend at cards."

"Exactly so. Anyway, that night, Simón won the game."

"He won by cheating, Alberto. Papa didn't admit that explicitly, but it was more or less clear."

"For goodness' sake, Serena, you're always the same." Poor Alberto. He's watching his favorite hero crumble, and he can't do anything to stop it. "It looks like you've got a grudge against Simón."

"All right. Whether he cheated or not, Simón won the game. The following day, he finally made his longed-for debut. If you like, we could linger over the enormous success he had, the intensity of the applause, the deafening final ovation, the director's congratulations after the performance—"

"There's no need to linger over all that, though it's important for understanding Salgado's jealousy."

Poor Alberto was walking directly into my trap. And the best part was that he was taking his own steps without my having to lead him. All he needed was the final shove. I gave it to him, but gently.

"Of course, because that very night, Salgado, dying of envy and fearful that the director would never let him play the role of Don Juan again, waited until he found Simón alone. He told him if he didn't disappear from the company, he'd break both his legs."

Alberto was enchanted. The moment to launch the final attack had arrived. The only way of attacking I know is with questions. I have no other weapon. "And what did Simón do?"

"He did what anyone would have done in his situation. He got into his car and disappeared."

"That same night?"

"The sooner, the better."

"And Amparo?"

"What about her?"

"Doesn't it seem that the normal thing to do would have been to take her with him? After all they'd been through?"

"Maybe she didn't want to go."

"Of course not. She was pregnant with his child, but she preferred to stay with the company."

"Come on, Serena—"

"And so Simón goes and gets himself killed. What a coincidence."

"No, not a coincidence. Simón was killed because he was driving on a terrible road and it was nighttime and he was going too fast—"

"Just a moment, Alberto." All I had to do now was close the trap. "The terrible road went to Cuenca, didn't it?"

"I believe so."

"But it wasn't the main highway, right? It was an unpaved forest track with more bends than a bedspring, and it went right through the woods. What was the name of that forest?"

"The Rodeno Woods, I think."

"Thank you, Pablo. The Rodeno Woods. Does it make sense that Simón would have chosen that road?"

"To me it does."

"Well, naturally, Alberto. Because you're even more pigheaded than Simón. But I think that if he wanted to get away from Salgado, the natural thing to do would have been to take the main highway. And it seems even more likely if we're talking about a man who barely knew how to drive. Besides, why was he going so fast? And why at night? Couldn't he have waited until the following morning? Don't tell me you've never asked yourself these questions."

"You and your fucking questions." Alberto couldn't take it any longer. "If you know so much, answer them yourself."

"Because he was being chased, brother dear. I've been trying to tell you that since yesterday, but you won't listen. No one behaves the way Simón did unless somebody's after them, and I doubt very much that it was Salgado. If your enemy's running away, build him a silver bridge, as the saying goes. That's why the detail of the stolen car, even though you refuse to accept it, is so important. Dear old Alfonsito might have been an arrogant rich kid, but I don't think he was a complete idiot. What did he do when Simón didn't return with the car? He told his father everything. And what did his father do? He called the police. Use your head a little. The police didn't have to do much investigating to uncover the relationship between Simón and Amparo. They'd probably been tracking them for days by the time they got to Teruel. And what did Simón do? Give back the car and ask for forgiveness? Take into account the fact that he hadn't been capable of confessing his lie to the director when it still wasn't a crime, and ask yourself if he was likely to do so now. No, Alberto. He got into the car and ran away. That's what thieves do. At night, at speed, along a deserted road."

"And he was killed," Mama interjected suddenly. "Very good, Serena. Boys, I don't know about you, but I'm convinced. Now, I don't want to spoil anybody's party, but we should be getting back."

"Then I don't understand anything." Alberto began to give the orders necessary for the *Amen* to catch the wind and carry us back to shore, but he kept murmuring to himself the whole time. "Not a bloody thing."

I sat down beside him. "What don't you understand? Tell me."

"Many things. But there's one that's bothering me more than all the rest. I don't understand why Papa invented this whole tale."

"I can tell you that," said Mama, who had come up behind me, as if she didn't want to miss the epilogue to the story. "I mean, I'm the logical choice; it's not that I know some secret. I think Amparo never wanted to tell her son that Simón died in that way, and so she invented a tale that was very much like the truth, with the same dates and places, but without the true reasons for what happened. But don't go blaming Amparo. Think about what you would have done in her place."

"Okay, Mama." I understood what she was saying, but I wasn't completely convinced. "Papa may have done nothing more than repeat the story his mother told him, but it's impossible that he didn't harbor at least same of the doubts I've always had. And he obviously added some imaginary touches."

"Don't be so sure."

"But I am sure. Do you know why? Because the story of Simón's death is too much like the story of Li Po's exile."

"Just what we needed," Alberto said, laughing for the first time. "The Chinaman."

"Yes, the Chinaman. Substitute the characters. The director is the emperor. Simón is Li Po, obviously, and Salgado's the jealous eunuch. The role of Don Juan takes the place of the poems, and the final flight is equivalent to the exile. The two stories don't just resemble each other, they're absolutely parallel. Doesn't that seem like too much of a coincidence?"

At this moment, the port shroud broke. Nothing serious. In fact, at first, we only noticed the noise, a twang like the sound a guitar string makes when it snaps, but a little louder. As soon as Alberto heard it, he rushed to the foot of the mast to keep it from falling, and started giving instructions. Luis and Pablo hauled the sail halfway down to decrease the pressure on the mast. I had to move to the starboard side, next to the other shroud, to make sure it didn't break too. If we had lost that one as well, the mast definitely would have fallen. Alberto was concentrating on repairing the ruptured shroud. Fortunately, it had broken near the end, so he was able to make it fast again. Since the mended shroud was now shorter than the other one, the mast leaned a little, just a few millimeters, to port. I think Mama was a little afraid. Luis tried to cheer her up: "Grandma, you're not going to die. You already died in Guatemala."

The east wind was blowing stronger, but it wasn't exactly a cyclone. We all agreed we should keep the sail at half-mast, thus reducing the possibility that the big spar might give way. Alberto used his belt to secure the shroud more tightly. Since only half the sail was spread, the return voyage went more slowly, but it was lovely. We sailed along in silence, all of us concentrating as if our lives depended on a length of braided steel.

When we arrived in Malespina, I suggested the others drop me off at the lighthouse so I could collect my car. Mama said it was more urgent to go straight to the house to check on Papa, and that she'd drive me to the lighthouse herself later. Sometimes I'm so naïve. It never occurred to me that this was just an excuse so Mama could talk to me alone. We didn't even go inside. When we reached the house, the men got out of the car, Mama stationed herself behind the wheel, and we set off for the lighthouse. Along the way, we talked about what had just happened, about Simón, about Amparo, about Papa. She congratulated me. It made her happy to see that I'd finally succeeded in reconstructing Simón's story without resentment and without looking for someone to blame. She said that it would be very good for me. By the time I realized she was luring me into a trap, we were already at the lighthouse, parked next to my car with the engine turned off, talking as if we were old friends. The view was impressive.

"So peaceful, isn't it?" Mama said.

"Yes, I was thinking the same. I'm not surprised that the lighthouse keepers always ended their reports with the same sentence."

"'Nothing new is known to have occurred . . .'"

"Mama, how the hell do you know that?"

"How do I know what?" She looked uncomfortable and fell silent for a few moments, thinking. "From your father, I suppose. Or did you think you were the only one he told his stories to?"

"No, I'm just surprised, that's all. Because he never used to talk about the lighthouse keepers. At least—"

"Then you must have mentioned it at some point."

"If I did, I don't remember."

"Well, so what?" She seemed impatient. "You know, it's about time you forgot about all that. Especially in your condition," she added suddenly, putting a hand on my stomach. I wanted to sink into the earth. "You're going to have to learn to think about the future."

"How did you know? Can you tell by looking at me?"

"No. You don't look any different. Luis told me."

"I'm going to kill him. When I get my hands on him, I'm going to kill him."

"No, Serena, you're not going to kill anyone. But seriously, what are you going to do? Are you going to keep it?"

"I don't know, Mama. I think so, but it's a little complicated. The father—"

"No, wait," she interrupted me. "Don't tell me anything more until you decide what you want to do. Let's do things right for once. I don't want any more Simóns in the family. We've had enough legends."

We went back to the house in two cars. My suitcase is packed, because we're all leaving tomorrow. When I came here, I thought I'd stay on a few days after everyone left, so I could keep on writing. I don't know what. Simón's story? That's cleared up now. In fact, all my questions have been resolved. All the important ones, at least.

As soon as we got home, I asked about Papa, and they told me they'd found him out on the terrace, sitting on a chair, covered with his coat, and sound asleep. I went to have a look at him, and he was still there. On the table next to him, the same table I'm sitting at now, he had his old telescope. The old rascal had been spying on us while we were sailing. I picked up the telescope and looked at Papa. His coat was slipping off, so I covered him again. "Did you have to come outside?" I said, scolding him. "You're going to catch a cold, and . . ."

But he looked at me with a strange smile on his face. I shut up. For the first time in a long while, we held each other's gaze, until finally he turned his eyes away and fixed them on the sea.

"Jury-rig," he suddenly said. Then he took the spyglass out of my hands, placed it in his lap, and pointed to the sea with a vague, slow, sweeping gesture, as if he were indicating life itself. Then he repeated his words: "Jury-rig."

I'm leaving tomorrow. I'll bring my notebooks with me, but I don't know why. In the beginning, I thought it was a good idea to leave a written inventory of borrowed words, but now they don't interest me so much. Maybe Mama's right: no more Simóns. And no more digging around in the past; even today seems remote. Time never stops. Now, more than ever, it's pulling me forward. I need new stories, my own words, something I can lend to the future. Even if I have to invent it. For example, a hypothetical eighth proverb of Li Po: "Truths and lies are jury-rigs. They keep us afloat in the shipwreck of life." I'm not sure, but I think Li Po never saw the sea.

SOME REFERENCES

In order to authenticate the real events in some of the stories told in this novel, I would—given its nature—have to write another one, which might be entitled *More Lies*. And what's worse, it would have to be even longer. Nevertheless, it seems only right to point out a few of the present work's brushes with reality.

Some details of Li Po's biography are remotely accurate, although a simple search will reveal the existence of at least fifteen different versions of his life and death. The one included in *Poesía China: del siglo XXII a.C. a las canciones de la Revolución Cultural* (Madrid: Alianza Editorial, 1973), selected by Marcela de Juan, strikes me as especially beautiful.

There was a Russian couple living on the Costa Brava. A glance at any of their biographies will suffice to show that they are not the couple in this book.

The historical Battle of the Formigues Islands transpired in a way quite similar to the account given here. It's strictly accurate to say that the discrepancies between the chronicles of Desclot and Montaner make it impossible, once again, to choose a version that could be considered strictly accurate. In any case, read as works of fiction, the chronicles are fascinating.

Anthropologists have investigated the treatment of death in different cultures with much more rigor than my characters. The results of such investigations have been published in hundreds of texts. Two works that I found particularly useful are *Celebrations of Death: The Anthropology of Mortuary Ritual* (Cambridge University Press, 1991), by Peter Metcalf and Richard Huntington; and *Death and the Regeneration of Life* (Cambridge University Press, 1982), edited by Maurice Bloch and Jonathan Parry. Isabel avails herself of the richness of the information they contain, and I, for my part, am grateful for their help.

A book deserving of special mention is *Consuming Grief: Compassionate Cannibalism in an Amazonian Society* (Austin: University of Texas Press, 2001), by Beth A. Conklin. Although Isabel makes some of this author's conclusions her own, in no way could she aspire even to reflect the immense knowledge that informs Ms. Conklin's work. Her study of the customs of the Wari is a document at once dense, academic, and profoundly moving. The present novel owes Ms. Conklin's text an unpayable debt, not only for the huge quantity of new data it provides, but also for the impressive learning with which its author interprets the information.

Malespina, October 2002

ACKNOWLEDGMENTS

Yolanda (Juarroz, 1/51).

Óscar, intelligent enthusiasm; Rosa, *apelotante*; Horacio welcomed me at last; Antonio's Puerto Vallarta saw the birth of that first page, which is never really the first one; Juan Gabriel, brother; José, eight tango steps; I owe Juan Royo and Dr. Seuba Borrell much more than a dinner; Juan Carlos was capable of honoring friendship with his blessed incredulity; in the background, Chet played *Leaving* and Astor answered with *Oblivion*, two lies; Luke, Kirsty, I've spent half my life, et cetera; Daniel dared, which is no small thing, and Josep took care of it, which is a lot; Santi almost believed all of it; Juan, master, I'm out of words; Antonia knows the value of silence; Dani Fotovski, you know what I mean, comrade; Mariana, what water?; Carina and Gloria, what patience; Pere, for what should have been, almost was, and perhaps will be; Laura C. Dail blessed me in advance with her faith; Nat Sobel, *hermano de repente.*

I assume the debts this novel owes you all.

ENRIQUE DE HÉRIZ was born in Barcelona in 1964. He has worked as an editor and translator of such authors as Annie Proulx, Stephen King, Peter Carey, and John Fowles. He lives in Barcelona.

A NOTE ABOUT THE TYPE

This book is set in Fournier, a digitized version of the original font cut that was part of the Monotype Corporation historical typeface revivals in the 1920s. Fournier was created by the typographer and printing historian Stanley Morison (1889–1967) and grew out of his admiration for the type cuts of Pierre Simon Fournier (1712–1768).